FIRST RESORT

NANCI LITTLE

Works by Nanci Little:

Thin Fire
The Grass Widow
The Maiden: a reworked classic (poetry chapbook)
First Resort

FIRST
RESORT
NANCI LITTLE

Odd Girls Press, Anaheim, CA

Original cover art and cover design by Lisa Conant. Original pen and ink drawing of Catawamteak by Lisa Conant. Lisa may be reached via the Internet at email: lisaconant@earthlink.net

This book is a work of fiction. Any resemblance to real characters or events is entirely coincidental and unintentional.

Printed in the United States of America on acid-free paper.
First edition, December 1998. Second Printing, July 1999.

10 9 8 7 6 5 4 3 2

This book was reformatted for the second printing resulting in a different page count from that of the first printing. Aside from the correction of typographical errors, no text has been removed or added to this novel.

The publisher gratefully thanks Veronica A. Shoffstall for permission to include her poem "After a while" ©Veronica A. Shoffstall, 1971.

Library of Congress Cataloging-in-Publication Data   98-71170 CIP
Little, Nanci, 1955-
First Resort / by Nanci Little
p. 240   cm. 14 x 21
ISBN (trade paper): 1-887237-01-1

1. Women golfers — Fiction
2. Domestic violence — Fiction
3. Lesbians — Fiction

DEDICATION

To the women
who came into shelter
hungry to taste life of a different
flavor and color and texture:
the depths of my respect
for your fear
and for your courage.

◆

And to Jan and Doug,
for so many lessons
that have so much more to do
with love than golf.

◆

Thank you:

my wonderful parents, for your unfailing support.

Margaret Gillon, for your patience.

Diane Benison, for the education.

Nan Amodeo, Susan Antoniewicz, Chris Brennan, Mary Demorest,
Judy Deschaine, Sue Foley, Margaret Gahles, Shizuko Hood,
Virginia Hood, Charlotte Luksa, Bernice McConnell, Penny McHatten,
Deborah Peifer, Karin Spitfire, and Jean Stewart, for your
women's wisdom.

AFTER A WHILE

Veronica A. Shoffstall

After a while you learn
the subtle difference between
holding a hand
and chaining a soul
and you learn
that love doesn't mean
leaning
and company doesn't always mean
security.
And you begin to learn
that kisses aren't contracts and
presents aren't promises
and you begin to
accept your defeats
with your head up and your eyes ahead
with the grace of a woman
not the grief of a child
and you learn
to build all your roads on today
because tomorrow's ground is
too uncertain for plans
and futures have a way of falling down
in mid-flight.
After a while you learn
that even sunshine burns
if you get too much
so you plant your own garden
and decorate your own soul
instead of waiting
for someone to bring you flowers.
And you learn
that you really can endure
that you really are strong
and you really do have worth
and you learn
and you learn
with every goodbye
you learn . . .

CATAWAMTEAK

CONTENTS

Catawamteak was a grand resort in the old Maine tradition: a rambling profusion of Victorian elegance, its verdant summer expanses dotted with Adirondack chairs and fringed umbrellas, and croquet wickets that humped like inchworms across manicured lawns, and the fluttering flags of eighteen holes; its interiors were oak and brass, pale pastels and French mural wallpapers; its staff was handsome, courteous, and ubiquitous. People went there to suppose they were Gatsby and Daisy, or that those fictional luminaries might join them for gin on the lawn, and the pretense was easy; built in the opulence of the second industrial revolution, Catawamteak had, in the next hundred years, been frequently and fastidiously freshened, but only marginally refurbished, and to enter its aura was to enter a time of self-confident indulgence, a place where people could be carelessly rich together.

The inn stood on a promontory fifty feet above and eight hundred feet back from the shore of Penobscot Bay, an ornate centerpiece on the meticulous carpet of the golf course. Two sweeping wings met under a towering rotunda. Each wing was bordered by broad verandas that overlooked the fairways and the sea; the verandas were liberally appointed with swings, and high tea was served in the afternoons of summer. Turrets rose from the centers and ends of the wings; the turret suites had balconies, and were highly prized. Every window in every room was shaded by a green and white striped awning that could be opened or closed by the whim of the guest and the strong arm of a valet.

The ground floor of the rotunda was a sprawling lobby, with chairs and divans for those who wished to linger in admiration of the seaward panorama. Down the corridors were an open parlor for casual players of billiards-bagatelle, and a closed chamber for those who took their games more seriously; there were rooms for table tennis and cribbage and backgammon, and one dedicated to the pursuits of rambunctious toddlers on rainy days. There were rooms for the conference of two or twenty or two hundred (for it was not always well or possible to entertain one's guests in private quarters or public spaces). There was a lounge for reading and writing, and a newsstand, and a small emporium where forgotten or expended necessities of toiletry and nicety could be replaced. The stairways and elevators leading to the three floors of guest quarters were discretely away from the central bustle of the lobby; the broad staircase curving down to the lounge and dining room was elegant in the center of the rotunda.

People of the middle class came once to Catawamteak, and they stayed their weekend or week and backed away uneasily, intuiting that they could be there forever without ever having arrived. The wealthy arrived, sanguine in their indulgences: they golfed carelessly, played tennis carelessly, ate and drank and smoked carelessly, and there were careless clutches of them scattered about the parking lot and lobby on the afternoon that Jordan Bryant made her entrance in cream colored flannel trousers and a pale lilac silk shirt open at the throat, cream silk tie raked casually down, pith helmet tipped back on meticulously cut dark hair. A '33 Packard phaeton glimmered under the entrance canopy, a slightly awed valet standing guard.

She cruised a look around the lobby, taking in fluted pillars and Aubusson carpets and ornately plastered ceilings hung with chandeliers, the massive oaken registration desk to her right and gaming parlors to her left, the windows overlooking the links and the brilliant ocean beyond, the pair of handsome young men in snug formal uniforms with the Catawamteak crest embroidered in gold on the breasts of their black vests. In the center of the lobby was a polished granite obelisk; she went to read the words carved in it. "Built in 1886, this Grand Resort commands the site where members of the Passamaquoddy Nation first welcomed white settlers to the waters they called Catawamteak . . . safe harbor," she read, and murmured, "And then if they ran true to form, the white settlers repaid that hospitality by murdering the welcoming Passamaquoddy and assuming ownership of their safe harbor."

With smiles that were a few degrees warmer than professional welcome, the valets started to approach her. She stayed them with a tiny shake of her head, for a tall, broad-shouldered, cruelly-jawed man of some fifty years had come around the registration desk as if he had well greased bearings instead of joints; he had boot-black hair and a butler's tux and a smile hinting that the best deals were out back and he'd tell no one but her about them. Jordan Bryant tilted back her head and watched from under a sweep of dark lashes as he came at her, and she thought: *now here we have a snake oil salesman in the thirty-first degree.*

"John G. Laing," purred the snake oil salesman. "It is our greatest pleasure to welcome you to Catawamteak, Maine's first and finest grand resort. And how may we be of assistance to you this afternoon, madame?"

Oh, the imperial we. Can we get over ourselves. She took a slim gold case from her pocket and selected an English Oval. John G. Laing offered flame. She drew and blew, and finally offered an unenthusiastic hand and let him do that calculated cross between a wring and a pump that oozed subservience before she said, "Jordan Bryant."

Well, didn't that *just tighten up the balls in his bearings,* she thought, for he dropped her hand and took a step back, and she gave him the same not-quite-smile she'd worn in arriving, a smile that (married to her custom clothes and her classic car and her carelessness) had made him sure she was a guest. He cleared his throat. "Miss Bryant."

She tapped ashes onto the carpet and smoothed them into the fiber with a wing tipped toe. "Ms.," she corrected gently. "This is quite the place we've got here, John."

Something twitched to and from his lips; it looked more like gas than a smile. "Mister, to you. And this place has ashtrays and you will use them."

She tasted her cigarette and blew smoke at the floor, her smile suggesting she was finding something very droll. "So where might I find the bar, Mister To You? I've managed to locate the golf course." She had managed the golf course quite well, in fact, paying its three digit greens fees and shooting three over (with assistance from an excellent caddie) on her first trip in ten years around an eighteen renowned for its challenge.

"You," he said evenly, "are not getting off on the right foot with me, young lady."

She drew on her Oval, and rolled the smoke forward on her tongue so she could inhale it with her nose, and pursed her lips and gently blew the smoke at him. "Touché, Mister To You, said the young lady."

Jordan Bryant was a licensed clinical social worker and a certified massage therapist; she had ten years' experience behind a bar, and in her young adulthood she had won a number of respectable, if not major, professional golf championships. Tall and grey-eyed, at thirty-seven she had a fluid grace and a disturbing — to John G. Laing, at least — suggestion of sensual ferity; she was as arrogantly, carelessly handsome as any guest to walk through Catawamteak's oak and brass and beveled glass doors, and he hadn't been the one to hire her and he knew now that he didn't want her, but he needed her. She needed him not at all, and they both knew it. "Come, then, *Ms.* Bryant," he said tightly. "There are papers to be signed."

"That one," said one of the handsome young men in black and white uniform, when the door gold-lettered 'General Manager' had closed behind Jordan Bryant and John G. Laing, "is gonna give Big Bad John a wedgie of major proportions."

"*Going* to? Girl, his shorts are so far up his crack right now! Don't I love those tall, cool dykes, honey. They're *so* damn bad to the hets."

TWO YEARS LATER

Ten years of on-again, off-again time behind a bar and a handful of respectable, if not major, professional golf trophies amounted to dual citizenship for Jordan at Catawamteak. As head bartender she worked the bar from seven to one — two on Fridays and Saturdays — and then slept in the apartment provided by the resort; in her real job as Director of Golf and teaching pro, she golfed most of her days away with guests in need of companionship or instruction.

Handsomely compensated to do things she enjoyed and at which she excelled, she understood the bottom line of her job. If guests needed competition she competed. If they needed to win she lost by a whisker, making them work hard enough to be able to believe in the victory. If they wanted to learn, she taught them. The two pros on her staff gave half-hour private or one-hour semiprivate lessons, keeping close schedules; Jordan booked two partners a day, allowing time for nine leisurely or eighteen carefully paced holes with each, and the people who sat at her bar in the evenings were frequently those with whom she had golfed that day. They came to continue conversations that often rambled on all summer, for Jordan was a teacher, a companion, a listener . . . and perhaps, if it suited her, a lover.

The chef loved her and fed her for free, and threw a passionate snit the day Big Bad John complained; hers was the only educated palate in the place, Gaston screamed, and if he wanted her to taste, she would taste, or he would not cook! He threw his hat to the floor and stomped it, and kicked it at Laing, who muttered something about French faggots and shot a murderous look at the grinning Jordan Bryant before he turned on a well-polished heel and simmered out of the kitchen. "Dat asshole," muttered Gaston, who was not French but Acadian, and not a faggot but hungry for Jordan no matter how many times she told him no. He kicked his hat under a table and got another to settle onto his glossy black curls. "And you! You come here to torture me! Go play, Zhordaan. Must I learn golf to get to play with you?"

In front of Jordan was a plate that had held a pheasant breast smothered *aux champignons* on a bed of wild rice garnished with fresh artichoke hearts. Only sauce was left; she traced a fingertip through it and licked it off in slow suggestion. "It's a magnificent game, *mon frère*. It's so long and delicate . . . like foreplay, hmm?" She teased him with a tender lack of mercy, for it amused them both. "Try marjoram instead of savory, and maybe a soupçon of szechuan pepper instead of white, half as much? It wants something for a signature." She stood to give his scratchy cheek a kiss. "Thanks for the compliment to my palate, *chère ami*," she grinned, and strolled to the clubhouse to meet her noon appointment.

◆

Well, isn't this nice, she thought, approaching the first tee and the tiny woman who had a foot on a bench, tying her spikes: she was forty-three, or maybe forty-seven; her hair was not blonde, not brown, not auburn, but sunlit hints of all, with a shimmer of encroaching silver. She was trim and tanned and as gracefully dignified as the clothes she wore, not pretty or beautiful but . . . *lovely? Now there's a word I never use, but she surely is — and either my gaydar's on the fritz or she's straight as a one-iron.* And wryly, she smiled. *Probably just as well. On second glance, she almost puts me in mind of my mother.* For there seemed to be a gentleness to her, a softness that hinted of children, and breast-feeding, and nurturing through years of meeting the needs of others before she considered her own.

The probably straight and definitely lovely woman looked up in tentative welcome when Jordan said, "Gillian Benson? I'm Jordan Bryant," and offered a hand.

Gillian Benson's returned handshake was firm and warm; her smile wasn't reserved as much as it was a little shy. "It's a hard G, actually. *G*illian. Like having to do with fishes breathing." She looked at Jordan with a raise of the eyebrow that wondered *have we met before — ? . . . Well, maybe not.* "I'm so pleased to meet you, Miss Bryant. Peony Watkins tells me you're the best teacher she's ever had." Her accent was softly Southern, not so much a drawl as an essence.

"Peony Watkins told me she'd never had a lesson in her life," Jordan smiled, "which makes her praise of somewhat dubious merit, but it's kind of you to repeat it, Mrs. Benson. Will we be nine or eighteen today?" Mrs. Benson seemed most pleasant, and Jordan hadn't had a pleasant partner for days — Peony Watkins, Valium Queen, included. It was beyond her how any woman medicated to the point of barely-upright could be so mean.

"Oh, you won't be able to stand me for more than nine! I'm not really a golfer, Miss Bryant. I just love the game."

"Jordan. If you love the game, you deserve to play it as well as you can. I'd like to help you get there." *I usually say 'it's my job to help you get there,'* she thought, and then wondered where the thought had come from. "What's your best club?"

"Oh — sometimes I don't slice my drive. I think I've hit two hundred once or twice with Barb's Big Bertha." Jordan glanced at Mrs. Benson's golf bag; nothing in it remotely resembled Callaway's famous driver. "My fairway woods and long irons fade as often as I slice my drive," Mrs. Benson added, "but my mid irons are fine. My short game isn't too awful, but a sand trap is an exercise in humiliation for me. Sometimes I can make up for it with my putting. Not always."

"I've had a few expensive sand mistakes." And she had, back on the Tour; one had turned a major tournament win into second place in a play-off. The price tag for that mistake had been in the thirty-thousand-dollar neighborhood.

She shook off the memory. *Not a golfer? She sure seems to have a handle on her game, for someone who's not a golfer.* "Two or three strokes to get out of the sand can surely give you the yips on the green. But putting's won me some up-and-downs that I was fairly sure were going to be bogey . . . or worse."

"Up and down," Mrs. Benson said dryly, "is not a phrase I use often."

"You love the game. That's all it really takes to make a golfer." Jordan pulled her glove from a pocket of her shorts. "What I suspect you're looking for is consistency. Let me round up my caddie" — Ric Bolli was apparently Mrs. Benson's pick for the afternoon (or, knowing Ric, more likely he had picked her) — "and we'll see if we can't add a few more up-and-downs to your vocabulary."

◆

"You've got a solid, athletic swing," Jordan said to Mrs. Benson on the second tee, watching her student's drive fade to the right and trickle to a stop a hundred and fifty yards down the fairway. "I'd like to see you get away from that baseball grip, though. It doesn't give you enough control over the club."

Mrs. Benson looked at her hands. "I used the interlocking grip for years. Barb Maxwell — one of the women I golf with back home — told me I should try this. She's so much better than I am, I thought I should listen."

"Have you ever taken lessons?"

"I — no. Not really."

"If you ever do, stop listening to everyone else. Pick your teacher and stay there until you outgrow her or him. And tell people you're taking lessons. That usually shuts them up if they love the game too. If they don't . . ." She shrugged.

"I take it I've outgrown Barb?"

"Probably before she started talking, if she's telling you to use a baseball grip. You've got small hands. You need all the control over the club you can get. I could get away with a baseball grip" — she held out a broad palm with long, smooth fingers — "but the interlocking grip is incredibly precise once you learn how to use it. When you pick up the club, what do your hands want to do?"

Mrs. Benson let go of her driver, letting it drop against her thigh, and made her grip again, raising the head of the club over her shoulder to show Jordan her right pinkie embracing her left forefinger. "Twenty years."

"Go back there. We'll adjust it so it works. May I touch your hands?"

19

Mrs. Benson glanced up as if the automatic question had surprised her. "I — why, yes. Yes, of course."

"Thank you. If you think of the shaft of your club as a clock, with the head of the club at noon and the end of the grip at six o'clock, you want the thumb of your left hand at one o'clock and the thumb of your right at eleven." She moved Mrs. Benson's thumbs on the grip. "Like that. Good. Now — " She positioned Mrs. Benson's right forefinger. "You want a little gap between this finger and the next one, but no space between your hands. Your right forefinger and thumb should be pinching the grip. That keeps the club from rolling in your hands when you make contact with the golf ball."

"It feels awful funny," Mrs. Benson murmured, her hands seeking where the newness fit in them.

"Everything different feels funny the first time you do it. Now —" She glanced at the first green; the foursome behind them was still putting. She teed a ball. "Show me your approach."

Shyly, Mrs. Benson addressed the ball.

Jordan thought again of her mother, shy every time her professional daughter offered guidance, and the memory softened her voice, making her advice sound more like a confidence than a lesson. "See how the ball's in the center of your stance? Try lining up with the ball inside your left heel — so that if you dropped the club the end of the grip would land on your left thigh. This is how I do it." She dropped a ball in the tee box and sighted down the fairway before she stepped to the ball. "Step up with your right foot, set your left where you want it, and then adjust the right foot. You end up in the right place every time."

Mrs. Benson broke her grip, adjusted her visor and sunglasses, and lined up on the teed ball. Jordan watched her remake her grip; not many of her students remembered the pinch on the first lesson, but Gillian Benson did. "Good approach; good grip. Now hit the ball."

"No practice swing?"

"I hardly ever do, except on the putt. Your practice swing is usually your best swing. Address the ball and then forget it's a ball. Pretend it's a dandelion and take your practice swing at it."

"That doesn't look a thing like a dandelion," Mrs. Benson murmured. "Maybe I'd better buy some yellow balls." She drew a deep breath and let it out and swung the club. They watched the ball land thirty yards ahead of her first one and more to the center of the fairway. "Well," she said, when it finally stopped. "I do like that."

"So do I." Jordan teed a ball. "Watch me. These are the things I'll try to teach you to do. Pinch the grip. Ball inside the left heel. Turn the left toe out a hair. Hold a basketball between your knees. Weight on the balls of the feet, a little to the inside." She demonstrated what she did automatically in her pre-shot routine. "That's the grip and address. Now an easy backswing; you want tempo here. The power's in your downswing, not your backswing. Straight left arm and wrist. Draw a semicircle with the club head. Then break the wrists here, at ninety degrees. Keep your head still until your shoulder forces it off the ball. Your backswing should finish with the shaft of the club pointing at your target." She stopped there, feeling Mrs. Benson trying to absorb what she was saying. "Don't try to remember it all now. Just remember later that you've heard it before. Now start down. Straighten out the wrists at ninety degrees. Contact" — her driver made that sweetly musical sound of a ball well hit — "and follow through as if you were throwing the club after the ball. Your left upper arm should be well away from your body. When you complete your swing, your belly button should be pointing at your target."

Mrs. Benson watched Jordan's ball. "And you did that talking all through your swing," she murmured, when Jordan's Top-Flite trickled to a stop fifty yards nearer the green than her own second ball. "I'll never remember all of that! Did I hear you say something about basketballs?"

Jordan smiled. "I'll tell you about the basketball as soon as you remind me you've heard it before. For now, just remember your grip and your approach. You've got a good inherent swing. You're not afraid to hit the ball. You just need to nail down some fundamentals." She bent to retrieve her tee. "What do you do besides golf?"

"I . . . play bridge. I — god. I read. I don't know."

Midlife crisis? "What does your husband do?"

"He sells — sold — he sold cars. He died last year. In October."

Big-time midlife crisis. "I'm sorry." Jordan apologized as much for her own innocently untimely question as for Mr. Benson's untimely demise. "It must still be hard."

Mrs. Benson shied her eyes away too quickly for Jordan to identify what might have been in them. "It has its moments. Ric, did I put my water bottle in my bag? Would you be a dear and look?"

◆

"I wonder if you have some back problems?" Jordan asked as they strolled toward the clubhouse after nine. "It seems as if you're protecting something in your body on your follow-through."

Mrs. Benson glanced at her; Jordan sensed, in that glance, that Gillian Benson was protecting something in her heart that had to do with her back before she said lightly, "After forty, we all have back problems, don't we? A twinge here and there."

Jordan let it go. "Maybe a couple of aspirin before you tee off. The biggest problem I see with your game is that you neglect your even-numbered irons. That's a throwback to the old three-five-seven-nine 'ladies bag.' I see it fairly often."

"Especially among us elderly women, I'm sure," Mrs. Benson drawled; Jordan flicked a look up from their scorecard and saw indulgent humor in the deep brown eyes. "You're right; I don't play those clubs much, but I think today I suffered from nerves more than anything. You make it look so easy I wonder why I can't do it."

"It's not easy." Jordan frowned at the total on the card and added again, and shook her head and handed the card to her caddie. "I just play eighteen or twenty-seven holes a day from the time the greens thaw in the spring until we get snowed off in the fall — and then I spend as much time as I can wherever I can golf in the winter."

"It sounds as if you eat, breathe, and sleep this old game of golf."

"It helps to be obsessive," Jordan admitted.

Gillian Benson peeled off her glove and ran a hand through her damp hair (it had rained hard in the dawn and turned off hot; steam fairly rose from the fairways), and Jordan wondered again what color that hair was. The closest she had come to description was that it was all of the colors of the handsome tigereye necklace that Mrs. Benson wore tucked into the throat of her shirt. "Lacking much obsession on such a muggy day," Mrs. Benson said, unaware that her hair so fascinated Catawamteak's Director of Golf, "might I buy you a drink?"

Jordan checked her watch. "Do you want to try the back nine? I'll introduce you to one of the most diabolical greens on the eastern seaboard."

"Oh, that's just what this three-putter needs! Do we have time for the drink?"

"If you want it. I'm yours until five. We can go as far as we can."

"I'm awfully thirsty. Would you order me a Stoli and tonic in a tall glass, no lime? I need to powder my nose. I'll meet you in the bar. Make sure you put yours on my account, too."

◆

"So what d' you think, Jordan? Do we fight over her?" Ric Bolli was a brutally handsome rake, black-haired, blue-eyed, bronzed from long days in the sun; he got more than his share of action from the bored married women who golfed at Catawamteak. "She looks wicked good going away."

"You could be replaced by a cart," Jordan said mildly, and something in her eyes assured him that she was not amused, and asked if he had perchance forgotten just who was the boss, and suggested that not amusing the boss might not be in his best interest if scoring bored married women was still high in his career plans — and that not only would they not fight over the attractive Mrs. Benson, but that if he offered anything she could even construe as a move in that direction, he'd be looking good going away, too.

His eyes said he understood all of that, right down to the last unspoken syllable. Jordan turned and went into the clubhouse. "Damn you, Jordan," he muttered. "Another nine holes and I'd've had her."

22

"Have you always pissed through your brains, or is this a recent phenomenon?" Carla Stern fed coins to the soda machine and pushed Moxie; a can of LaBatt's Blue rolled into the chute. "Ever occur to you that some women might actually want to golf instead of getting pronged by every links Lothario batting his baby blues at her?"

"You dykes piss me off," Ric grumbled. "I figured you for my side, you know? I know you got it bad for the boss."

"Oh, yeah. Right." Carla sat on a bench in the shade and went to work on Jordan's clubs; she wiped them off after each stroke, but between rounds she dug every speck of dirt out of the grooves. It wasn't that Jordan asked her to; she just knew Jordan appreciated it, and as far as Carla Stern was concerned, she existed on the face of the earth for no other reason than to be Jordan Bryant's caddie.

◆

"Stoli-tonic tall no lime and a club soda with, Artie," Jordan said to the clubhouse bartender, and she waited for the drinks and took them to a table overlooking the vista of the bay and the first holes of the back nine. She watched as Gillian Benson came toward her. She seemed to be as gracious as any woman Jordan had met in her time at the resort; many of her students were as careless with her and the caddies as they were with the Titleists and Top-Flites they left in the roughs. She had the potential to be a fine golfer: she listened intently, applied what she was told or shown, and remembered the instruction the next time the situation arose. But she was disturbingly self-deprecatory, her conversation scattered with 'I-can'ts' and 'I'm-nots' as if she needed only to be considerate of others, at whatever expense to herself.

"Why, thank you." Mrs. Benson smiled when Jordan stood to hold her chair. "The last time my husband held my chair for me I was still Gillie MacAllister."

Jordan's eyebrow raised in succinct opinion of the late Mr. Benson's omissions of courtesy, but she withheld any other comment. "Will it offend you if I smoke, Mrs. Benson?"

"Of course not, Jordan. Feel free."

◆

They turned their putters over to the caddies after an intensely instructive back nine; even running late, Jordan was patient, and Mrs. Benson less nervous — but not much less self-deprecating — on the second half of the course. Jordan added up the card. "Fifty-four on the back . . . that's a respectable one-oh-one, Mrs. Benson. This is not an easy eighteen."

"Damn that thirteenth green!" Gillian muttered; it had nearly reduced her to tears while she six-putted it, sending her score into triple digits for the first time in years. "What kind of a flaming sadist would design a green like that?"

Jordan laughed. She and Stewart Stedman, the greenskeeper (other courses might have superintendents, but Stedman was a greenskeeper by his own assertion) had dreamed up that treacherously undulant green one late night over a twelvie of Irish beer and a computer program that allowed them to manipulate virtual landscape until they arrived at a green they high-fived as mowable but unplayable. Then they convinced Michael Goodnow — Catawamteak's owner and Jordan's mother's older brother's wife's brother — to let them build it, after some four-wheeling punk destroyed the existing carpet one moonless fall night. The green had been featured in several golf magazines; the Stedman/Bryant Nightmare was considered a marvel of both audacity and landscape engineering, and making par on Catawamteak's 562-yard thirteenth won golfers bragging rights in any clubhouse. "I've been called a lot of things for that green," she smiled, "but I do believe that 'flaming sadist' is a first."

"You did that! Good heavens, have you considered psychotherapy?"

"I *am* a psychotherapist. Isn't that frightening?"

Gillian took a step back, wide-eyed in mock horror. "It's been just lovely knowing you, Miss Bryant, but I think I'd best amble on back to Atlanta now."

"Sounds like a bump-and-run to me."

Gillian Benson's laugh made Jordan think of wind chimes on a soft summer evening breeze. She welcomed the company of wealthy straight women about as often as she used the word lovely, but she couldn't deny that she had enjoyed Mrs. Benson's company as much as she had been intrigued by her potential, and her column on the white board in the pro shop was still mostly empty for the next week. "My Nightmare aside, you could be a really good golfer, Mrs. Benson. I mean it when I say we can take ten strokes — maybe twelve — off your game. It'll take time. But a brief obsession now could make a difference in your game for the rest of your life."

"Ten or twelve strokes? Oh, you're just teasing me now."

"I can see you shooting consistently in the low eighties. If you want to go there, just let me know how intensely you'd like to obsess. We can work out a schedule."

"You have more faith in me than I do! But if it amuses you to beat your head against a brick wall, I'll briefly obsess."

Gently, Jordan touched a hand to Mrs. Benson's shoulder. "The biggest part of the game is believing you can play it well," she said quietly. "Give me a week, and then twice a week, and I'll bet that at the end of a month I'd be willing to play for money with you on my team. Mrs. Benson, I live for students like you."

From his office window, John G. Laing watched the exchange at the pro shop door. Jordan was too close to the woman, her touch lasting too long; the hand at Mrs. Benson's shoulder slipped down to hold her elbow for a moment, and when she bent her head he was afraid Jordan intended to kiss her right there in front of god and everybody. "That queer bitch," he muttered, and reached for his phone.

Jordan had bent her head in an attempt to catch words Mrs. Benson was saying too softly for her to hear. "I'm sorry, I didn't — oh, John, what!" she almost snarled, when her beeper erased all hope that Mrs. Benson would repeat words that had surely been important. "Damn the man. I'm sorry, Mrs. Benson. Can I write you in tomorrow?"

"Damn him indeed." Mrs. Benson gave Jordan a slightly strained smile. "One o'clock? Pray for a breeze."

◆

"You keep your goddamned hands off the guests," Laing growled as soon as she closed his office door. "Jesus Christ, Jordan."

She sank uninvited into a chair. "Don't curse at me, John."

"Your behavior down there was completely inappropriate. I don't ever want to see a display like that again."

The sign on his desk said *You Are Permitted To Smoke Provided You Do Not Exhale*. In the band of her pith helmet were two English Ovals. She selected one and lit it with a match from a glossy black book with her signature blind-embossed on the cover. "Don't tell me how to do my job, John. And don't interrupt me in conversations with guests. Not given how handsomely Michael pays me for my education in psychotherapy." She tossed the matchbook to his desk; she knew they irritated John G. Laing far more than her smoking in his office. "Does it occur to you that if this woman goes home after her summer here feeling better about herself, she might not only come back next year but brag to all of her equally wealthy friends about the Catawamteak experience? And they'll come too? They call that bottom line, John. I know the bottom line of my job whether you do or not, so back off and let me do it."

"Don't ever think I can't burn you, *Ms.* Bryant."

"Mister, if you could burn me, I'd've been toast two years ago."

◆

"God, what a pain in my ass," Jordan muttered, leaving Laing's office and heading for the bar. She asked Cindy, the afternoon bartender, if she might cover until eight; the extra hour wasn't a problem. In her apartment, she took a long shower, and read for half an hour, and dressed; her bar uniform was nearly a military mess white, snug and sleek and formal. Perfecting her bow tie in the mirror, she wondered what progress she and Gillian Benson might have made had John not gone into his snit. Without him, the time she'd spent reading might have much better served that lonely, troubled woman. She hadn't renewed her license in the two years she'd been at Catawamteak, but still, she'd done a lot of *pro bono* therapy over drinks in the clubhouse bar.

Resigned, she shook her head. John could (and should) have worried about her with any number of women she had golfed with over the past summers, but Gillian Benson? She had responded shyly to the smooth good looks of Ric Bolli (who had shown remarkable restraint on the back nine; Jordan had to give him credit, for she knew his seductive charm was almost irrepressible), but her only response to Jordan (who had some seductive charm of her own and had caught herself applying it a few times, knowing she was gut-checking, for she couldn't deny Gillian Benson's attractiveness and straight didn't mean latency wasn't straining at its chains) had been ingenuous friendliness.

She might have preferred straining latency to the intrigue of coaxing out pain to be tamed, but she knew two things: Mrs. Benson had pain that needed coaxing, and Jordan needed something to occupy her besides teaching golf and tending bar, for it was July, and July was a treacherous month for her.

She caught herself whistling on her way down to the bar, memories of classic perfume and sun-glinted hair of an unidentifiable color Sunday-driving down the back roads of her memory, and she shook her head with a tiny smile. "Don't go there, J.B."

She poked her head into the kitchen on her way by. "Gaston! *Ça va, mon frère?* You feed me tonight, or did the man he scare you?"

"De man to scare me, he ain' been born, Zhordaan. Feesh, fowl, or peeg?"

"Never pig. Fish," she said, and a smirking waiter delivered mussels in sweet cream sauce, vegetables tempura, crisp French bread. Throughout the next two hours she reduced a woman at the end of the bar to glazed-eyed desire as she licked cream from the soft folds of the mussels in between making daiquiris and martinis and Manhattans, drawing drafts, grinning as she mixed a steady run of Slippery Nipples for a pair of hard-toned, dark-tanned women at table six; she knew more than nipples would be slippery there before the night was through, and was well aware of what she was doing to the handsome, hungry woman at the end of the bar.

"Two fussy martians —" That meant stirred, not shaken, with flamed lemon and one olive; the couple who ordered them were sweet old farts who owned an adjoining condo and stayed from Memorial through Columbus Day weekends every year. "— Stoli-tonic tall no lime, Nipples for the dykes at six," Rafael said, "and beer for the band."

Stoli tall, no lime? She swept a look across his section to find Mrs. Benson at tiny table nine in the corner, a shy smile of greeting there for her when their eyes met. She smiled back and poured generously, and squirted in tonic and remembered to forget the automatic lime. "Say hi to nine from me, Rafael."

26

"Ooh, fresh meat for Jordan! Start the betting pool; will it be tonight?" He snuck a look at table nine, rechecking. "Eewww, J.B. I don't think so. She looks like my mother, girl."

"Which is why I said say hi instead of join me at the bar, Twinkie. What d' you need, Bart?" It was Saturday; the jazz was a cool acoustic jam, the bar was packed. She had no time to spar with Rafael.

"Ginmerrywidow mudslide sevenandseven strawberrydaiquiri twice pinetreefloat and a gang-bang tidal wave for table twenty-two."

"What the hell is a tidal wave?"

"Tell me. They're hammered; make something up in a mai tai bowl and toss a shot of one-fifty-one in the middle."

She looked at table twenty-two, not recognizing anyone in the happy gaggle. "Are those guys aliens or guests?"

"Registered. They can drunk-walk home."

Occasionally through the evening came an order for Stoli-tonic tall, no lime. She looked up near eleven to find the hungry woman at the end of the bar gone, and wasn't overly surprised; she tried to remember what the woman had been wearing and couldn't. A man who had made her an explicitly rude proposition on the seventh green a week ago claimed the empty chair at Mrs. Benson's table. Jordan kept an eye there as she worked, and when he started leaning forward and Mrs. Benson started leaning back, she called the front desk. "Darlene? Jordan. When Mr. Ferland shows up at the desk, tell him the lady said she'd wait for him in the gazebo." And coolly, she laughed. "Never mind what lady, hon. I owe him this one."

She went around the bar to slip a hand across his shoulders. "Mr. Ferland, someone's asking for you in the lobby," she purred into his ear. "She wouldn't leave her name." She stepped away from the hand he reached for her ass as he excused himself importantly and lurched toward the stairs.

"Thank you." Mrs. Benson's relief was obvious.

"Not a problem."

◆

"Last call," she said into the bar mike at one-thirty, her voice a gently amplified suggestion over taped music; the band was packing up, and Mr. Ferland had not returned (the groundskeepers would find him in the morning, peacefully snoring in the gazebo). "Time, please. Coffee's on the house."

"Are you trying to get out of golf tomorrow, or do you just mix a fierce drink?" A few minutes ago she had glanced at table nine and found it empty, and assumed Gillian Benson gone with the end of the live music; she turned to find her leaning on the bar where the hungry woman had been, looking past both her limit and her bedtime. "I'm half in the bag, Jordan. But what the heck; I'll have one more."

27

"You sure?"

"I probably shouldn't, but if you'll make it I'll drink it."

Jordan made it light and waved off the offered five-dollar bill. "Everything okay?"

"Um. Do you always work a double shift?"

"The first one's nothing I wouldn't be doing anyway."

"Was there really a lady in the lobby?"

Jordan glinted a smile at her. "Nuh-uh. And she didn't wait for him in the gazebo, either."

"You're a devil — and a gentleman."

Jordan raised an eyebrow at her choice of words. "It's a tough job, but somebody's got to do it. Please excuse me for a minute?" She lined up glasses: whiskey sour, Manhattan, the last two Slippery Nipples, a Rob Roy and a Ward Eight for Rafael; a raft of frozen daiquiris for Bart. "Grab the tabs so I can cash up, guys."

"That sounds like my cue," Mrs. Benson said.

"Don't hurry. I'll be here for a while yet." She opened the dishwasher, wiping glasses as she slipped them into the overhead racks.

Mrs. Benson drew a manicured fingernail across the wet circle her glass had left on the bar. "How long have you worked here, Jordan?"

"This is my third summer."

"Hey, doll, vodka rocks chop-chop." He was slab-jawed and flint-eyed, with a still-short necktie and a smile as hard as the ratchet of a handcuff.

"Can't do it, sir." Jordan barely glanced up. "Last call's fifteen minutes out. State law."

"Aw, doll, give me a break. I was in the men's."

"Mm-hmm. And I'll be six to nine months in the women's if I serve you, Dick Tracy. Sayonara."

He started to argue; she froze him with a look, and he turned with a muttered opinion: *fuckin' lesbo.*

"So's your sister and I'll testify," she muttered back, and put a coaster under Mrs. Benson's glass. "God, I hate it when men call me 'doll.'"

"I thought that what else he called you was quite more ungracious."

"It probably wouldn't have been my choice of words for self-description," Jordan allowed. "Where were we, before we were so rudely interrupted?"

"Oh, yes. Phil and I came four years ago, which is why I asked how long you'd been here. There's something so familiar about you. I've been chasing it all day."

"I spent a few years on the LPGA Tour. That was quite a while ago, but if you watched a lot of golf on TV, you might have seen me a time or two."

"That must be it. I do love to watch it. It bored Phil to tears. He always said that the woman who could putt hadn't been born."

If he were here, Jordan thought, *I'd trot him right over to the Night-mare and invite him to put his money where his mouth is.* She'd heard a little history on the back nine: Philbrook Benson the Third had inherited his father's Ford/Lincoln dealership in Atlanta, added BMW just as yuppies discovered Beemers, picked up Mazda in time for the Miata, dumped Mercury, added Infiniti. He seemed to live a charmed life until the day last October when the floor jack in his home garage, in the manufacturer's delicate phrasing, 'effected a terminal malfunction' and parked a 1972 Lincoln Town Car on his chest. He left Philbrook Benson the Fourth with five locations in Atlanta and his widow with more money than she knew what to do with. It had crossed Jordan's mind that most insurance policies paid double indemnity for accidental death.

But what Jordan remembered most clearly was what Philbrook Benson's widow hadn't said: nothing in her words or how she said them intimated that she grieved the husband she had buried ten months ago. She mourned something, but not the man.

"I loved Maine," Mr. Benson's widow said. "He always wanted to go to Atlantic City, or Vegas. Probably because he was lucky at roulette."

"I've never seen the appeal of roulette." Jordan dumped the ice bins into one of three sinks. "I'd rather test my skill than my luck."

Mrs. Benson smiled. In another drink she'd probably be bleary, but right now she was still just softly tousled. "So far, you seem to be good at everything you do. Now if you could just tell me why I keep trying to call you Jordan Baker, I'd be happy."

"You're not too far wrong. I was named after her. She was a character in *The Great Gatsby.*"

"Yes, of course! The golfer. But — don't I recall that she wasn't a very nice person?"

"Incurably dishonest, in fact." She replenished napkins, swizzle sticks, paper umbrellas.

"Why in the world would you have been named for a character like that?"

"My father had a very unusual sense of humor," Jordan Baker Bryant said with a faint, cool smile that said, end of subject, please and thank you.

Gillian was drunk, but not drunk enough to have missed that cue. "What a long day you put in! Do you have to drive far to get home?"

"I don't even have to walk far. I have an apartment here."

"So you sleep here? Work here? Eat here? Play here?"

"I exist here. It's like a permanent vacation. The neat part is, they pay me."

Slowly, the bar cleared. She paid the band and invited them to come back the next weekend, for the band she had booked had canceled; they accepted. Bart and Rafael brought tabs and glasses, wiped down tables, joked back and forth with each other and Jordan, and finally clattered up the stairs, Rafael leering a last grin at her for the company she was still keeping, and Jordan sat for the first time in six hours, her fingers automatic on the keys of the calculator as she cashed up while the dishwasher thrummed through its last load of the night. She signed the tape, zipped it and the receipts into a bag, tossed it into the safe, and spun the dial. "Last call, Mrs. B."

"I wouldn't want you to go to jail."

"Any slick who wears brown wingtips, drinks pine tree floats all night and all of a sudden wants high-octane after last call's a dick. The G.M. keeps a very close eye on me."

"And what, pray, is a pine tree float?"

"Ice water and a toothpick." She scooped ice from the sink, made herself a scotch rocks, and killed all the lights except the neon Clydesdale over the back bar; she leaned against the sinks. "So what's on your mind?"

"Do I look like something's on my mind?" Mrs. Benson nudged her glass across the bar.

Jordan turned her back to pretend with the vodka and cover the ice with tonic; Mrs. Benson was already flirting with a long prayer session at the great porcelain god. "You look like alone isn't your first choice for the next little while," she said, delivering the drink, "and I'm in no particular hurry."

Mrs. Benson tasted, and looked at the glass, and tasted again before she put it down. "Did I really hear you say that you're a psychotherapist?"

"Licensed clinical social worker, technically. In most places they're pretty much terminologically interchangeable. But I haven't practiced for a year or three."

"And a bartender. My dear Jordan, you get more frightening by the very moment." She wasn't slurring her words as much as she was slowing them down, enunciating carefully. "Doesn't your husband hate it that you work all day and night?"

Jordan couldn't help the twitch of a smile. "I'm not married."

"Why not? Forgive me, that's none of my business, but I'd think some man would have snapped you up long ago. You're really very lovely, you know."

Jordan lit a cigarette. "I don't care for men," she said quietly, and dark brown eyes came to meet hers in cautious question. "Not an 'effin' lesbo'," she said, "but yes, I am a lesbian. If that changes our plans to golf tomorrow, that's all right."

"Why . . . of course it doesn't, I just — I — it's — I had no — " Mrs. Benson faltered.

"My feelings won't be hurt if you'd rather work with someone else."

"Jordan, don't mish — mis — understand. I'm not — I'm just — it just seems that you're so — oh, dear," she mourned. "I've had too much to drink. I can't even talk."

"You don't need to explain, Mrs. Benson. Either one of my pros could —"

"But I like you. I mean — I like *you*. And the other pros are men and I don't —" She stopped, looking surprised, almost confused; she blushed, hiding behind her drink for a moment that stretched in silence. "Sometimes I don't care very much for men, either," she said at last, softly. "Thank you for getting rid of that Ferland for me. I thought I'd have to leave, and the jazz was so good."

"They were good, weren't they. I considered the end of the breakwater instead of the gazebo," Jordan smiled, "but it's such bad publicity when drunken guests drown at midnight."

"Then I'll stay away from the beach tonight." She took the last of her drink. "And of course I want to golf with you. But look at me keeping you working late! Help me up the stairs, Jordan, and I'll toddle off to my room."

Jordan poured her drink into a styrofoam coffee cup and lidded it, and killed the Clydesdale over the back bar and went around to offer her arm. Mrs. Benson took it and Jordan guided her up the stairs, clipping the thick velvet rope that served as a door behind them. "Oh, my," Mrs. Benson murmured, almost tripping over a design in the carpet; gently, Jordan steadied her. "I'm really quite under the weather, I'm afraid. Would you mind . . . ?"

"Of course not." She walked Mrs. Benson to the elevator and rode up with her; Gillian leaned into her support. Gently, she took the key when Mrs. Benson fumbled with it, and unlocked the door. "Will you be all right?"

"Saving horrid morfi — morci — mor-ti-fi-ca-tion. I really don't do this."

"I didn't suspect that you did. Is there anything I can do?"

"No . . . no. But thank you."

"Good night, then, Mrs. Benson." She turned.

"Jordan . . .?"

She turned back to see Mrs. Benson leaning against the doorjamb; she looked tired and vulnerable and desperately lonely. In the lobby, Jordan had wondered if Gillian Benson might be asking for more than an arm upstairs; in the elevator, she had been almost sure of it. "Yes," she said quietly, answer to whatever Mrs. Benson might ask her, or ask of her.

"I won't remember" — her words slurred softly — "so I can be honest, too. I hated him. They made me marry him, and then he beat me, and hulim — hum — humilerated me in public, and — and he — He was a cruel, malicious bastard. Don't ever think I won't play with you just 'cause you have the guts not to put up with what I did for twenty-four years. There were times — "

She caught herself; it seemed as if she almost choked on the words, and Jordan took a step forward, but Mrs. Benson moved unsteadily away from the support she would have offered, finding the door for balance instead. "I'm all right. Tomorrow, Jordan Baker — Bryant — my lord, you are so sweet. Good night." Abruptly, however gently, she closed the door.

That the door was closed was a mild surprise to Jordan, but not a disappointment. She was well aware of the pliant poignance of virgins under the influence: liquor let them free long-closeted desires, relieving them of their fears of what they were doing, or what was being done with them and for them, and being the one to help them make those discoveries was a position in which she usually liked to find herself.

She was sure Mrs. Benson would answer if she knocked; she was almost sure that if, when she answered, she stepped inside and closed the door and offered her arms, Mrs. Benson would come to her. She would cry; she needed to cry, to be held for as long as that lasted, and if somewhere in the holding Jordan kissed her hair, she would know by the response whether she might brush her lips against her cheekbone when the tears were done, for that could be easily forgiven as compassion if Mrs. Benson drew away.

But if she didn't . . .

Jordan could almost taste her: the soft breath of surprise at the first touch of another woman's kiss, the tentative acceptance as Jordan's tongue traced her lips, and if arms came around her to draw her to awakened hungers, she would know. And then . . .

"Men make love like the interstate," a long-ago lover of hers had said. "You take the back roads." She suspected that was true of many men, but she knew, too, her destination once the clothes were on the floor: that place where she arched over a first-time lover's body, her knees between smooth thighs, her hands holding soft shoulders as helpless new desire pulsed against her, breasts rising, breath rasping as she bent to take a creamy nipple into her mouth one more teasing time, tasting, coaxing out the gasp of *god please, oh god yes* before legs used to men's ways tried to wrap around her and she broke that grip in her smooth slide to a new beginning, her lips whispering 'let me' against a body no longer able to say anything but yes.

She raised her hand to knock.

Oh, my dear sweet Jordan Baker Bryant. A few drinks to loosen inhibitions is one thing. A few too many is a cat of a different stripe. Softly, she sighed; she turned, and with her drink in one hand and the other in a pocket, she scuffed slowly down the hall.

32

◆

So you sleep here. Work here. Eat here. Play here.

I exist here. She leaned in a doorway of her apartment: an immense bedroom; a room half as big that was both kitchen and dining room; a bathroom half as big as that because it was half a room. The other half might have made a small sitting room; she had her stationary massage table there, and two comfortable chairs with a tiny table between them, and a barrister's case filled with titles like *Myofascial Pain and Dysfunction* and *Physical Examination of the Spine and Extremities* and *The Theory and Practice of Therapeutic Massage.* Her portable table was cased in a corner.

The staff apartments had been taken from the first floor of the west wing of the inn; the rooms overlooked no greater panorama than the driveway and tennis courts, and had never been popular with guests though they were larger than other rooms. During the Thirties the owner had converted them to quarters for managers and pros and chefs, spending a little to save a lot in salaries. Jordan figured it cost her four grand a year for an apartment roughly the same size as the space Gillian Benson was spending twenty-six hundred dollars a week to enjoy.

She could afford a house — owned one, in fact, in the western part of the state — but she didn't see any reason to buy a home in the surrounding towns of Lime Harbor or Bayview or Hylerville; she had lived her adult life in a series of apartments, and now she wasn't a collector of things beyond books and CDs. She was an avid reader and a good carpenter, and her bedroom, with its floor-to-ceiling bookcases on three walls and windows inviting with their padded seats, was more like a library that incidentally housed a bed. She liked the feel of being surrounded by centuries of thought while she slept.

But tonight, more than the books drew her, Gillian Benson's words disturbed her.

You sleep here. Work here. Eat here. Play here.

"So you get paid to play." She shrugged out of her jacket. "Some days you get Gillian Benson. Some days you get Vance Ferland. One day eat chicken; next day eat feathers." She unlidded the drink she had made in the bar and poured it into a glass. "To existing here," she toasted herself. "The neat part is, they pay you lots of money you don't spend much of. Medical, dental, room and board and Jesus, J.B., how long since you had a woman in your bed?"

That didn't mean not in any bed since she'd been there; of course not. Her voice was low and vibrant, her smile a curve of assured suggestion, her eyes long-lashed and direct, and there were weekends, weeks, months. But those women of the weekend or week or month were guests; they had homes, and when they were scheduled to leave they left, and they rarely wrote to Jordan at Catawamteak; she didn't expect them to, nor did

33

she miss them, because none of them had slept in her bed. She had been twenty-six years old the last time she had said *I love you* to a woman — the last thing she said before she closed the door on the piece of her life that had held Aiga Barrett and the LPGA Tour.

She went to the bedroom and hung her jacket; she toed out of her shoes and nudged them under the dresser, and tasted her drink again. "Director of Golf. Bartender. Shrink-in-residence. Midnight cowgirl. Caterer to the careless. Aren't you just special." She picked *The Great Gatsby* from a shelf and turned to the near-last pages: "They were careless people, Tom and Daisy — they smashed up things and creatures and then retreated back into their money or their vast carelessness . . ." She read the last two pages, and shook her head and closed the book gently in her hand, and holding it, standing there, she thought of Gillian Benson, and some uneasy thing muttered through her. Mrs. Benson was outrageously wealthy, but by accident; she seemed surprised by it, uncertain of what to do with it or how to be it. The late Philbrook Benson, on the other hand, had been (Jordan suspected) as viciously rich as the worst of the wealthy who had ever walked through Catawamteak's beveled glass doors, as vastly careless as Tom and Daisy Buchanan — and of all the things Mrs. Benson had said this day, Jordan Baker Bryant's mind could echo back only three words:

There were times —

"Oh, Gillian." Her hand tightened on the book. "Should I have stayed with you tonight?"

Pray for a breeze, Mrs. Benson had said, and Jordan hadn't, but there was one anyway, scudding sailboats across the bay, snapping the awnings over the windows and the eighteen green and white flags of the golf course; she appreciated that breeze as she kicked the ass of one of last night's Slippery Nipples on the tennis court the next morning, knowing she was taking unfair advantage of a hangover. "Bitch," gasped the hung one, shaking her hand across the net. "You beat me last night, you beat me this morning."

"You asked me to pour. You asked me to play. You didn't ask for mercy either time," Jordan grinned. "I didn't even expect you to show, Olathe."

"Oh, girl. We got so squiffed! Wine coolers after last call."

"Eewww. You guys got a death wish?" She toweled her face and hair and the grip of her racquet; even with the breeze, it was hot. "How's Park?"

"Girlfriend!" Olathe had a slow, rich chuckle of a voice. "She was OUI last time I saw her, if getting in and out of the tub is operating. But hey. What about my buddy Rocky? Did she make it out upright? She babied them, but I figured one more and you'd've been right into home delivery."

"Who's that?"

Olathe held up a hand. "Guest; I'm cool; sink no ships. It's just, we've hung out some: croquet, out-and-about, that shit. She's way too cool for an old straight jane. Most of the hairdos around here just drip snot."

"Who in the hell are you talking about?"

"Benson. I call her Rocky 'cause she's way tough. She comes on like fluff, but baby, don't play poker with her. That one's spent mucho time keeping her cards close and playing them careful, and you know she knows how to bluff, girl."

"Yeah." Gillian Benson had been an uneasy presence in the back of Jordan's mind for most of the morning; Jordan wasn't sure why. "She got home all right."

Olathe sparkled a grin at her. "But you weren't there long enough to break her in! And I know you wanted to, girlfriend. I know you. Pretty little virgins all in a row."

Jordan grinned. Olathe and Park had been coming to Catawamteak for three years, and she considered them friends; most of the staff knew that, and Darlene, the assistant night manager, was an insatiable gossip. "I see the rumor mill is still grinding away."

"Never stops. Want the consolation prize? A long hot — and mm-mmm, I do mean hot — shower with me?"

35

Jordan shook her head, her smile lingering. "I'd love to, but I've got another gig."

"Damn! It's Sunday, girlfriend. You need time off, and honey, I can make a shower feel like a holiday — and an hour feel like a three-day weekend."

She hung her racquet in her locker and snapped the padlock. Olathe was vividly beautiful, blatantly sexual, and it was easy to imagine that an hour with her would leave one needing a holiday to recover, but Jordan liked Park too well to risk the friendship. "You're bad, Olathe."

"You know it, sistergirl." Olathe almost purred it, peeling out of her sweaty shirt. Jordan didn't mind being teased, and Olathe was innately teasing with her clothes on; watching her get out of them was probably the most fun she'd have all day. "Bad to the bone." Olathe ran down the zipper of her shorts, opening the cloth in pure suggestion.

Jordan took indolent stock of that nearly naked body; it was magnificent, and tempting. "Call me for a massage. I'd love to get my hands on you." She knew how to purr, too. "But you know that table's sacred, sweet Olathe. No fun and games there." She stroked a slow fingertip across Olathe's sweat-wet throat. "Ta, darling. Give my love to Park."

◆

A shower erased Olathe's effect, but not her lingering image, and dressing, Jordan smiled at the memory. Gaston fed her an exquisite seafood alfredo and let her read his *New York Times Book Review* in the kitchen. She went to the water's edge for her cigarette, watching a tiny tide pool, wondering why she couldn't identify more of the living things in it. By quarter to one she was in the pro shop, cleaning up paperwork and swapping famous-course lies with Bill Marston, her junior pro, while she waited for Gillian Benson.

At one-thirty she called Suite 316 and let it ring ten times. She looked up the hill toward the inn; no Mrs. Benson coming down. She rang the lobby. "Blake, d' you know Mrs. Benson in three-sixteen?"

"Itty-bitty forty-something, kinda reddish-blonde? Real nice lady?"

"That's her. You seen her around?"

"Not today."

"Did she call for room service?"

"I don't think so. Let me check." She waited. "Nyet. Something wrong, J.B.?"

"I don't know. Call her suite. If you get her, keep her on the line. I'm on my way up."

It was a long uphill from the pro shop to the inn; she liberated a golf cart and drove it instead of walking up a sweat. "You get through, Blake?"

"Not yet. She got pretty well hammered last night, didn't she? Darlene said you practically had to carry her to her room."

36

"Darlene's got a mouth like a fucking jaybird," Jordan muttered. "Give me a key to the suite."

"Jordan, you're gonna get me in trouble — "

"Don't whine, Blake. Give me the key or I'll sure as hell get you in trouble."

The elevator made her wait; she took the stairs and knocked. No answer. She knocked again. "Mrs. Benson?"

She rattled the key on its brass tag. She rattled nervous knuckles against the door, sharply this time, remembering Gillian Benson almost choking on her words: *there were times* — The memory had disturbed her through the morning; it was like fingernails on a chalkboard now. "Mrs. Benson! Are you there?"

Silence.

"Damn it — " She keyed the lock and pushed open the door; she stepped into the suite and closed the door behind her. "Mrs. Benson, it's Jordan Bryant. Are you all right?"

No answer. No sound of water running. The parlor of the suite was immaculate. Feeling more than a little intrusive, she tapped on the bedroom door. "Mrs. Benson, it's Jordan Bryant. Are you here? If you don't answer I'll have to come in. Please . . ."

Nothing. She tried the knob; it turned in her hand. She drew a steadying breath. *I hated him. He beat me — humiliated me — cruel malicious bastard and there were times —*

Jordan Bryant knew the choked denial that had been in Gillian Benson's eyes last night, a look that said he was dead but the scars would never heal, and there were times when instead of shaving her legs she sat in the tub staring at the razor, seeing what he had taken from her, and made her into; there were times when she wondered what had ever happened to those old so-called safety razors, where all you had to do was unscrew the handle and that thin blue sliver of steel was in your hand.

Gillian, be all right. There are things I just couldn't handle, and being the one to find you not-all-right is at the top of the list in gorilla print. Please *be all right.*

She shuddered, and swallowed, and pushed open the door. "Mrs. Bens — oh, god! I am *so* sorry, Mrs. Benson, please forgive me — "

Damply naked, wearing only the golfer's tan Jordan knew from her own mirror, Gillian Benson froze in the breath-caught panic of finding another being in her privacy as she emerged from the bathroom, unable for a moment even to cover herself with the towel trailing from her hand, and Jordan gasped her apology and closed the door and was halfway across the living room when she heard, "Jordan Bryant, don't you dare leave — " and she halted as if she were a private and Mrs. Benson a general, and she knew exactly how much fun Big Bad John was going to have with this. *But she's okay. She's all right. Thank you, goddess, for sparing us both.*

Shakily, she sighed, and went slowly across the parlor to lean against the French doors that led to the turret suite's balcony. Looking out over the bay, she rubbed her forehead in a slow, distracted massage; wearily, she wondered how much trouble she was in. John couldn't hurt her directly, but she knew that given an inkling of provocation he'd shoot a complaint upstairs at the speed of fax; she knew that Michael Goodnow wouldn't be her benevolent uncle-by-marriage if he determined a guest had reason to complain of impropriety. "I think you just let your heart overload your ass," she murmured. "Next time send Security, you think?"

She heard the bedroom door open, and Mrs. Benson's quietly neutral voice. "Well, Jordan. Hello more properly."

She turned. "Mrs. Benson, I'm sorry," she said quietly. "No matter how concerned I may have been, I had no right to invade your privacy."

Not looking up, Mrs. Benson adjusted the bow on the belt of her white silk kimono. "I take it you didn't get my message. I left it with — what's his name? Your shop super?"

"Ray. No. I didn't." *God, I hate that bastard.*

"Well, you had reason enough to check on me, then. I know what shape I was in when you brought me home last night." She looked up, finally, and Jordan saw the residue of what must have been a flaming blush; Mrs. Benson barely met her eyes before she ducked her head away again.

Jordan shook her head with a soft sigh. "Yeah. I knew, too. I'm sorry, Mrs. Benson. I was worried. I called from the pro shop at one-thirty. Then I had Blake call from the desk. I knocked — "

"I was in the tub with Mozart on the Walkman. You could have broken down the door and I wouldn't have heard you." She turned to face Jordan, managing a smile. "Please stop apologizing. Did you really think I'd call that glorified butler downstairs and demand your head on a platter because you were kind enough to make sure I hadn't managed to drink myself to death? You startled me, yes, but honey, I'm not angry. Now why don't you call down for coffee while I dress, and maybe we can both stop blushing."

Jordan watched Mrs. Benson to the bedroom door, a distracted part of her thinking, *Ric, old kid, if you think she looks good going away in golf duds, you should see her in white silk and nothing else.* More consciously, she tried to identify what was nagging at her, and finally she came up with it: *Another era. That's what it is: she sounds like another era, like she was forty-five forty years ago, when people still knew how to be gracious and unabrasive. And she's all right. Thank you, goddess. Thank you.*

She rolled back her eyes with a wobbly sigh and reached for the phone, grateful not to be calling an ambulance, grateful to still be employed . . . and unable to shake the certainty of the answer to a question from yesterday: whatever colors her hair glimmered in the sunlight, Gillian Benson was a natural blonde.

◆

She ordered croissants with the coffee, and they and Mrs. Benson — dried and dressed and more composed than Jordan was yet — arrived together. The owner of the room answered the door, and thanked and tipped the valet, and poured for them both. "Recover, Jordan," she chided gently. "You're the last person I'd have expected to be so rattled by a naked woman."

Jordan smiled weakly, accepting the offered cup and saucer. "I'm sorry, Mrs. Benson. If I hadn't been worried, I wouldn't be rattled."

"Well, I'm as fine as anyone with such a god-awful hangover can be. And is it against the rules for you to call me by my name instead of my husband's? Given that Lurch or Laing or whatever his name is, I'd hardly be surprised, but when he pays my bills, he can make my rules. Please, call me Gillie. Olathe tells me Benson is my slave name."

"Gillie, then." It made it somehow easier to accept the memory of her smooth, golden nudity. "Olathe's a trip, isn't she. Did she tell you how she got her name?"

"Isn't that wonderful?" Olathe didn't have a last name; she was simply Olathe, a name she had chosen with a map of the United States and a single dart that landed in eastern Kansas. ("Lucky for me I didn't hit Shaft Ox Corner, Delaware," she had laughed, tossing her mane of shimmering black hair back over bronzed shoulders before she smacked Park's croquet ball out of contention.) "She's the most exotic woman I've ever seen. I've enjoyed the time I've spent with them."

"I really like them both." Jordan added a tiny splash of cream to her coffee and stirred. "Have you seen any of Park's photographs of her?"

"Not yet. They asked me to come over for a drink next week. Thursday, I think."

Jordan suspected that the photographer and model wouldn't share quite the same prints with Gillian Benson that they had shared with her. "You need to be comfortable with a certain level of erotica," she suggested; almost all of what she had seen were nudes, some of them explicitly erotic.

Gillian raised an eyebrow. "I'm a big girl," she said mildly. "I think there's quite a difference between erotica and pornography."

"Yes." Jordan cleared her throat. "So. Do we golf?"

"Oh, dear! Teach me cribbage or backgammon or something. I can't possibly golf today, Jordan; I'm too miserable." She sank to the other end of the sofa with her coffee, tucking her feet under her. "Are you mine until five, like yesterday? Do you work tonight, too?"

"No." She peeled flakes from a croissant and nibbled nervously at them, and wondered why she was nervous, and wondered why she wondered; she knew what residual adrenaline felt like. "I have Sundays and Mondays off."

"That's your weekend? But . . . Jordan, why did you sign on for golf with me today? I don't want to take your weekend away from you."

Jordan tasted her coffee. "I'd have been golfing anyway. I figured I might as well have a partner I'd enjoy."

Gillie looked up, and away, in shy surprise. "Well, thank you. But — oh, Jordan. If you want to golf, don't let me keep you. When I claimed you for the afternoon I had no idea this was your day off."

"I seem to recall you being on my schedule today by my suggestion. You're not hard to spend time with, Mrs. . . . . Gillie."

Brown eyes came to hers, surprised again, but Jordan wondered: was there a deep hint of caution in them this time, too? "Why, Jordan. What a lovely thing to say."

She put her cup and saucer on the coffee table and stood, not knowing if she was suddenly uncomfortable so close to Gillie or if Gillie was suddenly uncomfortable that she was and she was just picking up on it. "Gillie, I — " She turned to meet dark eyes. "Mrs. Benson, I enjoy your company, but that's all I'm asking for. I understand that you're not — "

"Oh, sugar!" Her laugh was soothing, reassuring. "Are you trying to say I'm safe with you? I should think I am! And nothing you can possibly say can prove that more than you already have. No one with less than honorable intentions would have let such a multitude of opportunities slip away, would she? I couldn't be less concerned, and I absolutely adore you, so can't we just be friends? — and Jordan, I do insist you not call me Mrs. Benson — or is friendship between guests and staff against Mr. Laing's precious rules, too?"

Jordan shook her head, not in answer (for it was indeed against the rules) but in disbelief; with the exception of Michael Goodnow, she didn't think she'd ever met anyone as deeply and inherently civilized as Gillian Benson. "He only signs my check, Gillie," she said quietly. "I make my own rules."

◆

"What did you do before you came here?" Gillie stood at the end of the breakwater that thrust across the throat of the harbor, a sweater tossed over her shoulders and tied at her breast; Jordan had insisted she eat lunch, and with more in her stomach than coffee and a croissant she'd felt up to tackling the hike in the bright afternoon. "Or did you do this, just somewhere else?"

"Therapy." Jordan sat cross-legged at the edge of a huge block of granite, trying to work a pink shell from between her seat and the block adjoining without breaking the fragile thing in the process. "Practicing more than receiving," she added; Gillie smiled. "Seemed like a great idea at the time, combining psychotherapy and massage therapy, and it still could be for the right person, but after four years I figured out that I wasn't the right person."

"Massage? You do that, too?"

"Certified massage therapist."

"Well, you're a woman of many talents. But how did you get from professional golf to that? And then back again?"

Jordan glanced up. "Kind of like the cover of *Rolling Stone*. What a long, strange trip it's been." She returned her attention to the extrication of the shell, and Gillie thought of the wall behind the counter in the pro shop, where there were framed photos of Pro Bill and Pro George, but none of Pro Jordan with her putter aloft after the winning stroke of some tropical tournament victory, and she wanted to ask why not, but something warned her not to.

"I coached at a private school in Tampa for a few years," Jordan said (Gillie thought she sounded almost reluctant to divulge that tidbit of personal information), "but I'm a golfer and a tennis player. Trying to cover field hockey and soccer didn't work, for me or for the kids. I could lie to myself, but I couldn't cheat the girls."

"You like children."

Jordan glanced up at her. "Yes. I never particularly wanted any of my own, but I do like them. They seem to like me."

Gillie smiled. "I'll bet you'd be a wonderful aunt, or grandmother."

"Hard to do without being a sister or a mother."

"That's true." She watched Jordan work at the shell. "How did you end up in Maine from Tampa?"

"I'm native." She gave the shell the right tweak and it loosened into her fingers. "Native Mainiacs who leave home seem to do one of two things: they never look back, or they can't wait to get home again." She wet her thumb with her tongue and dusted off the shell. "Footloose or rootbound. I guess I'm rootbound." She stood, brushing off the seat of her shorts. "How's your hangover?"

Gillie shuddered. "My head feels like it's full of dryer lint and little curly pieces of scrap metal."

"Eewww. Bad one. It's not the cure recommended by the APA, but Artie down at the clubhouse bar makes a wicked Bloody Mary. Can I buy you one?"

"Nor AA, either, I suspect, but lord, Jordan, it'd taste so good. Oh, you got your shell out. Let me see?"

Jordan offered it. "Watch your step." The breakwater was, at its purest essence, the mother of all New England rock walls, a mile long and eight feet higher than a normal high tide, great stacked slabs of rough-hewn granite that twinkled pink and pearl in the sunlight. Her first summer at Catawamteak, a big man had slipped, driving his foot into a crack between the massive blocks, crushing his ankle, and it had taken paramedics and firemen hours to free him, and a helicopter to carry him away.

41

"What a pretty shade of pink." Gillie offered back the shell. "I'll have to look for one. Do you know what kind it is?"

"No. I was thinking earlier that I ought to brush up on my marine biology. I don't know much about it. No, keep it. My bookcases are covered with them."

"But you worked so hard to get it, Jordan."

"Something to do with my hands. Please, keep it if you like it."

"I do." Gillie dropped the little shell into a pocket of her shorts. "Thank you, Jordan."

They picked their way along the breakwater, Jordan offering an occasional steadying hand at Gillie's elbow; once when she did, Gillie reached for her hand when she would have slipped it back into her pocket after the assistance was no longer needed. "You have the most beautiful hands, Jordan. I noticed them yesterday. Do you still do massage?"

"Sometimes." It felt odd to be strolling hand in hand with Gillian Benson when she wouldn't have considered doing it in public with a lover, but she remembered her 'other-era' thought and knew that in other eras no one would have thought twice about two women holding hands. "We get a lot of weekend-warrior athletes here, especially in the spring. People who haven't golfed or played tennis all winter and then try to go thirty-six holes or a full match the first day out. Massage can help push the lactic acid through, and make the strains and sprains feel better. And I've got a little cadre of other massage therapists I work on. That way I get rubbed, too."

Ruefully, Gillie smiled. "Does it work on a hangover?" She kept Jordan's hand long enough to steady herself over a broad space between two slabs of granite, and let it go.

"It does, actually."

"I wish you'd said so before I got my mouth all set for a Bloody Mary. When I hurt my back" — she hesitated, a bare, brief pause, and Jordan knew the story inside that pause was old and long and dark — "I went to an old-school osteopath. He had beautiful hands — like yours in a size male. Sometimes I went even when I didn't hurt, just because it felt good."

"There's nothing wrong with giving yourself a gift." And even though something nudged her to leave it alone, she offered the question like flicking a dry fly to the edge of a stream where she didn't expect a trout to be: "How did you hurt your back?"

Gillie stepped across three big gaps between the stones of the breakwater. "I irritated my husband," she finally said. "If I ever get married again — probably in my next life — I'm picking a man who's not big enough to throw me across the room like some brute of a farm boy with a bale of hay. What possible satisfaction can it give a man six-foot-four to use someone my size for a punching bag?"

Jordan was surprised she had risen to the bait; she played the subject cautiously. "There's a whole theory that I won't bore you with, but it boils down to power and control. Domination. They compensate for the power they don't have outside the home by controlling their families with an iron hand. It's like kicking the dog."

"He did that, too." She reached for Jordan's arm as they walked, needing a balancing point; the breakwater wouldn't have been an easy walk had she not had a drink for a month, and she had that hangover feeling of still-slightly-drunk. "I'm sorry for last night. I said I wouldn't remember, but I do. You didn't need to hear my dirty laundry."

"Someone did, if you needed to say it."

She stopped on a level slab, shivering in the warm breeze. "I did need to say it," she whispered. "I never dared to before."

"Which part?"

"That I hated him. Not even to myself. I was afraid he'd hear me."

"How did you feel when he died?"

Gillie looked out across the bay. Some oblique part of Jordan's mind thought that they must make a lovely picture, windblown and pensive in the middle of that thin finger of granite; would an observer from the shore sense the sudden intensity of them in the slanting mid-afternoon sunlight?

(Park Webster, responsible for half of the Slippery Nipples at table six last night, glanced out the window of her third-floor room just as Gillie stopped, and she scrambled for her Hasselblad and a 1000mm lens.)

"I felt," Gillie said quietly, "as if the car that crushed his chest had just been lifted from mine. And I felt as if that would surely win me a seat in hell right beside him, but I felt it anyway. I feel it every morning when I wake up not having to wonder if I'll live through the day."

"Do you still feel as if you've won a seat in hell for feeling it?"

Gillie looked away again. "I don't know." She slipped her hands into her pockets; her right one found the small, smooth shell Jordan had given her. She closed her hand around it, looking at the granite at her feet. "It's been hard, Jordan. I catch myself missing him and wonder how I can miss someone who made my life more hell than Saint Peter could ever assign me. But he came home most nights, and it wasn't always bad, and when it wasn't, he could be . . . charming." Softly, she laughed. "He was like a knife with a good blade and a bad handle. Sharp, but poorly balanced. You never know when you reach for it if you'll have all your fingers when you're through — but I missed him last night. Or maybe . . ." She looked up, and away. "Maybe I missed — I don't know, I just know I was lonely. And so drunk."

"Do you remember what you thought about last night? After I left?"

Gillie looked at her. *Damned sunglasses,* Jordan thought, and a muscle in Gillie's jaw jumped and eased and she looked away again. "Weren't we on our way to a Bloody Mary or five?"

"I'm sorry, Gillie. I had no right to ask."

Gillie's smile was weary, accepting. "Dear Jordan," she said softly, and touched the backs of her fingers to Jordan's cheek. "You ask me whatever you want to. I'll know that when I least want to answer you, that's when it's most important that I do."

"Careful." Gently, Jordan took Gillie's fingers in her own, leading them away from her face. "You being safe with me doesn't mean my heart's safe with you. I'm liable to fall in love with you."

Just as gently, Gillian laughed; she leaned into Jordan for a quick, warm hug. "No. No, Jordan, you won't. I don't believe you ever waste your time."

◆

I can't believe you said that! Jesus, are you out of your mind? I cannot believe you said that — !

They had gone to the clubhouse for Bloody Marys, sitting at a table for four with their feet on the extra chairs to keep the glowering Mr. Ferland at bay, and they lingered over their glasses when they were empty. The bartender caught Jordan's eye and raised an eyebrow; she nodded. Fresh drinks appeared and they loitered over those, too suddenly shy to talk much, not sure how to part. "I didn't mean that," she said finally. "Out on the breakwater. It was a bad joke in bad taste, and I apologize."

Gillie roused from what had appeared to be a sleepy study of the driving range. "What, Jordan?"

Jordan knew that look, too; it was the mask battered women wore so well, the mask that allowed them to hide from truths they didn't want — or couldn't bear — to face. "I said, how are you feeling?"

"Bless hair of the dog. The little curly sharp things are gone. Just dryer lint left."

"Sounds like an improvement."

"Vast — although I suppose such improvement means I can't beg the massage."

"Like I said: there's nothing wrong with giving yourself a gift."

"I will, one of these days. What will you do tomorrow? Your half a weekend, god love you for giving me half."

"I thought I might drive over to Bethlehem." *Oh, great. All systems red alert: Jordan's doing July again this year.* She stirred her drink with the celery stick. "Have you ever been there?"

"No. No, I haven't. That's inland, isn't it?"

"Yes." Lightly, nervously, she coughed. *Jordan, don't do this. Just shut up and leave it alone.* "It's a nice drive over. It's in the mountains."

"I haven't seen much of Maine. I've just been along the coast."

"Well — " *No. No. Don't say this.* "I don't mind company, if you'd like to ride along. Bethlehem is one of the three old grand resorts left in Maine. The food is five-star . . . and the front nine is absolutely brilliant."

"Aren't you sweet to offer! But Jordan, really. You don't need to entertain me on your day off."

Jordan lit a cigarette. She knew she would go with or without Gillian Benson, and no matter what that nagging part of her advised, she knew that if Gillian went with her she might survive the trip. "That course is probably the biggest reason why my short game is so strong. It'd be a good challenge for you."

She had time to imagine several gracious refusals that amounted to fast retreats in the pause between invitation and answer: "You know the shortest distance to my heart is golf, you stinker. What time will you want to leave?"

I shouldn't leave at all, and I sure as hell shouldn't take you with me. "Is eight too early? Nine's okay."

"Eight, if you take care of getting my clubs."

"Great, Gillie." *Great; yeah, great. J.B., you are an idiot and by tomorrow night she'll know it.* "I think you'll really like the course. I grew up on it."

"Well, I expect to hear all about it on the way." Gillie took the last of her second Bloody Mary. "And I promise I'll be on time — at least, I will be if I quit drinking now. Where shall I meet you?"

"Under the canopy. I'll have my car there."

◆

"Jordan? You want another drink?"

Artie's voice penetrated a remote analysis of her caddie's swing; Carla was at the chipping green, pitching shags toward the pin like a metronome. It was easier to watch Carla than to think. "No, two's my — oh, hell, why not. I don't work tonight. You got your liquor order ready, Art?"

"I'll bring it over for you to sign. June coming back?"

"Huh?" She was still in July, trying to avoid its dark corners. "In eleven months, I suppose. It usually does."

"No, I mean your drinking buddy, there. June Cleaver. Man, ain't she special." It wasn't quite an insult; it certainly wasn't a compliment. "I think a couple of decades slipped by without her noticing, my dear Jordan."

"Give her a break," she said, irritated, surprised to be — and not surprised at all. "We get too much Bette Davis around here to bitch about Grace Kelly when she walks through the door."

"Well, excuse me," he grinned. "Guess I know where you got your sights set for the summer, rotsa ruck in my humble opinion."

"Piss off, Artie." She didn't want the next drink now; she stopped in the pro shop to ream Ray's ass about not giving her Gillie's message before she went slowly up the slope to the inn and her apartment. She closed the door behind her and leaned against it, breathing shallowly.

Be careful . . . I'm liable to fall in love with you.

I can't believe you said that! Jesus, are you out of your mind? I cannot believe you said that — !

Bryant's First Rule of Survival: You are their servant, not their friend. Never, ever, seduce their hearts, or allow them to seduce yours; just sing along with David Lee Roth and whoever did it first: 'just a gigolo, everywhere I go, people know the part I'm playing — '

No. Every weekend, every week or month before that's all you've been, all you've wanted to be, and it's been okay, you never cared about them or wanted to but this time —

This time you care. God only knows why, but you care.

She thumped her head back against the door. "Jesus, Jordan, she's straight and you care about her and you're taking her to Bethlehem? In July? Are you out of your fucking mind?"

Jordan had asked, as teenagers will, for a car for her sixteenth birthday; her father — he of the unusual sense of humor — had given her one. It had been his father's, and hadn't been driven, or even started, since the old man didn't come back from the War; it sat in the barn under its dusty brown canvas, mice storing seeds in the seats and wasps making paper in the trunk. He took her to the barn on the day she turned sixteen and dragged the tarp from it. She gaped at it, at him, at it again. "You're giving me the Packard?"

"And this to get it going. It won't be enough unless you do the work yourself." He took a check from his pocket and tossed it onto the driver's seat. "Or get a job. Never been a Bryant too proud to work."

She had been hoping for a Mustang, her first vehicular love. But the old ragtop had always fascinated her; she did some research and came away believing that a prewar Packard was *très* cool wheels.

There was the requisite battle with the powers-that-be at Chadbourne Academy. In 1969, even in private high schools, girls weren't supposed to take auto shop; they were supposed to take home ec. But a job would have cut into her golf time, and the shop teacher's eyes glazed over when he heard why she wanted the course; he agreed on the condition that the phaeton be the shop project for the spring semester. They towed it in, and twelve boys and one girl swarmed over it for five months. By May its twin-six engine purred like a mother cat suckling kittens; its wiring harness was a rainbow of color; its ragtop, leather seats, and oak body framing had all been recreated by hand; it sat on gangster-whites with two on the fenders, chrome spokes glittering in the overhead lights. She'd had to fight to share the work, right down to the primer, but Mr. Albert threw the boys out when it came to the paint. She and he spent two weekends at the school, him coaching as she sprayed coat after coat of tawny lacquer, both of them rubbing it out between coats. Halfway through taking off the masking paper, seeing what it would look like at last, Jordan had to stop and throw up, and she loved him for turning his back while she did her business into an empty paint can, and for offering a clean rag when she was through. "Ask the man who owns one," he said roughly. "I'm proud of that goddamned car, Jordan, but I'm more proud of you. You earned every inch of it."

Her father said, "Don't take too much credit, young lady. It isn't as if you turned every lick yourself — and why in hell did you paint it yellow?"

"Just to piss you off," she said, and loved the car in spite of him.

ASK ME, invited the plates. It was the only car she had ever owned. She was the only member of Catawamteak's resident staff with garage space. It had cost her an annual grand of salary to coax that space out of

Big Bad John; that the Packard deserved it was the only thing she was sure they agreed on.

"Isn't this beautiful," Gillian Benson said wistfully at eight-ten, finding Jordan in cream-colored flannel plus fours and a matching jacket lined with the same pale lilac as her thin cotton shirt, a weathered tartan four-in-hand raked down and tucked between the buttons, argyle socks in lilac and cream over wingtips the same colors; her pith helmet was tipped back on her dark hair. Hands in pockets, frowning at the car, she looked up when Gillie spoke.

"You look like you belong in it. You're right out of the Thirties." Gillie walked around the car in slow admiration. "Is this a Packard? It must be; look at the license plate. My grandfather had one of these. Maybe a few years newer, but still prewar. It was years and years old, like him, to me when I was a little girl. I loved to ride in it. It felt so elegant." And she looked around, assuming Jordan had been frowning because the long-nosed touring car was where she wanted hers to be. "But where's your car?"

Jordan, who had been frowning over wondering how the Packard would look if she painted it cream with lilac fenders to match her clothes, reached to open the passenger's door. "Right here, my dear Gillian."

"Jordan, you're joking! Aren't you?"

"If I am, whoever owns it'll be some old ugly to find it gone. Some people have children. I have the Packard." She smiled. "I'll grant you there've been times when I've thought children might've been easier to maintain."

In the lobby, John Laing watched, tight-lipped, as Jordan handed Mrs. Benson into the phaeton. He went to the door. "Ms. Bryant?" His voice was unctuous. "A moment with you?"

Jordan snapped a look at the door, not trying to hide the habit of irritation. "Excuse me." She pulled on driving gloves as she went up the steps. "We've got a ten-thirty tee time at Bethlehem, John. We can just make it if we leave now."

"You're aware, of course, that the personnel policies of the Resort prohibit fraternization with guests in your off-duty time. There are very sound reasons for that policy."

"The Resort's Director of Golf is taking a guest golfing."

"It's still fraternization."

"Would you like to tell Mrs. Benson she can't golf at Bethlehem?" Politely, she asked. "Or that she can't choose with whom she spends her time while she's a guest here? Or that if she wants to golf at Bethlehem with me, she'll have to take her own car? If you want to tell her any or all of that, by all means" — she swept an arm at the car — "be my guest. But if you don't, you're wasting my time and hers."

"You're not above the rules, Miss Bryant."

"Ms.," she corrected gently. "It's *Ms.* Bryant, Mister To You."

♦

"I'll go anywhere I damn well please and golf with whomever I damn well want to! Who in the hell does he think he is?"

"Gillie, he's disliked me since the day he laid eyes on me and he'll dislike me until one of us dies. I just work around him." Jordan wheeled the phaeton down Catawamteak's winding drive. 'What was that all about?' Gillie had asked, and Jordan had told her; now, she regretted it. The only other time she had heard Gillian Benson swear had been Saturday on the Nightmare, and then she had been frustrated nearly to tears.

"It's your damned job to improve my game!"

"John could give a whooping damn about your game. He knows I'm a lesbian," Jordan said. "I don't hide it, and that drives him crazy. He's a raging homophobe, and one of the symptoms of homophobia is a belief that all homosexuals — excuse me — fuck like bunnies. If he sees me talking to a woman, he assumes I'm trying to get into her knickers. If he sees me talking to her again, he assumes I succeeded. If I got as much action as he thinks I do, they'd erect a statue to me on the front lawn."

"It's none of his business whose knickers you're in — or who I let into mine, for that matter. I'm going to talk to him, Jordan."

"You won't change him, and he'll just come back at me."

"Well, he can kiss my grits. Why should he be able to treat you that way?"

"Because technically he's my boss. I was hired by the owner and I can only be fired by the owner, and that drives him crazy, too — his favorite crack is that if it wasn't for nepotism I wouldn't have a job, which may or may not be accurate — but on paper he's my supervisor, and as far as he's concerned that gives him the right. But he never learns that I'm not the one with the knife in my guts. He just keeps walking up to me with a knife sticking out of his, and I can't resist twisting it. I bring a lot of it on myself. If I'd kiss his ass like he wants me to, we'd get along fine."

"I'd rather kiss a frog," Gillie grumbled.

"At least with a frog, you've got a chance for a prince." Jordan oogahed the horn for the benefit of a small boy on a bicycle, gaping in wonder at the Packard. "One of the favorite senior staff games here is called Jerking John. For example: he nicks me a grand a year for garage space for my baby." She patted the steering wheel. "Last weekend I drove to Portland to take my national certification boards with the American Massage Therapy Association. I had less than a quarter of a tank when I parked back here. When I fired her up this morning, the needle showed full. I didn't put gas in the car. I never do when I park it here, but every time I start it in that thousand-dollar stall, it's full. I don't ask questions. I just thank the goddess for my magic gas tank and try not to drive more than two hundred and fifty miles at a crack."

"Jordan, you're bad," Gillie grinned, appeased. "You are a devil."

She touched her breastbone with her fingers and raised an eyebrow, the epitome of innocence. "Me? No! I'm lucky, dear Gillian. I've got a magic car."

"You've got a marvelous car. Tell me all about it — and about this old golf course you grew up on. Tell me everything about you, Jordan."

◆

Route 17 unrolled beneath the Packard's slender whitewalls as Jordan drove and talked and pointed out pieces of the landscape; days like that Monday were why ragtop touring cars had been invented, Gillie thought, reveling in the wonderful car, the glorious scenery — and the indulgent self-assurance of Jordan Bryant as she told stories on herself that made Gillie laugh: "So they wanted me to do a TV commercial endorsing this 'feminine deodorant product' — do you remember that stuff? Every gynecologist in the world said not to use it. And I said — forgive me, but I quote: 'for Christ's sake, guys, you might's well call it Pussy Perfume in a Penis' — it came in this obscenely phallic can, I'm saying, whoa, dual-purpose packaging or what — 'and will someone please tell me what this has to do with golf?' The boys get to hustle balls and clubs — consider that imagery, if you will — and Bryant gets Wuss Fresh? I told 'em if they'd package it with two appropriately-positioned golf balls, we could talk. They were not amused. Hell, I thought it was a great idea. Can't you see me now, holding up something that looked like that?" She chirped in brutally perfect imitation of a breathless TV-commercial airhead, "Hey, girls! Smell good when he's home, but don't go without when he's gone! Buy Fresh'n'Full today!"

Jordan kept the stories coming as she drove and smoked and every now and then sent Gillie a smile that said 'I'm enjoying the hell out of this day, and you're the biggest reason why.' That didn't bother Gillie Benson at all; she was enjoying the day, too, and knew that Jordan Bryant was the biggest reason why.

They stopped in Winthrop for coffee. "How much farther?" Gillie wondered, and Jordan allowed it would be perhaps an hour and a half, and admitted that they didn't have a tee time: "John's so anal about punctuality he can't even make someone else late." She opened the passenger's door. "Don't get mad again. When you're all wound up about him, he might as well be in the back seat."

They ambled along dubious pavement Jordan called 'two-nineteen' as if the road were an old friend; sunlight glinting through over sweeping trees made a dappled Appaloosa of the phaeton, and Gillie could imagine this car and this road when they both were new and every trip an adventure — for this felt like an adventure, going somewhere she'd never been with someone she barely knew in a car that reeked of elegant indulgence, and she watched the scenery on Jordan's side of the car because that way

50

she could watch Jordan, too, as she lolled in the driver's seat as if it were an easy chair, handling the wheel as if it were soft-bitted reins to a spirited horse, trailing her fingers in the breeze like a child; she watched the road the way an eagle watches a field where a mouse might be, the way a mouse watches a sky where an eagle might be.

She was not beautiful. Gillie remembered calling her lovely and wasn't sure that was the word she should have used. She was striking, but that was her eyes, big and long-lashed and soft as grey flannel; she was attractive, but that was the unremarkable regularity of her features. She was handsome, but that was too masculine a word, for Jordan Bryant whispered femininity from her every curve and angle; no one seeing her in that man-tailored suit with its carelessly raked-down necktie could or would have accused her of being male. She was tall and lithe, but not thin; she had breasts and hips without being voluptuous. She simmered with feral sensuality, and murmured calm restraint; she seemed at times as dangerous as a scrape of sound in an unfamiliar dark . . . and as safe as a mother's lap. She was an old Kristofferson song: a walking contradiction, partly truth and partly fiction — and the fiction, Gillie knew, was provided by the surmise of the one viewing Jordan Bryant, who relinquished just enough truth to make fiction beg to fill in the blanks of her offered history.

Gillie had questions: why did you leave the pro tour, why aren't your trophies and photos in the pro shop with the others, what happened to you in those times your eyes say you don't want to talk about? For Jordan had talked (she was quiet now, engrossed in a road that threaded roughly around the lakes and over the foothills of the White Mountains), but the stories she had told were generic, offering no answers; when she said 'once' or 'we' Gillie wanted to ask when and who, but knew, somehow, not to.

And there were other questions, more intimate and disturbing, questions that she felt more than thought: why don't you care for men, haven't you ever . . . how did you know? She had never been with a man before Phil, and her soft virginal fantasies of sex had been shattered on that first night with him. The next time she saw him was six weeks later, to tell him she was pregnant.

"You might as well get used to it. I'm a fucker, not a lover," he said on their wedding night, and that was what he did then, and after that; he never made love to her the way magazines told her men made love to women. Sometimes he didn't touch her for months and she knew he was seeing some other woman, but then late one night he'd come home drunk and crowd her into the bedroom. It would go on for a few months — maybe a year — before one night he just came home and spent the evening with her and went to bed without demanding of her, and she could sum up the first part of her marriage this way: When he was fucking me he didn't talk to me, and when he was talking to me he didn't fuck me. She lived the talking times in an odd suspension of relief and confusion, wondering why she could only care for her husband when he was getting his sex somewhere else.

His dalliances were a relief to her until 1982, when he brought home a particularly virulent dose of clap. Before then he'd been casually abusive: a slap here, a cuff there, a shove out of his way some other time, but when she confronted him with the accusation of that diagnosis, he took after her with a savagery that could still make her spine prickle in its memory. She stopped loving him that day, not that George Jones would ever immortalize that particular cessation of affection for the edification of country music fans. "Leave the son of a bitch," said The Girls, that indolently wealthy gaggle with whom she played bridge and golf. "Take half of what he's got and you'll have ten times what he gives you now, honey." She tried, once, but he found her and took her home. He threw her down the stairs that night, and stood over her as she wavered between two worlds of consciousness, feeling the spray of his spit against her face as he hissed at her that if she tried that specific brand of shit again he'd kill her. She had no reason to doubt him.

Even with the Valium she was murderously proficient at bridge, and managed to keep up with The Girls as they sped around the local golf courses. She had learned more of the game in eighteen holes with Jordan than she had learned in twenty years of playing twice a week; with The Girls, golf was only an excuse to get to the clubhouse bar, and they played it the way she played bridge: with bleak competence, just to get it over with. She didn't miss them, or their abuse of a game she admired, or their jocular prescription-swapping.

She realized, on a thin and winding Maine back road on the twentieth of July, that she had no friends. She watched trees and rock walls and occasional blue flashes of water on her side of the car until the quiet tears came under control. "What's this lake?" she asked at last, testing her voice; it wasn't strong, but it didn't break.

"Bryant Pond. No relation. What's wrong, Gillie?"

She glanced over, but Jordan was watching the road. She started to say 'nothing,' but the thought of saying it hurt like a lie. She wondered why it surprised her that Jordan could sense the ache when it happened, and supposed she was surprised because it had been so long since anyone had bothered to be attuned to her feelings. Phil never had been, and her children had long since given up on her. She wondered if they knew she was still off the drugs. She wondered if they cared.

"Is it something I did, or said?" There was no hurt in Jordan's voice, no suspicion or accusation; she simply asked if she had been the trigger.

"No. Jordan, no. I just — " She sniffed, tracing her fingertips under her eyes. "He didn't give me much identity, but it was all I had. I was Mrs. Philbrook Benson. It meant something in Atlanta, but now he's gone — and so is she. I'm not her anymore. Why would I go back? I've sold the house. There's nothing to go back to, but I don't know where else to go. Sometimes I feel like — like a husk, walking around. It just hits me. And it just did."

The tires of the touring car inhaled a mile of road. "I never knew Mrs. Philbrook Benson," Jordan finally mused. "I only know Gillian Benson. I don't know her well enough, but I know she's a survivor. If she wasn't, she'd be holed up in Atlanta worrying about this dime and that dime and whether she was going to piss off ol' Philbrook's ghost by how she spent them, instead of being cozied up in Maine's first and finest grand resort blowing through bucks like they were hers, which they are, because she suffered for every damned dollar. You know that viscerally, whether you know it intellectually or not. Your kids ever tell you to get a life?"

"Hello, my darling daughter Meghann. Just a week ago."

"Go for it, then. Pick the one you want. You can afford it — and damn, girlfriend, you earned it. I was born in that house." Jordan pointed to a farmhouse that blurred by, and Gillie wanted to say *Stop! Stop and let me see, let me feel that sense of place even if it's someone else's*, but the road curved and the home place was gone and Jordan's voice filled the hole it left. "Take back your maiden name. Throw a dart at a map and pick a new one. Move to Myrtle Beach. Move to Palm Beach or Tampa or Tempe. Move to Maine. Get a condo here and a condo there and snowbird. Be a golf bum. Go to Europe. Go to Australia — that's golf in another dimension! Then go to Scotland. You're going to be good enough for Scotland, Gillie. Go somewhere. Do something. God, you're young, you've got money, and thank god almighty you're free at last. What a gift! Blow a kiss-my-ass at ol' Philbrook's grave on the way by and fly the hell out of Atlanta. Gillian, you deserve a good life. All a man'll ever give you is heartburn and yeast infections. Once you know that — hell, after that it's all open road."

"Yeast infections?" Helplessly, Gillie laughed. "Oh, Jordan, you are so special! You'd better be careful. I just might fall in love with you, too."

Jordan sent her a half-grin that said, *yeah, right,* there and gone as she returned her eyes to the road: the eagle returning to the field, the mouse returned to the sky; suddenly, the intensity of that look was almost disturbing. "Nothing would please me more than you falling in love, Gillian. It would mean you care enough about yourself to take the risk — and that isn't the oxymoron it might sound like."

And new questions sidled into her mind, settling in to keep company with all the still-unanswered questions: *why aren't you in love, Jordan? Why aren't you taking that risk?*

♦

"Jordan! My god, child, look at you, plus fours and everything! How the hell are you? I figured you for lost to that high-falutin outfit-by-the-sea. Hey, Fred! Get your skinny buns in here!"

Gillie stood aside in almost awed amusement as the Bethlehem pro shop welcomed Jordan home. She'd played her first round here, she'd said, at the age of six; Fred, the wiry antique of a man holding her hand now, had caddied for her then, and then for twelve more years before she moved on to more prestigious, but not necessarily better, courses. But she came back; five or eight or a dozen times a summer she came home, driving past the rambling white farmhouse where she had been born, a house she still owned but couldn't bear to live in for circumstances she hadn't explained beyond "it was a really bad time for me."

On the pine-paneled wall behind the counter was the photograph Gillie had missed at Catawamteak: a twenty-something Jordan looking as if she'd won the world with her last putt; it was inscribed 'to Doc and Fred, who taught me this glorious game so well, all my love, Jordan. Hawaii '77: 67 + 64 + 66= #1' and flanked by a pair of framed magazine covers: a golfing monthly *(Bryant Brilliant at Bethesda)* and a sports weekly *(Heeeere's Jordan),* and she wondered what had happened to end such a glittering future.

"Still got Pappy's Packard." Fred looked out at the tawny phaeton gleaming in the driveway. "I know for damn sure the old fart never expected his four grand to go that far, back in 'thirty-three."

"I could've bought it new ten times for what the old bitch costs me," Jordan complained, and she reached for Gillie's shoulder, drawing her away from the magazine covers and into the familial circle around her. "Give the ancient history a rest, sweetheart. Guys, this is my friend Gillie Benson. Gillie, this is Fred and Doc. God love her, boys, she thinks I can teach her this game. Tell her the truth, Alfredo. Who knows more about golf than I do?"

"Any goddamn caddie worth his tip. I got my grandson Marc I'm breakin' in. Let him carry for you, Jordan. Give him somethin' to brag on over t'th'Academy." He nodded to Gillie. "That'd be Jordan's alma mater and as fine a school as is to be had, no matter where else she brags on. I'll teach you to golf, missy. I probably have already, if she's doin' your teachin'."

Jordan handed over the keys to the Packard. "Our clubs are in the trunk. Put her where she'll be safe, Fred; I'll take door dings out of your leathery old hide. Is Ruby still slinging the hash around here? My stomach thinks my throat's been cut, guys; I've got to stoke the stove if I want to be hot."

Her camaraderie didn't sound forced; she just didn't sound like the Jordan with whom Gillie had spent so much time in the last few days —

until she turned to say, "Gillie, hon, are you hungry?" and in that husky voice, in those direct grey eyes, was the Jordan Gillie knew. The touch at her shoulder slipped into an almost possessive arm around her waist, and Gillie wondered at how no one seemed to care: not the men who had known her all her life and surely suspected or knew her sexuality, not the interested foursome who'd been trying to pay their greens fees when Jordan caused her small sensation just by walking in . . . and not Gillian Benson, around whom that arm warmly was.

"I'm starved," she smiled. "You bragged about the food; prove it to me."

"You heard the woman. Doc, can you write us in for noonish and leave ten minutes behind us? I told her: you can golf all over Maine, but until you play Bethlehem you're only practicing. She's going to be good, and that bastard third hole'll make a golfer out of her or I'll eat my club covers."

Two people, Gillie thought. *She's two people: one for them, one for me.* Whatever Jordan's reasons, Gillie knew she had to play along; she rolled her eyes. "Make that a table for one for lunch. Jordan'll be having hers on the fourth tee."

Jordan — her Jordan — aimed a warning finger at her, a smile deep in her eyes, her hand slipping up her back to leave a squeeze at her shoulder before it left her. "You might get your feet wet down by the old mill stream, my dear Gillian. I've never seen Fred give a mulligan on three, and that brook's eaten more golf balls than the whole bay at Catawamteak. Doc lets 'em soak two days and calls 'em club specials."

"A week, I slice 'em up and call 'em club sandwiches. Go eat, ladies. I'll hold you noon."

◆

"Jordan, you really are a celebrity," Gillie said when they were seated in the dining room. "I'm impressed."

"Don't be. That's not why I brought you here." She looked, suddenly, as if being 'their' Jordan had been an effort after all. "Doc sticks that crap on the wall just as if anybody else remembers some also-ran for three years on the LPGA Tour. It embarrasses the hell out of me, but he gets to point at it and say, 'I taught her to golf.' How can I take that away from him?"

"Golf East and SportWeek sure didn't seem to think you were an also-ran."

"I won a few," Jordan admitted. "But no majors." And her eyes said *please don't push this now. I'll tell you someday, but today I can only laugh it off if you let me do it my own way.* "It was a long time ago."

"Well, you're special to them," Gillie said softly. "It counts, Jordan, to be special to someone. Don't ever think it doesn't."

55

Jordan looked up. "You're starting to feel special to me, Gillian," she said quietly. "I hope I didn't make a mistake today."

"A mistake how?"

"Bringing you here." And she forced a smile. "Here come our salads. We could use something a little lighter."

♦

The front nine was a par thirty, a finesse course with no room — but many opportunities — for error. Gillie contributed to next week's club sandwiches on her third drive. Fred had given her a four iron she never used instead of the three wood she only sliced half the time, and she gave it all she had and swore at the splash. He offered another ball. "Mulligan stew, missy."

"I don't need an exception, Fred. I need my three wood."

"Way too much club. Five wood, maybe, if you had one."

Jordan plucked her own four iron from her bag. "Try this, just for the sake of comparison. If you can't get there with this, try my five wood."

Gillie took a few exploratory swings, getting the feel of the club before she teed a ball and blasted it onto the green. "How come I can do that with your iron?" she murmured, looking at a birdie if she could sink a moderate putt. "What a nice club, Jordan."

"Isn't it? Seventy bucks, give or take, you can have one just like it."

"Seventy dollars? I hardly paid much more than twice of that for all my irons together."

"Attention, K-Mart shoppers; we've got a blue-light special in sporting goods."

"Well, it was ten years ago," she defended, a little sheepishly.

"Yeah, and that was ten years ago. Welcome to now. How tall are you?"

"Five-one. Why?"

"Fred," Jordan said. "C'mere." She turned away from Gillie to consult with him; the old man listened: nodding, shaking his head, then nodding as if in some final agreement before he handed Gillie's putter to Jordan and jogged away with her bag.

Gillie eyed her. "Jordan, what are you up to?"

Jordan smiled and teed up an orange ball, giving it a six-iron clout onto the green. She knocked four white ones after it, hitting the green with three of them. On the green, she offered Gillie her putter and used Gillie's herself for the four white balls after Gillie secured her birdie. She took back her own putter for the orange ball, sinking it as Fred wheezed up with a soft purple leather bag filled with nine graphite-shafted irons and four metal woods. "Here you go, Mrs. Benson. Now we can play some damn golf."

Gillie almost recoiled at the names on the clubs. "Jordan! Good lord, I can't — "

"Damn, Gillie, spend his money. He doesn't care anymore."

"But I — Jordan, you need clubs like this. I don't — "

"Just try them. Please? If you don't like them, Doc'll take them back."

They were good, but they didn't cure her slice; she put it into the rough on the sixth. Jordan hooked to the other side, landing in a deep bunker. "Shit and two is eight," she grumbled. "Which is probably what I'll end up with on this fucking hole. Sand wedge, Marcus — thank you. Talk her out, Fred. See you on the green."

"Fred?" Gillie had looked at her lie; it wasn't bad, but it gave her time to ask. It was the first time Jordan had been out of hearing. "Why did she quit the pro tour? She's an incredible golfer."

Fred squinted at the flag, and at her ball, and offered a wedge. She took the grip; he held the head, his old blue eyes watering with the pain of walking the wire between love and despair. "Her goddamned father cut the heart out of her. He was my friend, right up 'til he did what he done, and now every time I see her I damn that son of a whore to hell." His voice was a rough rasp. "Plenty people around here can tell you what happened. She's the only one can tell you how it was for her. Best you wait until she wants to say it. Now you're going to lob this sucker out of here. Widen your stance and swing full and smooth. Make a picture in your head of that ball sailing high and landing on the green, missy. Make her proud of you. She loves you half to death."

"By the old lord, Fred," Jordan grinned on the green; her ball was four feet from the cup, Gillie's just under ten. "Does she have potential? That was a great wedge shot, Gillie."

She accepted the hug Jordan squeezed around her shoulders. She didn't mind being loved half to death, but she wanted to ask a dozen questions; she wanted to ask one question: *What did he do to you?* "I can see why you're so good, if he taught you."

"Don't let him take all the credit. Doc helped."

Jordan made the turn at the ninth with a four-under twenty-six. "That's positively intimidating," Gillie grumbled.

"I've been playing this course for thirty-odd years." She added Gillie's score, wrote it in, showed her the card. "That's not bad, Ms. Gillian."

"Thirty-eight? Oh, that can't be right."

"T'ain't. Thirty-seven," Fred said. "I said to give her the mulligan on the brook."

"Sorry." Jordan adjusted the card. "Force of habit."

"I never shoot thirty-seven. Or thirty-eight. It felt like a good round, but —"

"It's an executive course, Gil. It's only a par thirty."

"But that's still only seven over. Check your math, Jordan."

"Check those K-Mart clubs at the door, girlfriend. My math's fine. You up for the back nine? That's a par thirty-six; it'll give those woods a workout. Bet you dinner you come in at forty-five or under."

"That's going to hell with the joke! Do we have time to drink to the front nine first? If I really shot a thirty-seven, I need to celebrate a major life event."

"Order me one too? Stoli's fine, but I like the lime. I'll be back."

On her way back from the ladies' room, Jordan stopped at the pro shop. "Are those new clubs or rentals, Doc?"

"Rentals if she doesn't take them."

"She's taking them. She just doesn't know it. What's the damage? She needs a putter, too; she might as well be putting with a crowbar now."

"I'll throw in that damn purple bag. I haven't been able to give it away." He tickled his calculator. "Nine hundred bucks with your discount, give or take an Andy Jackson if you got your tax number. You doin' all right, dear?"

She knew what he meant. "So far. Crazy to be here, but what else is new." She took a slim wallet from an inside pocket of her jacket and selected a credit card.

"Expected you tomorrow. Glad you came early and brought help." He ran her card through the machine and wrote the authorization number on the slip. "She's a fine-looking woman, Jordan." He offered the receipt for her autograph.

Jordan glanced up. "She is, isn't she," she smiled, and signed the slip. "She's just a friend, Doc."

"Mighty gift for just-a-friend."

"She won't do it for herself." She selected her copy of the receipt and tucked it into her jacket pocket. "My brand of shock therapy. If she surprises me, which I doubt, just credit my account."

"Shock therapy." He gave back her card with a shake of his head. "I thought you didn't do that psycho-hooey anymore."

"I make the rare exception. Thanks, Doc. They fit her just right." She plucked a putter from the rack, imagined herself nine inches shorter, stroked a couple of times, and took it out to the patio. "Here," she said to Gillie. "Try this, while you're trying."

◆

They had a quick drink, and tackled the back nine; Fred kept handing Gillie clubs she thought were too short for the lie, and she kept making shots she'd never thought she could. He was a bold, articulate teacher, but on the twelfth, when her ball alit fifteen feet from the pin but in a ragged patch of grass on the fairway edge of the apron, even Fred puzzled over what club to offer. When Jordan said, "Four iron," they both looked at her as if she'd dropped in from another planet.

"I don't have a four iron."

"Oh. So you don't. Well, use your five and close it up."

"And do what? I'm fifteen feet from the hole."

Jordan placed a ball in a similar lie and demonstrated; it was a strange stance, a strange swing, but her shot left her six inches from the pin. Gillie looked doubtfully at her.

"Hold the club in your left hand, left foot behind the ball — hell, I could talk all day. Hang on." The fairway was empty behind them; she lined up half a dozen balls a foot apart. "C'mere; I'll show you. Can I touch you?"

Gillie had resisted lessons for years, wanting no part of the sort of instruction she knew Jordan intended now, but she was afraid Jordan would misunderstand if she refused. "Yes." She accepted her five iron from Fred and stepped up to the first ball. "Yes, of course."

Jordan's body was as close as a shadow behind her. "Club here — " Her hand closed over Gillie's on the grip. "Hips back — " A fingertip brought her into the curve of Jordan's belly; she bit her lip, knowing she was expected to mold herself to the body behind her to feel the swing. "Okay — damn, I need my right arm about six inches longer for this. Finish your grip — " The hand at her wrist was as impersonal as the touch at her hip had been, but Gillie shivered; she hated to be touched from behind, let alone held, and whatever it was in the name of, Jordan was holding her.

Jordan stepped away from her. "Is this uncomfortable for you?" she asked gently. "I can talk you through it if it is."

Unhappily, she smoothed her club head against the grass. "It's not you, Jordan." Fred, who had been watching with some interest, suddenly found a patch of crabgrass for his grandson to help him pull. "It's Phil stuff. I know that's not fair to you, but — "

Jordan took off her sunglasses and blew dust from inside the lenses. "There's a useful little word that I understand perfectly well," she said quietly. "It's called 'no,' and all you ever have to do is say it. There's any number of ways I can improve your game, but physical contact will only work if it's comfortable for you." She settled her glasses back on. "Ready?"

She demonstrated; she talked. Gillie tried. "Oh, to hell with it," she muttered six failed attempts later, while Jordan retrieved the shags Marc was tossing across the sharply-cresting green. "Come on, then," she almost snapped. "Show me." Jordan looked at her over the tops of her sunglasses. "Well, I'm too stubborn to quit and apparently too stupid to learn any other way."

"Don't even take into consideration the shortcomings of your instructor," Jordan said dryly, and stepped behind her. "And I don't remember saying I was willing to listen to you berate yourself in front of me." She set the club, her gloved hand lightly over Gillie's; she placed her feet with a touch of her own, and drew her hips back with a barely-there fingertip. "You okay? Yes? I'm coming under your arm with mine —" Her upper arm came warmly across Gillie's breast. "Make your grip — Gillian, pay attention to my hands." And in that directed moment of focus, with a flick of their wrists, she understood the shot. "Good. I felt you feel it. Step to the next ball; I'll come with you."

She was utterly neutral, purely instructional; Gillie eased into the feel of her there. By the sixth ball they were nearly one entity on the odd, chopped swing. "There." Jordan retrieved the shags and lined up three and a new Top-Flite. "Solo flight. Last one's your score."

"I miss the crutch," she murmured. Jordan twitched a smile. She got close with two, holed the last practice ball, and ended up with a foot-long putt for par. "There, damn it, and more lesson than one learned. Thank you, Jordan."

"Il n'y a pas de quoi."

Fred shouldered Gillie's bag. "Give her the one she holed," he said on his way past Jordan to the next tee. "She earned it."

◆

"We might as well eat," Jordan suggested, totaling their card as they exited the eighteenth green, "since you're buying, dear heart who shot a forty-four to come in at a very respectable eighty-one. It'll be eight by the time we get back to Catawamteak. You think?"

"I want to see that card, Jordan Baker; you cheat. I'd be prostrate from starvation by eight. No wonder I never lose any weight; golf makes me so hungry." She was mellowly in love: with Bethlehem, with Fred, with Jordan, who finally seemed her easy self again. She didn't know when she had last gotten so much from a day.

"That's Fitzgerald's Jordan Baker who cheats, thank you very much. And you don't need to lose any weight."

"But you can't add. I shot five on the twelfth, which makes it dinner on you. And always ten pounds, since I turned forty."

"Fred's the official scorekeeper here, and he gave you the one you holed. And your ten pounds sounds more like emotional baggage to me, Ms. Gillian."

"How can I argue with you? After all, you've seen me naked. Just don't forget you'll be forty someday."

"I wasn't going to mention that, but since you did, I rest my case. And I'll be forty real soon, if I live long enough to see it."

◆

"What's the Academy?" Gillie asked as they browsed their menus in the restaurant. "Your alma mater, Fred said?"

"It's a private high school." Jordan lit a cigarette. "Half the kids here go there — or at least they did when I went. It's no big deal. We had a choice. Bethlehem High or Chadbourne."

"Chadbourne?" Gillie looked up. "But that's a good school, Jordan. We considered it for Four, when he started acting up on us. I remember it being in Maine, but I guess I didn't connect it with being here."

"It's not usually considered to be a disciplinary academy. Where did he end up?"

"Detailing trade-ins at the dealership for a summer, under JoeJim Hayden's merciless eye. You'd have to know JoeJim. He's a great one-eared redneck brute of a man — a rough, tough cream puff, but he never let Four know he was anything but rough and tough. Four was happy enough to behave himself at the local high school the next year."

"Had enough of old JoeJim, did he?"

"And too much. I think I'll have the baked ham," Gillie said, and Jordan flicked a look at her that said *don't order that.* It was more plea than suggestion, and reminded her of the look in those grey eyes over lunch, the look that had asked her not to press the subject of her time on the tour. She looked at the menu again and pretended to discover the Front Nine Prime Rib, and knew Jordan's tiny sigh was bald relief.

She pushed aside that disturbing look as they reviewed the round hole by hole, almost shot by shot, Jordan providing as much instruction off the grass as she had on it. Gillie would have been glad to stay the night and play eighteen in the morning, but that wasn't an option; Jordan had an early appointment.

"So what did you decide about the clubs?" Jordan asked as they went back to the pro shop. Behind the counter, Doc looked up.

She hesitated. She'd played a better-than-ever round, but she was more willing to credit good teaching than good equipment, and some uneasy thing in her balked at spending so much money on toys. "I don't think so. I hope it's not too much trouble," she apologized to Doc. "They're beautiful, but they're just more club than I need. But please let me pay you for your time. I know you'll need to clean them, and —"

Doc shook his head. "You can't do a thing but ride home with them, dear. They're paid for and in the car."

Gillie blinked. "I'm sorry?"

"Don't talk to me; I just work here." He nodded toward Jordan. "Talk to that over there."

Jordan held up her hands, palms out. "Don't kill me here. I'll tell you on the way home."

Just-a-friend, is it, Jordan? Doc watched Gillian Benson look at Jordan, a look that was bewilderment and umbrage and some deeper emotion so fresh it was like a wound with the shock still in it, too new to know yet that it was bleeding. He watched the suspension of their breaths, and the soft sigh of Gillie deciding to make her objections elsewhere, but still their eyes held. Finally, her voice low and controlled, Gillie said, "Then we should be heading back."

Jordan lifted a hand to Doc. "See you in a week or three."

"Make sure we do. Mrs. Benson, you come back and see us. We can give that seashore outfit a run for its money."

"I'm sure of that." She was still giving Jordan a look that made Doc know the ride home for them was going to seem much longer than usual . . . or not nearly long enough. "It's been a pleasure. You have a beautiful course. A wonderful challenge."

"We like it. Lift the lid while you got light, Jordan. Smells like rain later."

"Love you too, Doc." She held the door for Gillie and sent a last, helpless look over her shoulder that asked, *How much trouble am I in?*

Oh, a lot, Doc looked back. *You forced a hand that didn't want the forcing just yet, and you picked a hard day to do it.* "Fish or cut bait," he said. "Give me a call in a couple of days."

"I will, Doc. Thanks."

Gillie was in the car, elbow out the window, fingertips drumming nervously on the belt line. "Do you want me to put the top up?" Jordan took off her jacket and draped it over the back of the seat.

"Not necessarily." It wasn't said coldly, or curtly; it was simply brevity from someone who was not, in Jordan's experience, particularly given to it. Jordan turned the key and pushed the starter button and eased the Packard onto the main street of the village to drive with studious attention through town. "May I have the sales slip, please?" Gillie asked when she stopped for the only light. Her voice was gently polite. "I'll make you a check when we get back to Catawamteak."

Jordan glanced at her, but didn't offer the receipt; they were nearly to Chadbourne Mills before she said, "I knew you wouldn't do it for yourself."

"I don't need fifteen-hundred-dollar golf clubs."

"Everyone who golfs needs the best clubs they can afford. But if you want to return them, I'll turn around."

Gillie knew it would embarrass Jordan in front of her friends to return what they thought was a gift. It occurred to her that they undoubtedly assumed Jordan was her lover ('after all,' she had laughed in front of Fred, 'you've seen me naked') and something low and strange queased in her at the thought.

"He sure trained you well," Jordan said quietly. "You think you don't deserve them."

"Jordan, that isn't the point."

"I think it is. And I think you do deserve them. You could be so good! Gillie, it breaks my heart to see you playing those pot-iron pieces of junk and trying to call it golf. Please. Just play them for a few rounds. Then make a decision."

Gillie studied her in the slanting light of the early evening; Jordan didn't seem uncomfortable under the scrutiny, but she kept her eyes on the road. "Jordan, why?" she asked at last, softly.

"I just told you why."

"You gave me an excuse. I'd like a reason."

"I gave you the reason. You want an excuse."

The words were obtuse, and somehow made perfect sense; she could find no answer to them. The sun sank below the dark clouds of the impending front, taking the warmth of the early evening with it; she shivered. Jordan offered her coat. Gillie tucked it around her to find Jordan's scents in the cloth: a subtle, dusty mix of colognes, and something more personal: her skin, her hair, her self. She remembered Jordan's arm around her in the pro shop when they first went in, and how she had searched that touch then, looking for desire, finding only affection. She remembered Fred saying *she loves you half to death*, and the neutrality of her shadowing touch on the twelfth green, and her awareness when even that impersonal contact was too much to bear; she remembered being captured by eyes as soft as grey flannel when Jordan said *you're starting to feel special to me*, and the warmth that had given her.

She let the coat drop away from her face. "Jordan — oh, god." Shakily, she sighed; she shielded her eyes with her hand. "Jordan, I'm sorry. I'm just not comfortable with it."

"What bothers you?"

She ran a hand through her hair; the motion brought Jordan's collar to her face and again, she caught the subliminal scent of her. She folded the coat and put it back over the seat. "I don't know. It's just — something doesn't feel right."

You forced a hand that didn't want the forcing just yet. Doc hadn't said it, but Jordan had heard it, and she knew that he or she or some innate combination of their understandings had been right. She eased the car to the side of the road and got out, and raised the top and fastened it down, and got back in and tinkered with the heat controls.

"I'm warm enough," Gillie said.

Jordan killed the heat. "You're angry."

Gillie laughed, a short, strangled laugh. "Jordan, you can't begin to know how hard this is for me! You treat me better than I ever dared to wish he would. You treat me like — " She drew a deep breath. "Jordan, it's — It's as if you're courting me," she whispered. "I can't accept that. I don't want to hurt you, but I have to be honest. I'm not — "

"I know you're not. Gillian, I'm not courting you. I'm treating you like a human being. Showing you common courtesy. Respecting your abilities. That's how people treat each other when they're not hurting each other."

"Fifteen-hundred-dollar golf clubs? Jordan! That's not common courtesy, or respect or — that's a — a — a diamond, for god's sake! What were you thinking?"

Jordan looked at her for a long moment in the dying light before she shook her head and found her cigarettes in the jacket Gillie had rejected; she took out an Oval, but didn't light it. "You're not hearing me," she said softly. "It's about how *you* feel about you, not how I feel about you."

She waited, but Gillie didn't speak, or look at her, and finally Jordan sighed. "Okay. Why don't I just take you home."

Tiny towns slipped by in the gathering dusk: South Woodstock. East Paris. West Sumner. North Turner. Wayne. The road was rough; their silence was thickly painful. It was dark by the time they got to Winthrop. "Would you like a cup of coffee?"

"No. Thank you." But Jordan wheeled the phaeton into a mom-and-pop and got out. Gillie watched as she stalked to the store, lithe as a hunting cat in the glare of mercury lights.

A teenaged boy approached the car in appreciative awe; Jordan showed at the door, and Gillie heard the sharp edge of her voice: "Leave it be. I'll get it." Startled, the kid looked up, and Gillie closed her eyes, knowing he had taken a shot aimed at her, and then she heard Jordan again, closer, her voice soothing: "I'm sorry, man. I'm kicking the dog. The cap's right here. Ten dollars, super-hi. You ever seen a twelve-cylinder engine before? I need to check the oil. C'mon and take a look."

He said something too shy for Gillie to hear. "Packard's motto was 'ask the man who owns one,'" Jordan said. "Two hundred thousand on 'er and she never skips a beat. Ask me if Packard made an automobile." They talked, terms like four-forty-five cubic inch twelve-banger and synchro-mesh trannie and vacuum-servo brakes flowing from her until she said, "Whoa, Jim, we've got twelve in there already," and they walked back to the store still deep in car talk; at the door she threw back her head and laughed, and gave his shoulder something between the easy slap of male camaraderie and a seductively feminine caress, and he grinned as if he were half in love.

Gillie shivered a sigh. Jordan had soothed the boy's injured pride like calming a puppy. She knew it was too late for it to be so easy with them; she knew that wasn't Jordan's fault. She pulled the jacket around her, breathing the scent of Jordan in the cloth, missing her with a dull ache.

"Gillie?" The soft voice startled her; she had been nearly dozing, nearly crying. "I'm sorry, were you asleep? You sure you don't want coffee? They've got Green Mountain hazelnut. It's good."

"I . . . Yes. That would be good. Thank you."

Jordan paused so long Gillie knew the question she asked wasn't what she had wanted to say. "Decaf or high-octane?"

"Regular. One cream, please."

That long, considering pause again, as if something ached to be said into it. "I think I'll get a sweatshirt. Put on my coat if you're chilly." Jordan scuffed back to the store, and Gillie sat forward to slip into the jacket; the heater was too warm on its lowest setting, but without it the night was too cool for the thin shirts they both wore. Adjusting the jacket, she heard a crinkle of thin, crisp paper, and knew what it was.

Bethlehem Pro Shop

C1357/5-9(3w)/PZ5	$1,450
pro disc 40%	580
subtotal	870
tax exempt #95CW863	
total	$870

She was wounded that Jordan had let her argue on the basis of the retail price; she knew that she wouldn't have paid nine hundred dollars any faster than she'd have paid fourteen-fifty plus tax, and that Jordan's point was painfully accurate — *all right, all right, I get it* — but still, the slip of proof in her hand hurt. She heard the jingle of the bell at the store's door and jammed the receipt back into the pocket of the coat.

Jordan came back wearing a sweatshirt that said *Maine: The Way Life Should Be* over plus-fours and wing tips; she looked ridiculous. She offered coffee, and their fingers avoided each other on the cup. "Are you warm enough? I'll get you a shirt — "

"I'm fine. Thank you."

Jordan seemed to hover on the edge of saying something; Gillie didn't dare look at her. Jordan huffed a sigh and turned the key and thumbed the starter button, and the V-twelve growled to life.

♦

The rain caught them in Augusta, drumming on the ragtop; they used the noise as an excuse not to talk, though both of them, at least once, spoke the other's name in soft hesitation and received no answer, and they hid behind the rain until the canopy at Catawamteak left them in a silence that had no more excuses. Finally Jordan said, "Should I take your clubs to the pro shop, or do you want them upstairs?"

The question forced a choice she couldn't possibly make tonight: which clubs? "The pro shop's fine. Thank you."

Jordan's hand brushed her shoulder, a hesitant touch. "Gillie, I'm sorry. I wish there was something I could — "

"There isn't. Not now. Please." She didn't mean to be abrupt; she was just too tired and confused to try to fix things at such a late hour after such a long day. She opened the door and reached behind the seat for her spikes. "Good night, Jordan. Thank you for the good parts of the day."

She didn't see Jordan's face. She only heard her low, husky voice: "Good night, Mrs. Denson."

The Packard slunk away like a lion in the rain. The canopy over the front door protected Gillie from the weather, but not from the echo of Jordan's parting: "'Good night, *Mrs. Benson?*'"

She was curled into a corner of the love seat in her suite, a drink in her hand and silent tears slipping from her, before she realized she still wore Jordan's jacket, and that was too much; she buried her face into its silk lining. "God, Jordan! What are you doing to me?"

◆

The rain had been relatively gentle all the way in from the capitol, but by the time Jordan got to the clubhouse it was coming across the bay in wind-driven sheets. She was soaked by the time she wrestled open the sticky lock of the pro shop door and got the bags from the trunk and into her office. "I didn't need this," she gritted, fighting the dead bolt again on the way out, but at last she got the catch to work. She drove to the maintenance barn (that lock worked smoothly enough) and parked the car in its stall and got out, searching for her wallet so she could tuck a ten-spot under a wiper for Farley, the vehicle super, for he'd wash it (and replenish the magic gas tank) by mid-morning if she left him that signal.

But she didn't have her wallet. She didn't have her jacket. Gillian Benson had her jacket. Jordan leaned with a weary, "Awww, shit," against the car to run her hands through her dripping hair. "God, Gillian —" Chilled, listening to the rain hammering on the metal roof of the maintenance barn, she wondered why she had even bothered to try. "Goddamned straight women! They're more trouble than they're worth. When will I learn?"

She locked the barn and trudged up the hill, not hurrying; she couldn't get any wetter in the time it took her to get to the lobby. "Hey, Darlene. Any messages?"

Darlene looked up from a rerun of *Murphy Brown*. "Nuh-uh. But Big Bad wants to know what time you guys got in tonight. What d'you want me to tell him?"

Jordan blew a breath. "Tell him four past midnight and we pulled up in a fucking pumpkin with all of his brother rats for footmen. Tell him we didn't come home at all. Tell him whatever you think he wants to hear, because frankly, my dear, I don't give a damn." She turned, and turned back. "Thanks, Darlene. Tell him the truth. It's usually easiest." She slogged to her apartment and took a shower and ran the blow dryer over her hair, and pulled on jeans and a shirt and went reluctantly up three flights of stairs.

◆

Gillie was into her second drink, her second round of tears, leaning against the French doors in the living room of the suite, staring out at the rain and the blurry wink of the lighthouse at the end of the breakwater. She wondered if a person could make it through the storm to the end of that mass of granite to dive off the end, or if they'd get blown into the bay mid-hike. Wondering what difference it would make made a laugh rasp

66

from her. She wondered if she should pack up and go back to Atlanta, or go find a new resort *(but not Bethlehem)*, or stay where she was and get drunk, or go find Jordan *(good night, Mrs. Benson)* — or go to bed, or draw a hot bubble bath and try to soak up the courage to cut her wrists, or call Jordan and beg her to come up so they could talk *(good night, Mrs. Benson)* — when a soft rap of knuckles came at the door. She jumped — "Jesus, Jordan!" — and tried to get back the rhythm of her heart as it ratcheted in her chest.

She thought about not answering even as she reached for the lock, knowing that if she didn't answer, Jordan would be back with a key. "You want your jacket." She turned, wishing she hadn't cried, not knowing how she couldn't have, not wanting it to show. "I'm sorry. I should have rung a boy to take it to you, but your wallet's in it and I was — I didn't know — your credit cards — I — you — oh, god." She broke. "Jordan, I'm sorry — "

"Gillian — " It was a bruised whisper. "Honey, come here."

She collapsed. Jordan caught her, and held her, and she wrapped her arms around Jordan's waist and let the tears go.

And when she came back from the grief — for that was what it felt like: loss and shock, denial and anger and fear — enough to know she was being held, she knew Jordan hadn't kissed her, or whispered false promises that everything was fine; she had just held her and let her cry herself out. "Thank you," she whispered.

"I'm sorry." Jordan kept her face in the hollow of her shoulder with a hand in her hair, her other hand smoothing across her back. "I don't know how it all went to hell so fast, Gillie."

She realized she had handfuls of Jordan's shirt; she let go and then didn't know what to do with her hands. They found each other behind Jordan's waist and held on. "What did you say about it being bad publicity when drunken guests fall off the end of the breakwater and drown?" She shivered a laugh. "It was on my list."

Jordan's hands closed hard against her shoulders. "Don't say that. Don't — god, Gillian. Don't even joke about it."

"Jordan — "

Can we stop on the way back? I'd love to see where you grew up . . .

She had asked, in a comfortable space between words, after the farmhouse but before the golf course.

No. And there had been no question, and no comfort, in Jordan's abrupt refusal. *No. I — I don't go in there. I don't even know why I mentioned it.*

I'm sorry, Jordan; it just looked like such a nice place —

It was. It — it — was. It's just — bad memories. A really bad time for me. I should sell it. It's stupid not to, but I — it's — the taxes aren't — I — oh, never mind. Just forget it.

67

And in her suite at Catawamteak, too many unspoken words and too many hours later, her hands found Jordan's back, and she felt the subliminal hum of pain — deeper than pain — and knew that 'a really bad time for me' had been brutally understated; she knew that right then, Jordan needed her more than she needed Jordan. "Jordan, I'm right here. I'm here. I'm not going anywhere."

It was long — almost too long — before a shaky sigh warmed her hair. "Thank you — " and then Jordan was subtly more distant, a retreat of essence, not presence. "Gillian, are you all right?"

She realized (*are you, Jordan?*) that she was, that needing, and being needed, had healed her. She wondered how long it had been since she'd had a real human exchange. There had been perfunctory hugs at Phil's funeral from her father and brother and children, but those hugs had been as artificial as her grief; her family held her without respect. The Girls, that bridge-playing, golf-abusing gaggle, had doled out their squeezes and kissed the air beside her cheek and headed for the buffet.

"Jordan — " She wasn't ready to let go, or to be let go of. "I wish my writer would give me better dialogue, but . . . god, I can't tell you how much it hurt — 'Mrs. Benson'? I've never felt anything that felt so much like goodbye."

"I didn't know what you wanted, Gillian." Her fingers squeezed a gentle pressure at Gillie's shoulders. "But since the first time we played the back nine here, I've known what you don't want. I understand that, Gillie. Please believe me."

"I do." She drew back enough to look up, to find Jordan's eyes. "I trust you, Jordan." She knew that was true, but the next thought hit her; she leaned into Jordan's warmth. "God, this has got to be hard for you, too."

Gently, Jordan broke away from her, turning to run a hand through her hair, and finally she turned back to look at Gillie. "It seems as if as soon as a straight woman knows I'm a lesbian — " A caustic laugh bit from her. "Friends? How do I get there with someone who's afraid to have me touch them? I can't show affection. I can't touch without asking. I can't do anything that might be misconstrued. You see what happens."

She started to protest; Jordan's eyes stopped her. "I thought we'd settled this yesterday, and all of a sudden you're backing up and I'm standing there with my heart hanging out? Yeah. That's hard."

Her voice made Gillian think of some strong, proud animal struggling in snow too deep while grinning wolves closed in. "I haven't thought so much about my daughter and my mother," she said quietly, "as I have in the last few days."

"I thought that was where we were going," Jordan said softly. "All that woman stuff that doesn't need to be lovers, and then — blam. Projectile pain. God, Gillie, the last thing on my mind was trying to seduce you."

"Why did you go home today?"

Jordan recoiled. "I can't do that. Please. We can go anywhere but there."

"I'm sorry." She reached to touch Jordan's wrist, wrapping her fingers around the feel of gooseflesh. "I'm sorry, Jordan. When you're ready."

"I shouldn't have taken you with me today. This annual p-p-pilgrimage of mine is so — so — so — and I dragged you into it and I'm so-s-sor — I'm sor — I'm so — I regret that." She turned away. Gillie, unnerved by the sudden stutter, watched the effort it took for Jordan to gather herself. "I needed something stable," Jordan said softly, "so I used you and I t-t-tr — I tr — god damn it." She drew a deep breath, and when she went on her words had a careful rhythm. "I tried to make up for it with the clubs. I did mean what I said in the car; it just wasn't all of the truth. I don't think I knew all of it then to be able to say it. But I caused this, and I apologize."

"Jordan, no. I'm the one who said I accepted you for who you are. I'm the one who said we could be friends, but friends don't do to each other what I did to you today. You were right; you treat me the way people do when they're not hurting each other, but I'm not used to it. That's not an excuse, just an observation." Hesitantly, she reached to touch Jordan's shoulder. "Jordan, I like how I feel about myself when I'm with you. I know I probably sound like a stuffy old fart most of the time, but please, don't ever take that as condescending, or — "

"Will you stop?" Jordan turned, reached, stopped; she jammed her hands into her pockets. "What's wrong with being gracious? Gillie, I think about you in words I never use, like gracious and lovely, because you — and you — god, you're everywhere. All over my head. And half of that is making me crazy and half of me knows you're calming me down and I needed that today. I needed that so I dragged you into my p-perversion, but not the one — " She blew a breath at the ceiling. "Do you remember what I said about intellectual and visceral understanding? In the car, on the way over —"

"Yes. Jordan, will you — I have scotch. Stay? Talk to me."

"God, yes. Thank you."

"Come sit down — by the windows. I like to watch the lighthouse at night."

"So do I," Jordan said, and that small normality of conversation eased them both; they touched on their ways — Gillie to the bar, Jordan to one of the comfortable wing chairs by the balcony doors — a short, squeezing hug of fingers that dared what their voices couldn't say.

"So there must be more to that." Gillie tonged ice into glasses and poured drinks bartenders would be fired for. "Intellect. Viscera."

Jordan watched the light at the end of the breakwater: bright white, soft green. "Yeah. It's psyche, if you remember your Freud."

Gillie wrapped a tray's worth of ice in a hand towel. "I majored in Mediterranean history. I did crossword puzzles through psyche."

"Tut, tut," Jordan said dryly; Gillie snorted a bad-pun laugh. "Sorry," Jordan smiled. "Comic relief however bad. Can I interest you in Jordan Baker Bryant's infamous 'Pervasive Homophobia' lecture?"

"You're an incurable teacher, aren't you."

"Incurably impressed with the sound of my own voice, I've been told. Thank you for a kinder interpretation." She accepted the offered glass. "Whew. Remind me not to let you fill in behind the bar."

"You looked like a double."

"Keep this mix up and I'll be seeing double."

"You could put me under the table — well, maybe not. But I like the sound of your voice, too. Tell me about intellect and viscera and psyche and Freud." She tucked herself into the opposite chair and touched the ice pack to her cheekbone. "Excuse me. When I cry, I swell up. If I don't do this, I'll look like Mrs. Philbrook Benson in the morning."

"Gillie, I'm sorry I hurt you. I swear to god I didn't mean to." And hearing herself, she laughed bitterly. "Yeah. Isn't that what they all say."

"Only the ones who can even be bothered to apologize. And I know you mean it," Gillie said quietly. "Maybe honesty hurts, but that's not the fault of the truth. I think we both meant everything we said, but not the way we took it." She moved the ice pack to her eye. "So what's the lecture? I don't think I've ever talked psychobabble with someone who had a degree in it who wasn't trying to convince me that my mother was the root of all evil."

"Eww. Tough crowd tonight. You know what a Freudian slip is? That's when you say one thing and mean a mother."

Gillie crossed her eyes. "Go directly to lecture."

"Okay. Short course preceded by a disclaimer: I think Freud was a spineless wimp who had some good ideas but allowed them to be perverted by the prevailing psychiatric opinions of the time, consequently doing more lasting harm to women and homosexuals than any other human in the last two centuries. End of disclaimer, start of lecture. There's solidity in some of his thought processes, and psyche is one I believe in. So . . . six letter word meaning soul."

"That was in the *Times* puzzle last week. I had to work out three letters before I got it."

"Wrote it right in. It wouldn't be Sunday morning without that puzzle, would it."

"Did you get 'Wang Lung's wife'? Four letters, ends with 'n'?"

"I wrote in 'iron' — "

70

"Oh, stop! God, a side of you I haven't seen: the bad joke queen of Catawamteak. Quit with the warm-up and educate me before I get too far into the liquor."

Jordan flicked a look at her. "You keeping an eye on that?"

"Yes. And now, ladies and gentlemen," she drawled, her soft accent lengthened by the day and a little more vodka than she was used to, "y'all please welcome Jordan Bryant, tonight presenting her infamous 'Pervasive Homo — ' "

"And that's exactly the point: straight people's fear of the pervasive homo."

Softly, Gillie laughed. "Jump right on in there, sugar."

"Don't mind if I do. You asked for it, you got it. Tonight's lecture sponsored by Toyota."

"Shut up and talk."

"Yes, ma'am. According to our old pal Sigmund, there are three essential parts to the psyche: ego, superego, and id. For our application, ego, which is conscious and mostly in touch with your external reality, is intellectual and understands the wrongness of homophobia. You understand homophobia?"

"When you get down to business, you get down, don't you." Gillie shifted in her chair, sitting up to pay more attention. "Yes, I think I do. It's what I did to you today, isn't it? It's what John Laing did. Is it fear of the unknown? Anger at the unattainable?"

"And why would you be angry at the unattainable?"

"That's Lurch. I'm afraid of the unknown."

Jordan flicked a half-smile at her. "Okay, we'll go with that. You know how they say to George Bush, 'You just don't get it'? Ego gets it. But the superego — the internalization of the imposed morals of early societal teaching — I'm sorry; am I lapsing into jargon?"

"Yes, but I'm following you. Parents, church, school, peer pressure. All that happy crap."

"Right. Superego has had the idea drummed into it forever that homosexuality is wrong. Superego doesn't get it, and given that its job is to censor and restrain the ego, when the intellectual ego says, 'okay, she's a lesbian, no sweat,' the visceral superego says, 'bullshit, this is the dyke from hell, I'm outta here.' Is that about what happened today?"

"Sounds close." Gillie nibbled at the edge of her glass, and sighed. "And not the first time."

Jordan raised an eyebrow.

Gillie sent her a small smile. "My college roommate." She brushed a wisp of hair away from her eyes. "Riqui. I knew when I walked into the room and she had art posters instead of rock stars on the walls that we could get along. I ended up loving her more than I've ever loved anyone outside my family tree — " She had been talking into Jordan's eyes; she looked at her drink, suddenly shy. "We spent every free minute together for three years. And . . . we touched a lot. Held hands. Hugged. I don't know how many times we fell asleep together, reading . . . Proust. Camus. Easy to fall asleep to. Once . . ." She dunked her ice cubes with a mani-cured fingernail. Finally, reluctantly, she said, "One night she kissed me. No tongues, but it was . . . a lot more than I expected from another girl."

"Were you frightened?"

"I — " She looked up. "Yes. I was. It was the Sixties, and the Age of Aquarius, and if it felt good we were supposed to do it. And it did feel good, but . . ." She shook her head. "But that was so scary for me, Jordan. I come from a very conservative family. And . . . I don't want to say I was repulsed, because that's not the right word, but something didn't feel right. I don't know if it was her or me. I just . . . couldn't."

"Gillie, it's not uncommon for straight women to have a lesbian ex-perience. Most of the time they amount to a lot more than a no-tongues kiss. And sometimes they screw up the friendship. Everybody's super-ego kicks in and they withdraw from one another and never talk about it. Did that happen with you and Riqui?"

Gillie shook her head. "She wouldn't let it. She promised me it would never happen again, and I spent a few really nervous weeks, but it didn't." She ran a hand through her hair. "Somewhere in there Phil asked me out. Talk about one-eighty out — I should have known when I met his par-ents. A vulgar man and a beaten woman. They came to a football game — he played linebacker. But that's all beside the point. We went out for most of my senior year. He finally talked me into having sex with him. It was awful. I gave him back his ring."

She brooded over her glass for a long moment. Finally, gently, Jor-dan asked, "Did you consider an abortion?"

Gillie looked up, and at her glass again. "Riqui tried to talk me into it. She said she'd arrange everything. Go with me. Keep me safe. But—" She gave a tiny, wounded shrug. "I believe every woman should have the right to choose, but I couldn't."

"Was that your son or your daughter?"

"Four. Phil the Fourth. He's his father's son, all right."

"You mentioned your daughter in the car, but I've lost her name."

"Meghann." She looked at Jordan over the edge of her ice pack. "Can we talk about the kids some other time?"

"Of course. So what happened with Riqui? Are you still in touch?"

"Christmas cards. She's a political activist. Gay rights, people with AIDS. She thinks I'm happily married with two-point-four children and a Lincoln Town Car in the garage." She snorted a brittle laugh. "What the hell. Two out of three ain't bad." She moved the ice to her other cheek-bone. "I didn't do cards last year. I don't know what I'll tell her this year."

"Whatever's real when you write the card."

"I guess. Anyway, she's been with the same woman for years. If she's happy, I'm happy for her. I still care about her." She drew a deep breath and let it out softly. "Jordan —" She lost her nerve, and toyed with the ice in her drink, and finally dared a glance up, and shied her eyes away again. "I'm sorry. That would be awfully personal."

"I can't think of much I'd hide from you right now," Jordan said quietly.

"How does a person ever admit to being homosexual? How do you accept it without coming unglued? I'd have been so much better off with Riqui, but I just couldn't do it."

"Some people are straight," Jordan said. "Try not to think of it as a handicap."

"You are such a wiseass. Please, Jordan. It felt good when she kissed me, but I couldn't even think past that." She leaned her head against the winged back of the chair. "Frightened, yes," she said softly, her eyes closed against her own words. "But not terrified, and I spent a lot of time there with Phil. Tell me who you are, Jordan. The lecture's fine if that's how you want to do it. But I have to understand more about both of us, or what happened today is going to happen again."

"So the question was, how do you look at yourself in the mirror and see a lesbian looking back and not come unwound?" She tasted her scotch. "A lot of people do. It changes everything about the way you look at yourself. In my master's thesis I said it was similar to the grief process. Now I think that it is the grief process. I had to mourn the person I'd thought I was. Textbook Kübler-Ross: denial, anger, bargaining, depression — and *that* sucked. Acceptance, finally. Part of the reason I majored in behavioral psych was to try to get through that." She huffed a little laugh. "But I think the more letters social workers have after their names, the crazier they probably are. I'm glad to have the education, but I'm glad I'm not making a living at it anymore."

"You seem . . . comfortable with yourself now. With what — who — you are."

"Thank you. It is who I am, not what I am. I love women. I don't think that's a bad thing."

"It doesn't look bad to me," Gillie murmured, and chased that thought through half a dozen interpretations, none of them leading anywhere she wanted to go; she was glad Jordan didn't pursue it, either. "But we're off track — oh, yes. Intellect and viscera. Ego gets it, guts take a case of the vapors, and I have this incredibly Republican reaction. You might as well know; I voted for Nixon."

"How often do you think I admit that I campaigned for him in '68?"

"*You?* A Young Nazi for Nixon? I'll hold that over you until doomsday," Gillie grinned, and Jordan aimed a swat at the foot she had hanging over the arm of her chair. "Cross my heart and hope to die, I'll never tell a soul." She sipped her drink. "What am I afraid of, Jordan?"

"Good question. Tell me tomorrow."

"You and Herr Freud may go cordially to hell. Pick up John Laing on your way. We hurt each other today, Jordan. I hate that. Help me understand what happened."

"You mean, beyond the fact that I fucked up?"

"That's a little strong, I think."

"I crowded you. If I can lapse back to the lecture for a minute: Look at your emotional estate this way. Your body is your house, and your aura" — Jordan's hands described that psychic circle of protection around her own body — "your aura is your yard, complete with fence however high. I thought about this on the way home. It didn't seem to bother you when I touched you, except once, and you explained that. So I could touch you; that's like, I'm welcome in the front yard. Following me?"

Gillie nodded.

"Okay. Then I told you that you're special to me, and that was like the first time your next-door neighbor did a knock-and-walk-in. You weren't really sure at the moment that you wanted that to happen, but after you had some time to think about it, it was okay. This is ego — the lady of the house — processing things, using logic and reasoning. Still with me?"

"Mm-hmm."

"With the clubs, I hopped the fence into the back yard after you'd gone to bed for the night, and your watchdog — Superego — started barking in response to an unidentified threat. So you had to wake up, get dressed, go downstairs, and identify why the dog's barking. You find your neighbor in your back yard in the dead of night with a reason that doesn't sound as quite logical as you'd like it to. The dog picks up on your reservations and continues to growl. Am I still making sense?"

"Yes," Gillie said slowly. "And now the problem is settling the dog down while the lady of the house decides if the neighbor's excuse is one she's going to accept."

"I still like reason better than excuse," Jordan said with a tiny smile, "but barring semantics, you've got it."

"Reason, then. So what we're doing now is letting the dog make sure you're the same neighbor I've already established is welcome to knock and walk in?"

"Yes. And this dog is a Siberian Husky, a malamute — a wolf breed. Very sensitive to your feelings. She knows you're still not sure the neighbor didn't screw up." She smiled ruefully. "And puppy knows the neighbor thinks maybe she did, especially since while she was standing on top of the fence Doc was asking what she was doing up there."

Gillie almost flinched at the thought of Doc — and caught herself. "Ouch. I see what you mean about pervasive. I remember thinking that they — he and Fred — probably thought you — um — I thought they must think you're my lover. That made me so uncomfortable."

"Does it still?"

She looked up, and away. She tasted her drink. "Yes," she said softly. "I'm sorry, Jordan, but it does."

"Don't apologize for your feelings. Why does it?"

"Because I'm not — oh, no. That's more of the same, isn't it. It shouldn't matter if I am or not, or what they think. Obviously it didn't matter to them." Wearily, she ran a hand through her hair. "This is hard stuff, isn't it."

"Yes. Usually the only reason straight people ever make as much effort in their entire lives as you've made in the last ten minutes is that they discover someone close to them is gay and they have to deal with it on a personal level. My father — "

She stopped so abruptly, and such deep pain flickered on her face, that Gillie started to get up. "Jordan — ?"

"No." Jordan held up a hand, stopping her. "I'm sorry. I'm all right."

"Like hell. Jordan, I've been watching this all day. What — "

"Gillian, please. I'm not going there. Not tonight."

Gillie studied her for a long, silent moment. "All right," she said at last, quietly. "I'm sorry. Finish the lecture."

"Thank you." She drew a ragged breath, and ran her hands over her face, and looked up, and Gillie knew that for another moment, she was back in control. "Where was I? Oh, yes: how hard you're working, and how easy it's coming to you. You recognize your homophobia. Once you do that, you can identify why you had the thought: they said in church, or school, or whatever. Then you calm down the wolf. When you do that often enough, you effect change. What you're doing is parsing your thought process in order to retrain your superego. And yes, it's hard. People can ignore huge truths until all of a sudden they find themselves caring about someone who's something they've been taught to hate. Fuck with your mind? You bet, Mrs. Benson."

"Mrs. Benson," she muttered. "I haven't been that scared since Phil — " *Since Phil what,* she wondered. *Died? Thought about killing me the last time?* "Since Phil."

"Sorry to speak ill of the dead, but I've grown a real dislike for him."

"Join the club." And something in her voice made Jordan look, but Gillie was hidden behind the last of a Stoli-rocks. "How's your drink?"

Jordan checked her glass; it was half-full. "Sure, Gil, if you're getting up. You could top it off. Just add an ice cube and some water." She smiled at Gillie's raised eyebrow. "If you splash, splash gently. I've got to work in the morning."

Gillie splashed twice, once hard, once within the bare limits of Jordan's request. "So is there more to the standard spiel, my pervasive homo?"

Jordan almost choked on the cigarette she was lighting; she blew out the last of the laugh with the smoke. "Olathe told me not to play cards with you."

"How often do you do this?" She offered Jordan's glass between her thumb and forefinger.

"Do what?" She reached for the glass. "Thank you."

"Dedicate yourself to the education of straight women."

"I've never done it before in my life. Straight women are usually so far away from where I am, politically and spiritually and holistically — Why waste the time on someone I'll never have anything in common with?" And she shook her head. "I'm sorry. That probably sounded pretty bad."

"I knew what you meant. What makes me special?"

Jordan looked up. "Natural ability." She tasted the mix and put it down to let the ice melt a little more.

"Except in bartending, I see. Sorry; I'm used to my own wrist. So we've got the lady of the house and her wolfen watchdog. Wasn't there a third essential part?"

"And I thought I never lost the thread," Jordan smiled. "Id. Id is the flower in *Little Shop of Horrors* that says 'feed me.' Id is the part of you that says, 'give it to me and give it to me right now.' Id asks — demands — immediate satisfaction of primitive needs."

Thinly, Gillie smiled. "Like the part of a man that takes over when he can't hear a woman say no anymore?"

"Yes," Jordan said quietly. "Rutting is id-driven."

"So — bear with me; I'm still trying to calm down the wolf." She tasted her drink. "Rutting is procreative. Homosexuals being — um — not that, does it follow that they can alter the demands of id, the way the superego can be retrained? And if homosexuals can, so can anyone else?"

"I don't know if id can be subverted. I think men are id-driven to conquer. Look at the differences in sexuality between women and men." Jordan's hands spanned something light-years apart. "Men's orgasm is part of their reproductive function, but there's no proven physiological reason for woman's orgasm except to get her to agree to the act. Why else would she go through that? Sidebar: that makes lesbian orgasm purely spiritual, since there's no procreational basis for it. Return to text: a woman can be distracted from orgasm while she's having one, let alone how easily she can be distracted from even starting to have one, but men — bearing in mind that I've never had sex with one — "

"Never?" Gillie looked up, partly amazed, partly curious. "Really?"

"Really. But that's not to the point, except to define my experiential basis — which is to say, I'm talking out my ear now; correct me if I'm wrong."

"Like I'm an expert on male sexuality," Gillie grumbled.

Jordan sent her a rueful smile. "So we theorize together. As I understand it, men reach a point beyond which they're — primal. Whatever the quality of their performance up to that point, once they reach that point, their only focus is the achievement of that primitive procreational need, whether the . . . receptacle of their seed, if you will, enjoys it or not. That becomes a non-issue."

"In other words," Gillie said dryly, and tasted her drink, "in the purely heterosexual interest of procreation, they reach a point where they fuck like bunnies."

Jordan nearly blew a mouthful of scotch across the table; she managed to swallow without choking on the laugh that bubbled up around it, but it was a moment before she regained control. "I think you've got that one parsed," she coughed. "Try not to kill me next time you see the light, okay?"

"It seemed like it was my turn." Gillie got up to take her ice pack to the sink; she shook out the towel, and wrung it out, and wiped up around the sink with it, and hung it over the faucet. "About the clubs, Jordan—"

"I'm sorry for that. If you don't want them — "

"It was never that I didn't want them. I'm not used to having money, Jordan. I had to answer to him for every dime, let alone every dollar. Fifteen hundred dollars for golf clubs — "

"I get a pro discount, you know."

" — would have been worth a week in the hospital, and I wouldn't have had the clubs when I got out. Just the scars for thinking I might."

Jordan, caught in mid-sip, looked at her over the rim of the glass.

Gillie offered a small shrug. "I told you he beat me. Jordan, maybe you crowded me today, but I was coming from all over the place with my reactions, too. Don't say you're the one who screwed up. I'm still afraid of him sometimes, but he's not here so I transfer it to other people. And . . . " She came back to her chair, but she didn't sit. "The last time I had a lesbian friend I ended up in hell," she said softly. "The only reason I ever went out with Phil Benson was because I was running away from her. But tonight when I thought — well, this sounds wrong, but it feels right — when I thought I'd lost you. I was scared. I was hurt and angry, but here —" She touched her fingertips to her heart. "It felt like two cups of coffee too many, and I've been scared often enough to know it when I feel it. So how can I be afraid of you and afraid to lose you at the same time?"

"I don't know," Jordan said quietly. "What do you think?"

Gillie sat. "Go shrink on me," she grumbled. "Make me figure it out for myself. Thanks a lot." She reached for her drink. "I'm lonely, I suppose. I know I am." She laughed, a tiny, bitter laugh. "Why else would I catch myself missing him? God. That's like missing a toothache."

"Breath in the dark. As long as you could hear him breathing, you knew you weren't alone. It's hard to learn to live with yourself when you've spent your whole life with someone else in it," Jordan said gently. "But you learn. After a while, you learn." She took the last of her drink, and looked at her watch, and sighed to her feet. "I think we both could use some sleep."

Gillie looked at her, and away; she closed her eyes for a moment, and swallowed, as if she were swallowing tears. "Thank you for all of today," she said softly. "Even the hard parts." And she stood, and walked with Jordan to the door. "One of the things I hated about group therapy was the space invaders who'd come lurching up to people and say, 'You look like you need a hug.' I don't like to be touched, let alone glommed onto by someone I hardly know, and I really resented being told what I needed. But —"

Jordan managed a smile. "But I look like I need a hug?"

"Trust a mother," Gillie said quietly. "You do."

Holding Jordan, she could feel a bare tremble of something deep and malignant, and she knew Jordan's night sprawled long and dark in front of her. "Will you be all right?"

"I'll get through it," Jordan said softly. "I always do."

"Me, too." It was a shivering sigh before Gillie broke from her warmth. "Good night, Jordan."

Jordan waited outside the door until she heard the snap of the dead bolt. It was something she'd done dozens of times, leaving a guest's room late at night, waiting to hear herself locked out of a life; it was a sound that had left her with a vague and resigned hollowness before. This time it was more than vague, more than hollow, and as she went slowly down the hall to the stairs, she felt the hot burn of tears.

She let them come. Somewhere between the end of the pro tour and the end of the Thorazine, she had learned that tears were all that would ever save her.

"What the hell are you pissed off about?" Park Webster complained, aced on the serve for the third time in a row. Friday she'd beaten Jordan Bryant by a hair, just squeaking out the tennis match, but today Jordan was silently unbeatable, providing no instruction other than the challenge of a formidable opponent. As the winner approached the net Park was reminded of nothing so much as an irate cat, the way she blew out her breath in sharp hissing huffs. "Damn, woman. You thought about electrolysis for that hair across your ass?"

Jordan dredged up a smile. She knew she could go another match with a fresh player and still be quivering with barely-bottled intensity. "Sorry. PMS, I guess. Good match, Park. You really made me work. Thanks."

"*De nada.* I saw a bumper sticker on a pickup truck on the Beltway? Says, 'I have PMS and I have a gun.' I knew the fuckin' feeling."

"That's about where I'm at." PMS had nothing to do with it, but she tried for some normalcy for Park. "I'll be better company in a few days." That much, at least, was probably true.

"And easier to beat, I hope." She walked with Jordan to the locker room. "You were out on the breakwater Sunday afternoon, right? You and Rocky?"

Jordan regarded her with mild caution. "Yeah . . . why?"

"I think I've got some photographs for you. The proofs're excellent, but I need to blow them up to know for sure. I've got some lab time rented tomorrow afternoon. They won't be great — I need my own equipment to make 'em great — but I know they'll be good. I'll call you when I get 'em done. We were going to have Rocky come up to our crib anyway to look at some of my work; she'll like these, too. You guys can come over and we'll drink some wine or something."

"Sure," Jordan murmured, and hung her racquet in her locker and closed the door.

Park looked closely at her. "You okay, Jor? You look like you're off your feed, girl."

She managed a smile. "Sure. Not enough sleep last night."

"Hoo-wah," Park grinned. "Give up your hand, sister. Let me smell that deflowered virgin. Am I right?"

"No." She turned. "See you later, Park."

◆

"Why didn't you wait until today, so you could really torture yourself?" Jordan leaned on her hands against the cool tiled wall of her shower, letting steaming water pulse across her shoulders. "You are so sick! You could've taken her to the Samoset or Rocky River or any-elsewhere, but noooo. You had to go to Bethlehem." And she laughed, a brittle, cold laugh. "Of course you had to go to Bethlehem. That's the ritual, shit-for-brains. Go to Bethlehem. Manage to come back alive. Drink yourself into a stupor. Manage to wake up alive. You are truly sick, J.B."

She twisted off the taps and stepped from the shower, glad the mirrors were fogged; she didn't want to see herself. She had never wanted anything as much as she'd wanted to sleep in someone's arms last night, but she had left the bar alone at one, not quite lonely enough to pick up a stranger, not quite drunk enough to go up three flights of stairs and beg at Gillian Benson's door, not quite crazy enough to join Park and Olathe, however sure she was that they'd think that was icing on their personal cake.

She supposed she must have dozed; she knew she hadn't slept. On the worst of her July nights — and last night had been the worst she could recall in years — when she dozed, smirking malignancies oozed around her in the dark. Sleep was like being ricocheted into the most horribly seductive pages of a Stephen King novel, and she fought it out of an elemental fear of never being able to get out from between the covers of that darkness once she had been spiraled into it.

She toweled off in black silence, and ran a comb through her hair and deodorant under her arms; she stepped under an automatic cloud of cologne and tugged on shorts and a pale lilac polo shirt with the Catawamteak logo embroidered on the breast, and stuffed her feet into her Birks and slapped her golf glove and pith helmet from the kitchen table on her way out the door.

She didn't want to eat. She'd played a full match of tennis on a slice of toast and a glass of tomato juice, but she knew she needed more than that if she expected to get through nine holes, let alone eighteen. Gaston usually had lobster salad hanging around for nibblers like herself; that and some cottage cheese, maybe. Then maybe just being with Gillie would lay down the nerves.

She pushed open the kitchen door thinking about Gillian Benson and lobster salad . . .

. . . and met the sweet, smoky pineapple-and-cloves aroma of baked ham ready to come out of the oven.

The memory slammed into her.

"Oh, god! No — " Her stomach rose; she retreated blindly, instinct getting her to the women's lounge ten steps away. She barely made it to a toilet before what remained of her breakfast made violent exit. Fighting for control, losing, she sank to her knees. "God damn you," she choked, retching, sweating, shivering. "Oh, Daddy, god damn you — "

This time it was the flies: the new yellow floor, the thickening, darkening puddle, the dull, witless buzz of busy blue flies . . . *tell me! you saw it, god damn it look at all your fucking eyes you saw it — tell me! tell me why —*

After a while, it was only dry heaves.

◆

"Jesus, J.B. You look like shit."

She knew how she looked, and that was considerably better than she felt. "Thanks, Ray." She had inherited the pro shop supervisor; she had never liked him, and liked him less every day. "Get Mrs. Benson's bag, please. The new purple one. And mine. They're in my office."

"You're dreaming. You'll do good to make it to the tee, let alone eighteen holes. You're sick, doll."

"Just get the damn clubs, Ray! Just — " She turned from the counter, her stomach roiling; she swallowed. "I'm — " *sorry? Bullshit times two, apologizing to this twerp.* "It's nerves. Just nerves. I'll be okay once I get out there."

He shrugged, turning. Jordan ran a hand over her face, searching for her belly, her composure. Ray came from her office with a bag over each shoulder; he parked the clubs by the door and went back behind the counter. He rattled the assortment of things in his pockets, studying her for a long moment, and finally he leaned onto his elbows on the glass-topped display case; he picked one of her business cards from the holder by the cash register. "Might be I could recommend something for those nerves, doll," he said softly. "Help to settle you down."

For the first time in an hour she focused on something: one sharp, silver hair in his beard, sparkling like a long-awaited opportunity. "God, yes," she whispered; it was so easy, today, to sound so desperate. "Anything, Ray. This is — I can't golf like this. I'm too wired."

He scraped her card edge-down on the glass; it screeched thinly. She seriously considered breaking his nose. "It isn't legal," he said quietly.

"Like I never inhaled. Help me out, here, Ray. Christ, look at me."

He did, for a long, silent moment, before he straightened up and slipped his hand into his pocket. She reached for a scorecard, letting her hand linger on the glass, and received a tiny vial into her palm. "Go easy," he warned. "It's pure."

She closed her hand around the vial. "It's all pure, isn't it, Ray?" Her guts lurched hard; she battled with them. "Give me your keys. You're history."

She had heard the expression about peoples' jaws dropping, but she'd never seen it happen before; it was actually fairly amusing — or would have been, had she been capable of being amused. He looked like one of those bug-eyed tropical fish that spend their lives kissing their own reflections on the walls of the tank. "You said *what?*"

"You heard me. Goodbye, Ray."

"Jesus Christ, Jordan, I thought you — fuck! I'm trying to help and you fuckin' set me up!"

"I don't need that kind of help in my shop. Give me your keys."

"But — Jordan, come on! I need this — "

"I don't give a good god damn what you need!" It was a raw flare; he stepped back, wary even with the counter between them. Outside, eight caddies' heads swung to look in the pro shop window as if a puppeteer had them all on the same string. Artie came to the door of the shop from the bar; Jordan saw him and shook her head, letting him know that she still had the upper hand. "Give me your keys, Ray. Right now."

Cautiously, he worked them from his ring.

"I'll have Personnel forward your check," she said with deadly control. "I'll ask that you get two weeks' severance."

He shouldered past her, bumping her hard; she managed to keep her balance, and followed him to the door. He turned, stabbing a finger at her. "This'll cost you. You don't fuck with me, bitch."

"Another word and I call security."

He simmered a malevolent look at her, considering, but finally he turned. "That queer fucking cunt! I swear to fucking Christ — " she heard, before his car door slammed against the rest of it.

She leaned in the doorway, trying to look casual, trying not to let her knees go out from under her. She ran her gaze across the interested caddies gaggled by the soda machine. They were under-twenty-five boys, mostly, earning pizza and beer money and getting a free shot at one of New England's best eighteen; none of the kids were options for the spot behind the counter.

There was Barry, thirty-something, tall, muscular, shyly intense; she thought he was gay, but wasn't quite sure. He summered at Catawamteak and wintered in Miami, making all he wanted on tips. When her glance touched him he ducked his head, knowing what she was looking for, not wanting to be it.

There was Carla, her own caddie, with a fresh phys ed degree and no job offers, dependable as a railroad engineer's pocket watch in her sixth summer at Catawamteak. She knew Carla was carrying a little torch for her *(you could have called her last night) (sure, and you'd have gotten up this morning with more trouble than you've got now which is plenty and enough, thank you very much)*, but she worked around it or with it or whatever she did. Carla was a bright kid, a solid golfer, a good caddie, and that little torch never seemed to get in the way. And she looked ready to leap, ready to catch, her eyes asking what the hell was going on; Carla knew more was wrong than the stress of an on-the-spot firing.

And there was brash, handsome Ric, raising a seductive eyebrow as if to say, matters not to me, Boss; I'm holding out for nailing you to the sheets. *And you don't have a clue that I'm in trouble at all, let alone how much trouble. You asshole.* "Carla. I need you in my office, please?"

Carla closed the door behind them. "Jordan, are you all right?"

"I just fired Ray. Do you want his job?"

"Of course I do. Jordan, are you — "

"It's year-round, full benefits — medical, dental, 401K, cost plus ten equipment discount — "

"Yes! Yes, okay? Jordan, are you all right? You look like — "

"I know how I look. Never mind. Just take over." She pulled the phone to her. "Cash up the register so you start honest," she said, pushing buttons. "Tomorrow I'll — Farley? Jordan. I just fired Ray Phelps and he's pissed to the max; lock that Packard down tight. And if you'd have Brownie send someone over today to change the locks on the clubhouse, I'd love you forever. Ten keys." Grimly, she smiled; not only did she get rid of Ray, she got rid of that sticky dead bolt on the pro shop door after fighting it for two and a half years.

She called John, and squelched his protest that he did the hiring and firing. "He was dealing drugs. I've got the proof in my hand. Just call Personnel; I promised him two weeks severance. Oh, John, give it to him! Maybe he'll snort himself to death. Carla Stern's the new shop super."

She listened, rubbing the back of her neck; Carla watched her, wondering what she was supposed to do if Jordan did what she looked ready to do, which was faint. "John, try to visualize this: it's nineteen-ninety-two. Your Director of Golf, female, just hired a shop super, female. Do you deal with it, or do I have to call Michael and have him remind you who runs this goddamned country club? Put her on a ninety-day probation with a ten percent raise when she clears." She hung up, her stomach churning hard. "And that's settled." She tried for a smile she didn't find. "Can you fake it today, Carla? I'm in no shape to do orientation."

"I see this. Jordan, talk to me. Please. You look awful."

"I'll live. Put a staff meeting on the board for tomorrow at noon, noon-thirty, whenever it works, would you, hon? When Mrs. Benson gets here I'll be in the bar." She stood, finding her balance.

"Jordan?" Carla said softly. "If there's anything I can do —"

She managed a semblance of a smile. "I know. Thanks, Carla."

She barely made it to the locker room before her stomach deserted her again.

◆

That was where Gillie found her, huddled into herself on a bench in the most secluded corner of the L-shaped room, her spikes dug into the wood, her arms wrapped around her knees, her head buried in her arms. *I've never seen her like this,* Carla had said, and Gillie saw the war behind the caddie's deep blue eyes. *If you care about her at all, Mrs. Benson, she's in way-bad trouble. I tried, but I don't think she'd ever forgive me for knowing.*

"Jordan," Gillie said softly, not daring to touch her; she knew how it felt to be so close to the edge that a touch could be a push. "What can I do?"

Barely, Jordan shook her head.

The door banged open; laughing voices tumbled in. Jordan recoiled, drawing closer into herself. "Gillie, please. Please keep them away from me —"

It may have been five minutes; it felt like hours to both of them, Jordan hearing, Gillie forcing herself to laugh and joke with the women asking her how Bethlehem had been, and when would she stop monopolizing Jordan so someone else got a chance at her, and how about her firing Ray? Where's Babs gonna get her toot now? It's for damn sure that little sports dyke out there isn't holding — I bet they're lovers. Oh, you know it! Look at her, and Jordan doesn't hide — Honey, that Jordan! Mmm-mmm! If I swung that way I'd swing her way — god, those eyes of hers! I'll bet she's got a tongue like a butterfly — Gillie! you're damn near living together, spill your guts! Oh, what guts, Gil, you're so fucking suburban! It's the chance of a lifetime! Try honey instead of sugar — Oh, shit, you're hopeless. We'll see you out there —

Lockers slammed and spikes clattered out and the sudden silence echoed; in it, she could hear Jordan's shallow breaths. "Jordan, you can't stay here. You don't have to talk, but please let me take you where it's quiet."

She almost flinched when Jordan looked up; never, not even in the mirror, had she seen eyes so hollow.

Her goddamned father cut the heart out of her.

"You come with me." It wasn't a request; it was her Mother voice, her I've-had-just-about-enough-of-you-for-one-day voice, and Jordan blinked and got to her feet, and followed her.

"I'm all right," Jordan said woodenly, halfway up the hill to the inn.

"Jordan Baker Bryant" — she used all of Jordan's names like a mother's privilege — "you just come with me."

◆

"All right," Gillie breathed in the parlor of Suite 316, backing Jordan toward the sofa; her biggest worry had been John Laing, but he had been absent as they came through the lobby. "Sit, honey."

Jordan sat. She put her face in her hands, a hard shiver driving through her. "God, th-th-th —" She drew a deep breath and hissed it out slowly. "Thank you."

Gillie sat beside her on the sofa, reaching to turn Jordan's face toward her; meeting resistance, she abandoned the effort, but left her touch. "Jordan, please tell me what this is. Please."

Jordan clawed her fingers through her hair, locked them behind her neck, held her head as if to keep it from exploding. "God, why did he — Jesus, Daddy!"

Her goddamned father cut the heart out of her. . . .
Every time I see her I damn that son of a bitch to hell.

♦

At twenty-five Jordan Bryant had a raft of amateur trophies behind her, her first three years on the pro tour pointing to a meteoric future: Consistently making the cuts, winning major minors, rising relentlessly in the money standings, wearing shirts from a club manufacturer and visors from a big name ball; making headlines and money in a tough field for either, she was the odds-on favorite to win the Women's Open a week before it happened. But it all blew apart the July afternoon she wheeled the Packard into the driveway of the rambling white farmhouse outside of Bethlehem, a winner's check in her wallet, a new endorsement contract in her briefcase, gratis graphites in the trunk. Her mother's promise of her favorite dinner was upheld before she opened the kitchen door: "And I'll put sixty-six cloves all over it, baby — I can't even look at a clove without seeing a little black golf ball on a tee — that's what you shot yesterday, wasn't it? Sixty-six? Honey, I am *so* proud of you — "

I am.

Not *we are.*

She smelled those cloves, and the sweetness of pineapple, that mouth-watering ham-and-baked-potatoes smell making her stomach growl as she pushed open the door . . .

. . . and screamed. "Mama oh my god Mama no! Oh god Mama no Mama no oh no Ma no Ma no god no Ma no oh god Mama no —"

And she didn't stop screaming, somewhere in her mind, for six months. It was that long before she could think of her mother without seeing her staring up from the kitchen floor, drying blood trickling from her mouth and nose and a ghastly spray of it splashed across new yellow linoleum, the front of her pale blue blouse soaked dark, her hands smeared brown where she had reached in dying confusion for the strange new hole in her chest.

Her father was in the dining room. What was left of his head was impaled on the barrel of his hunting rifle. What was gone of it splattered across a table set for dinner, across the table and the ceiling, the gore barely clotted across a two-tiered cake that said in lilac letters over cream-colored frosting *U.S. Women's Open Go For It Jordan*, across the scrap-book open to Monday's glowing story in the paper pasted there, across the framed magazine covers on the wall, across her trophies on the shelf behind him.

He was splattered across everything he had ever said he wanted for her, everything he had made her into, everything she was.

She didn't remember the next few weeks — maybe the next month — at all; that time had spiraled into oblivion, lost to her. She only remembered the headaches: the blinding, on-your-knees-bitch domination of headaches that felt for hours and days like what he must have felt for the fraction of a second that he could still feel while his head was exploding — and the pain pills the doctor gave her, pills she finally ate all of one night when her lover was out of town on business she hadn't been able to hand off. She puked most of them out and was lucky, in a reverse-luck sort of way, not to have choked on her own vomit, but she revived two days later and woozed out to get the scrip refilled, ready to try again. The pharmacist took one look at her and called Someone, and Someone put her Somewhere Safe, and when at last she went back to the farmhouse the bodies were gone and the blood was gone, the cake and the ham and even the hole in the ceiling were gone.

But the sweet, smoky scent of charred ham was still there (for when she bolted, of course it never occurred to her to turn off the oven, and by the time the police and the ambulance got there the ham was a blackened lump and the house was full of smoke; she had wished a thousand or a million times that it had burned to the ground), along with her cleaned trophies and her cleaned pictures on the wall and a scrapbook with two pages carefully razored out, but her brilliant career was there down to the last victory, that gore-stained record replaced by Someone.

◆

That was July twenty-first, 1978.

And on July twenty-first, 1992, she walked into the kitchen at Catawamteak to the smell of cloves and pineapple and ham and baking potatoes, and now she was curled into herself on the sofa in Suite 316 with Gillian Benson holding her the way a mother holds a dying child, willing her to stay, and in some subliminal place in her she knew that without that firm and urgent touch she wouldn't still be there; she'd be in the Packard headed for that long-locked farmhouse, headed for the end of the line while the Traveling Wilburys told her it was all right, that vapid, empty phrase that was never true. It wouldn't ever be all right, not as long as she carried the memory of her mother sprawled on a new yellow floor with a potholder caught in her hand, looking startled and terrified and too much as if her last sound had been the first syllable of her only child's name while fat blue flies worked busily at the thickening splatter of her blood. That was never going to be all right, and every mid-July she remembered that; every mid-July she knew she was wrong to go to Bethlehem, wrong to drive Pappy's Packard past the old place, wrong to play the old course where the three of them had spent so much of her youth, and every mid-July she did it anyway, and this time it had caught up with her. And with Gillie wrapped around her, holding her as if to let her go would be to let her go too far, in that deep-shadowed place in her that hadn't dared to sleep last night she knew Gillie was right not to let her go; she knew what would happen if she did.

◆

Gillie didn't know if Jordan slept or simply hovered in some uneasy exhaustion of awareness; she was afraid to break their physical contact, afraid she might be all that was keeping Jordan calm, but finally nature demanded otherwise. She withdrew her touch gradually, and watched her for a long moment before she went to the bathroom, and came back to find Jordan leaning against one of the French doors, her hands in her pockets and her eyes unfocused, or focused on some thing Gillie couldn't — could never — see.

"Jordan?"

Jordan stirred, but didn't leave her study of whatever she watched beyond the windows. "Thank you." Her voice was low and hoarse. "I'm all right now."

"Are you sure?"

"Yes." She turned, allowing Gillie to see for herself. Gillie went to her; Jordan let herself be held, and held her in return, a weary recognition of so much left unsaid. "I've got to go to work," she said at last, softly; when she had looked at her watch she had been shaken to find it almost five: more lost time.

"Jordan, you can't. Not tonight."

"I can't think about it. Down there I don't have time to." Gently, she broke from Gillie's arms. "I tend bar because it takes as much or as little attention as I choose to give it. I can do it on autopilot, or I can immerse myself in it. Bury myself in the rest of the world's alcoholic excesses."

"Would you mind if I came down for a while?"

Shakily, Jordan smiled. "No. No, Gillian, I wouldn't mind."

◆

Gaston came wearily in at ten; Jordan automatically poured his white wine when he flopped onto a barstool. "Zhordaan, cherie," he smiled tiredly. "All de day I don' see you, my heart he break. But you look so sad! Tell Gaston."

She reeled a piece of tape from the calculator and wrote, and passed it to him. *If you love me, never cook ham on or about 21 July again. Jordan.* He looked up, puzzled. "You don' even speak to me, Zhordaan?"

"If I say it, you might forget. If I write it, you might stick it on your fridge and remember. Please, Gaston." Through the early evening the cloying, unmistakable smell of baked ham had drifted into the bar from the restaurant, and Jordan had done that night what she had never done in twelve years of tending bar: she drank on duty, sipping Stolichnaya instead of Poland Springs water, not enough to lose her functional edge, just enough to soothe the raw ends of her nerves, and she kept a constant

87

cigarette going. They weren't the English Ovals she favored five or six of each day, and she didn't smoke them; she just let them burn to the filter so the stink would mask the smell of ham, if only for a few minutes.

"I am confuse', but I am in love. I am suppos' to be confuse'." He slid the note back across the bar. "You write on him, 'my Gaston dat I love,' an' dis I do for you."

'My darling Gaston whom I love more than any other man,' she wrote at the top of the note, and gave it back, and Gaston kissed the paper and buttoned it into his jacket pocket. "Close to my heart, an' dem pig, he be never in Zhuly."

Gillie came in at ten-thirty, and looked at her and said, "You've been drinking," and Jordan nodded wearily and set up glasses and constructed sours and fizzes, collinses and coolers, and Bart and Rafael took them away, looking worriedly back at her; she made Gillie a drink and freshened her own. She ran the cash register and sparred with her barflies and kept taped music flowing; she saw the fight brewing in the corner even before its participants were sure they might be going to fight. She spent some minutes at that table, standing, then sitting, talking gently, her hands as graceful as doves delivering her peaceful words to them, words that apparently made great sense, for the men shook hands sheepishly, and with their differences settled and Jordan back behind the bar, they spoke in minute detail of what they'd give for and do with a naked hour with her.

At half-past-twelve she announced last call and filled the last rush of orders and had everyone out by one-ten. Gillie waited while she cashed up. "Jesus, I need some air. There must be someplace on this planet where I can't smell baked fucking ham."

The bar opened onto a patio. They went out with their drinks, avoiding the lobby and the eyes of the talkative Darlene. A breeze came off the water; the moon was nearly full. They walked in ghostly silence down the slope toward the bay. Catawamteak's seaside lawn was the front nine of the golf course, meticulously landscaped and maintained; sprinklers wept softly over the gardens and greens. There were Adirondack chairs by the seawall that edged the thin beach and they sat, watching the ripple of the moon on the water and the metronomic wink of the lighthouse at the end of the breakwater: white, then green, and when it blinked green Jordan thought of the green light at the end of Daisy Buchanan's dock, of Jay Gatsby standing on his lawn across the bay with his arms outstretched in the unquiet darkness, believing in some orgastic future. "Well, it's technically tomorrow." She lit a cigarette and hissed out smoke. "I made it that far into the green light, thanks to you."

"The green light?"

"Nothing. Obscure literary reference."

"How about the rest of theoretically tonight? Will you be all right?"

88

Jordan rested her head against the back of the broad, comfortable chair; she finally turned enough to study Gillie's profile in the moonlight. "I'd say no," she said quietly, "but I don't want to put you in the position of feeling as if you need to respond to that. I'll get through it. I always do."

Jordan drank right-handed, Gillie with her left; she studied the inches between their hands in long silence before she breathed a tiny sigh and reached to cover Jordan's hand with hers. Jordan turned her hand; their fingers laced together with almost painful pressure. "Peony Watkins tells me I'm missing the chance of a lifetime by not sleeping with you," she said softly.

"Peony Watkins is like a fucking moth in a roomful of candles."

"Jordan, if it would help — "

Her eyes were closed; tears glinted on her cheeks. "I gave you my word, Gillian."

"I can't change my mind?"

"You can't change who you are."

They sat in silence, hands entwined; Jordan's cigarette smoldered away unsmoked. "But thank you," she whispered at last, and Gillie squeezed her fingers in acceptance of words and reasons too hard to say, and they let each other go. They drank, the ice in their glasses chattering in the night.

"Jordan, can you tell me what happened? I still don't know."

Jordan lit another cigarette off the butt of her first one. Her voice, when she finally spoke, was soft and raspy. "Fourteen years ago today — yesterday — the twenty-first, anyway — my father shot and killed my mother and then killed himself."

"Oh" — it oofed from her, a breath of pain — "my god. Jordan—"

"She had a ham in the oven. It was just starting to burn when I found them."

"You found — oh, Jordan. Oh, my god."

"So I walked into the kitchen here — fourteen years practically to the minute — and smelled ham and pineapple and baked potatoes and I disintegrated. Clinically. PTSD is a bitch."

"Is that what that was? Posttraumatic stress disorder?"

"That's my diagnosis. But what do I know? I'm only an LCSW — L as in lapsed, now." She shook her head. "The pill pushers called it bipolar disorder — what they used to call manic depressive illness. They walked the ol' Thorazine right to me. I'm lucky to be out running around. Without Aiga — she was my partner; she was — is — a lawyer — I'd probably still be white on white. Padded walls and a way tight coat."

"Where is she now?"

"Tampa." Jordan shook her head at Gillie's stricken look: *how could she leave you?* "A few weeks after it happened she had to go to Tallahassee to try a case. I was all right as long as I wasn't alone, but without her — " She shook her head again, a weary whisper of a laugh slipping from her. "I ate a bottle of T3 — "

"What's that?"

"Tylenol with codeine. She got me into a decent hospital, and she got me out. She made sure I got back on my feet again. But she felt guilty, and I felt guilty, and we started fighting, and that made me feel guiltier. The headaches came back, and the pills came back, and she didn't trust me with them and we fought about that — I left her. I had to just . . . start over. By then it was pretty much a relief for both of us." She tasted her drink. "But we've healed. I see her every winter when I go down. We're friends again."

"No chance of getting back together?"

"I think Cheryl might object. They've been together a few years now." She flipped her cigarette butt over the seawall. "She always seems glad to see me, but she loves Cheryl. And Cheryl loves her. They're good together."

Gillie smoothed the moisture from her glass with a fingertip. "Have you loved anyone since her?"

Jordan shook her head.

She watched Jordan's stillness. Finally, softly, she asked, "Why do you think he did it?"

Slowly, Jordan shook her head. "I keep telling myself that if I could just know why, I could deal with it. But I think I know, and I don't want to know, because if it's true I couldn't deal with it. And I'll never know, but if I only knew — " A harsh laugh bit from her. "I've been doing this for fourteen years. Sound bipolar to you?"

"I don't know anything about that, Jordan."

More gently than she had that afternoon, she raked her fingers through her hair. "He really only tolerated me." Her voice was shaky. "They used to fight about it. He wanted a son and got me, and she couldn't have any more children — he blamed me for that, but he didn't tell me that until later."

He cut the heart out of her — "Oh, Jordan. What a cruel man."

"Yeah. Well. I tried to be his boy. I lettered in three sports. Restored the Packard. Got an athletic scholarship to college — and then my sophomore year I told them I sleep with women. Don't sons do that?" She huffed a sardonic breath of a laugh. "After that, it was like — the more I won, the more it looked like golf was really where I was going, the harder he came down on me. I know he was afraid of what the next headline might say. And then in '78 — "

She lit a cigarette and smoked in long silence. "By July of '78 I'd won two of seven with three seconds — one of them a major by playoff — and a couple of thirds," she said at last. "I was way up there with the money leaders. Then there were endorsements." She said names: ball, club, shoe, timepiece. "Mama was so proud, and all he could say was 'someday we'll read about you in the paper.' That's the last thing he ever said to me." She shuddered a laugh. "I got plenty of press after he — after I — "

Gillie waited; Jordan's silence stretched long. "Did it come out? In the media?" Finally, quietly, she asked. "Who you are?"

"No."

"Do you hate him, Jordan?"

"I hate what he did. I'm still so angry at him. He took everything I had — everything I was. He took my mother away from me — I wasn't ready to lose her. You never are, but — god, it was so selfish of him. He destroyed us all. He meant to. He did it on purpose."

She picked up her glass, looked at it, put it down without tasting. "I was late that day — almost an hour. They'd been dead less than an hour when I found them. He might as well have waited for me." And she shook her head. "Jesus, J.B., listen to yourself. Wallow, why don't you."

"Oh, Jordan. Honey, I wish I could help."

Jordan's smile was small and tired; she reached to brush her fingers across the back of Gillie's hand. "My dear Gillian," she said softly. "You help; god, how you help."

◆

"Darlene's got a straight eyeshot down this hall," Jordan said at the elevator. "If I go up with you, we're tomorrow's gossip."

"We're yesterday's gossip and I don't care. Just walk me up."

As the elevator doors closed, Jordan saw Darlene's registration of the fact. "If she was malicious, I could despise her or something." Hands in pockets, she leaned against the wall of the cage. "But she isn't. She's just got a mouth like a tent flap in a tornado."

"Come in for a minute," Gillie said at her door; uneasily, Jordan did, remembering what had been offered and how hard the no had been to say. She felt shiveringly cold; Gillie looked warm, and calm, and safe.

"Jordan — " Gillie took both of Jordan's hands in hers. "I think you should stay," she said softly. "Please."

"Gillie, I can't."

"Jordan, please. I'll worry all night."

"I'll be all right."

"I wish I could believe you."

"The check's in the mail," Jordan said softly. "I'll respect you in the morning. I'm from the government, I'm here to help you."

"Three in a row."

"I'm all right," she whispered, turning.

Gillie watched her down the hall to the elevator. "Jordan," she said just before the doors opened. "I'm here if you need me."

She hated to let those grey eyes go.

91

"I guess you all know Carla's the new shop super." Jordan roamed her glance around her staff, thinking they were a fairly fidgety bunch on such a glorious day, but she knew she looked (as the absent Ray might have said) as if she'd been et by a buzzard and shit off a cliff, and perhaps they were just concerned for her. Or embarrassed for her. Or maybe Carla and Barry were the only two who gave a jolly dwarf's whistle about her at all and the rest of them just wanted her to get on with it so they could grab some lunch. "Legal tells me it's okay to do random drug checks, so you all can expect to have to whizz in a jar at least once a month. Pros too," she said. "Sauce for the goose, all that good shit. If you're caught, you're gone. Those are the new rules, so if you can't respect the resort, turn in your ID cards and/or your keys."

Certain eyes shied from hers when she met them. She knew she'd be Pro George and at least two caddies short before too long; recreational pharmaceuticals wouldn't have time to clear their systems before she popped the first test on Tuesday. "In the interest of rumor control: yes, I had a very crappy day yesterday, thank you all for your concern, but as Elton John says, the bitch is back, so don't let the bags under my eyes fool you. Barry, I'd like you to hold my bag; check with me before you take a gig. Any questions?" There was general head-shaking. "Then we're done. Go do great things. Carla, can I see you, please?"

"Rumor control, my rosy red ass," she growled in her office, kicking out of her Birks and sticking new insoles into her golf shoes. "What's the chit-chat?"

Carla closed the door behind her. "Ray sold you some bad toot. Your AIDS test came back positive. You're bagging Mrs. Benson. You're bagging me. Maybe you're bagging us both at once; I don't know. What about you? Are you okay?"

She slipped into footies. "I had a bad day. We're all entitled, every so often."

"It looked pretty cruel, Jor."

"Yeah, well. It was." She worked her left foot into its shoe. "I got through it."

"Yeah. I just — I mean — if there's anything, you know, that I can do, I . . . you know. I — um — I — "

Jordan glanced up. Carla was never so inarticulate.

"Jordan, I love you," Carla whispered. "Please, if I can help — god, Jordan, I'd do anything for you. I mean it."

No. Oh, god, no, I didn't hear that, I can't deal with this now — She bent to put on her right shoe, and straightened up to find dark blue eyes brimming with tears. *Yeah, you heard it. And no, it can't wait; you deal with it now.* "Oh, Carla," she said softly. "I don't know what to say."

"I can sure think of things I'd like to hear." It was half-laugh, half-sob as she turned her back and Jordan ached for her, for knowing how it felt. She'd had a hugely painful crush on her college golf coach *(and when you told her, you were both naked in ten seconds, too, and that's pretty close to what Carla's hoping for, right here on my office sofa, just like me and Lorette on hers).*

"It's just — I — when you gave Barry your bag — it hurt, Jordan. It really hurt. *I'm* your caddie, you know? People ask what I do, I say I'm Jordan Bryant's caddie. I mean it's like that's who I am, and now it's like — I'm not."

"Now you're the pro shop supervisor at Catawamteak. Not a bad résumé bite, Carla."

"It's not the same. It's just — not the same. I won't be with you."

Jordan leaned against her desk. "Carla, you've dealt with this for three summers. Why — "

From the look on Carla's face, Jordan figured she might as well have slapped her. "You knew?"

"Of course I knew," she said gently. "And I'm flattered — I know that's not what you want to hear, but I can't say what you want to hear. I like you, Carla. I like you a lot. You're the best caddie I've ever had. It was hard for me to give you the shop job because I know I'll miss the coach out there, but you've earned — oh, Carla, please don't cry, I know I'm hurting you and I hate it — "

"Jordan, you're all I think about! I've never loved anyone like this and I can't — Jordan — " She hid her face in both hands, the first sob breaking from her before she took two blindly wounded steps, trusting Jordan to be there for her to walk into.

She knew she shouldn't hold her; she knew she had to. "I'm sorry," she whispered into golden hair, and Carla broke, sobbing into her shoulder. "Oh, Carla, I'm so sorry —"

For almost three years she had avoided encouraging her; it wasn't that she didn't find Carla attractive, for she had a hard weakness for small blonde women, but her affair with her coach had ended badly. When she recovered, she knew Lorette had used her position to gain advantage over a vulnerable heart, for students fall in love with teachers the way patients fall in love with therapists, and it was the responsibility of the teacher or the therapist to draw that line in the sand.

Or the boss. Yes, she feels good, and yes, you need someone and your chances for who you really want are zero

(You didn't think that, you didn't even think that)

(Yeah, you did)

but let her cry herself out and reestablish the distance ASAP. Sleeping with your employees is bad form no matter what, and loving me today could be getting me fired tomorrow. You'd be just as wrong and nowhere near as lucky as Clarence Thomas.

93

"I don't suppose you'd kiss me now." Carla shivered a laugh into her shoulder and broke from her arms. "I'm sorry; I didn't say that. Thank you. Now you can fire me."

"Go back to work," Jordan said quietly. "We can be friends, Carla; that's a good thing to do with love. But we can't be lovers."

"I knew that. You're so fucking ethical." She sat tiredly on the little bench beside Jordan's golf bag. "Now I'm like, so totally embarrassed. I'm sorry, Jordan."

"Don't be. Embarrassed or sorry, either one. Remind me someday to tell you about Lorette." She got a flat of cigarettes from her top desk drawer and peeled the cellophane from it. "And not that it's anyone's business, but I'm not — disgusting phraseology, this — bagging Mrs. Benson, either. You can spin that out in the shop if you want to."

"Yeah, she's a little straight, I think. Tie your shoes. You can say no, but you can't keep me from loving you, and I don't want you to break your neck. And no, I won't mention it again. We need pink balls in the display case, and we're low on club specials, too. Got some somewhere?"

Jordan bent to make the bows. "Only god and Ray would know. I'll show you how to do a purchase order."

◆

"Hi, Jordan. I'm sorry I'm late. Park and Olathe are hard to get away from," Gillie said at ten past one, finding Jordan behind the first tee box, desultorily clipping heads off clovers with her three-wood; she looked tired, almost drawn, and impulsively, Gillie went tiptoes to brush a kiss against her cheek. "How are you, honey? And what happened to your shirt? You're dampish."

Jordan smiled wanly, touching her fingertips to the wet spot on the breast of her polo shirt. "A broken heart rested there to bleed."

"Come again?"

"Carla just told me she's in love."

"I'm more confused by the word, Jordan."

"With me."

"Oh, my."

"Oh my, indeed." A ball was set between the blue tees; she stepped up to it, and glanced to the green and back at the ball and drew back her potent swing; they watched the ball soar straight and long and stop dead, with no bounce or roll, where it landed. "I don't think I'm going to like that lie at all," Jordan murmured.

"And so you broke her heart? Jordan, how could you."

"Don't joke, Gillie. I feel awful."

"I know you do, but you obviously care for her, Jordan. Why not—"

"She's twenty-two. I'm thirty-nine. I'm her boss."

"And she's a sweet girl and she must love you terribly or she never would have told you." She walked to the red markers; whether she played the blues and whites with Jordan, or the reds by herself, depended on how her back felt, and she'd gotten out of bed that morning with a low, familiar ache nagging around her hips. But she hit the ball well, with just the barest fade; it rolled lazily down the back side of a little rise and came to rest a few yards ahead of Jordan's. "We're using a cart today?"

"Carts don't gossip." Jordan kicked the pedal. "When I was twenty-one I had an affair with my golf coach. She was forty. It was great while it lasted, but the age difference killed it. She broke my heart into five or six hundred pieces. I got over it, but — " She scowled at her ball; it was half-buried in the soft dirt of a fresh divot some careless player before them hadn't bothered to patch. "These morons who don't repair their divots piss me off. Does that look like a deep rut to you?"

"I'd certainly think so if it were my ball."

"Ground under repair; free relief." She dug the ball out of the dirt with her turf lifter, dropped it over her shoulder, and retrieved the strip of grass to tamp back into the bruised earth. "I don't believe in May-December relationships. There's too many differences in basic values. I grew up with *Leave it to Beaver*," she said, remembering Artie's June Cleaver remark, "and Carla probably never even saw an original issue of *All in the Family* or *M*A*S*H*. I remember where I was and what I was doing when I heard JFK had been killed. I'll bet you do, too, but to her he's just another dead president." She stroked her eight-iron, picking up a long divot; the ball dropped short of the green. "Jesus, Jordan, pay attention. That's pathetic." She bagged her club and repaired her divot and moved the cart twenty feet to Gillie's ball.

"Would you have made her shop super had you known?" Gillie picked a club from her bag and took a practice swing.

"I've known since the first time she laid eyes on me. You'll over-shoot the green if you hit that hard with a five-iron, Gillie. Try your six." She waited; Gillie's ball lofted to the far side of the green and rolled back a little, leaving her lying on in regulation with a long putt. "Good shot, Gil. You could have used your seven — and I should have used mine. But she's been dealing with it. At least I thought she was dealing with it."

Gillie watched Jordan's lob wedge leave her a six-foot putt and wondered what it would take to throw off Jordan's game. They had stayed out in the night by the third green until almost three; she knew Jordan had played an early eighteen with Peony Watkins — Pee Wee, who thought Jordan would have a tongue like a butterfly, who Jordan thought was a light-struck moth. She looked exhausted from yesterday, possibly more so in the wake of Carla's disclosure, but her swing was as balanced as ever; she golfed innately, as if it were part of her. "Will you still be able to work together?"

"I don't see why not. Read your green, Gillian. It breaks harder left than you think." She moved her shadow out of Gillie's line of putt and watched critically; the rest of her life notwithstanding, she was a teacher and Gillie her student. "Lying two, play the break and go for the three-foot circle. You've got room for error and can still make par."

Gillie stroked. The ball rolled to the barest lip of the cup and seemed to hesitate there; "Drop, you bastard," Jordan coaxed, and pumped a victory fist at the familiar rattle as the ball went down. "Yes! Nice bird, Gil. You played this hole just about as well as it can be played."

"Thanks to you, but thank you."

Jordan lined up and stroked; the ball ran out of gas, and she turned a disgusted circle and went to tap in the six-incher for a bogey. Gillie wondered if she'd been premature in wondering about the quality of Jordan's game today. "Do you think Carla will just keep hoping? That would make it awfully hard for her, wouldn't it?"

Jordan bent to retrieve her ball. "It's hers to deal with, Gillie. I won't fire her for it, and if she takes that as encouragement — " She shrugged. "Like I said. It's hers to deal with."

"So she'll do a lot of dainty laundry in the sink that she wouldn't be doing if she wasn't with you."

Jordan laughed. "You do have a way with words, dear Gillian." She piloted their cart to the second tee. "I bogied, you birdied. You're up."

Gillie blasted her drive off the tee; it sliced hard, bouncing off the cart path and into the right rough. "Shhh — oot."

"Cheer up; that much hook would've had you pitching up over the seawall. That's a bitch of a shot, I'm here to tell you, having done it a time or five."

Gillie stared at the deep rough. "What am I doing wrong? That's so discouraging!"

"You swayed. That finishes your swing with your weight on your back foot. Try walking through the shot . . ." She demonstrated; Gillie raised a dubious eyebrow. "I'm serious. Gary Player does it."

"I've never seen you do it before."

"It's a slice correction and I'm a hooker — no comments from the peanut gallery, thank you. Try it. It's almost as if you're taking the first step towards your next shot."

"Yes, but you're graceful. I'll trip over my shoelaces or something."

Jordan shot her a tolerant look. "Gillian, you move like a dancer. Why are you so hard on yourself?"

"Force of habit, I guess," she said softly, shy in the compliment.

"Bad habit. I wish you could see yourself the way I do just for a minute." She smiled. "'Course then you'd have to get a new visor. That one wouldn't fit the swelled head you'd have."

"Oh, you. No wonder Carla's in love with you, if you're as sweet to her as you are to me. Come show me this swing thing; my slice needs all the help it can get."

"It don't mean a thing if it ain't got that swing," Jordan grinned.

"I'm not that old!"

"Neither am I, but I can like the music. Remember what I said about ending your follow-through with your weight on your back foot? If you take those ten pounds you think you need to lose —"

"You go to hell, Jordan Bryant."

"Me and John Laing, duly damned. This way — can I touch you?"

"Jordan, please. You don't have to ask. Just teach me."

Jordan laid down her driver and stepped behind her. "What I want you to feel is the shift of weight," she said, reaching around to close her hands over Gillie's on the grip of the club. "This way. Feel me — "

And an image from deep in the restless night surged hotly into Gillie's consciousness:

Feel me — Jordan as close as a shadow behind her, breasts and belly and thighs against her, hands slipping softly down her arms to find her wrists, her hands, weaving their fingers together, but there was no club, no grip; there were only long, slender fingers entwined with her own, arms enveloping her, the smooth suggestion of a lithe body closer to her than clothes and she knew there were no clothes; there was only skin . . . and lips at her ear, a trace of tongue, a breath of words: *Feel me, Gillie. Feel how I want you to*

Feel how I want you to
Feel how I want you
Feel how I
want you

and she melted into her knowledge of that want, of her own aching need, and their hands slid from her belly to her ribs as Jordan's lips buried a whisper of desire into her throat and a hand cupped warmly around her breast and she gasped a breath of pure abandon in the velvet night —

— and in the steamy afternoon Jordan's arms closed around her and she jerked back to awareness: she jerked away from her, gasping her denial: "No — !" She turned in near-panic. "Don't — "

She had gone to bed unnerved by the lingering hollowness in Jordan's eyes, uneasy with what she had offered in an attempt to help her heal, grateful it had been so gently rejected, staggered that she had offered, wondering sickly what she might have done had Jordan said Yes, I need you, hold me, let me hold you, let me —

(feel me)

— and stark awake, she had tried to parse it, trying to (and desperately trying not to) imagine what might have happened had Jordan stayed; shivering, swallowing hard, finally she slipped into a restless sleep, and then —

Feel me, Gillie. Feel how I want you.

— and then it was Jordan real and warm and there, touching her, and parsing didn't help because she was sick-scared and there was nothing to say but that single simple word Jordan had promised she understood perfectly well.

"Gillie — ?" Jordan spoke her name in soft caution.

She lied. There was nothing else to do. "Damn you, Phil," she whispered. "Will you just die and leave me alone?"

Something flickered in the grey eyes, hinting that she knew — not what, but not Phil — before Jordan came to touch her arm; Gillie let her. To refuse her touch again would be to lose the safety of the lie. "Gillian, what happened?"

She bent to retrieve her driver. "I'm okay. I'm sorry."

"Don't apologize. Maybe we ought to just lose that kind of instruction," Jordan said gently. "Are you all right?"

"I'm fine. Please, let's just keep going. Have you driven?"

"No." Jordan teed a ball and took two slow, deep breaths and blasted it two hundred and forty yards down the center of the fairway; again, obliquely, Gillie wondered what it would take to throw Jordan off her game for more than one distracted bogey. She knew her own game wouldn't be worth scoring; it was going to be hard to golf with that shiver burning deep in her belly.

Jordan talked her out of the rough; she didn't get much distance with the punch-out wedge shot, but she ended up in the middle of the fairway, the ball perched on a tuft of grass to give her a perfect lie for her five-wood. "If I can't hit this, I might as well go home," she muttered, and addressed the ball.

"White knuckles, Gil. Don't try to kill it," Jordan said gently. "Ease up, hon."

"Right." She blew a breath, opening her fingers, making her grip again. "Thanks."

In the middle of her downswing, a ball thumped to the ground just ahead of them; she flinched from it and her ball squirted off the toe of the club, ending up back in the right rough. She almost sent her five-wood after it before she wheeled angrily back toward the tee. "How about a 'fore'?" she yelled up the fairway. "You think?"

"Whoa, Gillie!" Jordan reached, not quite touching her shoulder with a staying hand. "Take it easy, hon. That's about two hundred and seventy yards. He probably never thought he could reach." She offered a ball. "Place it, don't drop it. Reproduce the lie you had. No penalty."

"No penalty, my palpitating heart! If he does it again, I'll drive it right back at him."

"I don't think so. Go ahead and hit, Gillie. They'll back off."

She took a few breaths and approached her ball, and sizzled off a wormburner that might have survived a more level fairway, but it slammed into a knoll and one-hopped into a pothole bunker. "Damn it!" She thumped her five-wood against the turf. "Didn't I leave a good book somewhere?"

"It's not that bad," Jordan said quietly. "It's recoverable."

"Me in the sand? Recoverable? Bull."

Her first stroke with the wedge bounced the ball off the lip and back into the sand. Beyond frustrated, well into angry, she smashed an un-thinking — and perfect — sand wedge onto the green . . . and then three-putted from twelve feet. "God! Is it too early to start drinking?"

"Quite a lot." Jordan left a thirty-footer for birdie at the lip of the cup and tapped it in with the back of her putter. "All right. You had a bad hole." She replaced the flag and waved an all-clear to the foursome of men behind them. "Leave it here, Gillie. If you can't, you might as well quit."

Gillie slid her putter into her bag. "I know," she murmured, and dredged up a smile. "Hey. The third's a short par three. Maybe I can get an ace."

Jordan smiled. "Hey, indeed. I've seen it done."

She didn't ace it, but she did drive the green with her seven-iron, pin-high but twenty feet left. "Should we let these guys play through?" she asked, looking back to see the foursome on the tee.

Jordan waved, but got no response. "To hell with 'em if they can't pay attention. Take your time. Don't let them crowd you."

She left it two feet short of the hole; Jordan tapped in her own six-footer and stood back while Gillie secured her par. "Nice par, Gillie. Feel better now?"

She ducked her head with a small, embarrassed smile. "Yes. I'm sorry, Jordan. I just — "

"You got sideswiped. It happens, Gil." She socked her putter and tucked it into her bag. "Let's go. Maybe we can get ahead of these guys."

But the fourth was a long dogleg right, perfect for Gillie's fade but perilous to Jordan's occasional unintentional draw; she had to spend a moment finding her ball in the long grass of the left rough, and the men drove into them again, missing them comfortably but well beyond the etiquette of the game. "Gentlemen, you're starting to annoy me." Jordan found a book of matches in her bag. "Please either play through or wait for our second shot before you drive," she wrote inside the cover, and crimped back the cardboard so it would stay open and put it on the ground beside the offending ball. She was assessing the sand shot her second stroke had left her when she heard laughter behind them; she looked back to see a man in a red shirt lighting a cigarette — with one of her matches, she assumed.

And it didn't really surprise her when a ball thumped behind them before they'd taken their second shot on the fifth, but when one bounced past her while she was trying to read a birdie putt on the sixth, she picked up the offending ball and glanced at it before putting it in her pocket. "You're away, Gillie."

"These jerks are really getting on my nerves, Jordan."

"They were pretty well on mine two holes ago. I think it's time they got a refresher course in the etiquette of this gentlemanly game."

The seventh tee was over a knoll and through a thicket of trees; she parked the cart by the red markers and waited. "Almost bagged yourself a female there, Greg," they heard as the men drove up the path. "Suppose you can get her this time?"

"Short par three? Easy wedge," Greg said, and the men roared with laughter.

Jordan got out of the cart as the men parked by the blue tees. She strolled up to the first cart, using her sand wedge as a walking stick. "Good day, gentlemen. Which one of you is GB?" For the ball she had confiscated on the last green had GB markered on it.

"Hey, there, little lady!" The red-shirted man flipped a cigarette over the side of the cart and gave her a toothy smile. "GB, that's me, Greg Beame. Sorry about that last shot. Man, I've been nailing them all day. Surprised me as much as it surprised you!"

"That, I doubt. I think your good day is over, Mr. Beame."

He blinked, and lost the grin. "What the hell's that supposed to mean?"

The second cart edged up beside Jordan, putting her between the four men. "Don't get boxed in, Jordan," Gillie murmured. "I don't like the looks of these guys."

Jordan stepped back so that she could see them all; she leaned on her wedge, looking perfectly cool and relaxed, even smiling a little. "It means you're through playing golf at Catawamteak today."

"Like hell I am! I paid my goddamn greens fees, sweetheart. You don't like the way I golf, you can trot your dainty little ass right on back to the clubhouse and have a nice cry."

"Greg," said the guy driving the other cart; Jordan flicked a look at him and saw that he was eyeing the small LPGA tag that hung from her belt. "Maybe you should — "

"Got it under control, Dave," Beame snapped at him, and stuck out his chin at Jordan again. "I don't know who you think you are, puss, but it's gonna take more than some female on the rag to get me off this eighteen."

"Oh, I know who I am," she said with a small, cold smile. "My immediate guess would be that you don't."

"And I could give a fuck? Who your daddy was and what he left you doesn't count here, so don't push your luck, toots."

"I'm Jordan Bryant." She gave him time to wonder where he knew that name from before she said with icy gentleness, "Being Jordan Bryant would make me Director of Golf here at Catawamteak. And you, Mister

Beame, have pushed both your luck and me a tad too far. You're done for the day."

"Hey, now, wait a minute, lady. I paid your goddamn to-the-moon greens fees — "

"And we do so appreciate the donation," she said dryly. "But you're not hitting another ball on this golf course today."

Beame got out of the cart. "Now you listen to me — "

"Don't try to intimidate me." Her voice was deadly quiet. "I strongly suspect that at least one of your friends has the native intelligence not to let you do something really stupid."

He stared at her for a long moment. She didn't blink, or step back, or lose that small, cold smile.

"Greg," said the driver of the other cart. "Let it go. We've still got time to go up to the Samoset."

"I paid a hundred and ten bucks to golf here, and I'm gonna golf here."

"No," Jordan said. "You aren't."

"The hell you say!" He took a step toward her, his right hand raising. It might have been meant as punctuation; watching from twenty feet away, Gillian Benson recoiled from that upraised hand as if it were a physical threat. "I paid a hundred and ten fucking — "

"Greg, for Christ's sake! What're you — "

Almost reflexively — and almost because she had expected to have to do it — Jordan snapped the grip of her wedge into her left hand and planted the shaft of the club across his chest and pushed hard.

"Hey! What the — "

"Jordan! God, don't — "

"Greg, *back off!* "

More amazed into compliance than forced into it, Greg Beame stumbled backwards into the cart, as pinned to the seat by the dead cold grey of Jordan's eyes as by the shaft of her club. "You just pissed off the wrong woman, chummy." Her voice was a low, ominous purr. "You might think you own the golf course where you come from, mister man, but I've got news for you: Jordan Bryant owns enough of this one to throw you off it for the rest of your putrid life, and that's what she's doing. All four of you are going to die without ever playing Catawamteak again." She picked her club off his chest. "Don't even think about moving." He didn't; everyone at the seventh tee knew that Jordan Bryant was still vibrantly dangerous. "Now I'm going to follow you to the pro shop, and you four are going to turn in your tags. Don't think you aren't. One word out of you, Mister Beame, and I call in my rangers, and chummy, you don't *even* want my rangers taking you off this course. I don't hire them for tact. I don't hire them for grace. I don't hire them for brains. I hire them for muscle power, and if I tell them to remove you, they will do it, and they'll do it without the slightest bit of tact or grace. Do you understand me?"

He swallowed, and skittered a glance around; the only eyes there to meet his were Jordan's. "I got you. Yeah. I understand."

"Good. Now get off my golf course. Take your redneck pals with you."

"Nice fuckin' work, Beamer," she heard as they started away. "You've got shit for brains, you know it? Here I am, along for the fuckin' ride, and all of a sudden you get me a fucking lifetime suspension from the best eighteen in Maine? Jesus Christ, what a dickbrain . . ."

She turned on the men in the second cart. "Why am I still looking at you?" She went to slam her wedge into her bag.

The driver hesitated. "Let's go, Dave," said his passenger, "before the crazy bitch hauls out that wedge again and lofts us off her fucking course."

"Shut up. Christ, you're as big an asshole as he is." He got out of the cart and approached Jordan. "Miss Bryant —"

She turned, still cold enough to make him back up a step. "What do you want?"

He took off his hat. "I want — " He flicked a look at an impassive Gillian Benson, and swallowed, and looked at Jordan again, meeting her eyes. "I want to apologize," he said quietly. "Him being a jerk didn't mean I had to be. I'm his boss and I could have stopped him, and I didn't do it." Again, he looked at Gillie, dipping his head to include her in his act of contrition. "I apologize to you both."

Jordan glanced at Gillie: *is he for real?*

I think so.

Jordan took off her glove. "What's your name?"

"David Meyers." He drew a business card from his shirt pocket and offered it.

She glanced at it; he was a vice president for a company near Portland that was famous for its glass ceiling. "W. W. Green. Why am I not surprised."

"I'm in marketing, not human resources."

"I'll forgive you for using that as an excuse." She dropped the card into a cup holder on the dash of her cart. "You're on probation, Mr. Meyers. I'll let you golf here again, but one complaint against you and it'll be the last time."

"That's not what I was after. I mean — thank you, but I meant what I said."

"I thought so. That's why you got probation instead of life." She got into her cart. "See you at the pro shop."

David Meyers drove away, and for a moment Jordan sat with her hands on the wheel and her head on her hands, breathing shallowly. "I can't believe I lost my temper," she whispered. "Good Christ, I'll be lucky if the son of a bitch doesn't file assault changes against me."

Gillie looked at her and thought, *That was losing your temper? Honey, god help us all if you ever really do.* "I wouldn't worry about that," she said.

In the clubhouse, Gillie approached a sullen Gregory Beame. "Whatever you're thinking on, sugar" — Georgia wrapped itself thick and soft around her words as she teased her glove from her fingers — "you'd might ought to stop and ask yourself if you can afford to play lawyers with me." He stared at her; she gave him a smile as cold as old money. "No, darlin'. I didn't think so either."

Jordan didn't hear what Gillie was saying; she only saw the impotent rage in Gregory Beame's eyes when Gillie reached to pat him on the cheek with a tolerant schoolteacher's smile. "Next time you take a mind to be waving that thing around," Gillie said, still too softly for anyone but Greg Beame to hear, "you might want to stop and think about just who it is you're waving it at. Because sometimes, honey, we're just a little more than just a little woman."

◆

The clubhouse was crowded, more drinkers than golfers on a sweltering July day; Jordan got a bucket of ice from Artie and led Gillie to the air-conditioned privacy of her office. She opened a cabinet to expose a small, top-shelf bar; she made Gillie a Stoli-tonic and dumped some scotch over ice for herself. She found a flat of cigarettes in a desk drawer and filled her cigarette case. "Amazing how fast a day can go to hell, isn't it."

"I thought you handled that quite well."

"I was talking about his day. Mine was already shot."

"Well, thank you," Gillie drawled. "I was enjoying your company, too."

"Oh, quit. You know what I meant. What'd you say to him?"

Gillie tasted her drink. "Just passing the time of day."

"Tooth fairy," Jordan said gravely. "Easter bunny. Santa Claus."

"Isn't that nice. We share the same beliefs."

Jordan snorted a laugh into her drink. "You must know the joke."

"What joke?"

"I'll spare you the long, drawn-out version and my bad southern accent. Two southern belles are talking out on the veranda. One of them's going on about 'he gave me a Mercedes, he gave me a diamond, he gave me Thoroughbreds,' and with every 'he gave me,' the other belle says, 'Isn't that nice.' And finally the bragging one says, 'and what did your husband give you?'

"'He sent me to charm school,' she says.

"'Charm school! Why ever would anyone go to charm school?' And she says, 'That's where they teach you to say "isn't that nice" instead of — ' "

"Instead of 'fuck you,'" Gillie laughed. "A woman from Pittsburgh told me that one. It took her twenty minutes, and her accent was so dead-on northern Louisiana I'd have certified her as native."

"It's a good joke."

"It is."

And they spent a moment busy with their drinks. Jordan leaned back in her desk chair, opening her cigarette case again, extracting an Oval to smooth between her fingers. "Can I ask you something?"

"Of course."

"What happened on the second hole?"

Gillie hid behind a taste of her drink. "I triple-bogeyed, as I recall. You parred."

"Gillie — "

She looked up. "No," she said softly. "I can't talk about it, Jordan."

Jordan lifted her fingers in concession. She flipped through the mail Carla had left on her desk, finding nothing that warranted her immediate attention, and found a book of matches. She struck one and lit her cigarette. "We need to work on your irons. You never take your six out of the bag unless I say so. It could be a powerful club for you. You hit it well enough to drive some of those longer par-threes with it."

"I'm getting the feel of it. But I don't think I feel like going back out. My back's bothering me, and it's hotter than Tophet out there."

"Hotter than Tophet." Their sunglasses shielded them from each other; Jordan took hers off and put them on her desk. "My mother used to say that."

"So did mine," Gillie said. "Do you work tonight?"

"A fact of my existence."

"You should try to take a nap, then. You look terribly tired."

"Maybe I will." Jordan tapped her cigarette against the side of her ashtray. "You might want to spend some time on the driving range this afternoon. Try to figure out what you're getting for distance on your irons. You're still picking more club than you need."

Gillie stood. "I might do that later, if it cools off." She collected her glove and visor and took the last taste of her drink. "Well. I'll probably see you this evening."

"You know where I'll be." Jordan watched her out the door. She sighed softly and took off her spikes, and turned off her beeper and phone and stretched out on the sofa, knowing she wouldn't be able to sleep, but it was worth a try.

◆

"Twenty, forty, sixty, eighty, one. Twenty, forty, sixty, eighty, two. Twenty forty sixty — "

"Am I too late for last call?"

" — eighty, three. Send me to jail, honey; ice in the sink, vodka in the freezer, come on back and help yourself. Twenty, forty, sixty, eighty, four, and twenty." She entered it into the calculator. "I'd given you up for lost."

Gillie scooped a glass of ice out of the sink and covered it with vodka so cold it was thick; she leaned against the counter under the back bar. "I couldn't stay awake, but I couldn't sleep."

" — eighty, ninety, one. Your back bothering you?"

"Not so bad. I took a couple of aspirin."

"So what's on your mind?"

She sipped and listened by tens and fives and ones, credit card slips and room checks, as Jordan cashed up the night's receipts. "Who," she corrected quietly, when the bag was zipped and the dial of the safe spun; Jordan looked up. "*Who*'s on my mind, my dear Jordan."

Jordan shot the drawer back into the cash register and picked a footed rocks glass from the overhead rack; she half-filled it with ice, and filled it with Glenfiddich. "Is there more to that?"

"Quite a lot, if you have time."

Jordan tucked the bottle back to its place on the top shelf and found a pair of bar towels under the cash register. "Top off your drink and come down to the seawall. Watch the fog. Talk to me."

It had come in a low, grey bank early in the evening; the foghorn mourned in the ethereal dark. They walked on Jordan's memory around trees and rocks, flower gardens and bunkers, avoiding sprinklers they barely heard until they were in danger of a shower, so muted were the noises of the night. When Jordan had wiped off the Adirondack chairs at the edge of the bay and they were settled into them Gillie said softly, "I lied to you today."

Jordan raised an eyebrow. "Say again?"

"I lied to you. When you — when I — oh, god." She sipped her vodka, and drew a hand across her eyes; she sighed shakily. "On the second tee. It didn't have anything to do with Phil."

She heard the dull tap-tap of a cigarette against Jordan's slim gold case, and saw her profile in the brief flare of the match before the fog and the darkness dimmed her again. "So what happened?"

But she couldn't find words. Jordan waited; Gillie's silence stretched, and at last, quietly, Jordan asked, "Did it have anything to do with me?"

"Yes."

"Okay . . ." Jordan drew on her cigarette. "That's okay. I don't like to have men touch me. It's the same idea."

"No. No, it isn't."

"You were protecting yourself. I understand that."

"I'm not sure you do, Jordan."

Jordan undid her bow tie and opened her collar button. "Help me out here, Gillie. I have no idea where you are."

"Neither do I." The lighthouse winked blurrily: white and green, white and green. "I don't — I just — got scared. I'm still scared."

"Of what?"

She shivered. "I don't know. Of you, I guess."

The end of Jordan's cigarette glowed briefly in the darkness. "My word's still good."

"Don't misunderstand me. I trust *you*."

Jordan regarded her for a moment, and took the last taste of her cigarette and crushed it out in the butt can by her chair. "What are you feeling, Gillian?"

"I don't know. It feels . . . I don't know."

"Is it emotional or physical?"

"It's — both. Jordan, don't analyze me. Please."

"I'm not trying to. I'm trying to find out where we are."

She drew a deep breath. "Jordan, last night — and I didn't remember it when I woke up, I didn't remember until you put your arms around me on the tee — "

Jordan made a noise somewhere between a sigh and a laugh; it sounded like relief. "Oh, Gillie. Are we talking dreams here?"

She nodded, glad for the darkness to hide the hard blush she could feel on her face.

"God, hon, it happens. Don't worry about it. I don't sleep with men, but sometimes I dream about it — and graphically. That sure as hell doesn't mean I want to. Libido is a very weird thing. If I paid attention to all my dreams, I'd still be in a padded room."

"But it was so — so — "

"Real?" Gently, she asked; Gillie nodded miserably. "Look at the circumstances," Jordan offered quietly. "Monday night when we got back from Bethlehem we spent some time in close physical contact. You shared some old — and for you, very weird — stuff with me. You've got Peony saying you should sleep with me because she thinks it'd be fun. I was there, even if I was out of it; I heard what she said. You're not responsible for her fantasy, but you heard it. Subliminal assimilation happens."

Shakily, she laughed. "That's a heck of a bumper sticker."

Jordan's chuckle was low, soothing. "It is, isn't it. But there was all of that. Then you spent however much time yesterday keeping me from coming completely unglued. You held me — Gillian, you held me together. It had to have been emotional for you. It was also very physical. And then last night . . ." Slowly, she shook her head. "What you said — what you offered me — god, that was so special," she said softly. "And I

106

know how hard it must have been for you. You aren't Peony. That didn't come out of curiosity, it came from some — some innate decency running away with you, but god, it must have scared you."

"I was afraid for you, Jordan! You were so — lost, or — or — I was so afraid you'd . . . do something foolish."

"And you cared enough to compromise yourself to stop me? Do you know how long it's been since I've felt as if someone cared that much about me? Carla says she loves me, but where was she when I was falling apart? Worrying about her job? Jesus, I needed help, not some kid with wet panties. If it hadn't been for you — " She blew a sigh. "Yeah. Maybe. I was riding a really bad wave."

"But Jordan, how could you even think it? There are people who love you! who'd miss you terribly if you — "

"Not so many," she said softly. "Gillie, when I get that way, I feel like . . ." Her silence stretched. "Like one of those cardboard characters they put in theaters to advertise movies," she said at last. "All height and breadth, but no depth. I look at what I could have had, and how weak I was to let him take it away from me — "

Her cigarette had died; she relit it and held the match until it seemed the flame would burn her fingers before she dropped it. The fire sputtered out in the fog-dewed grass. "No. That's wrong. I had choices. I could come unwound, or I could grieve them and go on. He didn't destroy me; I blamed him for my own weakness and destroyed myself. I knew what he was afraid of, being afraid of my success. I don't know what I was afraid of, but I made damn sure it'd never be an issue. I quit. Oh, sure, I've obsessed on doing a dozen other things, but I quit what I wanted the most, and every year that chicken comes home to roost, and I have to talk myself out of quitting again." She drew on her cigarette and exhaled smoke in a sharp hiss. "I lose sight of the fact that suicide is the most singularly selfish act that any human being can possibly perpetrate, because sometimes when I look around it seems as if I'd go under without even leaving a ripple. I'm out of family — a couple of uncles and aunts and a few cousins is all — and here? They'd make Bill Director of Golf and Cindy head bartender, and Carla'd get over it — "

"I wouldn't," Gillie said quietly. "Jordan, I'd spend the rest of my life wondering what I did wrong, or didn't do enough of, or — "

Bitterly, Jordan laughed. "You'd do the same thing I did? Eat my Julys for me like some Appalachian sin-eater? What is it with women? We absorb all of this responsibility that isn't ours. We let the world beat us up until it knocks us down, then we get up and tell the referee we're all right and stagger right back to center ring for more. Are we any smarter than your average dog?"

"As long as you're meeting the bell, you're still fighting."

"Still fighting, or just taking punches?"

"Your father was a cruel man," Gillie said evenly. "He was weak and selfish and spiteful. You said last night that you thought that he might as well have waited for you — he didn't have to. You're doing a perfectly good job of it all by yourself. Did he know you'd do that, Jordan? Was it part of his plan? Because if it was, you're buying right into it and letting him win. Why don't you sell that goddamned house?"

Jordan looked at her for a long moment before a smile twitched to her. "And she defines the difference between a punch in the nose and a slap upside the head. I bet you're a great mother."

"I doubt that my children would agree with you."

"Probably not. They're still too young. At twenty-five I'd just gotten to a place where I understood what a wise woman my mother was, and then he took her away from me. We were just evolving out of the parent-child relationship — I never really had a chance to be friends with her. I guess that's part of why I miss her so much. Sometimes I want my mommy — but I want that best friend, too."

"Have you ever really talked about what happened?"

"Five years of therapy. And I'd say, 'my father killed my mother and then killed himself and I found them.' And the therapist would say, 'and how do you feel about that?' I'm a therapist, Gil. I know the jargon. I know how to defend against it. I didn't want to start what happened yesterday. Where was I fifty minutes into that? I'll tell you where I'd have been if I'd done it in a shrink's office: in some Ward Eight somewhere with nurses poking Thorazine up my ass. Again. Thanks anyway — and thank you. Ninety percent of the therapy in the world could be replaced by an intelligent friend."

"You're unkind to your old profession."

"I assisted more healing with my hands than I ever did with words." She shot her cigarette butt over the seawall. "How did this get to be about me? We're way off track." And she snorted a laugh. "You ran your mouth, J.B., is how it happened."

"What was that you said about not being willing to listen to me berate myself in front of you?"

"Ouch. Smack me again, why don't you."

"Only when you need it."

"Thank you, Gillian darling." She leaned her head against the broad back of the chair. "Not meaning to smack you back, but where are you with the dream? It doesn't feel resolved."

Slowly, Gillie rattled the ice in her glass. "I don't suppose it is," she said quietly. "It's — frightening, I guess. Or maybe that's too strong. Maybe 'disturbing' is a better word. It's been so long since I had any choices. This isn't one I'd really thought I'd ever consider . . ."

It trailed away, as if there might have been more; Jordan waited, but nothing else came. "My friend Casey and I went to Provincetown for Women's Week a few years ago," Jordan said at last. "Hats — god, we tried on so many hats. I've never laughed so hard. You'd have to know Casey. She's not a bulldyke by any stretch, but her in a pink silk hat covered with flowers was almost enough to make me wet myself." She chuckled in the memory. "She ended up with a black felt that makes her look like a cross between Billy the Kid and Indiana Jones. I wound up with another pith helmet. Last time we saw each other — just a few weeks ago — we were both wearing our P'town hats."

Gillie looked at her.

"I think that dreams are like Casey and me in those P'town hat stores," Jordan said quietly. "They're the dressing-room of the subconscious. It takes ideas in there and tries them on just for the hell of it, no matter what color or size they are, or how silly it knows you'll look in them. Usually you don't remember them when you wake up, but you got a trigger on that one too soon after the fact of it. It doesn't mean it's what you want; it only means that last night it existed in some . . . visceral possibility. I really wouldn't take it seriously."

"Visceral possibility." Softly, ruefully, Gillie laughed. "God, the things you come up with. While we're playing with visceral possibilities — " She ticked a fingernail against her glass. "God knows why I feel as if I need to know the answer to this, but — did you consider it, Jordan? I think that what started all of this was wondering what might have happened if you'd stayed last night."

Jordan sat back in her chair. She found her cigarettes; one-handed, she struck a match, and sighed out smoke in a weary hiss. "It's the hardest no I've ever had to say," she said softly, and then amended: "Maybe not. Maybe walking away from that next dose of Thorazine was harder. But it was the same feeling. Giving up the safety. Going out alone. I considered it, yes . . . but for all the wrong reasons."

"Then you don't — " She stopped. "Never mind."

"I don't what?"

"Never mind. It doesn't matter."

"Are you wondering if I find you attractive? Yes, Gillian. I surely do." Her voice was as gentle as the cool embrace of the night. "But I'd rather be the friend you can come back to than the lover you might always regret." And she stood, and went to the seawall, and stood looking toward the end of the breakwater, ghostly in pale flannel with the deep fog blurring her; her voice came softly back. "If there's a problem with women's relationships, it's that we tend to want every woman we love to be the mother we miss. We want that unconditional love to believe in. We're all Jay Gatsby, believing in the green light at the end of Daisy's dock . . . and we're all Peony Watkins. Just moths in a roomful of candles."

Gillie's night was restless with thoughts of Jordan and what she had said about moths and candles, and green lights and safety, and mothers and lovers and friends; she dozed, but she didn't ever really sleep. By refusing sleep, she kept the maybe of dreams at bay.

At seven she gave up trying; she dragged out of bed and showered, and called the Sales Office at eight, not expecting anyone to be there, but a pleasant woman answered the phone, and said she'd be more than happy to show her condos, come right on over.

From a living room window overlooking the fourteenth fairway, she watched a ruthless threesome of women browbeat their fourth into leaving a sliced ball in the bordering woods. She could almost hear them: "Screw the five-minute rule. Drop one. Let's go!" She shook her head, remembering The Girls and their haste to get to the clubhouse bar. She liked Jordan's pace of golf; with her, the game felt civilized, the drink between nines an indulgent reward for a round well-played, or at least well-attempted.

Indulgent. She wondered how many times that word had come in the same thought as Jordan Bryant. For there was something effortlessly indulgent about her: her car, her hand-tailored clothes, her gold cigarette case and imported cigarettes and matchbooks with her signature on their glossy black covers, her single malt scotches and classic perfumes. She thought, staring blankly out the window, that Jordan treated herself well, yes, but what were those few indulgences to a woman who worked sixteen hours a day? Who could criticize her for indulging in luxuries she could afford?

"You pinhead," she murmured. "For someone who admires someone as much as you admire her, you surely have a hard time listening to what she has to say." She turned to the saleswoman. "It's very nice," she said. "Thank you so much for showing it to me. I'll talk to myself and then call you."

She ran into Park and Olathe in the rotunda and allowed them to talk her into a leisurely brunch; they wanted her and Jordan to go to their suite that afternoon and look at Park's portfolio. ("Or some of it, anyway," Park said with a devilish grin, and Gillie puzzled mildly over that grin and Olathe's half-smiling, half-pensive contemplation of her.) She said she'd check with Jordan, and picked up the tab and a few postcards on her way back to her suite.

"Hi, IV & V," she wrote on the back of a postcard with an aerial view of the inn, and nibbled at the end of her pen. The last time she had seen her son and his wife, a week before she left for Maine, Four had been sullen and Valerie black-eyed with an arm in a cast, and she said to Val in front of him, "I see his father trained him well. Leave him before he kills you. I'll pay for whatever you need." It had made for a very short evening. "I love it here!" she wrote. "Great food & people, great weather — great golf! Playing better every day. Thinking of buying a condo. Price is right! Let me know how you are. Love, Mom."

"Leave him, Val," she murmured. "He's my son and I love him, but I hate what he does to you."

She addressed a postcard to her daughter. Her last phone call with Meghann hadn't gone well. The last words she heard before Meggie hung up on her had been, "Ma, he's dead! Get over it and get a fucking life!" They were slightly better than 'someday we'll read about you in the paper,' but as last words went, she didn't like them. She wished she could talk to Meghann, or that Meg would talk to her. And she sighed; she supposed it was a bit late, after spending most of Meg's teenage years in (as Meg had called it) a self-induced state of brain death, to expect them to have a relationship. She looked at the back of the postcard and knew she wanted to say much more than such small space allowed.

"Nothing ventured," she murmured, and reached for the phone.

"Lakeshore Battered Women's Project, Carol speaking. This conversation is being recorded."

"Hi, Carol. Is Meghann Benson around?"

"Tell her who's calling?"

"Her mother." And waiting, she wondered what she was going to say.

"Meghann Benson." Her voice was clipped and efficient.

"Hi, Meggie. It's your mother."

"Yeah, Mom." Her irritation was familiar. "What's up."

"I — um — " Meghann's shortness wounded her; she knew less what to say now than she had before. "I just thought I'd call and say hi. See how you're doing."

"I'm fine. You still in Maine?"

"Yes." She ticked the edge of the postcard with a fingernail, wishing she'd foregone the phone call in favor of Hi, having fun hope you are too, love Mom. "How's everything with you?"

"Fine. Like I said."

"I got your grades. You had a good semester."

"Yeah."

"How's work?"

"How do you think? It's hard. Guys beat up their wives and girlfriends and they come to us for help. At least the smart ones do."

She closed her eyes against the sting of the words, against the sting of tears. "I see," she said softly. "Well, I'll let you get back to it. Call me if you need anything."

"Yeah, right. You'll write me a check. See you, Mom."

She held the receiver for a long moment before she dropped it back into the cradle. She picked up her pen; deliberately, she wrote, "I think you're in the wrong line of work." She licked two stamps and took the postcards down the stairs, and shot them into the mail slot in the rotunda before she could reconsider.

She went to the windows overlooking the bay and leaned against the rail, glancing at her watch. Twelve-ten. It was too soon for lunch after her late breakfast with Park and Olathe, who, for whatever reason, had taken her under their wings. She enjoyed their company and their contrast: with each other (Park was brash, with barely-there hair and perpetual 501s and tight T-shirts over tautly muscular breasts, barely-controlled in her aggressiveness; Olathe advertised her sensuality in flowing ebony hair and softly laughing eyes and sultry spandex), and with anyone else she had ever known. Throughout the week they'd played at croquet and puttered at tennis; Saturday morning, before her first lesson with Jordan, they had driven the ten miles to Bayview to a hugely vibrant arts and crafts show, where Park bought a handsome market basket and shopped it full of locally-crafted jewelry. Back at the resort, Olathe pawed through the basket to find a stunning tigereye necklace to loop over Gillie's head. "We got this for you. It like matches your hair? Every color of gorgeous in the sun, and tigereye for courage. Don't even squawk, Rocky," she warned when Gillie tried to protest. "We got it for you." To be called gorgeous in any way by Olathe, who was the most conspicuously beautiful woman Gillie had ever seen, had warmed her as much as the gift.

The broad stairs in the rotunda led down to the bar on the left and the restaurant on the right; the smells wafting from the kitchen were seductive, even though breakfast had been late. Was that chicken cordon bleu . . . ?

Idly, she wondered if she'd ever be able to eat ham again (rumor had it that the row between Gaston and John Laing about not serving ham in July had been hilarious, Gaston putting forth grand theatrics, Big Bad John not daring, in the thick of tourist season, to antagonize the chef into quitting, so ham was off even the breakfast menu for the rest of the month [so it wasn't chicken cordon bleu]) or if she could, if she'd be able to taste it without thinking of Jordan.

Wryly, she smiled. She doubted a day in her future life would ever go by without a thought of Jordan Bryant.

She straightened up from her lean against the railing — it was the perfect height for her to lounge against, and she loved to watch the bay and the boats that skipped along the breeze and the view of the islands — and reached for the small of her back with a breath of pain that was part the unfamiliar moves of two-days-ago tennis, part impending period, part old insults acting up, and her mind tried to wonder if she should ask Jordan if they might . . . She pushed the thought away before it could complete itself. She was tired of the nagging ache, but that was a far cry from being brave enough to ask to be naked under Jordan's hands — hands that looked, to Gillian Benson, as if they had already sensed the feel of everything they would touch. "You're such a wimp," she murmured, trying to stretch out the stiffness. "Peony's probably right."

"Of course Peony's right! Pee Wee's always right!"

She turned to find Peony Watkins in golf clothes and the espadrilles that had let her come unheard across the thick Aubusson carpet. A small, quick, wiry woman, Peony looked, Gillie thought, as if she'd been carved out of ice with a razor blade, with her porcelain skin and sharp features and steel-blue eyes. Carla had called her a natural peroxide blonde; the crack had won a frown from Jordan, but Gillie still snickered every time she remembered it.

Peony was damply rumpled, but there was nothing in her eyes to indicate any rise of her internal temperature. That always stayed low enough to keep the ice sculpture frozen. "What the hell're you doing, standing here talking to yourself? And what am I right about this time?"

"Men being a collective pain in the butt." It slipped out in defense of her real thoughts.

"Oh, hell, yes. But honey, they do have their merits, as I just discovered about young Mr. Bolli," Peony grinned. "That's hung like a horse and knows what to do with every sweet inch of it. Not since college have I been balled like that! Up against a tree with my legs wrapped around that tight little ass of his? Rrrrrr. Get you some of that, sweetie; it'll calm you down. I swear to God you're the tensest woman I've ever met. I'd've thought Jordan would've loosened you up by now."

Faintly, Gillie smiled; she figured that to Peony, anyone not flatlined by ten mgs of Valium q.i.d. was tense. "She has," she said, not thinking how Peony would take it until it was too late to retrieve the words.

Peony haw-hawed. "I'll bet to hell she has! God, wouldn't I love to wrap my legs around her waist, too!" She laughed again, and Gillie wondered when she'd ever seen a laugh accompanied by eyes so razory. "Oops! Treading on Gillie's turf! But one of these days you're gonna have to talk about that tongue, Gillie-girl. I mean I want *de*tails."

She looked at her watch. Twelve-twenty. Peony Watkins cheated at golf and cheated at bridge and now, it seemed (what a surprise) she cheated on her husband, who was rather sweet in a bemused sort of way. Sunday evening at bridge he had spoken almost longingly of Clearwater; Peony told him to shut up because he knew he loved Miami. The look he leveled at her had made Gillie wonder how long it would be before he was driving back and forth across the bridges of Tampa Bay just so he could toss a baggie full of some frozen part of Peony over the edge each trip.

And Ric Bolli was a handsome boy, but just a boy nonetheless, barely older than her own son — and Gillie couldn't begin to imagine wrapping her legs around any man's waist and letting him take her against a tree, and (not to delve too deeply into the subject, but the thought had been raised) why around Jordan's waist at all, any time, anywhere? It seemed equipmental differences might render the gesture symbolic at best. "Pee

113

Wee," she said mildly, "when my brother was about fourteen my father told him, 'son; if you ever get lucky you'd best keep it to yourself, or the next time you go calling you won't find enough room at her porch to park your bicycle.'"

It was a three-count before Peony brayed a laugh. "Keep your damn secrets, then! See if I care. But — " She reached for Gillie's hand and poked something small and round and pale blue into her palm. "Jesus, loosen up, pup! The girls think you're stuffy."

Gillie looked at the tiny pill. She didn't need to see the letters; trade or generic, it was diazepam, ten mgs, and getting weaned from it had cost her thirty horribly expensive days of her life and money hadn't been the measure of the cost. It felt frighteningly familiar in her hand.

Maybe walking away from that next dose of Thorazine was harder.

She flicked the tablet from her palm with a thumb-powered forefinger. It skittered across the hardwood floor by the necessities shop; a man exiting reduced it to powder under his unknowing heel. "I don't give a flit what you and the girls think of me, Mrs. Watkins, and I sure as hell don't need to walk on your crutch."

"Well, who the hell do you think you are? Your insurance money's no goddamned greener than what I inherited, toots. It's just a whole lot newer, and you sure as shit haven't learned how to live with it yet."

"Money's got nothing to do with it. I said I didn't care about your opinion of me."

"Well, here it is anyway. You think you're such hot shit? You're just Bryant's piece of the week, tootsie. That's about all the longer it takes for new meat to start stinking. And I'll tell you what else, Gillie-girl: you get back in the real world and try messing around with the homos and see what it gets you besides shut out of everywhere you want to be."

My god, I spent twenty years with women like her? No wonder I took drugs. She looked at her watch as Peony stalked away. Twelve-twenty-two . . . and five months and six days since that last little blue pill had slipped dry across the back of her tongue.

Deep in her back, the ache throbbed like a heartbeat. She caught herself looking at the place where she had fired the pill, searching for it; sickly, she turned back to the view of the bay.

◆

"Hey, Ms. Gillian."

She almost came out of her skin. "Wha — god!" She had been way back: before Phil, before college, before puberty; she had been on calm fresh water learning how to thread a worm on a hook, her sturdy grey-haired grandmother in the stern of the canoe teaching her; when the unexpected touch came at her shoulder she wheeled with a sucked-in breath of *don't-touch-me!* before she recognized grey eyes and a smile that was fading fast under her reaction. "Jordan! I'm sorry — "

114

"*You're* sorry? Like I don't know better than to come at you from behind? Gillie, I apologize. I didn't mean to scare you."

"No — well, you did, but that's okay. I was — fishing. My grandmother used to take me; I was just — drowning worms. Hi." She pushed from the rail and felt the hard twinge low in her back; she tried to hide the wince.

No such luck. "What's wrong?"

"Oh, nothing. A snarl with Peony and a day away from my period. I'll be fine by Saturday." She waved a dismissing hand, burying the memory of a tiny blue pill and the ache of her phone call with Meghann. "I looked at the condos this morning. They're wonderful."

"Well, neighbor!" Jordan looked genuinely pleased. "When do you move in?"

In your ear, Peony. Let me know how you and Ric are holding up a week from now. "Don't uncork the champagne yet. I haven't made up my mind."

"So what's the problem? Not to sound like a true employee of Catawamteak, but these are just about the best resort-affiliated condos in New England, and you won't ever get a better deal than in this buyer's market. I've been thinking about buying one myself, just for the investment."

"It's not if, it's which. My pained indecision hangs on whether I want two bedrooms or three," she admitted. "Oh! By the way — " She found a folded check in her pocket and offered it with a smile. "For you. And for me."

Jordan opened the check. "Well, will you look at this. Somebody rolled out of bed on the right side of life this morning."

"Somebody certainly did, thanks in the largest part to you. Pay your VISA bill, sugar. I'm worth every dime and the condo too."

"You surely are." Jordan studied the check, a grin flirting with a corner of her mouth; the amount was to the penny. "You went through my pockets, you turkey."

"Well, of course I did. I went through your wallet, too. How could I resist that? I didn't learn a thing — except that your driver's license picture's a lot better than mine, your credit's triple-gold, and you carry a lot more cash than I dare to."

"Girlfriend, you are solid brass and a whole handful." Jordan found her wallet and tucked the check into it. "So what prompted this?"

"Well . . ." She leaned against the rail in their corner of the lobby. "I prowled the bed all night last night thinking about what you said."

"That doesn't tell me much. I'm always yapping about something."

"You're always yapping about something good. And I end up thinking about things I don't usually think about." Ruefully, she smiled. "I never knew how much I didn't think at all until I met you, my philosophical friend. This time it was what you said last night: friends and mothers

115

and lovers and — making a difference. Caring for someone — " Faintly, she blushed. "Being able to," she said softly. "It's been so long since I cared about anyone besides my children. Since my mother died, I guess. I haven't had a friend — or been one — for ten years. I didn't know how much I'd missed having a shoulder to cry on, and someone to trust, and talk to, and just . . . be with."

"Thank you," Jordan said quietly. "I know the feeling."

"It's so hard to care about yourself when you can't care about someone else — or maybe that's backwards, but when you said how long it'd been since you felt as if someone cared about you — " She hesitated; Jordan waited. Finally she looked up. "I do, Jordan. More than I ever expected to, and I . . . the other night, when I — "

Offered myself to you? Oh, I can't say that. She ran a hand through her hair. "Tuesday night, down by the seawall," she managed. "I was so afraid, Jordan. For you — and for me, too. You've made me look at myself. For the first time in years I like what I see, and a lot of it's because of you pointing me into the mirror. And if I had to be — your mother, or . . . or your lover, or whatever it took, I had to keep you safe so I'd be safe. You've showed me I have wings, but I'm not ready to fly solo yet. I know that sounds selfish — "

"No. No, Gillie; it's not selfish." Her smile was faint and bittersweet. "Jesus Bryant Christ, Tarvis used to call me. A parable for everything. You're it this time, Tarvis."

She found her cigarette case in her pocket and took out three: two for her hatband and one to light. She shook out the match. "I had a friend in Arizona — we went to college together. I was twenty; he was — oh, fortyish then. He was gay; I'd just admitted to myself that I was. I was having a hard time. I'd just come out to Mom and Dad, and that didn't go well at all. I was in love with my coach — or in lust; I don't know which. Anyway, Tarvis was my best friend. You made me think of him. 'Spread your wings,' he'd tell me. 'Flying's only part of it. The other part is being able to take someone under them.' The way he did for me. I'd have done anything for him, because I needed him, but it seemed like I was taking a lot more from that relationship than I was giving. I felt selfish. I worried about it to him one day and he said, 'hey, someday I'll need you as much as you need me now, and when I do, I know you'll be there for me.'" She put her hands in the pockets of her shorts. "Three . . . no. Four years ago he called me."

Gillie looked up. "This doesn't have a happy ending, does it."

"No. He had some weird, rare cancer — " She blinked back a quick shine of tears. "It wasn't AIDS, but it wouldn't have mattered to me if it had been. We had a month. God, we talked — there was so much I'd never known about him. I took the sunlight shift — he didn't like the nurses. He said I was the only one who could give diapers dignity." She hitched a tiny laugh, or a sob, and wiped a finger under her eyes, catching old pain. "I held him while he died. Asking him to let go was the hardest thing I ever did — and the easiest. I loved him. I knew he loved me. The last thing he said was, 'We came out even, J.B.' And we did. Accepting love is never selfish, Gillian. You come out even in the end."

"J.B." Gently, Gillie reached to brush a straying strand of Jordan's thick russet hair away from her eyes. It was a familiar intimacy: her mother had done it to her, and she had done it to her children; she did it now to Jordan, and felt her surprise at the touch. "I don't know how it happened so fast, but I do love you," she said softly. "Park and Olathe invited us up to look at pictures this afternoon. Want to go?"

"You mean instead of — "

"Ms. Bryant . . ." Dripping with disapproval, John Laing's voice interrupted them.

"Oh, Lurch!" Gillie turned, the low fume from her phone call to Meghann waking up to boil over. "I have *had* it with him!"

"Gillie, let me — "

She shook off Jordan's hand at her elbow. "No, Jordan. This time he's mine."

Jordan wondered who was more amazed, her or John, when Gillie went tiptoes to give her a kiss full on the mouth before she stalked across the lobby. "*Mis*ter Laing." She spat it out. "That's the third time that you have interrupted me in a conversation with a member of the staff of this resort." She was five-foot-one, he was well over six feet; she compensated by driving an italicizing fingertip into his solar plexus. "I find it way too interesting that it's always the *same*" — she poked, he stepped back, she followed — "staff member, and frankly, Mr. Laing, you are beginning to annoy me. If my business means so little to you that you can afford to *irri*tate me" — poke — "I can certainly take it elsewhere. I hear the Samoset has a lovely golf course, and I know Bethlehem does. And if you annoy me to the point that I *leave*, Mr. Laing" — hard poke — "neither do I buy the condo, which I'm sure you know I'm considering. And I assure you that if I don't buy here, Catawamteak's ownership *will*" — poke — "know" — poke — "why!" She snapped words over her shoulder — "Jordan, come find out what he wants." — and back at him. "Do please consider that we have a one-fifteen tee time, and that I am paying handsomely for Jordan's time this afternoon. Don't take much more of it."

"*Hoo*-wah!" Park Webster's laughing voice came from the necessities shop. "You *go*, girl!"

John found his voice, after jamming back a couple of choicely vulgar rejoinders. "Mrs. Benson, I beg you, please accept my apology." No way did he need Jordan Bryant's distant uncle Michael Goodnow hearing that — or why — a former guest was hiking down the road to the Samoset to buy a condo. "I give you my utmost assurance that it won't happen again."

117

"I'll take your apology under consideration. Just be damned sure she's not with me when you need her the next time, or the apology will be rejected in triplicate."

"Mrs. Benson, please consider the possibility of extenuating circum — "

"Extenuating usually means excuses, and you've wasted all of yours. I expect Ms. Bryant at the first tee in" — she glanced at her watch — "eight minutes. Good day."

Equally shaken, if for very different reasons, John and Jordan watched her away. "Remind me not to piss her off," Jordan murmured, and added — for John stripped publicly of his pride, she suspected, could and would be vicious — "I think that's what they call the insufferable arrogance of money." Her tone suggested that she was, for once, on his side. "What did you need, John?"

He salvaged something that bore faint resemblance to a smile. "In the wake of that tongue-lashing, I've completely forgotten. Go ahead; you're probably down to six minutes by now, and god forbid you should be late. If I remember it, I'll leave a message at the pro shop with Carla."

She knew there would be no message; she pushed open the door and let the laugh bubble from her. "Jesus, Gillie! I didn't know you had that much rich bitch in you. That was great!"

"Thank you," she heard, and turned to find Gillie leaning against the wall looking smug. "It took every ounce of starch I had, but lord, how he irritates me! I'm sorry for the kiss — I know it surprised you as much as it did him — but I could have talked all day and not said half as much."

Jordan grinned. "I'll take your apology under consideration, but if it ever happens again I'll be forced to accept in triplicate."

"Oh, you." She gave Jordan's shoulder a gentle push. "Are we golfing, or going up to see Park's pictures?"

"Don't call them pictures to Park! She's rabid about that. Photographs, thank you very much. But she mentioned wine, and I'm working tonight. Can we do it Sunday?"

"Sure. Let me give her a quick call from your office. Then we can see if this back's going to let me golf or if I have to ask about your massage rates."

Jordan smiled, too. "My massages are free to good homes. If you promise to feed it right and walk it twice a day, I'll give you the pick of the litter."

◆

"So what'd you and Peony get in a flap about?" Jordan asked as they walked to the first green while Barry raked her footsteps out of the bunker from which she'd holed a lucky birdie and Simon lugged Gillie's bag to the second tee. Gillie was lying five on the green of a par four, her swing hampered by the ache in her back.

"Oh, that! I could have killed her. She told me I was uptight and stuffy and put a ten-mg Valium in my hot little hand. She'll never know how it feels to withdraw from that stuff, but I do, and it wasn't long enough ago for me to be that close to it." She paused to putt; the ten-footer curled around the cup and angled back to leave her a six-incher. "Oh, come on! I've been robbed."

"I'll give you that one. Jeez, Gil. Valium's a bitch to kick. You did that?"

"Bitch doesn't begin to describe it. I'd have had more fun staked naked to an anthill and covered with molasses — which I more or less thought I was for two days." She shivered in the memory; she had thought only heroin addicts and stone boozers got the bugs, before she got them. "Anyway, I told her I didn't need it or her and she said the most vulgar thing and stomped off." She tapped her ball with the back of her putter, knocking it into the cup, and bent to retrieve it. "Most seventh-grade girls would have shown more grace."

As she started to straighten up something in her back grated, or slipped; pain flared hotter than ache, sucking the strength from her legs and driving the breath from her in a soft gasp: "Oh! god — "

"Gillian — " Jordan was there, her hands at her waist in time to keep her from going to her knees. "Easy — easy, Gil. I've got you."

"Mrs. Benson, let me — "

"No, Barry," Jordan almost snapped at her caddie. "I've got her. Go get a cart. Double-time, my friend. Simon, take our bags to my office." Barry cleared the green and took off at a dead run. "Gillie, breathe. Talk to me. Tell me what's going on."

Cold sweat washed across her scalp, between her shoulder blades, under her arms; she could only focus on the pain, and the hard delineation of Jordan's forearms under her hands. "I'm okay." Her voice sounded vaguely distant to her ears; sharp pinpoints of light twittered at the edges of her vision, and then started closing in. "Oh — maybe not. Jordan — oh, damn, I think I'm going to faint —"

"Come on, deep breaths . . ." Jordan's voice sounded as if chuckling bees were buzzing benignly around them both. "Faint in my arms and we'll be the talk of the season. Stay on your feet, hon."

"We're already the talk of the season." The thought distracted her; without her sharp focus on the pain, it ebbed. She managed to straighten up, wondering how she could feel so chilled in ninety-degree heat; sickly, she wondered what had happened in her lower back. "I'm okay," she said, as if saying it would make it so. "Really, Jordan."

"You, my dear Gillian, are full of shit." Jordan laid a palm against the small of her back. "Jesus, this is a real screamer." Gently, her fingers probed through the damp cotton of Gillie's shirt as she thought out loud: "You bent to get your ball, but you were looking at me. There's your ball on the ground, so you were coming back up when it happened. Extension

119

and contralateral rotation —" A fingertip touched a spot that made something deep in Gillie's back twitch in snarling irritation. "Bingo. Tell me as specifically as you can where the pain is."

It was fine for Jordan to tell her to breathe deep breaths, but it hurt to do it. "Left side, close to the spine above the hip — well, down into my hip, a little. It feels like someone stuck their hand into my back and grabbed any old handful of muscles and squeezed as hard as they could."

"That sounds extremely unpleasant."

"It hurts like a bastard, if you want the humble truth."

"I know it does. I can help this, Gillian," Jordan said quietly. "Would you let me try?"

She was as afraid of the thought of Jordan's hands roaming at will across her body as she was afraid of how long the pain would last if they didn't. "God," she whispered. "I didn't plan on this. Not now."

She felt the soft breath of Jordan's laugh. "Right. You should have been able to write it into your Day Runner. Thursday the twenty-third, one-thirty: major muscle spasm. One-thirty-five: equally agonizing decision process."

"Don't be such a wise-ass."

"Sorry. But you might as well line out the rest of the day, because with or without the massage, you're not going to be up for much. Here's Barry with the cart."

Barry skidded to a stop on the gravel path by the green and started toward them. "Mrs. Benson, let me help you — "

"I've got her, Bar. Thanks," Jordan said, and Gillie was grateful for the refusal; Barry seemed shy and gentle, but he reminded her uneasily of Phil with his dark-tanned, dark-eyed good looks. He hovered, ready to lend an arm if it was needed while Jordan walked her slowly off the green.

She eased into the seat of the cart, wishing it were her deep, soft recliner, with a stiff Stoli on the end table and something absorbing on the stereo — Mozart, or Beethoven. She let her back adjust to the feel of the new position; it took its time finding a place that was even tolerable.

"Thanks, Barry," she heard Jordan say. "Tell Stedman I tore the green, will you?" When she had jumped to catch Gillie, her spikes had wrenched the delicate turf of the putting surface. "He needs to patch it up and cut a new hole on the other side. Oh, and tell Carla I'm off call. If she beeps me, somebody better have died."

"New hole Stedman, off call Carla. Will do, Jordan." He hesitated, and took a half-step toward Gillie. "I — she's got good hands, Mrs. Benson," he said softly. "She's helped me out a few times. Probably she can help you, too. I — um — I hope you feel better, Mrs. B."

"Thank you, Barry."

She watched him halfway to the hundred and fifty yard bush, and then looked up the hill to the regal inn, its ensigns fluttering brightly from the turrets. Jordan's voice brought her back from an odd absence of thought; she looked over. "What?"

"I said, how are you doing?"

Slowly, she shook her head. Jordan reached to drop her ball into the cup holder on the dash of her side of the cart. She reached for it. Her back growled a warning, but she got the ball anyway, and turned it over in her fingers, finding markered initials on the Catawamteak-logoed Top-Flite. "This isn't my ball."

"No?"

"It's that guy's. Greg Beame. That's not my handwriting." Looking at it in her hand made her realize that she was trembling; she rattled the ball back into the cup holder. "So where do we do this?"

Jordan took off her glove and tucked it into her pocket. "The fitness center has tables."

She had been to the fitness center; it echoed with thumping aerobics music and the careless laughter of sleek, athletic people. "Not my favorite place."

"Nor mine," Jordan agreed. "I've got a table in my apartment, or a portable I can bring to your suite. Wherever you'll be most comfortable."

"What's easiest for you?"

"It doesn't make a bit of difference, Gillie. Whatever's best for you."

She considered possibilities, and their attendants. "My suite, if you don't mind. Give me time for a shower." She looked at Jordan with a wan smile. "Bring your patience."

"I don't leave home without it."

◆

"Where's Jordan?" Carla's voice was a sharp inquiry. "I need to talk to her."

Barry looked up from wondering why Jordan's golf bag was standing by her office door; he'd heard her tell Simon to put her clubs — and Mrs. Benson's — inside. Probably Carla hadn't let him in. Carla had managed to get awfully bossy in two days, he thought; he had always been able to talk to her with relative ease, but she tongue-tied his painful shyness now. "She's — um — off call."

"That doesn't tell me shit, man. Did I just say I need to talk to her?"

"She said — umm — " Jordan's sand wedge sparkled with the still-damp remnants of her birdie blast out of the bunker on the first; he pulled it from the bag and wiped the head with a towel. "She said not to beep her unless somebody died."

"Don't clean clubs in my pro shop! You think I got nothing better to do than sweep up after you? Take that crap outside. Shit, man. When I caddied for her I cleaned them after every shot. Where is she?"

He swallowed, feeling his cheeks flush hotly. "Mrs. Benson took a cramp and I guess she was going to work on it. You know. Massage it."

"Oh, Mrs. Benson took a cramp, did she? My ass. Mrs. Benson's test-driving a car she doesn't plan to buy, is what precious Mrs. Benson's doing, and Jordan's letting herself get suckered right into it." Carla slammed a handful from the last box of scorecards onto the counter by the cash register. "I hate these fucking rich bitches. I really do."

"She's not like that," he said softly. "She's n-nuh-nice, Carla. And she was really hurting. I was there. I saw — "

"*Good* morning! She's like sucking Karo syrup through a straw, for Christ's sake. She's — "

"Okay, Carla. That's enough." Bill Marston had been sitting silently in a corner of the shop, regripping an elderly putter for a guest; Carla had forgotten he was there, and wheeled when he spoke. "Yeah. How-do." He stood with a faint, cool smile. "You know, I could have been a guest, and I don't think Jordan wants some guest in her face — or Big Bad's face — screaming about what she overheard you saying about her, or her best bud. You need to keep that kind of yap out of the shop."

"You're not my boss, Bill, so spare me your advice."

"Maybe you should trot your tuchis into Jordan's office and take a look at the organizational chart on the side of her file cabinet, kiddo," Bill said coldly. "You'll find you're a level below me, which means when Jordan and George aren't here, I'm the man. You've gotten way too big for your britches since Tuesday. Barry might not tell you, but I sure as hell will." He stepped back to let Barry past him into the bag rack. "If Jordan says don't beep her and you got a problem you can't handle, you bring it to George or me. And just for the record, kid, this isn't your pro shop. Not until you hang that LPGA tag off your belt. You might run the cash register, but you're still just a glorified caddie, and don't you ever forget it." He wrapped a hand around Barry's muscular upper arm when the caddie emerged from the rack with Gillie's bag, his head still ducked and his cheeks still scarlet. "Stash those and grab your putter, Bar. Give me a lesson."

◆

Showered, wearing only her white silk kimono, Gillie waited by the French doors leading to the balcony of her turret suite. She watched a bright-sailed boat on the deep blue water; she listened to the thin whine of pain in her back and the dull flutter of her heart, the treacherously different rhythm of her body that for nine years had told her it was time for a pill; now, there were no pills. There was only the low-grade panic of waiting, one thought caught in her like a skipping record: *You shouldn't have put on the perfume*

the perfume
the perfume
you shouldn't have put on the perfume

and when the knock came at the door of her suite she absorbed it the way a boxer absorbs a hard left jab to the body. She half-turned — "It's open." — and sought the tricolored spinnaker of the sailboat again, remembering Jordan standing Tuesday where she stood now, the way she stood now, feeling whatever she had and hadn't felt, seeing whatever she had and hadn't seen, headlocked by the past.

"Are you all right?" Jordan's voice was quiet, half the room behind her.

She didn't turn. "I'm terrified."

"Would you rather not — "

"I'd rather not be afraid to be touched, but I am. I'd rather all those things — all those years — had never happened, but they did. I can't change them, but I can't live like this, and I can't imagine letting anyone but you touch me." *Oh, that sounded great, perfume and all. Why not just say let's skip the massage and go right to bed, my dear Jordan who finds me attractive. Why? I'm nothing but a walking bundle of neurotica.* "That didn't come out right."

"I knew what you meant."

"You would," she muttered, as if Jordan's understanding warranted accusation — and she turned to find Jordan by the wing chairs, almost close enough to touch. "I'm sorry. I told you to bring your patience. You'll probably need it all."

"I doubt that." Jordan had showered, too; the ridge her pith helmet left in her hair was gone. Other than that it was hard to tell; she seemed to have an endless supply of cream-colored shorts and pale pastel polo shirts with the Catawamteak logo embroidered over her left breast. "I think we both wish this had been more optional, Gillian. We'll work at your pace."

She made her table sideways on the floor, and turned it onto its legs, and made it up like a summer bed: fitted sheet, flat sheet, light blanket. "Come sit?" She offered one of the wing chairs. "I need to get your vitals and a little history."

Gillie sat, knowing she left a wave of scent in the air where she had been. "It was just force of habit," she whispered.

"What's that?"

"The perfume. It was just force of habit. I didn't mean — "

"You always wear perfume. Shalimar; you and my mother. Did you think you shouldn't?"

"I'm sorry. Homophobic reaction. Parse: two drops of cologne and you'll turn into a slobbering sex fiend. Jordan, I'm sorry. I'm just so nervous."

"That's okay." She opened a well-aged leather case and found a clipboard, stethoscope, blood pressure cuff. "Left arm, please. . . . Tell me about your back."

"I broke my coccyx in '86. I had surgery then, and again in '88."

Jordan pumped up the cuff, released the valve, and watched the dial. "Do you take blood pressure meds?"

"No. I'm just — it's usually fine."

She opened a fountain pen and wrote on a blank sheet of paper: Benson, Gillian. 23 Jul 92. Coccyx surg 86/88. 132/96. "How'd you break your tailbone?"

"I fell — " The lie was force of old habit; only she and Phil had ever known what really happened that night. Softly, she cleared her throat. "No. Phil . . . um . . . threw me down the stairs." *And it wasn't much of a crawl to the phone, only twenty feet or so, because I had to call the ambulance myself. That's how the lie started: when he didn't come down when the ambulance came. I said he wasn't home. I said I fell. Now ask me why I was protecting him.*

She looked up to find deep grey eyes watching her with neutral compassion — not pity. She would have known pity; she'd seen enough of it. Quietly, Jordan asked, "Is there more to that?"

"Yes," she said, just as quietly. "Let's do the intake first."

Jordan nodded at her clipboard. "Any surgically fused vertebrae?"

"No."

"Any other back pain besides low back? Diagnosed structural conditions? Sciatica, bursitis, radiation of pain or discomfort into the arms or legs, numbness or tingling in your fingers or toes?"

"Not all that. My neck, sometimes, when I'm tense. Headaches. I take aspirin."

"Any other meds? Any allergies? Cancer? Diabetes? HIV positive? Are you pregnant?"

Gillie stifled a nervous laugh. "No. Not that I know of."

"Have you had massage before?"

"No."

"Chiropractic or osteopathic adjustment?"

"Osteopathic, but it's been . . . three years, probably. At least three years."

"And you're five-one and you weigh, give or take — "

"One-eleven last week."

"Don't lose ten pounds; exercise if you want to look better in the mirror. I'll give you some exercises for your back that'll help tone your tummy, but your weight's just right for your height and build. Date of birth?"

"October tenth, nineteen forty-six."

This wasn't Jordan the golf pro, or Jordan the bartender, or Jordan her friend: this Jordan was professional to the edge of some oddly warm remoteness, and that was strangely calming. "Which makes you . . . forty-five." Jordan capped the pen and tucked it and the clipboard into her case; her Rolex and rings followed. "How do you feel?"

124

Gillie managed a wan smile. "I guess I've gone from terrified to just scared."

"That's an improvement. What about your back?"

She shook her head. "It's just waiting for me to move wrong again."

Jordan leaned against her massage table. "Can you give me an idea of how much contact you think you'll be comfortable with?"

"I don't know, Jordan," she said softly. "I just don't know."

"It's up to you. Whether you've got all of your clothes on, or none of them, or anywhere in between, we can get the work done."

"What do you prefer?"

Jordan shook her head. "Doesn't matter." She lifted the cuff of the top sheet on the table. "You're under this, Gillie. I move it around, but you're never exposed. If anything I do makes you uncomfortable, tell me. My ego isn't invested in my technique. You won't hurt my feelings by telling me the truth." She pushed away from the table. "The last thing I do before giving a massage is wash my hands. Why don't I go do that, and you can get on the table. Face up, head at this end, bolster under your knees. I'll knock before I come out of the bathroom."

"Face up?"

"Yes. What I learn from your neck will tell me a lot about your back."

Gillie drew a huge sigh when the bathroom door had closed behind Jordan. She stood, and looked at the massage table for a long moment, weighing her pain against her fear. "Trust her," she finally murmured. "She's never given you a reason not to." But still, she hesitated before she unbelted her robe and tossed it across the back of the sofa; self-conscious in her nakedness, she slipped between soft flannel sheets and searched for her breath.

She heard Jordan's knock. "I'm ready," she said, and added in a whisper, "I hope." She closed her eyes and waited.

She didn't feel Jordan's hands as much as she sensed them, a calm presence near her head, and in the moment of quiet before Jordan touched her she felt them arriving at some mutual rhythm: of breath, or boundaries, or space, as if something had closed around them, enveloped them, protecting them. She felt the warmth of Jordan's breath across her face, and then her touch: a gentleness like music, as low and rhythmic as the pulse of the tide against the breakwater, and she knew that eventually the tide would win, the breakwater would be sand, the ocean would flow unfettered. "Oh, Jordan," she murmured. "I think I'm going to like this."

◆

Tensions that she hadn't known were living in her neck and shoulders dropped their guard under the persuasion of Jordan's fingers and thumbs and palms; she drowsed through adjectives, trying to find one that was just right. *Delicate? Subtle? Precise, gentle, strong careful connected neutral.*

125

talented. graceful. considerate. thorough . . .
Safe.
"Mmmm. Jordan, you'll put me to sleep."
"That's all right. It works either way."
Safe.
"This feels so good — "
"Okay so far?"
"Mm-hmm."
She's so gentle. I love to have her touch me. It feels so . . . loving. It feels so
(feel me, Gillie. Feel how I)
She stiffened, her breath abandoning her.
"Okay . . ." Touch went away; cloth murmured over her shoulders. "Gillian, breathe."
Deep as an instinct, something in her low back twitched nervously. "I'm sorry," she whispered.
"It's all right. What's going on?"
I love to have her touch me —
Oh, god — do I want more than this?
No. No. That's not it —
It seemed forever before she could imagine those hands belonging to the therapist instead of the smoothly skillful lover in that unexpected dream. *There's so many pieces of her — so much of her to keep track of! But I trust her — I trust her touch. It's mother-touch, grandmother-touch; I know I'm safe. I just got tangled up in a memory that wasn't right to begin with.* That felt right; she sighed a breath of relief. "I'm okay. Go ahead."
Cool air touched her, then the warmth of hands smoothing across her collarbones, cupping around her shoulders, slipping up the back of her neck. Jordan's voice was quiet. "Do you want to talk about it?"
"I'm not sure I could find words for it," she murmured. "It was just . . . something. Took me by surprise."
"Do you want to stop?"
"I miss my mother, too."
She felt a tiny hitch of the rhythm of those hands, like a skipped heartbeat, and then a small squeeze, a brief caress before affection detached from ability.
Fingertips coaxed through layers of tension at the back of her neck. Jordan said the names of muscles — trapezius, levator scapulae, scalenes, splenius, spinalis — and they meant nothing to her, but the murmur of unfamiliar words was almost hypnotically comforting.
She drifted in and out of awareness.

◆

Feel me, Gillie. Feel how I
no.

feel how I want
no.
want you
"Wait — "

No hands; no voice. There was only a patient silence. Finally, gently: "Do you want to stop?"

She shivered a sigh, barely awake, acutely aware. "I'm okay. Go ahead."

◆

"This is incredible," she murmured, when Jordan's quiet voice suggested she turn over. She felt her back and the table for their limits and turned. The drape felt like feathers above her, warm but not in the way. "No wonder you're such a good putter. What a touch."

"Why, thank you, ma'am. Two compliments in one. Slide up — face in the cradle." Jordan adjusted the drape. "I'll be starting at your feet again. When your back's better I'll give you a reflexology session. Your feet would love to be that happy."

"My whole life would love to be this happy," she mumbled, already halfway back to wherever she had been before the intermission. "Thank you for your hands. Thank you for your heart."

"Thank you for your trust," Jordan said quietly.

She heard that, before she slipped away again.

◆

Don't you ever *tell me no, you little bitch!*

"Phil please! Ogod Phil don't please — " She fought back in blind panic against the strength that restrained her. "Phil don't don't oh god don't hurt me don't — "

"Gillian, don't fight me — "

Arms locked around her, pinning her to a rasp of cloth at her breasts and belly and she tried to get her arms between her and the body that held her. "Phil, don't! Please — "

"Gillian, don't fight me. Please. I won't hurt you."

She only knew another body too close to hers, more strength than she could break keeping her there. "Don't — "

"I'm not going to hurt you. No one's going to hurt you — shhh, Gillie. It's Jordan. You're all right. It's okay. There — "

Vaguely, she knew she had been on her belly and was now on her back and didn't know how she had gotten there; acutely, she knew she was naked. Jordan *(Jordan?)* filled her senses, but Philbrook Benson filled her memory. "Phil — "

"Phil's not here. You're safe, Gillian. This is Jordan. I won't hurt you, honey. Not ever."

127

"Jordan — ?"

"It's me. You're safe — " It was a warm whisper in her hair. The resistance drained from her; she submitted to the arms that held her. "There . . ." It was a breath of relief. "God, Gillie, I didn't know it was that bad. I'm so sorry."

"Jesus — " She buried her face in Jordan's shoulder, but it was a long moment before the panic let go enough for her lungs find their rhythm again. "I'm sorry," she whispered. "Jordan, I'm sorry —"

"Don't apologize. I'm going to lift your shoulders. Let me do it. Let me — "

She lifted her the way a mother lifts a baby, supporting her head while she got the drape out from under her, and Phil's voice sneered a warning at her: *she's strong enough to throw you halfway across the room.*

And then the table held her and Jordan didn't, and she curled up small under the cloth, shivering.

"Gillie, talk if you can. Let this go if you can. You'll never be more safe."

"I can't — " *tell you not you not Jordan it's she's too —* "It wasn't you. It wasn't — "

"I know. I'm going to get you a blanket. I'll be right back."

She finally found the right rhythm of her breath, and then the soft, familiar weight of the down comforter from her bed settled over her and the need to get small subsided; she shivered a sigh. "God, I didn't expect that."

"I almost did." She could feel Jordan wanting to touch her, to reassure her; that restraint hummed in the space between them, and she wanted to say *it's okay, you can* — but the words wouldn't come. "Sometimes touch triggers body memories. The safe space lets them release — sometimes with a vengeance. But if I warn you beforehand that it might happen, it's like a self-fulfilling prophecy."

"No wonder you quit doing this for a living."

"Fairly intense, twenty appointments a week."

She turned onto her back, drawing up one knee to take the pressure off her low back. "How tall are you, Jordan?" Her voice ached in her throat. "What do you weigh?"

"Five-ten. One-forty-five."

"God, I wish. It's so hard to be this small. Look at me next to John? Phil was bigger than him. He was — " A tiny laugh slipped from her. "Poor John. He got more than he deserved, but god, it felt good. Jordan, will you make me a drink? Please?"

"Alcohol and that much adrenaline will give you a hangover that'll make Sunday morning look like a walk on the beach. Would you let me try instead?"

She looked up, and away; Jordan's voice was calmly professional, but her eyes held too many emotions to sort through. "I'll say yes. I don't know what will happen."

Jordan slipped her hands under her head, supporting it in her palms; her fingers stroked in slow rhythm at the back of her neck. "I want you to remember two things," she said quietly. "He's dead and you're safe with me, Gillie. We might trip over the truth sometimes, but I'll never do anything you don't want. My hands will never hurt you."

It wasn't until she realized she was no longer trembling that she knew she had been. "God, your hands." It was a shaky whisper. "Thank you."

"Can you tell me where you were?"

"I — oh, god. Jordan, I — I've never really told anyone. I mean — some, at the clinic, but not — I just couldn't. Not what happened. Not what happens. It was too soon. I was still too afraid of him."

"Your body's breaking silence. Trying to show the pain its way out of you. I think you should follow it."

"I don't even know where to start."

"What did he do to your back?"

She huffed a choked laugh. "He never hit me in the face. That would have shown. I'd get small — curl up like I just did — and that was what he had to hit. My back. He was a big man — strong. He played linebacker — He'd wait for me to come through a door. Next thing I knew I'd be two feet off the floor." With Jordan's hands rustling in her hair she could barely hear herself; it made it easier, somehow, to talk. "I was always black and blue the next day — always there. First there. Five bruises to a side. Four in front. One in back. Fingers and thumbs." She shivered a sigh. She knew she would talk, but before she did, for a moment, she needed the compassion of Jordan's touch; she didn't want sympathy, or pity, or condolences; she only wanted the proof Jordan provided: that gentleness existed, for this moment, in her life. "I know I'll cry."

"I'll bring you ice."

"He threw me downstairs that once," she said at last. "He threw me upstairs — god, how many times?" A laugh jittered from her. "You've heard of dwarf-tossing? He could get four or five steps to a toss. I had them install the thickest carpet I could find — I learned how to land. He'd bounce me off a few walls on the way to the bedroom. Once that door was closed . . ."

It seemed long before Jordan's voice came quietly. "Breathe, Gillie."

She did, a few quick, rasping gasps. "Thank you."

"Take your time," Jordan said softly.

"There was nothing I could do. He'd throw me — against the wall, against the dresser — I'd end up on the floor. Just — praying. God, don't kill me — or do. Kill me and get it over with. He'd stand over me and — he'd have his — his penis in his hand, shaking it at me like it was a fist and it was; it was like a — god, Jordan, this is hard. It's so hard to say it."

129

"I know," she said quietly, and Gillie remembered her Tuesday, a huddled ball of exposed nerves; softly, she sighed.

"He'd hit me. Kick me. I think — just to hear me scream. I couldn't help it. He was so — " Deep in her hair, Jordan's fingers soothed her scalp; it was bizarre to remember the pain of Phil and feel the gentleness of Jordan. "He was just brutal," she said wearily. "It turned him on if I fought back. It turned him on if I didn't. It didn't matter. He just liked to hurt me. And he was — He'd get so hard — it always hurt, and sometimes he — he went — the wrong — he — Jordan, I can't. I can't —"

"You don't have to." Her voice had an edge like canvas ripping; her touch was calm and steady. "Say what you can, Gillie."

She shuddered a breath. "He'd hold me down. His hands were so big — I didn't know if I'd suffocate or . . . if I was lucky I'd faint," she whispered. "If I was really lucky, he'd be done when I came to. If all the planets were lined up in a row, I wouldn't wake up until morning."

She rested, absorbing Jordan's touch.

"When . . . the other night, when I — dreamed you. You were so gentle, you didn't — " She breathed a tiny, pained laugh. "You didn't. But — in a way you did, and it made me remember . . . He didn't always hurt me, but he was never gentle, and sometimes he was so vicious. I hate remembering that. Thinking that this time he'd kill me. I think sometimes that was worse than what he did."

"How long did it go on?" Jordan's voice had steadied; her hands had stilled, just pillowing Gillie's head in palms that were uncommonly warm.

"Well — since nineteen-eighty . . . two. Nine years?"

"How often?"

"Every few months. What's that, probably — thirty, forty times — " Her stomach lurched; she'd never really thought of it in a how-many way. "I knew my way home from every hospital in north Georgia. It always started with him grabbing me from behind. At first . . . only if the kids weren't home. When he figured out I wasn't letting them both out of the house the same night he just — went ahead. That's when I really started hating him. When I had to face my children in the morning and know they pitied me. I sent them to private school. I missed them — I took the Valium so I wouldn't feel it. Killing myself instead of killing him. Meghann called it self-induced brain death, but god, she heard me scream."

"Did he abuse her too?"

"No! I'd have known — god, Jordan, if I let that happen — no. I'd have known. I couldn't protect myself, but I'd have killed him if he'd touched her. I could have — " A harsh laugh escaped her. "I couldn't kill him for myself, but I could have for her. I love her — I loved my son" — (she didn't realize the past tense, but Jordan heard it and knew Philbrook Benson the Fourth was too much like his father for his mother to still love unconditionally) — "but Meggie was mine. Sometimes she was the only reason I had not to — just . . . quit. God knows I thought about it."

Hands murmured reassurance to the tension in her throat, tracing her shoulders, slipping below her collarbones, releasing her breath; again, those warm hands stilled, resting on her skin as if to protect her throat. "It seemed everyone — so many people — the girls I golfed with, Dad, my brother — " She felt as if she were breathing high mountain air, too thin to support her lowland body. " — asked me why I stayed. But nobody offered me a place to stay, or — they didn't . . ."

"Were you afraid he'd kill you if you tried to leave him?"

"God, yes. I did once. Stupid? Never run away from home on credit cards. He tracked me down — he just knocked on my hotel room door and I opened it. He was — it wasn't good, but at least he didn't hurt me. He tried to be — he apologized. He begged. And I believed him — I wanted to — but it was all a lie. Flowers, dinner — everything. He took me home and got drunk and threw me down the stairs. I think he was trying to kill me. He told me he would if — he wouldn't even call the ambulance for me. I was in the hospital for six weeks. Flowers every day. Too late. I didn't want to go back, but I didn't have any choice, Jordan. I didn't have any money. When I got back from the hospital — he'd gone through my purse. He took my credit cards away from me. Even my checkbook. After that I had credit. At the grocery, the pharmacy, the country club — they sent bills. Phil paid them. I had to beg him to get ten dollars to put gas in the car. I just didn't know what to do. I was so afraid of him."

Jordan rested one palm against the air a few inches above Gillie's breastbone. "This is your heart. Is it all right if I touch it?"

Gillie opened her eyes, looking upside down at her. "You did that a few days ago," she said quietly. "Yes. It's all right."

Hands settled onto her chest, a comfortable weight and warmth. "You said nine years, but you were married — what, twenty-four? What triggered him to start beating you? Do you know?"

"He cheated on me all the time we were married, and it was . . . almost a relief, really. When he was having an affair he left me alone. It hadn't been that bad but it wasn't — I didn't — enjoy it, but he didn't really hurt me. But then — I started having trouble — you know, feminine trouble — and I —" She drew a deep breath. "I had gonorrhea. I had all hell to pay getting rid of it, and when I — damn Nancy Reagan. Just say no? I just said no. He just broke six ribs. That's when it started. You told me to say no? Jordan, I hardly dare to. He beat the word out of me. I hate what he did to me. Not — what he did, but — that was bad enough, but — what happened inside me. Trust. Love. They should be so easy — they won't ever be easy. How can I get married again? God, sometimes just the thought of a man touching me —" She shivered. "He kept telling me he'd fuck me up. He did. Boy, he really did."

"You know you should be tested for HIV."

"Three times since he died. All negative." She laughed, bitterly exhausted. "Does that make me a virgin again?"

Jordan's hand rested against her cheek; Gillie knew that somehow, she understood all the cryptic things such seemingly nonsensical words had meant. "Do you think I could touch your back?" Gently, Jordan asked.

"Oh — " She bit her lip, searching for words, or for one word.

Jordan's hands cupped around her shoulders, as if to keep their palms warm for her. "It's all right to say no. I won't do anything you don't want."

"I know — " But still, it was long before she could turn; she felt herself trembling as Jordan adjusted the drape over her. "Jordan —"

"Yes."

"I trust you as much as I know how to. Please know that."

"I do. I'll start with the drape in place. Try to let go . . ."

She didn't know when she had ever known anything as gentle as Jordan's hands.

". . . try to feel it not hurt. Gillian, I won't hurt you."

"Mr. Goodnow, I appreciate Jordan's talents. I don't think I've ever met a woman who does as much as well as she does." John Laing sat back in his desk chair, the phone tucked into his shoulder as he cleaned under his nails with a corner of the matchbook Jordan had left on his desk a few days ago. "But the fact remains that she seems to have a studious disregard for certain personnel policies, namely the prohibition against fraternization between staff and guests. She's spent the last week in nearly constant company with the same woman, including both of her days off. She took this woman to Bethlehem, supposedly to golf — "

"That's Jordan's home course, John. She grew up in Bethlehem. You know that." Michael Goodnow had a calm bass rumble of a voice. "It's a beautiful course. Any golfer would jump at the opportunity to play it, and we can hardly fault Jordan for exposing a guest of Catawamteak to one of our other resorts."

"Be that as it may, guests are complaining that they can't access our star pro for lessons."

"Well, now, John, I know how Jordan schedules. It wouldn't be unusual for one student to occupy her for a week or so. I doubt that she'd let it go on much longer than that. She has a well-developed sense of fairness." He chuckled. "Unlike some of our guests, might I add. No, John, I'm not sure I'm ready to call it fraternization. Not from what you've told me so far."

John tossed the matchbook to his desk. Talking to Michael Goodnow about Jordan Bryant was always an exercise in frustration, but this time he figured he had an ace in the hole; he flipped it with a vengeance. "Two hours ago she and this woman were kissing in the lobby. I'm not talking a peck on the cheek. It was damned close to tongues."

"Well." Michael Goodnow's four-count pause was gratifying. "That's hard to believe, John. What's your source?"

"My own eyes. And then she" — he didn't bother to specify which she — "verbally assaulted me in the lobby for trying to tactfully stop them. Sir, I only mention it because she's a senior staff member. That's not setting much of an example for the kids — not to mention how seeing two lesbians necking in public rattled the cages of a couple of Baptist blue-hairs who were there to witness it. I've warned her I don't know how many times to keep her hands off the guests. She throws Uncle Michael in my face and does what she damn well pleases. At this point   " He let his shrug translate across the phone lines. "I had no choice but to call you."

Michael's pause was thoughtful. "What is it that you're asking me to do, John?"

"Give me some authority over her, sir. It's not in the best interest of the resort for her to be autonomous. She's openly disrespectful to me, and it affects the rest of the staff. Everyone knows I can't do anything to discipline her. She's made that clear."

"And what might you do with this authority, were I to grant it?"

Fire the bitch, John thought. "Sir, I'd let her know that she has to abide by the personnel policies or suffer the same consequences as any other staff member who doesn't. On the whole, she does good work for us, and she'd be hard to replace, but — "

"Replacing Jordan," Michael said mildly, "will always be my decision. I'll give your request my consideration and get back with you. If there's nothing else, then? Good day, John."

"You senile old fuck," John growled, jamming the receiver into its base, not knowing that one of Michael Goodnow's habits was to say goodbye, tap his pen against the mouthpiece of the phone, and not hang up. He'd learned a lot by hearing what people said while the handset was on its way from their ear to their desk.

Michael swiveled in his leather chair to look across his Boston office at the shelf on the east wall, where seven trophies and two framed magazine covers presided. "Jordan, Jordan," he murmured. "What is this senile old fuck supposed do with you, my little rebel?"

◆

"Gillian."

Who calls me that — ? Mom . . .

"Gillian — "

Oh, Mama. God, I miss you.

"Gillian, it's Jordan."

Jordan. Yes. She does, too.

"Can you start thinking about waking up, hon?"

"Hmmm?"

"You don't have to move. Easy — " A hand smoothed across her back; cloth between them was all that kept that touch from deep intimacy. It soothed the day's hurt, and the older, deeper pain; it left a last gentle touch against her hair, and she added one more Jordan to her list: Jordan-who-loves-me. "Wake up easy, Gillian." That voice was low, pacific. "You're safe."

The room was golden with slanting early-evening light. "Jordan . . . ?" She groped for awareness; impending dark and Jordan didn't fit properly together. "Don't you have to work?"

"Cindy's filling in for me. Glad for the overtime."

She sent an unfocused look at her wrist, finding only pale skin where her watch usually lived. "I fell asleep?"

"Yes. Can I get you anything? Water? Tea? The kettle's hot."

Gillie let her awareness wander around a body that felt too relaxed to be the one she was used to. "You might need a crane to get me off of here. God, I feel . . ." She searched for words and didn't find any that seemed to fit.

"A little disoriented? Like you're in someone else's skin?" She heard the smile in Jordan's voice. "We call it table-stupid. Do not attempt to operate heavy machinery."

"The keys to the steam roller are in my purse." She thought to turn over and found the drape suspended above her, Jordan holding it against the edge of the table with her thighs and up enough that she could move without getting tangled in the soft cloth. "Just toss the blanket over me," Gillie murmured. "Have them give me a wake-up call at six; I've got a seven-fifty tee time."

"How's your back feel?"

"Great, just lying here. What did you do?"

Jordan shrugged. "Swedish. Some neuromuscular therapy. Muscle currenting. Myofascial release stuff. Reiki. A little psychic surgery."

"Psychic surgery?" She opened her eyes.

"Yeah. I combed some of the dust out of your wings." She smiled at Gillie's skepticism. "You don't have to believe. But I think you'll find that tightness that nags between your shoulder blades is going to feel better."

Gillie felt for it with her memory and didn't find it. "I don't remember mentioning that."

"You didn't."

"God, Jordan. You get scarier all the time."

"It's not scary. Just experience." She rested a hand on Gillie's shoulder. "Where are you with Phil?" she asked quietly.

Gillie looked up at her. "My whole body remembers your hands," she said softly. "Phil will never be able to hurt me quite so bad again."

Jordan smiled; briefly, the backs of her fingers touched Gillie's cheek. "One for the win column."

Gillie closed her eyes. "Yeah," she murmured. "I'd say so." She sighed, a deep, grateful sigh. "I suppose I should get up, and not just lie here like a slug."

"Let me help you." Jordan's arm was neutral around her shoulders. "Don't sit up too fast — easy, Gil. Easy."

"What time is it?"

"A little past seven. Take this" — she handed a corner of the draping sheet over Gillie's shoulder — "and this" — another corner came over the other shoulder — "and when you stand up you'll have a toga."

She managed to stand, and hang onto the corners of the sheet; she yawned, and sneezed lightly. "'Scuse me. Dusty brains, I guess — to go with my dusty wings. After seven? I really slept, then."

"You had a little system crash. An adrenaline OD'll do that — whoa, hon. Steady." Jordan caught her when she wobbled.

"God, you've turned my entire central nervous system into tofu." She leaned into Jordan's warmth. "Mmm. Just take me to bed," she murmured, and felt a tiny twitch of Jordan's arms tightening around her, and a barely-there brush of lips against her hair that seemed as if it might almost have been a whisper, a whisper that she sensed more than she heard: *Gladly.* She dared to look up, dared to meet grey-flannel eyes. "Did you . . . say something?"

Jordan parked her gently against the table. "Find your balance, Gil," she said softly, and turned to get the orderly tools of her trade from their weathered black bag. "I'd like to get your blood pressure, if you can wift over to the sofa."

"Wift?"

Jordan smiled; it was a familiar smile, with no hint of anything more than her natural affection. "That's a word I came up with in massage school. Drift and waft at the same time. The walk of the table-drunk. I used to get off the table in school and walk into walls."

"I understand that." She wifted as best she could, and sank in barely-exaggerated collapse against the cushions of the sofa. "Did I wift wight?"

"You wifted wonderfuwwy."

She drowsed a smile, offering an arm; Jordan tucked her wrist between her arm and her ribs, supporting her elbow with one hand, pumping up the cuff with the other. Gillie watched as that dark head bent to listen through the stethoscope. She felt Jordan's warmth against her wrist; she smelled her powdery cologne, and heard her breath; she saw the feathery splash of dark lashes against her cheek, and the tailored cut of her almost-black hair, the rise of her breast and the graceful length of the fingers that supported her arm, and a slow, liquid warmth stirred in the pit of her belly.

"One-twenty-two over seventy-six. I like that a lot better, Ms. Gillian."

"So do I," she murmured, trying to figure out what that odd nudge of warmth had been.

Jordan gave her back the hand she had secured between her bicep and ribs, and loosened the cuff. The back of her hand brushed Gillie's breast, and that low warmth rolled deep inside her again, so surprising that she reached for it. *What in the name of —*

"Excuse me. My hands get klutzy when they're tired." She found her date book. "Let's see . . . tomorrow's Friday, we're on for golf — I don't know that you should golf tomorrow. Give your back a chance to catch its breath. I can leave my table here and we can work on it again tomorrow."

This again? Tomorrow? She groped for her awareness. *I'm not sure —*

"We can do Saturday and again Monday, and try to clear this up."

— not sure that's a good idea. What in god's name is going on? I feel like I'm — She found her voice, denying the one inside her. "But Monday's your day off."

Jordan glanced up. "No problem." She closed her date book and got her clipboard, and made a few notes and capped her pen. "I was going to ask if you wanted to run over to Bethlehem with me. I need to let the boys know I survived July one more time. They never believe me over the phone. We could leave early Sunday and stay over — "

Stay over. In Bethlehem. With you.

" — if you feel like golfing. If you don't — well, it's still a nice drive. If you're still here in leaf season, we'll have to go then. It's just beautiful when the foliage is peak. Anyway, a sauna might do you good. No one believes me when I say how great a sauna can feel in July, so we'll have the place to ourselves. Blanche DuBois understood, steaming up Stanley's bathroom. It feels so much cooler when you get out." She snapped the catches of her case and reached to cup Gillie's bare foot in her hand. "Gillie, I've got to tell you — "

She knew that touch was meant to be playful, but when Jordan's fingers stroked the sole of her foot that heat bloomed in her belly again; she felt her nipples crown hard against the flannel toga. *What — ? My god, I don't believe — I can't — this can't be what it feels like. It can't be. I'm not —*

" — of all the women who ever got onto that table, you were the first one with green polish on your toenails. That tickled me no end."

She launched from the sofa, fleeing that touch, that smile, that voice; she found herself on the balcony with her heart thudding in her and her thoughts laughing in nervous near-hysteria *don't take my blood pressure now, Jordan, all of a sudden I'm not vewwy damned wanguid —* and when Jordan's voice came behind her it seemed as soft as the step of a predatory cat and she turned in panicked defense, strangling back a breath that could easily have been — was very nearly — a scream.

"Gillie, no — Gillie, please. What's going on?"

"How many of you are there, Jordan?" It came out in a trembling whisper; she crossed her arms over her breasts, afraid of those deep grey eyes and what they would discover if Jordan only glanced down; her nipples were still painfully hard.

"How many . . .? Gillie, I don't understand. What — "

"There's Jordan-the-golf-pro and Jordan-the-bartender and Jordan-the-psychotherapist and Jordan-the-massage-therapist and Jordan-my-friend and Jordan-who — who — Jesus! I never know who I'm with! Maybe you can flit around all these personalities of yours" — *don't, don't blame her for this, you're not being fair* — "like some — some — butterfly" — *(tongue like a) (shut up, Peony!)* — "but I can't keep you sorted out, I can't" — *stop, my god look at her stop this you're hurting her —*

"flit or wift or dance fast enough to keep up with who you are or who you were a minute ago or who you'll be next or what to expect or — "

Jordan's palm met her face. It was barely a touch, but she felt the impact of a slap and the panic of words collided in her throat like a chain-reaction accident on a foggy mountain highway while she wondered if Jordan had hit her; she finally realized she hadn't but she reached for her face anyway, grappling for her breath through the wreckage of words still piled up in her throat.

"Gillian," Jordan said quietly, "forty feet up with nothing but a wrought-iron rail between here and eternity is a really bad place for a panic attack. Please come inside."

"You . . . you . . . oh, my — " She sank into one of the wicker deck chairs and buried her face in her hands. "Jordan, I'm so sorry, I — Jordan, I — oh, god, I need a drink. Jordan, please. Please."

Jordan turned; Gillie hugged herself, feeling exposed in a makeshift toga and nothing else but the lowering evening and the memory of that liquid, rolling warmth deep inside her. *I'm not asleep, I didn't dream that, it happened, I felt it and if I'd stayed there I couldn't have hidden it, you'd have seen it and by now you'd be kissing me and I'd be —*

By now I'd be begging for you. Come on. Come on.

It was more than a slow roll this time; it was a hard, hot surge.

No! I'm not a lesbian. I don't want this, I don't want her, I
(do)
don't! want! her! I've never ever been attracted to a woman never!
(So send Riqui a card and tell her: You have now.)

"Gillian, please. Tell me what's happening."

Her voice was close — too close. She rose blindly only to run into Jordan, and recoiled with a barely-whispered "don't touch me — " and found the door, but in the living room of the suite she didn't know where to go, and when Jordan spoke her name she sank to the sofa and did all there was left to do with the confusion: she cried.

And when Jordan's voice came near to her she flinched, expecting her touch to come with it; it didn't. "Gillian — " It was barely more than a whisper. "Please tell me. If I — "

"I can't! Jordan, go. Please go. Please. I can't — "

Finally, gently, the door closed, and she let the tears go: the deep tears, the ones that came on sobs so hard they hurt.

◆

It took a long time, but she cried herself out. At last she shivered up from the sofa and into the bathroom, and she took a steaming-hot shower, wary of where and how she touched herself; water beaded on her oiled skin to tell her where Jordan's hands had been. She scrubbed off that touch, wondering with a stark, angry weakness how she could have slept

138

through those hands slipping across her ribs, her belly, her buttocks, up the insides of her thighs . . .

Just the right touch, that's how. The right touch, the right hands, the right one. Imagine those hands —

"Oh, shut up!"

She found the thick terrycloth robe the inn provided with suites and wrapped into it, shivering; she wanted only a drink and fresh night air and the lighthouse to calm her. The drink Jordan had made for her was on the coffee table, its ice cubes melted small; she tasted it and dumped it and made a fresh one and took it to the balcony. Jordan's cigarette case was on the table there, with a book of her matches; she looked at it, but didn't touch it.

Somewhere on the grounds, people were partying. She heard laughter and music and wished they would stop, or take their jollity somewhere away from her hearing.

She drank her drink too fast, and got up to make another, and took it back out to the balcony. The moon was fat and full, coldly sterile in the night; she looked toward the seawall and wondered if it was Jordan or shadows she saw moving down there.

Reluctantly, she picked up the cigarette case. It was surprisingly heavy, the gold warming to her touch. She thumbed the catch. It had room for six cigarettes, and held two. There was a butt and a spent match in the ashtray. She held the case to catch the light and read the engraving inside the lid.

James Knox Polk Bryant
Faithful Service
1888 - 1938
Bethlehem Inn & Country Club

She wondered what Jordan's father had done for a living, and what his name had been; she wondered if he had carried this smoothly-aged piece of family history in his pocket until he died, the way Jordan carried it in hers.

She leaned back in the creaky wicker chair with a huge, shaky sigh. "Oh, Jordan," she murmured, and she sipped her drink away, watching the lighthouse: white and green, white and green.

We're all Jay Gatsby, believing in the green light at the end of Daisy's dock — and we're all Peony Watkins. Just moths in a roomful of candles.

Honey, that Jordan — mmmm-mmm! If I swung that way I'd swing her way; god, those eyes of hers? I'll bet she's got a tongue like a butterfly . . .

Maybe Peony's right.

Maybe Peony's right.

She knew that if she went to the elevator and pushed G, she'd end up six steps from Jordan's door.

She got to her feet and went slowly to the bar. There was no more ice; there was barely enough vodka to bother pouring. She poured it anyway, and drank it in a swallow, and leaned tiredly against the bar; she slipped her hands into her pockets and found James Knox Polk Bryant's reward for fifty years of faithful service.

◆

She got off the elevator and almost collided with Jordan in the hallway; she retreated a step. "Hi."

"Hi." Jordan's hair was damp; she had on jeans and a shirt that looked as if it had once belonged to a tuxedo. "Did I leave my cigarette case up there?"

"Yes. I was just — " She offered it, not daring to meet those dispassionate grey eyes, and missed its warm weight when Jordan took it from her hand. "I thought you might miss it."

"I did. But I — " Jordan stopped, and amended, it seemed: "I'm out of scotch."

"I'm out of vodka."

Jordan looked down the hall toward the lobby, where the stairs led down to the bar. "So. Buy you a drink?"

Gillie dared to meet her eyes, and then fled from them. "I don't — I — Thank you. Yes."

There was no band; the bar was lightly populated. Jordan offered an empty table in a corner, well away from the sparse crowd. Rafael was there before they were settled into their chairs. "Hey, women. What can I do you for? Stoli tall, Mrs. Benson? That pink's a great color for you."

"Thank you, Rafael. On the rocks."

"Heavy-hitting tonight! How about you, boss? Glenfiddich? Ice on the side?"

Jordan nodded, and toyed with her cigarette case until their drinks arrived. "Gillie — "

"Jordan, I'm sorry. I don't know what it was or where it came from. But it wasn't you, Jordan. It was nothing you said, nothing you did — it wasn't you."

"Are you sure? One minute you were" — a pained smile traced across her lips, there and gone — "wanguid. The next minute — "

"The next minute I was up to my neck in ancient history. It didn't have anything to do with you." *There; you've lied to her again. Explain it tomorrow night down by the seawall, if you can: sorry to have acted so weird, Jordan honey; it's just that all of a sudden this supposably straight woman wanted both of us to be naked.* "It's not your fault that I can't handle being cared about."

"It isn't that you can't — " It was a flare choked back almost as soon as it erupted; Jordan thumped her glass to the table, and leaned her head on her hands for a taut moment before she said softly, "I'm sorry. I'm sorry, Gillie. It's not my place — "

"It *is* your place! This is what I was talking about, Jordan! You're never who I expect you to be! If you care about me, be honest with me! If you're just my — my golf teacher, tell me, and I'll go to Bethlehem and let Fred teach me to golf! Will you pick who you want to be to me and be it?"

And she knew that had they been in her suite, or in Jordan's apartment, that in that moment Jordan would have closed the distance between them, closed her arms around her, whispered into her breath what they both knew: *I want to be your lover.* She saw it in her eyes before she closed them, in her hands before they fisted and opened again in an intensity deeper than fists had been, in the taut cords of her throat as she searched for control before she found herself again. "It isn't my choice! What I want isn't what's impor —"

"Why not? Why aren't you just as important?"

Jordan drew a hard breath; her fingertips sought her forehead for a brief, frustrated moment before she dropped her hand. "Because you've spent your life being whatever or whoever someone else told you to be or forced you to be. Not being allowed to choose or to find out for yourself what you are or who you could be. That's rape, Gillian, and I'm not going to be the next one to do it to you. I'll support you, I'll be here for you — I'll be all you said I was and whatever else you want to add to the list, but I won't tell you what to do or who to be."

"So it's all right for you to take the rape?"

"You can choose to play rough, but you can't choose to be raped. Rape is a condition of no options. This way we both have options."

"Choose to play rough?" She choked out a laugh. "Jordan, you always play rough! You're just so damned good at making me think you're gentle."

"When there aren't any rules all you can do is try to play fair. Sometimes that's the roughest way to play."

"God — " She turned in her chair, away from Jordan, hugging herself, trying not to explode into tears or a screaming shrew. " — damn you!" It hissed out. "You're everything I ever wanted in a man, Jordan, but I know there's not a man like you on the face of god's green globe — which really makes me wonder just what in hell I want. And that's the problem. I don't know what I want — why I want — what I'm looking for or what I — expect or need or — You're so good at explaining things away," she said softly. "Explain this away. When you touched me — not the massage, but after, when — " She swallowed. "Something sexual happened to me," she whispered. "I got — " She met the dark grey eyes. "Turned on," she said softly, trying not to cry. "I wanted — " She passed shaky fingers under her eyes, catching tears that had escaped her, and took a deep breath. "I wanted you to — I — wanted you," she managed. "And I got scared. I'm not a lesbian, Jordan. It has nothing to do with homophobia. I'm just not. I'd like to get married again — I'd like to think there's a man somewhere who'd love me for me instead of the money, and treat me . . . the way you do. And make me feel the way you make me feel. Maybe he doesn't exist, but that's what I want. I care so much for you, but not — not — and to feel that — this — because it's still there. And god, I'm afraid of it. Not of you, Jordan. Of myself. Of what I'm feeling."

Jordan studied her drink for a long moment; at last she looked up. "I'm just tossing this out. Is it possible that you're bisexual? Riqui — "

"No. No. It's not that you're a woman, Jordan — or maybe it is, but not — that's not what I want physically. It's just that I trust you and — need you. It's as if you're taking the place of everyone I miss: my mother and my daughter and my grandmother, all of that safety and healing and still, it's like — this much isn't enough? God, I'm not making any sense. I'm so confused."

"You're making perfect sense."

"You always say that." She plucked the napkin from under her drink and swiped at her eyes. "And you can always make me believe it. Sort it out for me, Jordan. God, I'm . . . lost. Just lost."

Jordan tasted her drink, and sighed and rested her elbows on the table; Gillie looked at Jordan's long slender fingers loosely entwined in front of her because she didn't dare meet her eyes. "Gillie, I don't think it's me you want," Jordan said quietly, at last. "I think it's love, and gentleness, and tenderness, and trust. You see it in me because it's all the women you miss . . . and the lover you never had in Phil."

Gillie looked up.

"You've never been made love to, have you."

She looked away, feeling the hard, hot flush. "No."

"And you trust me."

"Jordan, yes. But I'm not a les — "

"You don't need to be." Gently, Jordan interrupted the protest. "You just need to need, and you do. I'm possible. I'm safe. I want you. You know that. It has nothing to do with homophobia; it has nothing to do with gender. It has to do with being lonely, and what you need, and what you want. It's projection. I'm everything you want from a man without any of the risks."

"But that's not fair to you! It's like — like — using you for a Band-aid, to cover the wound and then throw you away when I'm healed. That's horrible."

"Would you throw me away? If we made love tonight, would you be embarrassed, or ashamed, and not be able to look at me tomorrow? Then I'd be a Band-aid, and no, it wouldn't be fair. Not to me, and not to you, because then you'd have a new wound and no friend to help stop the bleeding. Gillian, if all I wanted was to get you into bed, I'd have had you there or known I couldn't and been gone by now. I meant it when I said I'd rather be the friend you could come back to than the lover you'd regret."

"That's one of the things I love about you." It was half a sob, half a laugh. "Your fucking humility. God, Jordan, I can't imagine regretting you." She felt Jordan watching her, and wondered what she was seeing. "You're the strangest thing that's ever happened to me," she said quietly. "I don't know what to do next."

Jordan sat back in her chair. "Well," she said, "we could go back to my place, or your place." She opened her cigarette case, not looking at Gillie. "Or we could have dinner here. Or my place, or your place." She picked one of the remaining Ovals from the case and closed it with a soft click. "Or we could try to connect with Park and Olathe and do some food with them and look at Park's picture — photographs." There was a box of matches with the Catawamteak logo in the ashtray; she slipped it open and struck one. "Or we could sit here and drink too much on empty stomachs and go through this all again in a few hours, when neither one of us would have the judgment we have now, and end up somewhere one or both of us might regret." She lit her cigarette and shook out the match. "Or we could kiss the air beside each others' cheeks and say parting is such sweet sorrow, and go do whatever we do before we go to sleep."

"Do you ever run out of answers?"

"Every day of my life. I just hope I never run out of options."

Gillie looked at her: at her eyes, her lips, her hands. "You're not an option I ever thought I'd have to consider, Jordan," she said softly. "How hard is this for you?"

Jordan met her eyes, and didn't answer; she didn't have to.

"Call Park and Olathe. We've still got time for room service?"

"If Gaston's in the kitchen, we've got time for room service." And she looked up with a ghost of a smile. "Your place or mine?"

◆

"Cool!" Park said over the phone. "You guys want to come here, or do we invade?" And she laughed. "Rocky's crib? I'll bring the black book, baby. Maybe you'll get lucky later if the Rockette gets into that."

"You leave your black book right where it is. I appreciate the artistry of your pornography even though your subject matter isn't precisely my cup of tea, but I'm not sure Gillie would — appreciate it at all, or ever be comfortable with Olathe again if she saw it. Bring your tasteful stuff, okay? Land and sea. Mountains. Stuff like that."

143

♦

"You're good, Park. You really are," Jordan said. They had been through three of Park's binders of eight-by-ten black and whites, most of them making Jordan wonder what Ansel Adams might have done given the coast of Maine instead of Yosemite. "Where's the ones you took Sunday that you were bragging about?"

"Save the best for last." Park offered another book. "This is a good one. These happened in Mexico over the winter." She looked at Gillie. "Mostly nudes." It was a gentle caution.

Gillie reached for the binder. "Why does everyone think I'm such a prude? I'll have you know I subscribe to *Playboy*."

"No way!" Olathe poked her knife through a dwindling platter of Gaston's excellent stir-fry, finding a water chestnut. She sucked the crisp slice from the blade of the knife; Jordan, coming back from the kitchenette wiping her hands on a paper towel, couldn't help but watch.

"Well . . . it was my husband's subscription, but I renewed it. The articles are good."

"And the women are major babes," Park grinned. "But their photographers are great."

"So are you."

"Thanks. There's some good textural stuff in this series. Check it out."

The photographs weren't erotic because of what Park had done so much as they were erotic because Olathe was a purely sensual being. "Look at the background in that one," Park said. "I freaked out. She was cold, goose bumps all over, and the adobe behind her is almost exactly the same, texturally, as her skin — except in reverse. I love that photograph. I really do."

"Like being between mirrors," Gillie offered.

Park raised an eyebrow. "Thanks for the title, Rocky."

"I knew we picked up on this girlfriend for a reason," Olathe grinned. "You guys through eating? I'll put this junk back on the cart." They nodded absently, and Olathe cleared the table, tipping the last of the bottle of Chardonnay into Gillie's glass. "I know you didn't order just one jug of grape juice, Jor."

"Fridge. Corkscrew's by the sink." She paused behind Gillie, looking over her shoulder as she turned pages. "Oh, wow. That one's great, Park." The flow of Olathe's body mirrored the flow of the shoreline; a sunset took the same shapes, so that an upraised knee was a rock was the sinking sun, a breast was a rolling wave was a cloud, an arm was a branch was a contrail in the sky. "That's incredible."

"One negative. All that happened by itself. Awesome, huh?"

Gillie shook her head over the next one; Olathe was in a taut crouch, as ready to spring as a preying cat, her abdomen a light-and-shadowed ripple of definition. "How many sit-ups a day, Olathe?"

144

"Crunches." The model drew the cork on a new bottle of wine. "Three hundred in the a.m., three hundred in the p.m., with a twenty-pound plate on my chest. You like that belly?"

"I feel positively obese."

"Not. You've got a good build, girl. Just gotta work at it. Like the pecs. If I don't do the pec work, I've got big ol' tits. Can't deal with it. You get big jugs, that's all they look at. I'm like a total body, you see? One picture to the next, wherever she puts me, your eye never lands in the same place on my skinscape or her landscape. Some of that's Park's balance. Some it's mine."

"It's the balance between you, too," Jordan murmured. She knew enough about anatomy, and was enough of an athlete herself, to appreciate the work Olathe put into her body; although her massage career had taken different directions, she had majored in sports massage, and athletes who weren't hurt were still a pleasure to work on. "I'd like to get you on the table sometime, Olathe."

"Whoa! You want me flat and naked? Where and what time, babe? You know I've got major fantasies about those hands of yours, sistergirl."

Jordan sent her a reproachful smile. "God, Olathe. Don't you ever turn it off?"

Olathe laughed. "Can't. I'm a universe-class nympho, baby. Park's my main squeeze, but no one person's enough for me. I need too much of it."

Gillie looked a puzzled question at Park. "And that works for you?"

Park shrugged. "I love the girl, but she's just warmed up when I'm worn out. She could do us all and still be ready. The doc says it's a chemical thing. Wanted to give her some pills, man. She told the bitch to chill. She likes to fuck. I like to watch. I don't see a problem."

Gillie blinked. "You . . . watch?"

"Sure. Look, say her and Jordan. They get great sex — and you know it, too. I know what Olathe's like and hell, all you got to do is look at Jordan and know she's one extremely good lover."

Gillie didn't doubt that for a moment.

"So if they let me watch, I get to see two beautiful women doing the most beautiful thing women do — that, and nursing babies." Park leaned forward. "Good sex is art, Rocky. Great sex is great art. That's why I take photographs of it. Nudes have been art probably ever since the first cavewoman scratched a portrait of her ol' lady on the wall of their crib with a sharp rock. So what makes two nudes doing what comes natural obscene, instead of art? Violence is obscene. Two people loving each other's bodies — that isn't obscene, and it isn't pornography. That's fuckin' beautiful." She tasted her wine. "I got photographs of Olathe having orgasms — that's some of the best stuff I ever shot. Can I sell it? No; they call it degrading to women. But they can sell magazines of men hurting women? That's bullshit. Turn on the television, all those movies

145

of men beating and raping and killing women — shit. That's pornography, girlfriend."

"I see your point." Gillie turned a page to study Olathe's wet, flawless body dusted with sand against the same adobe background that Park had pointed out before; in this one, the sand was her gooseflesh. It was between the mirrors again; it was exquisitely different. "This one's good, too."

"Yeah. I like that one."

"How do you explain the black book?" Jordan had been watching over Gillie's shoulder as she went through the album, hoping Park had taken her at her word about that book.

"I had a lot of fun that day."

Gillie glanced up as Olathe tipped wine into their glasses, thinking that the model had sounded almost defensive. "Am I missing something?"

"No one got hurt," Olathe said.

"But the implication — "

Park cut Jordan off. "The reality," she said evenly, "is that a lot of women have rape fantasies. The implication in the black book is that she can satisfy that without getting forced."

Gillie turned a page to find evidence that Park photographed Olathe with other women; thighs and bellies were molded together, nipples and tongues barely touching, the other woman's body so much like Olathe's that they were images of one another. "This is beautiful. What's the black book?"

"Jordan thinks it's porn. Didn't even want us to bring it."

Gillie looked over her shoulder at Jordan. "Censoring for me?"

"Not really. I just wasn't sure that graphic rape fantasies were something you'd enjoy."

"I won't argue with that." She turned the page. "But if we're going to debate the subject of art versus pornography, I'm at a disadvantage by not having seen the same spectrum you've all seen. *Playboy* isn't pornography." The next photograph was a mouth and a breast, just the tip of a tongue touching just the tip of a hardened nipple; she flipped back to it when she saw the next one, to confirm that the close-up had come from the one that followed it. "Beautiful," she murmured, and was suddenly aware that the conversation had lulled. She looked up. "Is it twenty past, or my turn to talk?"

"Come again?"

"My grandmother said that when there's a silence like that, it's usually twenty of or twenty past the hour. If it isn't, the person who notices the silence is the one people expect to say something." Everyone checked their watches; it was 10:40. "Right again, Nana." She turned a page; a black-and-white Olathe arched into the kiss of the woman over her, her hands buried in hair as long and thickly dark as her own, holding that face deep between her thighs; every fiber of her captured body exuded

146

her pleasure. Gillie's belly flip-flopped a little; she restrained a jittery laugh.

She escaped the photograph only to be floored by the next one. It was the image from her dream, and that memory surged in her: Jordan behind her, holding her, one hand stroking to her belly, one to her breast, finding her throat with a whispering mouth, and what happened in her wasn't a little flip-flop. It was a surge so hard and hot that it left an ache when it finally subsided.

Olathe reached to trace a long fingernail across Gillie's cheekbone. "Look at that blush," she teased, as gentle as her touch. "Hot flash, Rocky?"

Gillie couldn't look away from the photograph. "Seduce Jordan, Olathe," she said shakily. "I'm straight, remember?"

"Straight's just a state of mind. Not that seducing Jordan isn't a most excellent idea." Softly, Olathe laughed. "You want to watch?"

"Don't promise what you can't deliver, Olathe." Jordan only glanced up; she knew that the image on the page had stirred something in Gillie that had to do with much more than generic eroticism. She was fairly certain that if she were to take the shoulders in front of her into her hands, Gillian Benson would come unglued.

She looked up to find Park studying her; the photographer raised a questioning eyebrow before looking at Gillie. "Whatchu thinking, Rocky?" Park asked quietly.

Gillie didn't look up. "To answer your question, Olathe, I think seeing the photographs is about as deep into voyeurism as I want to go." Her voice was softly unsteady. "But no, this isn't pornography. Not by any stretch. It's certainly erotic, but it's beautiful."

Park shifted in her chair. "Are you serious about wanting to see the full spectrum?" The spoken question was for Gillie, but she looked another one at Jordan.

Jordan raised her hands in defeat. "Don't look at me. It's not my decision."

"Full spectrum — ? Oh." Gillie gave the binder a tiny push away from her, still open to that disturbing page. "I . . . god, Park, I don't know. Tell me about it."

Park drew a black notebook from her bag. "This is the other end of it." She put the book on the table, keeping one hand on it. "Intimate body parts, up close and personal. It's about playing rough, Rocky, but it's still about playing. It looks like violence, but it isn't. You understand?"

"Are you apologizing or justifying?"

"Explaining. I know where Jordan's coming from trying to protect you, so I'm explaining. And we won't get warped if this is too much for you. Just close it if it is."

She took her hand from the portfolio; Gillie looked at it, but didn't reach for it. "Does this involve a man, or . . . men?"

Park shook her head. "Penetration, yes. Men, no."

147

"Olathe?" Gillie looked at the model. "Can I ask you a personal question?"

"Freshman year of high school, if 'have you ever been raped' is what you're wondering. The bastards hurt me, too. Three senior guys, one of me. They had some out-there ideas. One of them was beating the shit out of me. But they didn't kill me. They could beat me up and fuck me, but they couldn't fuck me up and beat me. Somebody went there on you, didn't they." Olathe sat at the table, reaching to touch the cover of the book, one finger straying to brush Gillie's knuckles. "This isn't about rape, Rocky. It's about power. Some women have this rape fantasy thing going on, and maybe that got taken away from you, but for the ones who can still go there, it's about walking that fine line and still having the power. It's a domination thing, but the one receiving is really the one doing the dominating. She's calling all the shots. You follow?"

"I don't know. I don't think so. I guess I can see what you mean intellectually. But viscerally — "

"Yeah. I hear your guts singing a different song."

"If I can't handle this, I don't think it'll have much to do with you. Or art. Or pornography. It'll be about . . ." She ticked a fingernail against the edge of the book. "Power I didn't have."

"Don't open it yet; I got a question." Olathe tasted her wine. "I don't get you, Rocky, probably no more than you get me. But I know everyone's got wants, and they're all pretty much the same. They just take different answers. You want what? Security? Someone who loves you in the bed and out of it? Some respect? Some physical comfort?"

"It would be nice to have all of that, yes."

"I've got all that," Olathe said gently. "I like my life. I like what I do and who I do it with, or I wouldn't do it. My way's way out there to most people, but it's all the same. Security and love and respect and physical comfort. I'm lucky to have Park. There aren't many people who'd understand that I'm not owned by my sexuality, I just indulge it while it's hot. What's in here isn't everybody's drug of choice. It's not mine, most of the time, but when I'm there, that's where I want to be. You understand that your hard times and these photographs, they've got nothing to do with each other? I've been both places, girl. I know what I'm saying."

"I'll take your word for it."

"That's all I wanted." Olathe smiled. "And if you're shocked, go ahead on and be there. Ain't nobody here who doesn't care about you."

Jordan didn't need to see her face. She could feel Gillie's reactions to the photographs through the energy of her body as she turned explicit pages. Some of them she flipped past quickly; all three women saw that the ones she didn't care to linger with were the ones where Olathe was facedown submissive.

Once she laughed in unfettered embarrassment: "God, Olathe! That's almost physically impossible, isn't it?"

Olathe roused from watching her face to see the picture she meant. "Yeah, that's big, but I was pretty horny by then. Took more of it than I thought I could."

Gillie shook her head slowly. "Your face," she murmured. "Your eyes, your mouth — everything. You're not faking this. You were enjoying it."

"You can't fake something that big," Olathe said quietly. "You can take it or not, and if you can, you like it."

Gillie looked at her. "You know I'll never see you the same way as I did before."

Olathe shrugged. "You'll just be deeper into me, like that dildo."

Gillie turned pages; at last she closed the book. All three of them knew she was shaken. "I might not call it pornography from this perspective," she said at last, "but if I saw it cold, without you to explain it, I wouldn't know what else to call it."

"I call it hard-core erotica," Park said. "We're pretty picky about who sees it."

"Why did you show it to me?"

"I didn't show it to you. I told you it was here and you looked."

◆

They left the Mexico book and two big white envelopes when they left. "These are the Sunday shots. A set for each of you. It's killing me not to see the looks on your faces when you see them, but this is something you need to do alone together." Park started out the door, and paused. "I can't sell them without model's releases," she said quietly. "That's up to you guys."

Gillie closed the door behind them and leaned against it to draw a shaky sigh; she flicked her eyes at Jordan, and away again. "God, I wish I'd listened to you." She went to the bar and opened the ice bucket, finding only cold water. "Damn," she muttered, and cracked the seal on the fresh fifth of Stolichnaya Jordan had spirited out of the bar.

Jordan emptied the water into the sink and went down the hall, and came back to find Gillie curled into a corner of the sofa, her head resting on one hand, an empty glass in the other, looking as if the reaction she had kept in check for Park and Olathe was straining, all of a sudden, to be free of her. "Gillie?"

She looked up.

"Do you want me to leave?"

She held up the glass. "Make me a drink? There's scotch there if you want."

Jordan mixed and delivered, and sat at the other end of the sofa. "Are you okay?"

"No." She tasted her drink, and ran a hand through her hair, and shook her head slowly. "How can she take so much pleasure from something that was so painful for me?"

Jordan lit a cigarette and blew out the match, dropping it into an ashtray. "Apples and oranges. She was having rough sex. Some women — "

"Rough! God, Jordan, it was brutal!"

"That's how it looked to you. Some women enjoy playing that game."

Gillie shook her head hard, hugging herself. "This afternoon you told me to only say what I could about — and I couldn't, but — well, pardon me for stepping out of my old-fart character for a minute, but I can say this now and I'm going to. Seeing a woman jammed into a mattress and getting fucked up the ass is hard for me! He did that to me and it's never going to be erotic for me to see it happen to someone else. The Mexico pictures, yes, but not that black book. I don't care how much fun she was having. Maybe Park's a genius with the camera, but I'm sorry — and don't tell me not to apologize — but if you tie potato peels and chicken bones up in a pretty pink bow, you've still got garbage."

"I hope you're not expecting me to argue with you."

"I don't know what I expect." She got up, pacing around the sofa. "Tell me the truth, Jordan. How does that hit you? The black book?"

"It's not to my personal taste."

"Do you think it's pornography?"

"If I were on a jury and had to answer that question, I'd say no."

"Why?"

"Because I agree with Park that for something to be pornographic, it has to have an element of real violence. The black book flirts with it, but it doesn't go home with it. It expresses what might be perceived as a dark side of mutual human desire, but it's the mutuality of the desire that sways my vote."

"Why did she think I'd want to see it?"

Jordan shook her head. "You'll have to ask Park that. I don't know. Why did you look at it?"

"I have no idea." She collapsed into one of the wing chairs by the French doors. "But I wish I hadn't. God, I wish I hadn't."

Jordan got up; she took both their drinks around the sofa, and coastered them on the table between the chairs. "You want to talk?"

Her laugh was small and unhappy. "No more than I wanted to this afternoon. But I probably will." A chill settled hard into her and she shivered; Jordan got the blanket she had folded over the back of the sofa, and shook it out and draped it over her. "Thanks," she whispered. "God, what a day this has been."

"Seems as if it's been rough. I'm a little pissed at Park for bringing that. I asked her not to." She tapped her cigarette over the ashtray on the table. "It isn't that I was censoring for you. It just didn't seem like good timing."

"It wasn't." Gillie worked a hand out of the blanket to reach for her drink. "Keep 'em coming, sugar. Just pour me into bed when it's over. Maybe if I get drunk enough, I'll let you take advantage of me." And she shivered again, and closed her eyes; she held the cold glass against her forehead for a moment. "God, Jordan, I'm sorry," she whispered. "That was absolutely vulgar."

Jordan reached for her drink. "Would it be easier for you if I went home?"

"No. Not that I'd blame you if you did, but — god, Jordan, I know it's stupid, but if you leave now all I'll do is sit here all night because I'll be afraid to go through a door for thinking he'll be on the other side of it. He's dead, he's dead, he's dead — and every once in a while I have a night of the living dead, and he's everywhere." She looked up; Jordan was still standing near her chair, her drink in her hand, looking as if she wasn't sure she should have mixed it. "Stay. Just for a while." It was a soft request. "And Jordan, honey, I trust you with every little tiny fiber of my being, but I just can't take having someone standing over me like that. Sit down. Please."

Jordan sat; she crushed out her cigarette. "Cellular-level trust?"

"What?"

"Every tiny little fiber of your being. Cellular-level trust." She smiled. "When I told my friend Casey I was going to take a workshop on cellular-level Reiki, she said, 'What's that? Reiki by car phone?'"

It felt good to smile. "Your friend Casey sounds like a pistol. I hope I can meet her someday."

"She's good people. If you buy the condo and want any remodeling done, let me know. She's a good carpenter, and she could use the work. She's had a rough year."

"Good people." Gillie rested her head against the wing of the chair. "Lots of hats."

"Hats?"

"Wasn't she the one you tried on hats with? Made me think of all of your hats. Jordan, I said awful things to you this afternoon. I've been kicking myself — "

"Gillie, don't. You do too much of that."

"Oh, I know, but sometimes it's deserved. There's no call for me to accuse you when all you're doing is wearing your hats. It's just that sometimes it's so hard for me to put all of you together. Most people are one thing, or maybe two things, but — "

"The diagnosis is 'compulsive overachiever.'" She found her cigarette case in a hip pocket of her jeans and put it on the table. "My résumé's been questioned more than once."

"I've spent enough time with you that your résumé isn't a question. I'm just sorry for what I said."

"Did it feel like the truth when you were saying it?"

Gillie looked at her. "I knew I was hurting you and I hated myself for it," she said quietly. "But yes. It felt like the truth."

"Then don't apologize for it. Yeah, it hurt when you said it. But when I had time to think about it, I understood it. I understand more of it now."

"All my secrets. I came here to get over one bad soap opera and I've walked right into another one." She blew a soft sigh. "Don't take that wrong. I haven't said anything right all day."

"You haven't done anything today but tell me the truth. It's hard to do and it gets taken wrong too often, but it's never not right, Gillie."

"But if I just keep saying awful things to you — Jordan, I'm afraid of losing you! God, you're the only thing that's made me feel — made me feel — made me *feel* for ten years! All that time, all that hurt, all that . . ." She drew a huge, shivering sigh. "Nothin' but the truth," she whispered. "All right: can you even imagine how many times I wished him dead, Jordan? I don't remember selling my soul to the devil, but sometimes it feels like I must have. I don't know how many times I screamed at him that I wished he'd die, that he'd have a heart attack or an accident — I can't forget that. I can't."

"Don't try to forget it. Try to put it into the perspective of where you were when you said it."

"Curled up on the bedroom floor getting the literal shit kicked out of me? I don't question why I said it. I question why that particular wish got granted."

Jordan reached for her cigarette case. "Deus ex machina? I'm not a fan of the concept of divine intervention, but if you can make it work for you here, use it. You got saved, Gil. Don't question — "

"Jordan, you'll never understand — "

"I understand you — and your daughter — more than you think I do, Gillian. He never hit me, and as far as I know he never hit Mom — except the once. But he had a razor blade for a tongue and he cut us both to rags with it. I don't want to get into comparing abuses, but I know how it feels to be that small in someone else's eyes. I don't like to be labeled, and I'm not trying to label you, but naming it helps to understand the concept of survivor guilt. You didn't kill him — "

"How do you know I didn't?"

Jordan felt the question like tripping into a three-strand electric fence — *good,* something in her whispered, nipped on the heels by *God!* — and for a frozen moment nothing worked: not her voice, not her breath, not her thoughts.

"And she has a moment of doubt," Gillie said softly. "Motive plus opportunity equals one great big payoff, and the money's nice, too. I knew the jack had a slow leak. He's not the first shade-tree mechanic to get squashed under his project car. I had a perfect alibi: seven other women in the house that afternoon, playing bridge and yakking up a storm, and they all testified in my behalf at the inquest, but as the insurance company's attorney so delighted in pointing out, I was the hostess of that little bridge party. I was in and out of the kitchen all afternoon, and the garage was right off the kitchen. Couldn't I have popped in there and turned that little handle and popped right back to the bridge game while my husband — whom the whole town knew was an abusive, philandering bastard — gasped his last under a 1972 Lincoln Town Car?" She looked Jordan in the eye. "Did I do it? Self-induced ex machina?"

I couldn't kill him for myself, but I could have for her.

"It seems to me" — Jordan selected a cigarette and closed her case with a slow click — "that the coroner should have been able to determine whether his injuries were sustained all at once or over a period of time. He must have tried to get out once he realized he was in trouble. The nature of abrasions. Fractures. That kind of thing."

"Even the way the creeper was broken." Gillie's voice was barely more than a whisper. "Four hours. They said it was probably four hours from the time he started fighting until the time he died. You know what saved me from a murder charge? His fingers. He tore his fingers down to the bone trying to claw himself out from under that fucking car while we gabbed and fought about who was kicking who under the table and had Linda Ronstadt cranked up loud on the CD player. They figured I couldn't have killed him that slow. And I keep wondering how long he screamed before he couldn't scream anymore. I wished him dead, but I don't think I can imagine a much more horrible way to die." She took a swallow of her drink. "So the girls went home and I was half-hammered, and after the fourth time I'd called him for dinner I finally went out to check on him, and he was dead. I just stood there for the longest time. I couldn't believe what I was feeling." A laugh gritted from her. "Not feeling. What I didn't feel was the worst. I was so full of gin and Valium I couldn't feel anything anyway. I was just as dead as he was." She emptied her glass and held it out. "Please?"

Jordan got up, taking both their glasses to the bar.

"So I called the ambulance. 'My husband is dead. Please come get him.' That's how I felt. They laid it down to shock. Put me in the hospital. And they finally figured out that if they didn't give me some Valium they were going to have a serious detox problem on their hands. Thank you." She reached for the glass Jordan offered. "How come you're letting me drink tonight when you wouldn't let me this afternoon?"

"This afternoon you were roller-skating on a razor blade. You know where you are now."

"You think I do." She tasted and winced at the smooth bite of the vodka. "Maybe you'd best start making them tall, hon. This hurts too good."

"If you'd had any tonic, that one would have been tall." Jordan sat. "Gillie — "

"I know. I'm getting drunk and yammering about my night sweats and avoiding everything. Including and probably mostly you. God, Jordan, everything I want's just one step out of reach — and I'm the one who keeps not taking the step. Can I have a cigarette?"

Jordan handed her case and matches across. "I didn't know you smoked."

"Not in five months." She extracted a cigarette, and lit and blew out the match, and closed the gold case and rubbed her thumb over the art deco JB in chevrons on the lid. "Was this your grandfather's?"

"Great-grandfather. What are you feeling?" she asked quietly.

"I'm not feeling anything. I'm just shutting down."

"Don't do that. You're still safe with me, Gillie."

"God, Jordan, I never question that. Never." She sipped at her drink, and at the cigarette. "Have you ever had that flu that hits you from both ends and lasts three days? I feel like the third day of that. I feel like the camel on the other side of the eye of the needle — or maybe the eye of the needle after the camel's been through. Stretched a little thin, either way." She jittered a laugh. "You know about being stretched thin. Tell me, Jordan. If you could be anywhere right now, where would you be? Genie in a bottle. Take you there."

Jordan raised an eyebrow. "Why waste the wish?"

She snorted a derisive laugh. "You must be joking." She offered the cigarette at arm's length. "Finish this for me? I guess I did quit."

Jordan took it. "Do you have any idea of how easy you are to like, Gillie?"

Gillie looked at her.

"You are. It's a pleasure being with you. Why would I want to be somewhere else?"

Self-consciously, Gillie smiled. "You don't get out much, do you."

"I meet enough people in the course of a season here, between the golf course and the bar, to know that I don't care if I never see most of them again." She blew a brief laugh. "Unfortunately, we become a habit for some of them. Every summer, here they come. Thank god for Park and Olathe. Without them, I couldn't deal with people like Peony Watkins."

"I can't stand her. To listen to her, you'd think she had a hundred dear close friends. I doubt it." She took a swallow of her drink. "God, I'm getting drunk. Well, what the hell. I walked away from Atlanta and don't feel as if I left anything there. It makes me wonder, Jordan. She's such a bitch, but she'll go back to Miami and have her little circle of pals, but when I leave here, what do I have? My son's the spit and image of his father. Looks like him. Sounds like him. Beats his wife like him. Meghann thinks I'm a vegetable. My father and brother wrote me off years ago.

My mother's dead. Here I am twisting in the wind, and you tell me I'm such a wonderful person — it's hard for me to believe that. Wouldn't such a wonderful person have someplace to turn after forty-five years?"

"What am I, chopped liver?"

Gillie looked at her for a long, brooding moment. "You, my darling, are pâté de fois gras of the very finest." She clicked open the lid of Jordan's cigarette case and regarded the single Oval left there, and closed it again. "And I don't have any frame of reference for how I feel about you," she said at last. "And that's so frightening. I don't have any perception of normal adult relationships because I've never had one, and I know this isn't what's meant by attention deficit disorder, but I was ignored for any value except as a receptacle for someone else's needs for twenty some-odd years, and I'd have to be a lot drunker than I am not to know that you give me a lot of attention and that feels really good to me. But you can't be everything to me, Jordan. You can't be all I have, or all I need."

"I know that. But you can't say you don't have any friends. You have one."

"Why? What do you get back?"

"Remember Tarvis," Jordan said quietly. "It all comes out even in the end."

"God, what do I do with you, Jordan?" She barely murmured it, not especially meaning for Jordan to hear. "What am I supposed to do with you?"

Jordan reached for her drink. "I'm usually pretty reserved with my personal life," she said, and Gillie thought that Jordan hadn't heard her, but wasn't quite sure; she was never sure where Jordan might come from. "I don't form relationships with guests for all of the reasons the powers that be had in mind when they put the no-fraternization clause into the personnel policy. They're sound reasons. The potential for fraternization to turn into something that's bad for me and bad for the resort is too high. In two and a half years here, I've violated that policy for three people: Park and Olathe, and you. I think there are people who transcend the normal order of things. Have you ever met anyone you instinctively disliked?"

"A few times."

"And did those people seem to like you?"

"No more than I did them."

"I believe the opposite happens, too."

Gillie smiled crookedly. "Love at first sight?"

"In a manner of speaking. Maybe we were friends in another life, or sisters, or mother and daughter — Casey and I did a past-life regression together and had an amazingly similar experience. Kind of a surprise to find out — if you believe in the whole idea of past-life regression — that we'd been father and son. She calls me Dad now. We both laugh about it, neither one of us is sure we really believe it, but still . . . She came for a golf lesson one day. We'd never met before, and by the end of nine holes we were planning a vacation together. The bond was just like that."

Gillie sipped and found her glass empty but for ice. The wine and vodka made her brave; she asked, "Were you lovers?"

"No. Oh, we got half in the bag and tried one night in Provincetown, but we're both butch. We wrestled for dominance for a while and ended up laughing for fifteen minutes. We finally gave up and watched Jay Leno."

"Butch." Gillie rattled the ice in her glass, a hint that Jordan ignored. "That word doesn't seem to fit you. It sounds so . . . masculine. I can see calling Park a butch, but — "

"I don't recommend it," Jordan smiled. "Not *a* butch. Just butch. Park is butch, I'm butch, Olathe's femme — but Olathe's not a good one to try to label. She'll all over the place. All butch really means, bottom line, is that we usually . . . lead when we dance."

Gillie smiled faintly, understanding what Jordan meant. "And you don't mind being labeled?"

"We mind like hell when straight people do it. I can call myself butch, but if John called me a butch I'd yell harassment at the top of my lungs and be within my rights, since Catawamteak's policy is not to discriminate on the basis of sexual orientation — for which I take quite a lot of credit. I told Michael I wouldn't work here unless he changed the personnel policy to include that phrasing. He didn't bat an eye."

"Michael?"

"Michael Goodnow. He's my uncle by complication. GRI — Goodnow Resorts International — owns Catawamteak. Three summers ago he lost his Director of Golf in a car accident. He just happened to have a niece who was qualified to be one. He called me."

"That's right; you said John said if it wasn't for nepotism you wouldn't have a job. He's a real bastard, isn't he. John, I mean, not your uncle."

"Yes, but he's really pretty good at his job. He knows the resort business inside and out, and he knows how to act like a subservient toad, which is what ninety percent of the RBs who come here want him to be. But we disliked each other on sight, and it grieves his control-freak soul that I have absolute authority over the golf course and the bar, and that I make as much money as he does — without having to act like a subservient toad. Would you buy me another drink?"

"Of course." She held up her glass as Jordan went by. "It's only there for you."

"Thank you," Jordan murmured at the bar. "Why did I think you drank it?"

"Vodka only. Well — wine, but this is my poison. Too much of it, lately — and yes, I've heard you twit me a couple of times. Another trip to Betty Ford if I'm not careful. A nice place to visit, but I don't want to live there." She rested her head against the wing of the chair. "They told

156

me I needed something to fill the hole I poured the Valium into," she said softly. "That sounds like full circle: no family, no friends — one friend," she corrected. "Black holes. So I said, I'll pour myself into golf. But golf isn't pouring itself into me. I love the game. I love it better now that I'm not slicing every other drive into oblivion, and I love playing it with you. But . . ." She looked up as Jordan came by her chair. "Jordan," she said softly. "Is it enough for you?"

Jordan put their glasses on the table. She slipped her hands into the pockets of her shorts, and stood there for a moment, looking at the floor. "It never has been," she said finally, quietly. "It's just been what I've had."

"What do you want? What do you need, Jordan?"

"I don't know." She reached, extracting her cigarette case from its warm place in the folds of the blanket covering Gillie's lap. "I don't know, Gillie." She put the case on the table beside her glass. "Sometimes I think, god, I'm almost forty years old and I'm not partnered — but I really don't think I want to be. I like the freedom, but I know there's something about being committed to another person that I miss. Sometimes I want to call Aiga and say, hey, this is where I am today, just to talk to someone who knows me at that depth. And her partner wouldn't mind. Cheryl's wonderful. I really like her. But my day-to-day shouldn't be part of their day-to-day. She's the last woman I loved, so she's the first one I think of when I think that's what I need. But it's — " She huffed a small, hurt laugh. "The one I really want to call is my mother, but she's not there."

"Oh, Jordan." Gillie blew a soft sigh. "I know. God, I know. And I wish there was some way I could — " She leaned to get her glass from the table, and sat back and sipped and shook her head. "Yeah, you wish," she murmured. "Lost cause."

"You wish what?"

"Meghann. My mother and I didn't have the best relationship in the world. There were times when I didn't even like her very much, but nothing in the world ever hit me as hard as losing her, and I know that's going to happen to Meggie. And she'll do the same thing I do: kick myself in the butt for not paying more attention to who Mom was and what she was living with in her own life."

"How old is she?"

"Meg? Almost twenty. Just finished her sophomore year at Smith."

"Good school. If it hadn't been for golf, that's where I'd have gone."

"She was an A student all through school, except in math. She needed a little tutoring there. A good athlete. I tried to get her interested in golf, but I guess if Mom does it, it isn't cool. She skis. Plays basketball, softball. Swim team."

"What's her major?"

157

"Women's studies. I'd argue with her about where she can go with that, but it isn't as if she's ever going to go hungry — or listen to me anyway. I let her do what she wants. As long as she keeps her grades up, I'll write the checks."

"What does she want to do?"

"I don't know. We speak, but there's not much substance to our conversations. I know she resents me sending her away to school, but god, Jordan, I couldn't keep her home. She came home one day — she'd just turned thirteen. She'd started her period for the first time, and I looked at her and saw this . . . this utterly beautiful little woman. Tall and slim, breasts and hips — She wasn't a child anymore. I was terrified that he'd see that." She raised a hand in defeat. "So. Boarding school and summer camps. I just wanted her to be safe, but it meant I had to give her away."

"Did you send — what do you call him? Four?"

She nodded. "I didn't want him to turn into his father. He did anyway. Too late, I guess. I told Val — his wife — don't ever not leave him because of money, I'll take care of you. Butt out, she said. What else can I do?"

"Leave the offer open."

"Jordan, I'm afraid he'll kill her."

"There's nothing you can do," Jordan said quietly. "You know that, Gillie. She has to make the decision herself."

"Yeah." It was a snort of derision. "Like I never did."

"Don't beat yourself up. Are you afraid Meghann might end up with someone abusive?"

"I don't think so. She works summers at a battered women's shelter. Calls her father 'that subhuman sack of toxic waste.' When she was sixteen she asked me why I didn't leave him. Well, god, I was a turnip by then. I just said, 'I can't.' She didn't understand . . . any of it. When he died she said to me, 'You finally got what you were waiting for. All that fuckin' money, Mom.' God, that hurt. And every time I write a big check I think of that. All that fuckin' money, Mom."

Jordan opened her cigarette case, and closed it again, and looked up. "How do you like your new clubs?"

Gillie studied her for a moment before a slow smile snuck onto her face. "I love them." She untangled herself from the blanket and the chair and stood, holding out a hand. "Can we do this? No wrestling for dominance; I just want some breath in the dark for a while. Leno must be on."

And they propped up the pillows and kept on everything but their shoes, and Gillie tucked herself under Jordan's arm, and laughed at Jay a few times, and was asleep before the monologue was over. Jordan watched, her fingers an unconscious caress in Gillie's hair, and when Leno said good-night she turned off the TV and extracted herself gently from Gillie's limpness, and she pulled the down comforter over her and bent to leave a kiss against her cheek. "G'night, Gil," she whispered. "Sleep well, my love. You're safe."

"Mmm," Gillie purred, and Jordan put their glasses in the sink, and emptied her ashtray and wiped it out with a damp tissue, and retrieved her cigarette case and locked the door on her way out.

Hey, Dad, it's Casey. If the weatherman's right we've got a couple of days of rain coming next week, so I can get at that cabinetry in your office. Give me a call if this isn't a good time, or I'll be filling your files full of sawdust the first muzzy day.

Jordan, it's Karin. I need a massage! I bet you do too. Call me and we'll swap.

Jordan. This is Michael. They may be nothings that John's whispering in my ear, but they aren't sweet. Call me when you can. I'll be in the office Friday and home all weekend.

"Oh, balls." Jordan, still towel-wrapped from her shower, refilled her coffee cup. It was ten past seven; she'd forgotten to change her alarm clock from its usual 6:45 setting, and she was feeling decidedly cranky after her fourth night in a row without much sleep. "Thank you, Gillie, for putting his pecker in a twist. Jesus, John. I can't believe you called Michael, you spineless turd."

She flipped through her Rolodex, finding Karin's office number; the rest of the calls would have to wait. "Hi, Karin," she said after the beep-beep-beep. "Jordan. You're right, I do, and we can. Call me at the bar after seven and maybe we can avoid more phone tag. Monday's my best day."

She dressed and went down to the pro shop. Stedman was sitting at one of the tables, drinking coffee and studying his blueprint of the course. "Hey, Stew. How's the green?"

"It'll live, if we can keep fumble-footed turkeys like you away from it." But his eyes smiled in the saying, and she drew a cup of coffee and sat with him. "You look like life's catching up with you, Jordan. How long you going to keep working that double shift?"

"It's starting to feel a little old," she admitted. "What're you scheming up now?" She nodded at the map. "Redesigning the back nine?"

"Just moving the pins." His smile was wistful; the last significant work the course had seen was the redesign of the thirteenth green. "But you know my old song about how fourteen through seventeen don't live up to the lay of the land. Hell, after the Nightmare they just coast into the clubhouse, birdie-birdie-birdie. No need of it."

"Know what I've always wanted to do?" Jordan touched a finger to the map. "Stretch that long par three sixteenth into a short bastard of a par four — "

"No room."

"There would be if we went into the pond with an island green. The first time I played the course, I wondered why they hadn't done it."

Stedman looked at the blueprint in front of him. "You're crazier than I am," he mused, tracing a finger from the current green to the middle of the six-acre pond beyond it. "There ain't a way in the world Mick Goodnow's going to go for that. Not with his short game."

"You may be right, but I've got to call him anyway. I'll put out a feeler." She glanced up as Carla came out of the office with *Director of Golf* gold-lettered on the door. "Hey, Carla."

"Hey. We need to order scorecards. We're on the last box."

"I told Ray to order some last week. Check my in box for the P.O."

"I did. Not there."

"My god, I'm glad to be rid of him. Wouldn't that be cute, no scorecards. Fax the order and put a rush on them if we're on the last box. They don't last long."

"How's Mrs. Benson?"

Jordan flicked a look at her; something in Carla's voice rendered the question less than heartfelt. "She had a serious muscle spasm yesterday. She won't be golfing today."

"So you're free this morning?"

"More or less. Phone calls and paperwork. Why?"

"Well, I'm kind of running blind here. You never did any orientation with me. I mean, I've been to Personnel and they got me signed up, and I pretty much know what to do, but a job description might be nice."

The edge that had caught her attention a moment ago was still in Carla's voice: a hint of sarcasm, or irritability, or petulance. "You're right," she said mildly. "I never did. How's ten o'clock sound?"

"What's wrong with now?"

"What's wrong with now," she said evenly, "is that I'm talking with Stedman now. When I get done talking with Stedman, I'll be talking with Michael Goodnow. When I'm through talking with Michael, then I'll talk with you."

Carla flushed. "I'm sorry. Ten's fine." She retreated behind the counter.

"Let's go in my office, Stew. If I'm going to approach Michael about revamping the sixteenth, we might as well look at the big picture. We both know that those last five holes are the only reason we're not in the running for at least the LPGA Tour."

Stedman rolled up his blueprints at nine and left grinning. Jordan allowed herself a moment of warmth in the reflection of his good humor before she punched a speed-dial button on her phone. "Michael. This is Jordan, returning your call. What's Big Bad John whispering in your ear?"

"Oh, John." His deep voice rumbled over the phone. "I'm slicing again, Jordan. I thought I might come up for a few days. See if you can't put me back in the fairway."

If he's coming to have a look for himself, I'm in deep shit. "I'd love to see you, Michael. I've been working with a slice for a few days. Making enough progress to hope I might be able to give you a tip or two."

161

"Better you than Fred. He hurts my feelings. You've always known how to soothe this old man's heart."

"Old man," Jordan scoffed. Michael Goodnow was a decidedly fit sixty-two, indulging himself in the rare cigar, a daily single-malt scotch, and an hour at the gym every day. "You'll outlive us all, Michael."

"Ugly always does." Ugly only worked if one thought a gentleman who bore more than a passing resemblance to Spencer Tracy might be called ugly. "Is your slice an old man, too?"

"Hardly." She didn't try to hide. "A very attractive widow, Michael. And if Fred had got hold of her twenty years ago, she'd be a few wins away from the Hall of Fame by now. A fine golfer with a solvable problem, so I'm obsessing on curing it. You know how I get."

"That's one of the reasons I hired you, Jordan: seeing what a week with you did for my game. An attractive widow, did you say? Do you suppose we could make it a threesome? Say . . . Sunday afternoon?"

"That's a nice segue into what else I wanted to talk to you about. Stedman and I were talking — "

"God help me. Was that the sound of a million dollars flying out of my wallet?"

"Not that bad. Just the last five of the back nine. Do you want me to fax you a sketch, or wait until Sunday and walk you through our daydreams?"

"Fax me a sketch. Is there room at the inn, or will I have to sleep on your massage table?"

"I'll connect you to the desk. It'll be good to see you, Michael."

"And you, Jordan."

She switched him to Reservations — there was always room at the inn for Michael; he had a suite on permanent reserve — and dropped the phone into the cradle. "Lurch, you're a major pain in my ass, you know it?" She photocopied the course map with the topographic daydreams she and Stedman had drawn up, and fired up the fax.

◆

Bill Marston did a knock-and-walk-in at 9:45. "Got a minute, Doctor J?"

"Sure. What's on your mind?"

He pulled the door closed behind him and sat. "I hate to dump a new turd in your lap, Jordan. I know you've had the week from hell, but you need to know about this. I had to pull rank on Carla yesterday. She was giving Barry a ration of shit he didn't deserve, and talking hard about a guest — Good Christ, Jordan, if other guests heard her blatter like that! It's just not good for business."

"Tell me what happened."

"She wanted to talk to you. Barry said you were off call. She ranked him about cleaning clubs in the shop — hell, all he did was wipe a wedge

162

on a towel. And then she made some crack about hating the rich bitches, specifically Mrs. Benson. By name, right out in front of god and everybody. I told her to can it. She told me I wasn't her boss. I know I'm not, but I pointed out the organizational chart to her. I don't know if she's on the rag or what, 'cause I don't remember her ever being so damn bitchy, but she's sure been playing high lady mucky-muck around here since you put her behind the counter. She'd have been my choice, too," he added, "but damn, who'd knew it'd go to her head? The caddies are all pissed off at her."

Jordan sighed. "Yeah. She copped a little attitude with me this morning." She looked into her coffee mug; it was empty. "I'll talk to her, Bill. If she doesn't clean up her act, I'll put her back outside and try Ric behind the counter. Where's George, by the way?"

"I haven't seen him for a couple of days. Wouldn't surprise me if he never showed up again. You know he'll never be able to pass a piss test. He smokes a lot of pot."

"I know that, but it never seems to interfere with his work. It isn't as if I never inhaled," she said, and Bill grinned. "Give him a call and see if you can round him up, would you? He's a good guy — and no one can teach putting like him. We can work something out."

"Sure will. Anything else?"

"You busy this afternoon?"

"I'm working wedges with a woman from Tampa. Good golfer." He rolled his eyes. "Then Peony Watkins wants help with her putting. George picked a fine time to disappear."

"Since the door's closed, I can say that you have my utmost sympathy." *But Bill busy means I have to go nine with Henry Matlin, because ol' Hank wouldn't be in the least bit sympathetic to my sleep deprivation problems if I called to cancel. Oh, well.* "Michael Goodnow's coming in tomorrow afternoon. Have the caddies and rangers run police call while they're out there. Cigarette butts and candy wrappers. And tell the rangers to watch for foot-draggers on the greens."

"Will do." He stood. "Get some sleep sometime, Jordan. You look pretty tired."

"I'll try that tonight. Send Carla in and cover the shop for her, okay? We won't be too long."

◆

"Close the door and sit down."

Carla looked at her, and did as she was told.

"The attitude will stop," Jordan said neutrally. "Talking disparagingly about guests will stop. Abusing the caddies will stop. Understood?"

Wavering between defiance and doubt, Carla held her gaze for a moment; Jordan kept her eyes steady, but she didn't try to hide her weariness. Finally Carla looked away. "Yes," she said, subdued. "I understand."

163

"Good. Anything to say?"

"Only that I'm sorry. I just — I — " She flicked a look at Jordan, saw her impassive composure, and canned the excuses. "I'm sorry," she repeated. "It won't happen again."

"Thank you. If you owe apologies, I strongly suggest you extend them ASAP. This is the chain of command: Me and Stedman, John Laing, Bill, George, you and Barry, then the caddies more or less in order of age and experience, starting with Ric like it or not. Your role with the caddies is as an advisor, not a boss. I expect you to treat them the way you'd want to be treated. If you have problems with them, talk to Bill or me and we'll either mediate or handle it completely. As much as possible, we keep John out of the business of the golf course. Understood?"

"Yes."

"Good. As far as sales go: Balls, hats, gloves, towels, shirts — everything except clubs — that's your department. If a customer comes in and picks a club, or even a set of clubs, off the rack and whips out a credit card without asking any questions, take their money. If they have questions beyond price, call whichever pro is in the shop. Helping customers select clubs is absolutely a function of the pros. Understood?"

"Yes, ma'am."

It was an automatic response to her authority, without a flicker of sarcasm, but it surprised her; she paused, but Carla didn't look at her. Finally she leaned back in her chair. "Okay, Carla. Tell me where you are."

"I just wish I'd kept my mouth shut, is all," she said, her voice small. "I'm embarrassed and I've been taking it out on everybody and I'm sorry. I hate it that you're mad at me."

"I'm not mad at you. How you feel is important to me, Carla, but how you deal with it is more important to me. I hired you because I want you in my shop, but you know there's no love lost between John and me. If guests complain about you, John will fire you, and I won't be able to protect you."

Carla looked up. "Would he fire you?"

"Stedman and I work for Goodnow Resorts International, not Catawamteak. John can't fire us. But the guy who can is going to be here tomorrow, and" — she hesitated, and decided sharing a little something with Carla could go a long way toward mending fences — "and I'm in enough trouble with him already without having staff problems in my department. So help me out, here, okay?"

Carla was itching to ask what trouble Jordan was in; she scored several points with the boss for stifling that curiosity. "You've got it," she said. "What else do I need to know?"

Henry Matlin, who was up near the top of Jordan's list of people who wouldn't hurt her feelings if they never found their way to Catawamteak again, scored points with Jordan, too, by playing a fast back nine and letting her go without his usual shot-by-shot rehash of the round. By three she was back in her apartment.

She called Gillie. "Hey. Did you get any sleep?"

"I just got up at one. I guess I'll have to help you close up the bar tonight. How about you?"

"If I don't get a few hours between now and seven, you'll have to do more than close up. Are you busy Sunday afternoon? Michael's coming up from Boston and wants to golf. I thought you might enjoy meeting him." It wasn't quite a lie; under normal circumstances, it wouldn't even have been a stretch of the truth. "Stedman and I are mapping out a new last five on the back nine. You can get a sneak preview of possible coming attractions. Help me talk the Old Man into it."

"How in the world would I do that?"

"Breathe a sigh of relief coming off the Nightmare and say something about it being all downhill from there, and make birdies."

"Oh, thanks for the pressure! Will par do?"

"You can birdie those holes. I can't remember the last time I didn't."

"Apples and oranges. But I'd be happy to meet him. You haven't said much about him, but it seems you're fond of him."

"Very fond of him. He's an old-school gentleman. Charming — and rich as Croesus. I've got to get some sleep, Gil. Come down for a drink after dinner."

Fifteen minutes later, her alarm clock set for 5:45, she was dreaming of an island green on the sixteenth hole of her golf course.

Jordan came groggily out of a deep sleep with that stupid Paul McCartney song buzzing through her mind, the one about someone knocking on the door and would somebody please do us all the magnificent favor of letting the numb bastard in before he rang the bell into oblivion and hammered the portal off its pins — and realized that someone was indeed knocking at the door of her apartment, not hammering but politely insistent; she rolled out of bed and found her robe, mumbling her ungracious opinion of whoever was waking her up at six in the morning when she'd worked until two the night before. "Hold on, I'm coming — oh, Carla, what!" She couldn't keep the irritation from her voice when she opened the door. "I work nights, too, you know?"

Carla flinched. "Jordan, I'm sorry." She offered a Styrofoam coffee cup like a peace offering, and wearily, Jordan regretted her shortness. "We knew you'd kill us all if we didn't get you up — and kill whoever did. I got elected to be the sacrificial lamb."

Jordan looked up from peeling the lid back from the coffee in time to see the end of a look she knew had touched her from her sleep-tousled hair to her bare toes, and as much as she didn't want to offer Carla anything remotely resembling encouragement, she couldn't help but feel complemented by the explicit appreciation in the deep blue eyes. "Elected to drag my antique ass out of bed at six in the morning when I worked until two and didn't have an appointment until ten? I can't even imagine how much I don't want to hear this. Come in, sit down, and don't start talking yet." She took the coffee with her to the bathroom and peed and brushed her teeth and washed her face, and ran through her hair with a brush, and came back with the coffee gone. "Okay. You can hit me now."

Carla drew a deep breath. "It's the Nightmare and seventeen. They're all torn to hell, Jordan. Stedman cried when he saw them."

"The *Nightmare?* Where in the merry fuck was security?" She almost screamed it. "Those greens are practically in the fucking driveway! Oh, Jesus, and Michael's coming today —" She paced around the kitchen, understanding Stedman for crying; she would have understood him for puking. He was probably the only one who loved those smooth bentgrass carpets more than she did. She felt sick herself . . . sick with a glittering rage, with a crystalline memory: *this is gonna cost you. You don't fuck with me, bitch.*

"Ray." It was a hoarse whisper. "Did you hear him, Carla? The other day, did you hear — "

"We all did, Jordan. Me. Barry. Ric. The kids. We were all there. That was the first thing out of anybody's mouth when we saw the greens. You fired him, he made a threat, and three days later we've got two fucked-up rugs? You don't need to be an ophthalmologist, you know?"

"Oh, god — " It was almost a moan. Jordan sat in a chair at the kitchen table, her eyes closed, trying to absorb the blow. "God! The Nightmare, Carla, that's my green, mine and Stew's — " She breathed shallowly. "How bad is it?" And she shook her head with a strangled laugh. "Stew cried and I ask how bad."

"He says he can probably have seventeen playable in two or three weeks if the weather holds. But the Nightmare —" Slowly, Carla shook her head. "Some of the ruts are a foot deep," she said softly. "Stedman said that's because it's so new, still soft, and it's got all that ripple so the guy's tires really dug in —" She stopped; Jordan looked as if she were hearing pathological details of the beating death of her best friend. "I'm sorry," she whispered. Walking up from the clubhouse, she'd been able to think of any number of reasons why she'd rather be making her first trip to Jordan Bryant's quarters. "I sure as hell didn't want to be the one to tell you, but poor Stedman's a basket case. I wasn't sending Ric."

"Thank you." Jordan looked into the foam coffee cup; it was still empty. "Did you call the cops?"

"They're on their way."

Wearily, Jordan got to her feet. "I'll be down as soon as I get dressed."

"Um . . . you want me to wait?"

"No, go ahead," she said, before she realized that Carla wanted to wait. "On second thought, if it's not a huge imposition, could you bring me another cup of coffee?"

"Sure, Jordan. Black, right?"

"One of those little tiny lumps of sugar. Don't lock yourself out."

◆

Stewart Stedman was a small bull of a man who had worked fifty of his sixty-five years at Catawamteak, starting as a caddie and working his way up to head greenskeeper; he had seen directors of golf come and go, and he had liked some of them, respected some of them, had no use at all for some of them, but only a few had earned his devotion. The only way to Stedman's devotion was to love the grass as much as the game and Jordan Bryant did, and he put his arm around her when she couldn't fight back the tears when she saw the remains of the Nightmare. "Oh, Stew," she whispered. "God, that used to be our green?"

It looked as if a tank had run around and around it, carving gashes to spill its dark earth-blood onto soft green sod, chewing its verdant skin into gaping wounds, spitting mangled pieces of it onto the apron; she stood fifteen feet from the first cut and there were pieces of the green at her feet. She recalled playing eighteen with Ray Phelps one day early in her first summer there; he had dug a fat divot with a three iron, and when Barry went to retrieve it he said carelessly, "Don't fuck with that. Stedman'll get it."

167

"You son of a bitch," she whispered. "I'll bury you for this, Ray. I swear to god I will. I didn't hurt you this bad then, but I will now."

"Wait in line," Stedman growled. "I get my hands on that pubic-faced prick and he'll rue the day that his daddy didn't strain that shot through the sheet."

"Stew — " She argued with her throat; her voice came out hoarse when finally she could speak. "Let's fix that little drainage problem we always had there on the south side."

"No doubt about it. But for now we've got to get this mess stitched together so people can play golf. I don't know how the hell we're going to do it, either. This end's all woods and water. Nowhere to mow a temp fairway."

"All we can do is cut a trail through the woods so they can get from the twelfth green to the fourteenth tee. From the sixteenth —" Her laugh was brittle. "Fuck, Stew, I don't know. Swim to the eighteenth tee?"

"It's not that much of a walk. No more'n from the fourth to the fifth over t'Rocky River." He bent to pick up a clump of sod, cradling it in his gnarled hands; Jordan could smell it like earthworms after a rain. "Let's face it: we've got a back seven for two, three weeks. Be up to eight by then. Or we could just close it and do the renovation, if Mick gives us the green light."

Jordan looked toward the end of the breakwater, to the lighthouse that blinked white and green, white and green. "He might not, now," she murmured. "It's going to cost a goddamned fortune to repair this."

"We need to draw some more pictures, J.B.," Stedman said quietly, "and get this unlucky son of a whore away from the road."

◆

"Either that, or we need to find a good old Maine farmer who knows how to build a rock wall," Michael Goodnow said early that afternoon. "A big christless rock wall." He had seen the wreckage from the driveway on his way in and stopped, ready to fire Bryant, Stedman and Laing en masse for starting construction without his approval, but one look told him that the Nightmare had become its namesake, trashed twice in as many years. It took less time than that for him to know that nothing in recent history had hurt his distant niece more than the destruction of that oval of turf. She and Stedman were there when he arrived, still trying to figure out how to keep the back nine open, even if it would be only seven holes. He put his arms around their shoulders and steered them toward his car. "You know, you two didn't have to go to such lengths to talk me into a few new holes."

"Mick," Stedman said sourly, "the day I'd do that to a green is two days after I'd fry for murder. The only time I ever expected that grass to be disturbed was the day they buried me under it."

168

"George," Jordan said in the pro shop, seeing her former next-in-command looking hangdog and worried and angry all at once. "I'm glad you're here. How's your flu?"

"Better," he said, grateful for the fib, and knew that circumstances had saved his job, at least for a while, but he hated the circumstances. "Doesn't this just suck, Jordan. What can I do?"

"Take my appointments for the next week" — she hesitated enough that Michael heard her stutter of decision — "except Mrs. Benson. The back nine's closed for play until we get a cart path cut through the woods from twelve to fourteen. You and Bill give lessons on the playable holes; that'll free up space on the front nine. That's going to look like an ant farm, if it doesn't already. Teach Carla how to fit clubs so she can cover if there's not a pro in the shop. God knows where I'll be, and we've got too many lessons scheduled for you guys to have to worry about one of you being in here for that. When I'm not here, Bill's got the reins."

George nodded with a wry twitch of a smile that acknowledged his loss of the assistant director's position. "Been a hell of a week, hasn't it."

"And another one on the way." She smoothed her hand from his shoulder to his wrist, took his hand, looked into his eyes and let him know his job, if not his life, was secure. "We'll be in my office. Can someone bring us a carafe of coffee?"

"I'm not questioning you," Michael said, once Jordan's office door had closed behind them, "just asking questions. What's going on with George? He's been assistant director here for ten years. I tried five years ago to give him the directorate, but he wouldn't take it."

"George is in one of those little sand traps of life. He just needs to get back in the fairway."

"Drinking?"

She shook her head, opening a file cabinet, finding the folder that held the paperwork from the construction of the original Nightmare. "These are the contractors who built the Nightmare. No reason not to use them again, unless you want someone else. That drainage thing was our fault, not theirs." She put the folder on her desk and fingered through files again. "I was thinking about your rock wall, Michael. It's a good idea." She pulled a file. "There's a quarry down in Port George that cut the granite slabs for the parking lot. If we had them make something that looks like a miniature breakwater between the course and the driveway all the way up to the woods, maybe we could keep these fucking cowboys off our greens."

"Bring it all the way down to the clubhouse," Stedman suggested. "Block 'em all the way."

"That sounds dear," Michael murmured.

"What are those greens going to cost to rebuild, Michael?" she snapped. "This is the coast of Maine. Granite's as common as seagull shit — and so, apparently, are assholes who've got nothing better to do than spin wheelies on carpet that costs a thousand dollars a square foot. If you can't be bothered to protect them once we rebuild them, find another director of golf, because I'm not going through this every two years."

Stedman blew a soft whistle through his teeth.

"Beautiful when she's angry, isn't she," Michael said dryly. "Point taken, Jordan."

She sat. "I'm sorry, Michael. I'm really upset, and you're here for me to dump on. If it means anything, it means I respect your ability to hear the truth without my having to filter it through civility I don't particularly feel right at the moment. Let me get coverage for the bar, and call my carpenter to cancel my cabinetry, and my massage therapist to cancel that, and I'll call Mrs. Benson to cancel golf for tomorrow — "

"Don't do that," Michael said. "We can play the front nine, or Rocky River. By then a round of golf will be good for us. Join us, Stedman."

"Second green at Rocky River," Stedman nodded. "Oh, I could study that evil son of a whore and think about our own seventeenth."

Jordan reached for the phone. *Personally*, she thought, *right about now I'd rather cancel the golf and keep the massage.* "Karin," she said after the beep-beep-beep. "Sorry, hon, but I'm going to have to beg off on the swap Monday. I'll call to reschedule as soon as I can."

◆

Gillie had heard; everyone had heard. Most of the golfing guests had walked down Catawamteak's winding driveway to see the destruction for themselves, and returned full of their own interpretations of the devastation of the greens. Gillie didn't go. To do so felt like watching in a window whose shades the neighbors had neglected to pull in the aftermath of some family tragedy, so that through that naked window one could watch their naked pain. She picked up the phone a dozen times, thinking to call Jordan. Each time she put it down again without dialing, as if Jordan were that neighbor whose pain was inadvertently exposed, and whom she wasn't sure was ready for the condolences of others. She wrestled with that indecision long enough that when the phone finally rang she jumped, and just caught herself before saying "Jordan" instead of "Hello."

"Um . . . hi. Mom?"

"Well. Meghann." She couldn't keep Thursday's wound from showing in her voice. "What a surprise."

"Yeah. Look, I got your postcard — "

It was on the tip of her tongue to apologize, but she heard Jordan saying *don't apologize for your feelings* and bit it back.

" — and I want you to know that I know I deserved it. I'm sorry for what I said. I'm sorry for a lot of things I've said to you."

"Uh — " She searched for something to say; it finally occurred to her that her strong suit was offering apologies, not accepting them. "I — yes. I mean — "

"Yeah. You're probably, like, blown away, right? Just let me talk, okay?"

"All right." She took the phone to one of the wing chairs by the French doors, glad her suite overlooked the breakwater instead of the back nine. "I'll listen."

"I was really, really pissed when I got that. I'm like, who the hell do you think you are? And I'm slamming things around and snarling at people and finally Carol — she's the director — hauled me into her office and asked what the hell was wrong with me. I'm like, 'oh, my fucking mother,' and she jumped my bones big-time, like, 'has your "fucking mother" ever sexually, physically or emotionally abused you?' And yeah, I'm pissed at you, but I'm going, 'no, no, no — all of that shit was Dad. That was Phil who did all of that.' And I —"

"Meggie — " She could hardly hear her own voice for the blood suddenly roaring in her ears. "Meggie, did he — Sexually? Did he —"

"He never touched me. But Jesus, Mom, knowing what he was doing to you — that was sexual abuse for both me and Four. It sure as hell wasn't teaching us normal. Look at my shithead brother, for god's sake. He learned that from Phil, the way he treats Val. So anyway, I showed her your postcard, and she asked me why you sent it, and I told her what I'd said about only the smart ones coming to us. Man, did she tear my head off. I mean, they know why I'm working there, you know?"

Gillie's belly gave an unhappy quease at the thought of her marriage being common knowledge at the Lakeshore Battered Women's Project, where she had never found the courage to go.

"Not like I've given a lot of details," Meghann said. "I mean, I said my father beat up my mother and I saw it, and for all they know it might have been once or . . . as often as it was, but they know you were an abused woman. So Carol says to me, 'Jesus, Meghann, what do you think you were doing to your mother the other day?' And I'm like, du-uhh. Three-point-eight at Smith and boy, can I be dumb. Hello! Can you say 'battering'?" She drew a huge sigh and let it out in a discouraged rush. "It's like . . . I spent all this time being so angry at you. For taking all of that shit from him, for putting us through it — You know, one of the biggest things we fight here is everybody asking, 'why does she stay?' How come women stay with men who abuse them. I do the workshops, I know all the words we're supposed to say to answer that, but it's like . . . I never felt them before today. I was mad at you for not leaving, but I didn't know jack about where you were. I think I was mad at myself as much as I was mad at you, because I didn't do anything to —"

"Don't." Gillie interrupted the rush of words. "Don't do that, Meggie. I'll accept your apology, and I'll accept your love, but I won't accept you regretting that you didn't do something about a situation that wasn't your responsibility to control."

There was a brief silence before Meghann said cautiously, "Man. Are you in therapy, Mom?"

Gillie smiled. "In a manner of speaking. It's a long, long story."

"Hey. Agency nickel. Talk to me and send a donation later."

Gillie tucked her feet under her in the chair. "Her name is Jordan Bryant . . ."

It was long and complex and delicate, their conversation; it was spilling forth and drawing back, listening and being listened to, laughing and flaring and realizing, listening again, being heard again; it was both of them knowing that some of their lives was for now and some for later in the process that was the beginning of their friendship. Gillie hung up two hours later drained, spent, cried out (for now), knowing that for all they both had said, there was much they both had guarded, not sure enough yet of each other to let that last percentage go into the infant trust between them.

◆

At nine that evening Stedman stood and stretched and said, "You two can keep this up all night if you want to, but my wife's already been mad for two hours. I'm going home."

Jordan snapped off the light over her desk. "I'm with you, Stew. I haven't had enough sleep in the last week to make a decent night. I've got to quit. Talk you into a nightcap, Michael?"

She looked as if another fifteen minutes awake was going to be an effort, let alone a civilized hour for a drink; he shook his head. "Thanks anyway, sweetheart. Do we have a tee time tomorrow?"

"Don't need one. I figured if we get there at two or so we'll have time for eighteen. It's a longish course from the whites." She looked at her desk, considered cleaning it off, and waved a weary hand at it. "Never mind. It's all right where we need it in the morning. I'll be here by seven."

"You'll be here all by yourself," Michael said.

"By seven I'll have people coming off the front nine and trying to sneak onto the back."

She roamed a glance across the bar on her way by, looking for Gillie, not finding her there, and hoped it wasn't too late to call. "Hey. Were you up?"

Gillie heard the weariness in her voice. "Of course. Tell me how you are," she said, and listened to Jordan's anger and frustration and said, "Come up. I've got enough scotch for one drink," and as much as she wanted to tell her about Meggie's phone call, she understood when Jordan begged off for reasons of exhaustion. She drank the last of the scotch herself because it was there and Jordan wasn't and she was out of vodka, and before she went to bed she wrote a check to the Lakeshore Battered Women's Project that equaled the price of several sets of graphite-shafted golf clubs . . . retail. "Up yours, Philbrook Benson the Turd," she muttered, and licked the envelope.

"Start us off, Michael." Jordan offered Catawamteak's owner the first drive on the first hole of the neighboring Rocky River Golf Course, a deceptively difficult nine-holer with two significantly dissimilar approaches to each green. Michael gazed at a long, sharply downhill fairway with the narrow Rocky River wandering through at about his optimal driving distance and muttered, "Thanks a lot." He unsocked his driver. He was a strong golfer and a confident man, but there were two people with whom he occasionally golfed who could rattle his game. One of them owned several green jackets; the other was Jordan Bryant. When he played with her, he could only remember hearing someone say of Jack Nicklaus, back when the Bear was in his prime: "He knows he's going to win. You know he's going to win. And he knows that you know he's going to win." He found a spot between the white markers and teed up a ball.

Jordan shook her head, watching his warm-up swings. "That's going to go right into the ninth fairway," she murmured, but she let him hit the ball; it was usually easier to show someone how to do something right when they had just seen the results of what they were doing wrong. His shot didn't quite make the ninth fairway, but it faded hard that way; the look he sent her was plaintive.

"You're swaying," she said, and Gillian looked up; she'd heard those words from Jordan often enough. "A couple of things going on, Michael. You lined up to compensate for a slice, which is okay if you're a consistent slicer, but you aren't. If you'd hit the ball well, you'd have ended up in the woods, which is where you were aiming. A fade ends you up more or less where you want to be. A hard fade or a slice . . ." She offered a hand in the general direction of his shot. "You end up over there anyway. Watch my hips." She swung her driver in a slow demonstration (Michael thought that watching Jordan's hips, whether or not she was his niece and employee, was not at all an unpleasant thing to do). "When you backswing, this is what you're doing." Her hips went right and her shoulders went with them; when she brought the club down, the face of it was open. "See what it does to the club face? That's a sway, and not only will it make you slice, or at least fade, it's hard on your back."

"My back's been bothering me," Michael admitted.

She checked the clubhouse yard behind them, figuring they had a few minutes before the foursome milling around a pair of carts would be panting to get onto the tee. "Turn around and face your shadow. You too, Gillie." She was close enough to touch Gillie's shoulder, turning her to see her own shadow in the mid-afternoon. "This works better at four o'clock, but if you watch your shadow, you can see all kinds of things going on in your swing." She brought back her driver. "Watch the

174

shadow," she said, and exaggerated the sway that plagued both her students. "See the hips? That's your swing. Now watch mine. See how my chin points to the tip of my left shoulder at the top of my backswing, and then to the tip of my right shoulder on the follow-through? That's what you're not getting. Try it." They tried; she watched. "Good, Michael. Do that when you hit the ball. No, don't aim for your fade. You'll go in the woods. And don't give it all you've got or you'll end up in the river."

"The thing is," he mused, watching his second ball soar straight and long down the fairway, dropping short of the water and rolling to a nice lie for his second shot, "your complete and serene self-confidence would irritate all hell out of me if you didn't improve my game so much."

She shot him a smile. "You take instruction well, Michael. That's more than can be said for a lot of men when it's a woman offering the wisdom. Gillian, that was a perfect swing. Tee a ball while you still remember what you did."

"Good lord." Michael thumped the head of his driver against the ground when Gillie's ball landed just past his. "That tiny little girl can outdrive me?"

"This woman can hit the ball," Jordan said quietly as Gillie picked up her tee. "John might have his shorts in a knot over the time I'm spending with her, but if we shave ten or fifteen strokes off her game, what do you think she'll brag about all over Myrtle Beach this winter?"

"You," Michael said, "but not necessarily Catawamteak. Stedman! You're up."

Stedman got off a good drive, but with three behind the water Jordan showed why she talked and they listened; her ball soared across the river, helped around a mild curve by a tightly-controlled draw. "That dog'll hunt," Gillie said. "Beautiful drive, Jordan."

"Thanks."

"Let's go, Stedman." Michael bagged his driver. "We're already playing catch-up, and there's no such thing as a friendly game."

◆

The women were a stroke up as Jordan drove the cart to the fifth tee, Gillie's long, well-read birdie putt compensating for Jordan's misread chip to the far side of the fourth green for a bogey. "Your uncle is very competitive," Gillie said.

"Not really. He just hates to lose to me. It's a guy thing."

"Losing to a pro shouldn't hurt anyone's feelings." Gillie examined the ball she had used on the last hole, rubbing her thumb over a scuff on the cover, and dropped it into a cup holder on the dash of the cart. "He seems like an awfully nice man."

"I like Michael a lot. Always have." Jordan set the brake and got out. The fifth was a long par five, a straightaway over water and then a sharp dogleg-left to an intimidating uphill fairway that was heavily rippled to

175

prevent balls from rolling back down the side of the mountain. "I don't know why he never remarried after Celia died. I know he loved her dearly, but it's been . . . six years? Time enough."

"She must have been young when she died."

"Seventy, not that that's old. She was almost fifteen years older than him. Heavy smoker all her life. She died fast, but she died hard."

"That must have been hard for him."

"It took him a long time to get back to himself." Jordan bent to pull a stray sprig of crabgrass from the tee box. "How's your back?" she asked, changing the subject as the men arrived in their cart.

"It feels good. I just can't see the ball leave the tee with this new swing."

"You'll get used to it. I'll spot you. You're up."

Gillie forgot not to compensate for her slice with her address; her ball cleared the brook and bounced into the tall grass to the left of the fairway. "Just this side of the red bush, about a foot in," Stedman said. "I wish I had your distance."

"I wish I had your aim," Gillie grumbled; Stedman's ball went thirty yards short of hers, but dead center. "Mr. Goodnow?"

Michael teed a ball. "I wonder if you might care to join Jordan and me for dinner tonight, Mrs. Benson."

Gillie raised an eyebrow in mild surprise. "Why, thank you. I'd be happy to."

"I'll look forward to it." He addressed his ball and drew back his driver, and they watched his ball fade into the woods to the right of the fairway. "In the presence of ladies," he murmured, "I refrain from comment."

Gillie smiled. "I usually just stamp my foot and say 'fuck.'"

Jordan snorted a laugh. "Don't believe her, Michael." She swung for her best drive of the day so far, but her ball hit the two-hundred-yard marker and caromed crazily off to the left. "Well, I've never done that before." She picked up her tee. "Michael, even if you can find it, it's probably unplayable. I've been in there. I'd hit another one and take the penalty."

"Do I remember an easy par three up next?"

"It's a par three," Jordan allowed. "Easy is debatable."

◆

They were even at the eighth tee. The sixth hadn't been easy at all, only Stedman getting up and down, but the short, level eighth lazed before them like a promise. Jordan had honors after a hard seventh, a forty-foot putt winning her the hole with a bogey; she surprised them all by unsocking Big Bertha. "A driver?" Gillie asked. "Jordan, you'll land on the clubhouse deck!"

Jordan smiled and swung, and Bertha sang her well-hit song and the ball spanged from the tee and soared and dropped and stopped fifteen feet from the pin.

"How'd you do that?" Stedman wondered.

"Sweet Jesus," Michael mourned. "Why do I golf with you?"

"You're up," she said, and retrieved her tee.

The hole looked like a simple par three, and it was, really, but Jordan had hit her driver; Michael hit his because she consistently outdrove him. They watched his ball sail past the green, past the apron, past the cart path, past the ninth tee and into the narrow depth of Rocky River that meandered between the ninth tee box and the fairway proper. He turned. "You sandbagged me," he accused.

She tossed him a Top-Flite. "Take a mulligan. Try a five wood."

◆

"Why in the world did you do that?" Gillie asked as Jordan steered their cart toward the green. "He isn't very happy."

"I hit a soft one-wood with a stop spin because that's what I felt like hitting. Why did he hit his driver as hard as he could on a hundred and ninety yard hole when he's been driving two-thirty, two-forty all day? He'll never beat me playing my game. He needs to play his own. That's why I did it."

"I think you're both playing head games. What's going on, Jordan?"

"Michael's got a feather in his ear."

"What does that mean?"

"Something a little birdie left there."

"I'd quicker think a big turkey named John Laing. How much trouble are you in?"

"I have no idea." She stopped outside the cart line behind Gillie's ball.

"Don't you lie to me, Jordan Baker," Gillie said in her Mother-voice. "How much does this have to do with me?"

Jordan squatted to line up Gillie's shot. "A soft eight iron, I think. Hit it just as if you were putting with it. A nice little bump and run."

"You know, Jesus was walking through Jerusalem one day," Gillie said, and Jordan looked at her in cautious amusement. "He went by the town square, and the people were getting ready to stone a whore. Jesus elbowed his way to the middle of the crowd and held up his hands and said, 'Stop! Let ye who is without sin cast the first stone!' This big rock sailed out of the crowd and hit the whore on the head and killed her dead. Jesus looked out into the throng and saw who'd thrown the rock and he said, 'Mother, sometimes you piss me off.'"

Jordan laughed. She pulled their putters and Gillie's eight from their bags, and stopped at Gillie's side of the cart; she touched her fingertips to

177

Gillie's chin. Softly, she brushed her lips across Gillie's cheek. "I love you, Gillian Benson. I really do."

"Michael's watching us."

"Never mind Michael."

"Why do you suppose he asked me to dinner with you two tonight?"

"Why would any rich, handsome man ask a rich, beautiful woman to dinner?" Jordan offered her hand to draw Gillie from the cart. "Birds of a feather. Hit your ball. The boys are both on."

"Why would he ask two at once?" She eyed the pin and took a practice stroke, and stepped up to the ball.

"Oh, Gil, beautiful shot — go, ball! Go, ball! Yes!" she cheered, when the ball collided with the pin and dropped. "Excellent!"

"You missed your calling, Mrs. Benson." Michael offered a congratulatory handshake. "You should have gone into golf."

"I did," Gillie said. "I started late, but you can do that when you find a teacher like Jordan."

Jordan exited the first nine at two under, Gillie at seven over; Stedman and Michael both made the turn at four over. "Looks like we buy the beer, Mick," Stedman said. "Jordan's always tough, and that Mrs. Benson's turned into one hell of a golfer in the last week."

"So I hear."

"Ayuh, straighten up that fade and give her a little more work in the bunkers and she'll be deadly." He squinted at the sun. "Hell, we've got time for nine more."

"Would you mind if Jordan rode with me? I could use some pointers on my short game."

"Bone up, Boss. Our new sixteenth is going to be a killer."

◆

"What are you doing with the house in Bethlehem?" Michael asked on the eleventh fairway.

Jordan left her seven iron shot just short of the green. "Nothing. I just pay the taxes."

"What kind of shape is it in?"

"I don't know. I don't go inside. Fred checks it out spring and fall. He says it's all right."

"Have you considered selling it?"

"Were you serious about wanting help with your short game?"

"Anything you can offer."

"Don't hit that as hard as you're swinging. Above this green is the worst place on this golf course to be." The green had a malevolent lie; it looked flat as a pool table, but took a downhill break that would suck a missed putt back into the sand trap on the low side. "Play it short and putt uphill." She waited for him to shoot. "So what's John's problem, other than Gillian Benson?"

He raised an eyebrow at her. "Pardon?"

"Michael, I hate this cat and mouse game. If you're unhappy with me, tell me. I'll do what I can to correct it. If you're unhappier than that, show me the door and I'll buff up my résumé. But I'm too busy to waste my time trying to figure out what kind of cockamamie bullshit my old buddy Lurch has decided to come up with this time. Let's get this out in the air."

Michael studied her for a silent moment; Jordan was always honest, but rarely so abrupt. "This is July, isn't it," he murmured.

"Yeah. It is." She took the driver's seat of the cart. "And it was a bad one for me, and a big part of the reason why I'm still your director of golf and not a mental health statistic somewhere is over on the other side of the fairway trying to blow out of the rough, so whatever John has to say about her, I don't care to hear. She was there when I needed someone, and all I can do to repay her for that is to carve strokes off her game. If John doesn't — "

"Jordan — "

"If John doesn't like that, he can go to hell. John might know how to run a resort, but I'm doing the job you hired me to do, and that didn't ever include putting up with misogyny or homophobia."

He waited for her to brake the cart beside the green. He got out to pull his pitching wedge and putter from his bag, and paused there until she came around the back of the cart. "Jordan," he said quietly, putting a hand on her forearm.

Across the fairway, Gillian Benson did the same to Stedman when he would have gone to his ball. She hadn't heard any of what was said between Jordan and her uncle, but she knew by the body language that it was tensely important. "Wait, Stewart. Let them finish this."

Stedman looked across the fairway, getting the same read on the non-verbal communication that Gillie had. "That fucking John Laing's in this mix somewhere," he muttered. "Pardon my French. He hasn't done squat for two years except try to get rid of her." He dropped a ball in the sand trap beside them and lofted it onto the green. "Well, Mickey-boy, here's the news. You fire my director of golf over that walking commercial for Bryl-Creme and I'm retiring. You can tend to your own goddamn nightmares."

"Jordan," Michael said, "I told you when I hired you, and I'll tell you again now, that your attachments are none of my business. In fact, I admire your taste. But I can't allow public displays of affection between two women on resort property. Not on the golf course, and certainly not in the lobby. Our guests are just too conservative."

"Well, I guess I missed the one on the golf course, unless you bought this one while I wasn't looking. Tell me, Michael: If I were straight and my boyfriend had given me a kiss in the lobby, would we be having this conversation?"

He leveled a look at her. "Work with me, Jordan. I know you understand what I'm saying."

"I understand perfectly. Don't let the closet door hit me in the ass on my way back into it, right? Michael, I heard that shit from my father for five years. He was too goddamned self-absorbed to accept who I am. It never occurred to him that I didn't offend other people the way I offended him. He took everything I loved because I wouldn't compromise my identity for him. It cost me my mother and my career and a couple of years of my life, and I'm sure as hell not going to compromise now for the sake of my job. I'm good enough at golf not to have to. But let me add one significant piece of information to your database, Michael: Gillian Benson is not my lover. Gillian Benson is straight." She snapped her lob wedge and putter from her bag. "Now that I know that the clause in the personnel policy purporting nondiscrimination on the basis of sexual orientation is so much eyewash, can we get on with our game?"

He watched as she punctuated "I'm good enough at golf" with a lob that landed on the green just above the hole; the ball hesitated and decided it wasn't through. It trickled back sixteen inches, kissed the pin, and dropped. She picked up her putter. "You're away. That's a three, Stedman."

♦

She shimmered with brittle intensity. Her drives were viciously long, her short game deadly in its accuracy. She didn't talk. Michael thought it wasn't so much that she didn't listen when he tried to talk to her as it was that she didn't hear him. She just hit the ball and told her score to Stedman, who was keeping the card: Three. Three. Four. Two. Three. Two. Three. She birdied every hole after the tenth. "Twenty-eight from the blues on the back," Stedman said to the club pro. "Sixty-one on the game. How many times you seen that?"

The pro whistled softly through his teeth. "If she'll sign it and you'll attest, I'll frame it. That's a course record by two."

"I expect she'll hold it for a while. This is a bitchy little course you've got here, Kris."

In the women's room, Gillie dared to ask. "Jordan, what happened?"

"Nothing."

"Like hell. You're sucked so far into yourself you're about to implode. What — "

Jordan slapped up her glove from the counter and pushed open the door.

"Jordan — "

"Jordan! Jesus Christ, you tamed my golf course, I guess! Sign the card for me, will you? I sure wish I'd been out there to see it."

She took the offered pen and slashed her signature across the card, dropped the pen, and went out the door. Kris Garrison blinked, looking after her. "That's one pissed-off woman for somebody who just played that kind of a round."

"He should've pissed her off on the tenth," Stedman growled. "Then she'd've had a twenty-seven." He signed the card in the space marked Attest. "Don't take it personal, Kris. She'll apologize all over hell and gone next time she sees you."

◆

Jordan had driven Michael's Mercedes to Rocky River; Michael drove back. No one spoke for the half-hour it took them to get to Catawamteak, saving a terse "take a left here" from Stedman when Michael neglected his turn signal on a meandering country road.

In the parking lot of the pro shop, Jordan got out, retrieved her spikes and pith helmet, and slammed the door. They watched her into the clubhouse. "None of my goddamned business, Mister Man," Stedman said, "but just so's you know: you fire her, you lose me too." He golfed in running shoes, so had no spikes to retrieve; he just slammed the door.

Gillie had ended up in the front seat by the default of neither Jordan nor Stedman wanting it; Michael looked wearily at her. "Your turn, Mrs. Benson."

"I don't know what was said," Gillie said quietly. "I do know that Jordan doesn't strike me as a woman quick to anger, but she's surely angry now. You might consider the possibility that you owe her an apology." She opened the door. "Thank you for the invitation, but I don't know that I'll be joining you for dinner tonight. Good day, Mr. Goodnow."

She didn't slam the door; she left it standing open. "And that," Michael said to his empty automobile, "is a woman who knows how to express her utter contempt in an utterly civilized manner." He reached across to catch the arm rest and slammed the door himself, and got out to get three sets of clubs from the trunk. Barry and Ric, who were lounging on a bench outside the pro shop and had seen the look on Jordan's face when she went by, made no move to help him.

◆

Carla watched in bemusement as Jordan seethed into her office, followed momentarily by Stedman, who risked the boss's wrath by not knocking before he pushed open the door, followed shortly thereafter by Gillian Benson, who knocked but didn't wait for an answer before she went in, too. When no voices rose and no bodies made violent exit, she followed them. "Coffee, you guys? Beer? Drinks?"

"No," Jordan said flatly, and Carla decided that her continued presence was unnecessary.

Jordan swiveled in her chair to look out the window that afforded her a view of the empty tenth tee and equally unpeopled eighteenth fairway and green. "I apologize to you both for my behavior," she said; her voice

181

was deadly calm. "I'm very angry, and I'm trying not to lose control of that."

"You still work here?" asked Stedman.

"I haven't heard that I don't."

"Does this have anything to do with the course?"

"No."

"Anything I can do to help?"

"I don't think so, Stewart. Thank you for asking."

"I'll be out and about, then." He tipped his cap to Gillie and took his leave.

Gillie waited. Finally Jordan turned her chair; she reached for her phone. "Artie," she said. "A bottle of Glenfiddich, a bottle of Stoli, a bucket of ice — " She looked at Gillie. "Tonic or rocks?"

"Rocks."

"That'll do. Thanks, Artie."

Not until the liquor was delivered and poured and Jordan's glass was empty did she speak. "What's worse than betrayal of friendship, Gillie?"

Gillie knew that Jordan was angry, but more than that she was hurt. "Betrayal of blood? What did he say, Jordan?"

"He's not my blood." She unscrewed the cap from the bottle of scotch and poured, and fingered the cap for a moment before she tossed it deliberately across the room. "And he's not my friend. He is my employer." She tasted her drink. "You might want to beg off dinner tonight. It's liable to be quite chilly at our table."

"I've already told Mr. Goodnow that I don't care to — "

The door opened; they both looked up as Michael stepped into the office. "Jordan, we need to talk." He set her clubs in their stand in the corner.

"This isn't a good time."

"I'd rather we clear this up before it gets any worse."

"It can't get any worse, Michael. It can only get older."

"You're blowing this out of proportion, Jordan. Surely you can see my point of view."

"I can see that you lied to me, and to every other gay employee of Catawamteak," she said evenly. "And there are a lot of us. I can see that you took John's word without so much as extending me the courtesy of asking for my perspective on the events in question. I see that I've been laboring under the apparently mistaken belief that our relationship was one of mutual respect. Michael, if it's blowing things out of proportion to recognize that as far as you're concerned I'm just one more homo that you can lock in a closet — "

"That's not true and you know it."

"How am I supposed to know it? The other day in the lobby of your inn, this woman took it upon herself to express her affection for me with a brief kiss. There's no way on god's green earth it could have been

182

construed as anything but an expression of friendship, but you're telling me that because it was two women, you won't tolerate it. What would you call that, Michael, except showing me the closet door?"

"Jordan, that's not — "

"Is that what all of this is about?" Gillie's question sliced into his protest. "Does that mean that I can't kiss my daughter hello in the lobby if she comes to visit me here, Mr. Goodnow, because it might be miscon-strued as lesbian activity? Or my daughter-in-law? Or my best friend?"

"I understand that you're not a lesbian, Mrs. Ben — "

"What difference does it make whether I'm a lesbian or not? The problem isn't who I am, it's your perception of lesbians. I could kiss my husband in the lobby, but not my female lover? I was under the impres-sion that you had a nondiscrimination policy here."

"The question isn't the conduct of guests, Mrs. Benson. It's the con-duct of staff."

"I kissed her," she said coldly. "Therefore, the question is indeed the conduct of guests."

Michael regarded her, a faint smile twitching at a corner of his mouth. "Are you an attorney, Mrs. Benson?"

"No. Another calling I missed while my husband — that person you'd find so acceptable for me to kiss in your lobby — spent twenty-four years beating me into wifely subservience. Mr. Goodnow, the consensus of opinion is against you."

"I see this."

"Good. I was afraid in order to get your attention I might have to jab you with my finger, the way I did Mr. Laing."

"Excuse me?"

She was tired of Michael Goodnow; she waved a dismissing hand. "Never mind. It's not important."

"I'm not sure of that." He tucked his hands into his pockets and rocked back on his heels. "He mentioned a verbal assault. Now that I think of it, he only said 'she verbally assaulted me' and I assumed Jordan. But given the lambasting you just gave me, I'm wondering which 'she' tied into him."

"I did. Verbally and physically. And that, Mr. Goodnow, still goes to the conduct of guests."

He regarded her for a long moment before he turned to Jordan. "Have you ever, in any of your conversations with John, referred to me as 'Uncle Michael'?"

"I haven't called you Uncle Michael since I was ten years old and you pointed out how stupid it sounds."

He went to the other end of her office and bent to retrieve the cap to the scotch; he put it beside the bottle on the tray. "Mrs. Benson, please reconsider joining Jordan and me for dinner. I'd like to pursue this further with you both after I've talked with John." He looked at Jordan. "Hoping, of course, that we might still have dinner?"

And in the length of her consideration he knew that what had broken between them had a chance, however slim, of being mended. "Seven-thirty, wasn't it?"

"Yes." He turned to Gillie, and started to offer his hand, for he respected her for her fire and her ice, but she turned both of those things on him with her eyes and he hid his hand in his pocket. "For Jordan, then," he said quietly, and left them.

Jordan added ice cubes to her glass and tipped the bottle over it. Slowly, she turned the cap onto the neck, and tasted, and took off her pith helmet. She picked the last cigarette from its band and lit it, and tossed the hat to the sofa beside her desk. "Damn you, Michael," she said softly.

"He's willing to listen," Gillie said gently. "Give him that much credit, Jordan."

"He should have listened first."

◆

"Mrs. Benson." Michael Goodnow stood as Gillie was shown to his table. "I'm glad you're here. I know it'll mean a lot to Jordan."

She had chosen a sage green 40s styled silk suit and pearls, and Michael's eyes reflected what her mirror had told her: she looked better than good. He held her chair. "You're a fine-looking woman," he said quietly. "A strong woman. I admire that. And I appreciate your loyalty to Jordan."

A waiter appeared. "A drink for Madame?"

"Spare me the Madame, Rafael. You know what I drink. Make it light, please."

Rafael, playing to the boss, bowed and exited. Gillie crossed her legs and opened her napkin. Michael had time to register the fact that at least one woman in the world still wore stockings instead of pantyhose when he detected the tiny bump of a garter on her thigh before she draped her napkin over her leg. "Mrs. Benson — Gillian? May I?"

"You may not. Don't try to charm me, Mr. Goodnow. You've known her all her life and I've known her a week, and I know ten times better than you do how horribly you hurt her today. I'm only here for her, and I'll pick up my own check."

"There's never a check at my table. Mrs. Benson, I know I hurt her. I can't begin to tell you how deeply I regret that. Please understand that I've always had to err on the side of caution with Jordan. She's my niece and I love her like the daughter I never had, but she can be strong-willed to the point of arrogance. If I allow her autonomy — "

"Erring on the side of caution gives you liberty to break her heart?" Gillie spat the words at him. "She respected you. She cared for you. She trusted you. And you took the word of that smarmy, brilliantined weasel over hers? You dared to question that woman's integrity? My family abandoned me, Mr. Goodnow. I know how she feels, as much as one human being can ever know how another one feels. You pulled the rug out from under her just like her father did, and you'll never have words enough to make that right. If you've got good genes, you might live long enough for your actions to earn her trust again, but I wouldn't count on it."

He sat back in his chair, smoothing his napkin on his lap, and reached for his scotch; he sipped and put the glass precisely back on the wet ring it had left on its coaster. "You don't pull any punches, do you, Mrs. Benson."

"No one ever pulled any for me." She looked up at Park Webster's laughing voice ringing out from a few tables over: *Look at you, my sistergirl! Damn, don't you be fine!* and saw Jordan, sleek in a lilac-colored tuxedo. "Here's Jordan. You know where I stand."

◆

"I've called the headhunters," Michael said, when Jordan was seated and drinks were delivered. "They can find me anything but the apology I owe you, Jordan."

She looked at him for a silent moment before she looked across the dining room, her lips tight as her glance touched the stairs, the doors to the kitchen, the distant bar, and he had time to see a quick shine of tears before she closed her eyes and nodded, as if to herself. A muscle in her jaw tightened, and eased, and the shine of tears was gone when she met his eyes; her voice was quiet and steady. "I'd appreciate it if you'd phrase it in the form of a letter of recommendation."

And he understood that her lingering glance had been a goodbye, that his careful phrasing had, in her mind, only confirmed what she thought she already knew. He reached to cover her hand with his. "You misunderstand me, sweetheart," he said softly. "They're hunting me up a general manager. They couldn't find me a better director of golf than the one I have now."

They watched it hit her: the dilation of her pupils, the drain of color from her face, the jump of a muscle in her throat. She pushed back her chair. "Excuse me —"

The best table in the house was a discreetly convenient distance from the women's lounge; she had time to get there without looking as though she had to. Mercifully, it was empty.

Gillie looked at Michael; he met her eyes briefly before he looked away in mild discomfort. "Perhaps I've been harsh with you, Mr. Goodnow."

"I was wrong this afternoon. We all know that. All I can do is try to make it right." He glanced at the door of the women's lounge. "She might appreciate you in there. Jordan has an unfortunate reaction to extreme stress." He smiled wryly at her questioning eyebrow. "She . . . is probably emptying her stomach."

On her way to the women's, she shook her head with a tiny smile at his delicacy.

"I'm sorry," Jordan whispered when Gillie's hand touched her shoulder. She groped for the chain of the toilet and pulled. "When stress hits me or leaves me too fast, I puke. I always have."

"I think I'd rather do that than get the trots. That's what happens to me. Throw up and it's over and done. All through?"

She sat back on her heels, embarrassed to the depths of them but not yet able to relinquish the support of the toilet. "I hope so."

The lounge was well-appointed; its sitting room had a cabinet with washcloths and hand towels. Gillie offered a cold cloth and a dry towel, and a paper cup of water so Jordan could rinse her mouth, and then the fat wedge of lime Rafael had forgotten to omit from her drink. "Bite. If that doesn't kill the taste, nothing will."

"Thank you — " She shuddered as the lime bit back, but it did the job. "Do you always bring your drink to the bathroom?"

"I didn't know how long we'd be. I brought yours, too. Come sit. Let me dust you off." She led Jordan to a chair in the sitting room, checked lapels and shirt front, brushed off her knees, and felt her forehead, still damp with the sweat of being sick. She rinsed the washcloth and smoothed it over Jordan's face. "You look incredible in a tux, Jordan," she said softly. "Not many women would dare."

She managed a smile. "It's a dyke thing. I figured if I was going to get canned for being queer, I might as well go out in uniform." She found Gillie's hand, taking the washcloth from her, refolding it and touching it to her upper lip. "Jesus, I can't believe he fired John."

"I can't believe he didn't fire him long ago. The man's a toad." She took the cloth from Jordan and dropped it into the hamper by the vanity. "Do you think you'll be able to eat?"

"Given that it isn't the last supper — " She stood, managing not to wobble, and reached to trace a hand down Gillie's arm, finding her hand, squeezing gently before she took it to her lips to leave a gentle kiss against her knuckles. "Thank you," she said softly, "for wearing your mother hat for me. Again."

◆

Michael stood as they approached the table. Jordan allowed him to hold her chair for her; he rested a hand on her shoulder for a moment before he played gentleman with Gillie's seat. "I'm so sorry for all of this, Jordan. There's nothing you've said to me today — either of you — that I can rejoin."

"Tell me why you fired John." Jordan was still pale, but her voice was calm and neutral, and Gillie had a moment's impression that Jordan was

186

the owner and Michael her employee, and that she expected a satisfactory answer and expected it soon, or his head would be next on the block.

Michael straightened his tie. "He lied to me at your expense. Maybe I'm old-fashioned, but to me, dishonesty at the expense of another is grounds for dismissal."

"That's not old-fashioned," Gillie murmured. "That's just good business. Keep the help happy."

He sent her an appreciative glance. "I've always thought so. And so now, in the middle of the season, I need a general manager. That won't be easy." He leaned back in his chair. "I suppose I could fill the chair with someone from GRI, but my people are valuable where they are. More so than I am. I'm not much more than a fancy signature pen. But I know my resort and how to run it, so until I find a handshake I like, I guess I'll stick around."

Gillie had watched Jordan's neutrality, and its effect of mildly unnerving her uncle, and when Jordan finally nodded and said, "It'll be nice to have you here," she knew Jordan meant it, but for reasons that were painfully different than they would have been that morning. She knew that had Michael ousted John simply to appease Jordan, Jordan would have quit. While being suddenly divested of his general manager, director of golf and head bartender at the height of the season might have amounted to little more than a significant inconvenience for Michael ("they'd make Bill director of golf and Cindy head bartender," she remembered Jordan saying, "and I'd go under without even leaving a ripple"), she knew that losing Jordan to his own impenetrability would have been a hard blow to Michael's pride . . . and his heart. She could tell from his gentleness with her how much he cared for Jordan.

"Mrs. Benson — " He turned to her.

"Gillian." She suspected that he cared neither for nicknames nor abridgments, and that allowing him the familiarity would help, in whatever small way, to ease the bruising she had dealt his pride that day, and knew she was right when a small smile crinkled the corners of his dark brown eyes.

"You seem to be an essential player in all of this, Gillian. Do you have questions?"

"Just one." There were a few crumbs on the tablecloth in front of her; she pushed them around with a freshly-polished fingernail before she swept them into her palm and dusted them onto her bread plate. "Is the reason that there's never a check at your table because there's never any food at your table?"

Jordan snorted a laugh. Michael leveled a grateful smile at her before he looked up to find Rafael and wave him over.

♦

Mother and daughter? Sisters? Lovers? He watched them through the evening and didn't know who they were to one another, those two handsome women who shared his table; their glances and touches roved through every women's bond he had ever witnessed. And he saw the differences of Jordan's affection: her easiness with Gillie, her reserve with him; sometimes he felt her warmth surround him, and then felt it die, and he knew her long habit of liking him wasn't sure of what to do with itself. And after Drambuie and coffee and the generic excuses of taking leave he stood for them, offering his hand to Gillian, first, and then to his niece. "I'll regret this afternoon for the rest of my life," he said quietly. "I miss you, Jordan."

She held his hand, and his eyes, and he saw the sadness in her. "All we can do is go forward."

"By the way," he said, not knowing if he should. "That was incredible golf you played today."

Her smile was slight and cool, and her eyes held a shadow of the afternoon, a shadow as mutable as muttering quick water under treacherous river ice. "Thank you. But I don't remember."

♦

The women walked slowly up the stairs together; in the lobby, Jordan paused. "Nightcap?"

"I'm sorry; I'm out of scotch. I meant to get some today, but —"

"It must be my turn to buy. I have vodka. Drambuie if you'd like."

"That would taste good again."

Jordan's kitchen was monochromatically black and white, scrupulously neat. Jordan got down snifters that gave a thin, crystalline ring when they tinged against one another, and opened a cabinet for the Drambuie. "You took ice?"

"Yes. Thanks." The knives magnetted over the counter top were *au carbone*, the pots hanging over the stove Calphalon; there were baskets filled with fruit and wooden spoons and tennis balls. The spice rack was a mismatched jumble of hand-labeled jars, a half-used garlic braid hanging from its side; Gillie thought that Jordan was probably an extraordinarily good cook, when she found time to cook. Over the table hung a nearly life-sized photograph of a woman in shadow, her reclining nudity a suggestion of soft curves; opera-length pearls glimmered against her skin. It was subtly erotic, surprising in the kitchen. "Park's work?"

"Mm-hmm. They gave it to me last year." She offered a glass. "It took me a while to get used to having Olathe naked in the kitchen, but I just couldn't bring myself to hang her in my bedroom."

"I guess I can understand that." She accepted the glass and sipped. "Thank you. You know, we never have looked at the ones they gave us. They're still on the table in my suite."

"Want me to run up and get them?"

"They can wait." She pulled a chair away from the table and shrugged out of her jacket, hanging it over the back of the chair.

"Let's go in here. I'm not a kitchen-sitter." Wearily, Jordan smiled. "Please don't take suggestion from my entertaining you in the bedroom. It's just that this room is where I live."

It was brass and glass and indirect light, framed art and expensive electronics and things to play on them, and window seats, and an antique gaming table with two comfortable-looking chairs — and books, thousands of books bound in cloth and paper and leather: a rainbow of novels, textbooks, reference books, literature, history, biography; and dozens of seashells and small polished stones scattered among them on the oak shelves . . . and almost incidentally, a queen-sized bed. "I can see why you live here," she murmured. "This is beautiful, Jordan. It's like a library." She touched the soft leather padding of one of the window seats. "These are wonderful."

"That's the best one; you can just see the lighthouse at the end of the breakwater. I sit there to read."

And Gillie knew Jordan had read or would read all of her books, curled into that window seat that showed her the barest glimpse of the tip of the lighthouse, capturing moments of peace in the only place in her life where she knew she had the last word. She picked a coaster from a basket on the game table and put her drink on it. "Are you all right, Jordan?"

Jordan unbuttoned the jacket of her tux, and undid her tie and cummerbund and slipped out of her heels, and sat at the game table to undo her cuff links; the cuffs came with them, and Gillie knew she hadn't taken off her jacket because she wore only a shirt front under it. "What did I shoot on the back nine?"

"Twenty-eight. A course record on the round."

She shook her head with an unfocused smile. "What was the old song? 'They're coming to take me away, ha ha, hee hee, ho ho, to the funny farm, where life is beautiful all the time — ' and then something about 'trees and flowers and chirping birds, and basket weavers who sit and smile and twiddle their thumbs — ' Trees and flowers and chirping birds. That's all I remember after I holed that chip on eleven. The sky was so blue. And there was a cardinal. I never saw him, but I could hear him calling the dog. Did you see those wild roses along the sixteenth, by the rock wall?"

"Yes. I also saw you get three-twenty on your drive on the twelfth."

"*Three*-twenty?" Jordan paused in mid-sip, looking at Gillie over the rim of her glass. "That can't be right."

"Stedman paced it off from the last marker. I've never heard a ball go off the club like that. I thought it was going to break the sound barrier."

"If Stedman paced it, I've got to trust him, but god, I've never hit a ball past two-eighty in my life. Not that since I was about twenty-five."

"We all had a fairly good idea of whose face you had painted on it. But it was scary for Stedman and me, Jordan. We didn't know why. We just knew it wasn't you out there. I think Stedman was ready to kill Michael. When we got back — maybe I shouldn't tell you this, but I'm going to — he told Michael that if he fired you, he'd lose him too."

"Thank you, Stew," she murmured, and slowly, she shook her head. "I was just — blank," she said softly. "Like the handle on the pisspot. I was there, but I wasn't in it."

"You didn't sweat," Gillie said. "You walked most of the course, all of those hills — but you never broke a sweat, Jordan. That was what scared me the most."

"I was cold," she said. "I remember that." She nudged her glass on its coaster, and shook her head; she got up and found a flat of cigarettes on the stand by the bed and came back to light one. "I guess Michael Goodnow is the only man besides Tarvis I can say I ever loved. I tell Gaston I love him, but — My father was — " Something of the afternoon flickered in her eyes; Gillie shivered. "I — " Jordan shook her head, and bumped her cigarette against the side of the ashtray, knocking off a resistant ash. "Aiga — I've mentioned her, haven't I? She was my partner when it all went to hell. She did everything she could when I had my shutdown, but she couldn't do it alone. Michael had my money, and that gave him the last word. But he listened to her — he really tried to work with her to get what was best for me. And I think that's why I was so— " She raised a hand, a tiny gesture of helplessness while she searched for a word. "Shattered, today. Like so much had just collapsed inside me. He was the last person in the world I expected to say something like that. He was the last person I could call family and feel that bond. I felt that break — " She raised her glass, sipped, held its coolness against her lips; Gillie watched the fog her breath left against its side. "And I just lost it. Was it Dickinson? Zero at the bone. A narrow fellow — a snake in the grass." She put the glass down. "All of that. You know, Gil, except for you, this has been a putrid week. Thank you for being here for me."

"I'm beginning to wonder if I'm what's bringing you the bad luck. This week has been so god-awful for you, and it seems I've been in the middle of it all." Ruefully, she smiled. "Not quite just the handle on the pisspot. You have to admit I'm the one who set John off the other day. All of this rift with Michael stemmed from that. If it hadn't been for me — "

"If it hadn't been for you I'd have had to put up with John G. Mister-To-You Laing for the rest of my fucking life. If you were the catalyst that got rid of that oily bastard, I should get on my knees and kiss your feet."

"But what about Michael? That's too dear a price to pay, Jordan."

She rolled the end of her cigarette in the ashtray, shaping the cherry to a neat cone. "Michael knows what he did. He admits it. Apologized for it. Did everything he could to make it right again. My mind is working hard to forgive him, Gillie, but my heart needs a while to catch up. I'll get there. We'll be all right."

"I hope so, Jordan. I know you love him. And god, honey, he loves you."

"Best father I ever had," she murmured, and shook off the thought with a visible effort. She looked up with a tiny smile. "He's quite taken with you, I think, is my Uncle Michael."

"Oh, please," Gillie scoffed. But she knew that he was, as well as she knew that his courteous interest had warmed her in ways she had not expected to be warmed — ways she wasn't at all certain she wanted to be warmed.

"Well," Jordan said, "I can't fault his taste." She toyed with her glass, moving the coaster around with the foot of it. "You might give it some thought. He'd treat you like a queen."

"I thought you didn't believe in May-December romances."

"I think we're talking more like June-September. You're both grown up."

Gillie stirred her drink with a finger. "I've got a lot of thinking to do before I get involved with a man again," she said quietly. "I'm still trying to figure out how I feel about you."

Jordan looked up, catching Gillie sucking Drambuie off her forefinger.

Gillie shied her eyes away. Meticulously, she straightened the hem of her skirt across her knee, avoiding Jordan's eyes. "Did I tell you I talked to Meggie yesterday?"

Jordan stubbed out her cigarette, chasing the embers around in the ashtray. "Who called who?"

"She called me. We talked — god, I don't know; it must have been two hours. I didn't even know I could talk on the phone that long. We got a lot of things sorted out."

"Gillie, that's great. I know that's been hard on you, being so disconnected from her."

"It has been. But I can see light at the end of the tunnel." She tasted her drink. "Apropos of — oh, something; I don't remember, but I didn't take offense — she asked if I was in therapy. So I was telling her about you, and I'd say Jordan the psychotherapist, or Jordan the golf pro, or the bartender, or the massage therapist, or my friend Jordan . . ." She gave a little laugh. "And finally Meggie said, 'Momma, Momma! How many women named Jordan are there up there?' I said, 'just one. I think.' She asked if I was sure you weren't twins."

"Just call me Sybil."

Gillie looked up; for a moment she hovered on the edge of her thought before the words finally came. "This has gotten me in trouble before. But sometimes it feels that way," she said quietly. "All those hats. You do all of those things, you're all of those people — and you come from all of those places just a little differently, Jordan. As if you have different levels of . . . distance that you allow yourself to close, or allow me to close, depending on what hat you're wearing."

Jordan ticked a fingernail against her glass. "Boundaries."

"I suppose. But sometimes it feels as if you're letting me inside you — your mind, or your space, and then . . . well, Thursday. That was — it was so — " She huffed a tiny breath of frustration, unable to find the right words. "I was — I don't know. That was my rotten day. That awful phone call with Meggie, and then Peony, and then my back. All I wanted was for that to go away, but I was afraid of how I might react, or — "

She seemed to stall, groping for words. "Breathe," Jordan suggested quietly.

She drew a slow breath, and let it out, and dared. "How can you be attracted to someone" — a faint blush touched her, but she forced out the words — "and still be so neutral with their naked body?"

Jordan toyed with her flat of cigarettes, opening it, closing it; finally she tasted her drink. "It isn't easy," she admitted. "But I take my professional ethics fairly seriously. If you'd looked up at me on the table and said make love to me right now, I couldn't have. Or if I'd said before the massage, this will cost sixty dollars, and you got off the table and said god, that made me horny, take me to bed and I'll write you a check later, I couldn't have. I've been in both of those places. I've learned how to deal with it." She shook her head. "But given that I was working in the capacity of your friend who happens to have those skills . . . if you'd gotten off the table and said take me to bed — " She smiled a little. "I would have had to search my soul."

"I thought I did get off the table and say take me to bed," Gillie said quietly.

Jordan met her eyes. "I didn't think you meant it."

Grey eyes and brown held for a long moment before Gillie looked away. "I didn't."

Their silence stretched; Jordan finally got up, offering a hand for Gillie's glass. "Refill?"

"Thank you." And she listened to the rattle of ice in the kitchen, and the pulse of blood in her veins; her stomach felt full of warm, sleepy-winged butterflies.

Jordan came back, both glasses in one hand; she put them on the table, but didn't sit. "Gillie — " She put her hands in her pockets and looked at the floor, and finally met her eyes. "The other night, when Park and Olathe came over."

"Please sit down," Gillie said softly. "I'm still not comfortable with you standing over me."

"I'm sorry." She sat. "That picture in the Mexico book. It hit you like a truck. What was that about?"

It was Gillie's turn to get up, to escape their nearness. "I — " She went to the window, and fingered aside the curtain to watch the lighthouse: white and green, white and green. "When I was talking to Meggie it seemed as if I was . . . I don't know. Pulling back from saying things," she said quietly. "Withholding things. As if — as if I wasn't trying to keep them from her as much as I was trying to keep them from me. As if there were . . . things I didn't dare to think even after I'd thought them. That photograph . . . " Slowly, she shook her head. "If you'd touched me then, I'd have fallen apart. You knew that, didn't you?"

"Yes."

"And you knew why."

She heard the scrape of a chair against the hardwood floor, and knew before Jordan's hands came to her shoulders that the touch was coming. She knew it would be unlike any other touch Jordan had given her, and it was: it was question and answer, desire and denial; it was sensuous and sensual and controlled. "What do you want, Gillian?" It was breath in her hair, lips at her ear; the butterflies in her stomach rose in a frantic, breathless cloud.

"I don't — " She drew a shaky breath. "I don't know. I don't know what I want."

Gently, Jordan turned her to face her; her eyes were deep fog and hard seas and moonless nights; they were the feathers of a dove and the fur of a sleeping cat and the touch of silk on private skin. "Do you want me to kiss you?"

"Jordan — "

"It's all right to say no," Jordan said softly. "I won't be hurt. I only want what you want."

"Oh, god — " She closed her eyes. "You know I do, Jordan," she whispered. "You know I do."

Lips met hers, more breath than touch, and that warm deep something didn't gently roll this time; it surged a hot, liquid ache into her and her lips parted in helpless answer to the delicate question of Jordan's tongue; she felt a burn of tears that were need and desire . . . and a deep, thrumming fear.

Fingers combed through her hair like her own on an indulgent morning. Jordan's lower lip trembled across her eyebrow, and both her lips tasted her forehead, and fingertips found her throat like the whiskers of a cat before they smoothed across her cheek, seeking her like a blind mother learning the face of her firstborn child, and her voice was as soft as her touch: "Should I stop?"

Feel me

193

Feel how I

"Gillie, do you want me — "

want you

" — to stop?"

She reached to find Jordan's face, searching for the courage for the words. "No," she whispered. "No. Don't stop."

Jordan's body barely touched hers, and touched her everywhere; one of her hands slipped into Gillie's hair, the fingers of the other tracing across her cheek with a gentleness that drew tears from her as Jordan bent her head to her, her lips seeking her mouth, her tongue tracing her lips. Lips went to learn her cheekbone, wandering to touch the tips of her eyelashes; she was hands and lips and tongue and everywhere, faces making love and then Jordan's mouth met hers as if she couldn't wait any longer, her tongue probing with a deep thoroughness that left Gillie gasping for breath. "Oh, god — " She didn't know how she had found skin but it was there under her hands, smooth and taut and warm; she felt her nails digging hard in her need and her need to control it; she wondered if she was drawing blood at Jordan's ribs. "Oh, my god. Jordan — "

"Say no if you need to." She could feel the restraint in Jordan's hands.

"No isn't even close to what I was thinking."

"What were you thinking?"

"That I don't know what to do with this much yes. I've never — " She shivered at the feel of Jordan's lips brushing hers. "I've never wanted like this," she whispered. "I don't know how to do this, Jordan."

"Just fall into the love," Jordan said softly. "That's what you give yourself to. Not me. Not my body. Our love."

She slipped her hands up Jordan's belly, her fingers stuttering when they found the rising softness of Jordan's breasts. "Oh — god, you're a woman, Jordan, this is so — oh, god." Jordan's tongue met hers, a bare touch and then a smooth caress; their lips had never parted. She remembered the feel of Jordan's hands against her naked, oiled skin as fingertips found the side of her breast, a slow brush and then the slower smooth of the backs of Jordan's fingers there. "I was so afraid Thursday that you'd make love to me. I was so close to wanting you to, Jordan."

"I did make love to you Thursday," Jordan whispered. "As much as it felt like we were ready for. God, Drambuie was made for kissing. You taste so good."

"I'll remember that next time I want to get seduced. Jordan —"

Jordan smoothed her hands down the length of Gillie's back, and back up enough to defeat the tuck of her blouse; Gillie's breath caught in her when one warm palm slipped under the silk. "I meant to tell you how good you looked tonight," Jordan murmured.

"I dressed for you," she whispered, and knew it was true.

Jordan's lips found her throat, and wandered up to her ear and across to her mouth. "Thank you." Her fingers found the button of Gillie's skirt, slipping it free, and paused at the zipper. "Yes?"

She swallowed, and nodded, and shivered at the feel of silk slithering away from her; like a dance, one hand at her shoulder and the other at her hip, Jordan moved her away from the crumpled pile of her skirt before she shrugged out of her jacket and let it drop to the floor. Her mouth found Gillie's throat, and then the hollow above her collarbone, and then the one below it, finding the trail the stopper of her perfume bottle had taken so that a whispering tongue could follow; fingers loosed the first two buttons of her blouse and lips touched the rise of her breast; an arm tightened around her waist when her knees forgot, for a moment, how to work. "Gillie — "

"Don't stop. God, don't — oh, god, what have we gotten into, Jordan, I am so ready for you — " She filled her hands with Jordan's hair and heard "Come on — " and felt arms around her, lifting her, and she knew the gesture was much more than symbolic when she locked her legs around Jordan's waist and their breaths mingled in a shared "oh, god — " as her wet warmth met Jordan's skin. She felt Jordan's face buried in her throat, and the scrape of teeth at her collarbone; she felt her heat rising like a dangerous summer storm and when Jordan's cheek scrubbed against her breast and her mouth closed over her nipple the storm exploded *come on, come on come on —*

◆

"Gillie?"

She drowsed into awareness: arms and legs and hands, breasts and bellies, bodies tangled together; lips and warmth, a deep, hot scent — Jordan, holding her in an oddly undulant confusion of sheets. "Hmmm?"

"Are you okay?"

She remembered Jordan's waist between her legs as she took her to the bed; she remembered their tongues slow-dancing with one another, and Jordan's hands making a lingering exploration across her skin: first palms, then fingertips, then the backs of fingers and the soft scrape of close-trimmed nails, and then palms again . . .

She remembered the feel of Jordan's still trousered leg between her thighs, and the sweet softness of breasts against her belly, and shoulders in her hands and thick hair between all her fingers as Jordan's hands cupped her breast, her tongue drawing wet circles around her nipple before her lips closed there and she drew that hardened bud into her mouth; she remembered the soft scrape of her teeth, and rising to the heat of her mouth, holding her head there, crying her name as an iris of color exploded inside her like a crystal world exploding in the arms of the sun. "Jordan — "

"Hey. Welcome back."

"I've never seen so many colors," she whispered. She could barely move, but that was all right; she didn't want to. She managed to hook an ankle around one of Jordan's, feeling summer-weight wool. "We were in a hurry, weren't we," she murmured. "God, Jordan. If that was an orgasm, I finally understand what all the press is about." Her eyelids lost enough weight for her to lift them; she reached to trace her fingers through Jordan's hair. "Incredible," she whispered, and felt an unexpected burn of tears trying to start; she closed her eyes, willing them back. "Oh, Jordan. How will I do without you now?"

Jordan touched a finger to Gillie's lips. "You'll always know where to find me," she said softly. "I promise." She bent her head to brush her lips across Gillie's breast, feeling the swell of response when the tip of her tongue found her nipple. "Mmm. Are we through?"

"I don't — oh, god, I think id's in control, here — "

"Could be," Jordan murmured, her hand slipping from her throat to her breast to her belly, a lingering intimacy against the quivering awareness of her skin. "What does id say?"

She caught Jordan's hand with hers; their fingers entwined as she led that hand back from her ribs to her belly. "She's only got one line," she whispered. "Give it to me and give it to me right now. Now, Jordan. Please."

"I love you," Jordan whispered, and gently broke the lock of their fingers. "I know you love me. Fall into the love, Gillie. Let it catch you."

"Oh, my god — " It was almost a moan as fingertips brushed the soft froth of hair at the tops of her thighs. "Jordan — " Gently, that hand slipped between her thighs. "God, you make me shameless, Jordan, you feel so oh god!" It gasped from her as one slender finger found the silken embrace of her wetness. "Oh, Jordan — oh, god, Jordan, I can't believe this — "

"Stay with me — " It was a brush of breath against her lips. "My god, you feel so — oh!" It was almost a breath of pain; Gillie realized her fingernails were dug hard into Jordan's shoulders and she opened her hands, but Jordan's teeth raked gently across her throat. "You don't have to stop. It feels good — "

Jordan's fingertip drew softly to a sensitivity that ripped a breath from her. "Jordan, it's too good, I'm — oh, my god. Jordan — "

"Stay with me, Gillie — oh, god, your nails, that's so good — " Jordan's tongue sought hers; she fought that probing tongue with her own, fighting the orgasm as Jordan's finger flirted with her need. "Gillie, can I be in you, please let me go inside you — "

"Yes oh god! Jordan — " She was aware of everything, of nothing; she knew Jordan's breasts against hers, Jordan's mouth against hers, her back in her hands and how Jordan arched *god yes* as her nails bit into sweat-slicked skin; she knew nothing more than that slim finger stroking a slow, slow rhythm deep inside her. She knew the scents of their mingled perfumes, and their own richer, more personal scents; she knew the sound of her own voice begging *please oh god more Jordan come on* — and Jordan withdrawing just enough to give her the more she had asked for; she knew the feel of Jordan's tongue against hers, the taste of their breaths together, and her need to break away from that for there was only one thing to know and that was Jordan inside her *stay with me* and that mouth seeking hers again, their breaths gasping against each other *Jordan more* and teeth bruising lips *Gillian oh god Gillie* and the rake of her nails down the length of Jordan's back and the rise of her hips and the thrust of fingers deep into her and Jordan's voice *stay with me oh god Gillie Gillian come with me*

and then knowing Jordan in her arms, breasts and breaths together, knowing both of them crying as the shudder slowly faded and she found Jordan's mouth with hers, finally, and tasted her lips and her breath and her tongue before she whispered, "I don't think I'm going to be worth a damn to golf tomorrow."

Jordan shivered a laugh; she raised to one elbow, and slowly, gently, she drew her hand from between Gillie's thighs. "Enough?" she whispered, and Gillie felt an almost painful jolt as Jordan took the tip of her longest finger into her own mouth before she bent to flicker her tongue across Gillie's lips.

Gillie tasted something softly salty and realized it was herself, her own taste, and she knew what Jordan meant; she knew if there was a last taboo, it was about to be broken. "No." She buried her fingers in Jordan's hair. "Not enough." It was a whisper, a growl, a hunger; it was a helpless, aching release. "I want all of us, Jordan. All of who we are tonight together. Give me that."

She was relatively certain when she woke up the first time that she was only dreaming she was awake; she'd never slept in a waterbed, she'd certainly never slept in a library, so there was no logic in waking up in a waterbed in a library. She turned over and went back to sleep.

She woke up an hour later in a waterbed in a library. The smell of coffee was fresh and strong, but she didn't need to taste that coffee to know the bed was Jordan's even though Jordan wasn't in it, and that the library must, by logical progression, be Jordan's bedroom; she didn't need the wake-up call of strong dark brew to remember lips and tongues and arms, hands and breasts and bellies, sweat and scent and the feel of Jordan Bryant smoothly naked between her legs. . . . Her body pulsed in helpless response to the memory, and she tried to sort out confusions and contradictions and couldn't, not with the evidences of the night still so close she could almost taste them. "Oh, my god," she whispered into her pillow. "What have you done, Gillian?"

She sat up to scrub her hands through her hair and over her face, and stifled a morning yawn and looked across the room to meet a grey-eyed study, a hint of a smile that stirred up butterflies she would have thought had been thoroughly settled last night. She was self-conscious in her nakedness, but thought it would be ungracious, after last night, to cover herself.

Sprawled gracefully in a window seat, Jordan closed the book she had been reading. "Hi." She wore a soft purple robe; carelessly belted, it showed smooth expanses of thigh and breast. Gillie wished for Park Webster's ubiquitous Hasselblad and wondered if, once she had the picture, she'd ever dare to look at it — or if she'd have it blown up to near-life-size so she could hang it over the kitchen table, an erotic surprise like smooth shadows and pearls. "Can I get you coffee, breakfast in bed, or privacy?"

"Coffee, I guess."

Jordan got up, allowing her a moment of privacy; a moment was all she had really wanted. A silk robe was draped across the foot of the bed. She took it to the bathroom.

Her suit was neat on a wooden hanger hooked to the back of the door; her blouse and hose, still damp from a sink wash, murmured in the breeze from the open window. Jordan's lilac tuxedo was crumpled in a basket by the tub. A set of towels and a new toothbrush were laid out on the vanity; she peeled the cellophane from the box while she peed, and brushed her teeth and washed her face and borrowed a comb to run through her hair. She was vaguely sorry — and vaguely relieved — that she hadn't awakened in Jordan's arms.

There was a delicate bruise on her collarbone. Seeing it brought back the feel of Jordan's teeth there, a composed urgency she knew she had asked for; warmly, she shivered. "Chance of a lifetime?" she whispered to her reflection; the woman in the mirror was sleepily smug. "Peony, you'll never know."

Jordan's Rolex was on the vanity; she glanced at it. Ten past eight. "Don't let me make you late for work," she said, going back to the bedroom to find Jordan putting a coffee tray on the game table.

"It's Monday. I'm off."

"I know, but — I suppose I assumed Michael would have dibs on your time." The thought of Michael raised a faint blush to her; she busied herself with tipping cream into a cup, and stirred and tasted. "Good coffee." She ticked a fingernail against the china, and finally turned to the window. "Well," she said softly. "What do we do now?"

She heard the soft sound of Jordan's cup meeting its saucer, and when hands settled gently on her shoulders she put her coffee on a bookcase and turned to her, and for a long, silent moment they held each other. "I didn't expect this, Jordan. God, I didn't expect it."

"Neither did I."

"I'm so afraid of hurting you," she whispered. "I care so much about you, Jordan, and you're a — god, you're an exquisite lover, but I'm not — "

"Gillie, I know. I know. I knew that one night wouldn't change that. That's not what it was about." She took Gillie's face in her hands. "It was about safety. And pleasure. Touch. You knowing it doesn't have to hurt. It was love" — grey eyes glimmered with tears — "and trust. And it was very much a two-way street. Those aren't things I give up easily, either."

"I know that. That's why I'm afraid of hurting you."

Jordan touched her lips to Gillie's cheek. "I don't expect anything except that we'll still be friends. I'm here for you, Gillian. Whatever you want me to be."

Gently, Gillie broke from her arms. "That's not fair to you."

"Why not?"

"Because it isn't. I can't say I can be whatever you want me to be, if you want — I can't — I don't know if I want this to happen again, or . . . I've never felt so loved, and it might be hard to let go of that, but I can't expect you to just — be here. You must have a life besides me."

Jordan snorted a laugh. "Sure; that's why I work sixteen hours a day. Gillie, I never expected this to happen at all. Why would I expect it to happen again?" She found her cigarette case in a pocket of her robe. "If you said you'd found your lesbian identity and wanted us to move in together and be life partners, I'd say no. It wouldn't have anything to do with you; I'd say it to any woman who wanted that from me. I've been single for a long time. I'm comfortable in it." She smoothed her fingers across the burnished gold in her hand. "Maybe that's selfish, but it lets me say things like that, because I'm free to be here for you, for talk or golf or . . . touch, if you need or want that — now, or some other time," she said quietly. "We fit each other, somehow. If our lives put us in a place where our physical paths cross again . . . Gillie, I loved loving you. It's been a long, long time since I knew it really meant something. And I'll hold that memory like — "

She opened her hand; the gold case gleamed softly in her palm. "Like this. Like the Packard. Like that quilt on my bed — my mother made that, every stitch by hand. Things that meant so much to someone else. Things I was . . . not given, so much as trusted with. I hope I'm making sense."

"Yes," Gillie said softly. "You're making perfect sense."

"And when some July hits me hard again I'll remember you, and I'll have something to hang onto. You'll always be a new July to me, Gillian. Whatever I gave you — if I gave you anything — you gave me July. I never thought I'd get it back."

"If you gave me anything? God, Jordan — " She took one of Jordan's hands in both of hers and took it to her lips and held it there, trying not to cry. "I never could have trusted a man — not to let go like that. There wasn't a moment — not a second — when I was afraid you'd hurt me, and I couldn't have felt that with a man. Not the first time, after — it was — god, don't laugh at this. It was like losing my virginity — the right way, this time." She sniffed a laugh. "God, you carried me to bed. That's the most romantic thing that's ever happened to me."

Shakily, Jordan laughed. "It's not all bad to be so small, is it."

"I'll remember that every time I have to use a step stool to reach the top shelf of the kitchen cabinets." And her laugh was stronger this time. "Damn, I shouldn't have said that. I will, now. You'll be sweeping me off my feet ten times a day."

"So, happy cooking," Jordan grinned, and Gillie's laugh was pure and real as she swatted Jordan on the shoulder, and they knew they could still be friends. "I make fairly good crepes," Jordan said, "and I've got real maple syrup. You hungry?"

"Famished. Do I have time for a shower first?"

"Plenty."

"And then what?"

"Well . . ." Jordan opened a closet door and studied what was there before she reached for a weathered plaid jacket and plus fours. "I'll call down to the shop and see if Michael and Stew can get along without me today. It is my day off, after all. And then why don't we throw our clubs into the trunk of that Lincoln Town Car of yours and head for Bethlehem. We can play a little golf, have a good meal . . . and I can talk to a Realtor about pounding a for sale sign into the lawn of that goddamned house. I think it's high time I got that particular monkey off my back."

"Bravo, Jordan! Is there a car dealer there?"

"Several. Why?"

"I want a sports car. That Lincoln just doesn't fit me anymore."

Jordan grinned. "We're getting busy. I might have to take tomorrow off, too."

"He owes it to you. You worked yesterday."

◆

"Go," Michael said, when she ran into him in the lobby on her way to the kitchen to borrow some eggs from Gaston and asked if she might have two days off to go to Bethlehem. "Take the week if you want to. God knows you've earned it." He found a key in his wallet and offered it. "Use my suite."

"Thank you." She slipped the key into the pocket of her jeans. "Can I afford to be gone all week? The thought's incredibly attractive, but we've got a lot to do."

"We won't chisel anything in stone until you get back. Oh, but speaking of chiseling things in stone, did you ever play a little executive course called East Bay down in — where is it, Saint Pete? Largo? — when you lived in Tampa?"

"Largo, I think. Yeah, a couple of times. Why?"

"Do you remember their hole markers? Polished granite, carved —"

"Yes. Really attractive."

"Well, we're getting a kind of a granite theme going here, what with the breakwater and the wall. I thought that might fit." He smiled. "As you pointed out, granite's cheap on the coast of Maine."

She knew it was a peace offering, forgiveness for the snarl she had turned on him about the rock wall when he had protested its possible expense. "That would look great, Michael. If you really want to carry the theme, make the bridge to the island out of granite, too. That'd look good."

"Yes it would." He cleared his throat. "So you're off to Bethlehem. Do you suppose that Gillian might care to have dinner with me one night while you're gone?"

"Um . . ." She felt the blush creep onto her face. "I — uh — no. I mean, not that she wouldn't, but . . . she's going with me."

She knew that he was a little of a lot of things: shocked and disappointed and hurt, before he said "I see," and she knew that he did. "Well. Perhaps we can all get together when you get back."

They were standing by the door gold-lettered General Manager; she remembered that it was Michael's office now, not John's, and she pushed open the door and stepped inside. "Please?" she asked, and he followed; she knew he didn't want to. She closed the door. "I didn't lie to you yesterday, Michael," she said quietly. "Last night was the first time, and it'll probably be the last. I still think she's straight."

"Jordan, I don't need to hear about your private life."

201

"You do when the truth today makes me look like a liar yesterday. I've always been honest with you, Michael. I always will be. I don't ever want you to doubt that."

He looked at the floor, and back at her. "I'm glad you still care about my opinion."

"Of course I do," she said softly. "Michael, I — " *still love you,* she wanted to say, but the words wouldn't come. "God, this is awkward." They both knew what she meant. Silently, she offered the key back to him.

"Go get your eggs," he said. "I'll call and have them dust the suite."

◆

They stopped in Augusta to look at BMWs, Corvettes, Miatas, MR2s; nothing captured Gillie's heart. They stopped at a real estate office in Bethlehem; Gillie browsed a car lot down the street while Jordan talked to the agent. Jordan appeared at her side with a handful of paper. "Find anything?"

"No."

"We need to go to Falmouth. Put you in a Mercedes."

"Too much money." And she smiled. "Don't buy me one!"

"No danger. Ready to golf?"

"Always. Did you get everything done you wanted to?"

"She said the sign should go up in a few days." Jordan looked at the paperwork in her hands. "I should have done this years ago," she murmured. "God, the things we hang onto."

"Pain can get to be a habit," Gillie said softly. "Maybe when you break this one, you can quit smoking."

"Don't start on that. Please."

◆

"Should we register before we tee off?" Gillie asked, when Jordan headed for the pro shop instead of the lobby.

"Michael gave me the key to his suite. We're all set."

"Michael has a suite here?"

"Michael owns here. Catawamteak, Bethlehem, Shipwreck Harbor. He collects grand resorts." She opened the clubhouse door, guiding Gillie through with light fingertips against the small of her back. "We should play Shipwreck. That's a killer course. Slice there and you're toast."

"I thought you loved me," she said, wondering if Michael Goodnow's suite at Bethlehem was like hers at Catawamteak: kitchenette, bathroom, living room, balcony . . . and one king-sized bedroom with one king-sized bed.

"I do love you. Hey, Doc! *Comme ça va?*"

"Jesus, two wrecked greens and you're here? What kind of a golf director are you?"

Jordan held up her hands. "Michael's there."

He laughed. "And now I know why you're here. How is he, besides running the show and pissing Stedman off? Hey, Mrs. Benson! It's good to see you again. How're those clubs doing you?"

"They're perfect. It's me that needs work — and the little girl's room."

She returned to find them deep in conversation about wrecked greens and course redesign, and she watched Jordan's calmness and wondered if July might really someday be hers again, once the house was gone.

They played an intense front nine, the par threes allowing Gillie to work on her wedges, the lingering weak spot in her game, and had a drink and tackled the back nine; it was hot, and they dragged back to the clubhouse sweaty and fatigued. "God! I'm beat. Why am I so tired?"

Jordan answered with a slow, deep smile, and she blushed to the roots of her hair.

◆

Kitchenette, bathroom, living room, balcony . . . and one king-sized bedroom with one king-sized bed. Jordan felt the uncertain change in Gillie's energy. "Have the shower first," she offered. "I've got to make a few phone calls." And while Gillie was in the shower she lifted cushions to discover a convertible sofa; she pulled it out and made it up and was lounging there, sipping a scotch and watching the news, when Gillie emerged in shorts and a tee shirt. She looked up. "Feel better?"

"Six hundred percent," she said, and Jordan figured the option of separate beds was at least half of that. "Where was Fred today? I missed him."

"Off. He'll be in tomorrow." She rattled the ice in her glass and got up. "Make you a drink?"

"That's the very next thing I need."

"Tonic or rocks?"

"Umm . . . tonic."

Jordan mixed and delivered the drink and a menu. "Preview of coming attractions. Any of that can come up here if you don't want to go down." She opened her garment bag. "Damn. I forgot my robe. Is there one in the closet in there?"

"I'm sorry; I used it. It's on the foot of the bed."

She came out wrapped in the thick terrycloth robe, her hair turbaned in a towel, and freshened her drink and lit a cigarette. "Are we going down for dinner?"

Gillie was watching *Jeopardy!*, curled into the corner of the sofa bed Jordan hadn't been in; she looked back over her shoulder. "Do you want to?"

"Not very bad. I could do with some fruit and cheese and be happy."

"Why don't we do that. Then we won't have to change."

Room service delivered apples and grapes and pears and melon, five different cheeses, a loaf of crusty bread, a bottle of Pouilly-Fouisse, and an extra robe. "Sorry about the robe," the valet said, his eyes flicking to the sofa bed. "We're used to Mr. Goodnow being alone."

"That's more than we needed to know," Jordan said when the boy was gone; she wedged a Granny Smith on the cutting board. "It's none of our business if he has a woman in every port."

"He doesn't strike me as the type."

Meticulously, Jordan pared the core from the slices of apple. "How does he strike you?"

Gillie glanced up from reading the label on the bottle of wine. "He's a gentleman. Don't try to play matchmaker, Jordan."

"You two wouldn't be a match, you'd be a merger." She offered the corkscrew; Gillie handed over the bottle, and Jordan pulled the cork. "At least neither one of you would have to worry that the other one was after your money."

"That much is true," Gillie conceded.

"I'm not trying to play matchmaker." Jordan tipped the bottle over glasses. "I thought you two might enjoy each others' company. You have a lot in common."

"Money and golf?"

"Friendships have been built on less." Jordan offered a glass. "I'm not trying to push you into anything, Gillie. I thought you might like each other."

Gillie shrugged. "He seems very nice." She sat in one of the wing chairs by the French doors; the suite was so much like her own at Catawamteak that she almost felt at home. "After eighteen holes of golf and an unusual dinner, what else can I say? He seems nice."

Jordan put the board of fruit and cheese on the table between the two wing chairs and sat. "When I was a little kid — five or six, I guess — he and Celia came for some family reunion. Maybe it was Celia's class reunion at the Academy. Anyway, it was the first time I'd met them. When they were leaving, Celia told me she wished she could take me home with them. I thought it was because she didn't have a little girl of her own. It was a long time before I knew that she thoroughly detested my father."

"They never had children?"

"No. I guess that's why they took so much interest in me. They got me my first golf clubs, and then a really good set a few years later when I started showing some promise as a golfer. They paid my tuition at the Academy. Stuff like that." She scooped up a slice of sharp cheddar with the blade of the knife, speared a slice of apple on the point, and offered it.

"Thank you." Gillie nibbled at the apple. "So I take it Michael had money when Celia married him? He'd have been a relatively young man thirty years ago."

"Old Boston money. What he spent on me was pocket change to him."

"How hard was that philanthropy on your father's ego?"

Slowly, Jordan shook her head. "My family's always been connected with Bethlehem, but in sort of a service role. Great-Grampa James K. was like Stedman: caddie to greenskeeper. Dad's father was head groundskeeper. Four generations of rubbing elbows with the rich and famous without ever being one of them. All that elbow-rubbing generated a certain amount of static electricity."

"I expect so."

"Dad was a really good golfer, but when he was young there wasn't enough money — it takes a lot of money to make a pro golfer. He saw Michael as a way to make it happen for me, and then resented that I was going where he'd never had the chance to be." She tipped wine into their glasses. "And I think when Michael bought the place, Dad just couldn't deal with it. Michael did what Dad and his father and grandfather had always wanted, and it was poison to him that it wasn't really family that finally got there. Add a queer daughter — here I was, on my way to everything he'd ever wanted, but I was this . . . aberrant thing. I really think that's how he saw me." She shook her head. "Somewhere in there, he lost it. His whole life was vicarious. I guess the only thing he could see to do was take it down. If he couldn't have it, no one was going to."

"Phil said that to me," Gillie said softly. "Just before he tossed me down the stairs. 'You say no to me and you'll never say yes to any other son of a bitch.'" And she tried to shift the subject: not to change it, in case Jordan still wanted to talk, but to lead it away from such treacherous depths. "Did your mother golf?"

"Loved the game. She wasn't very good at it, but she loved it. She got a hole in one once — my god, you'd have thought she'd won the lottery. High point of her life."

"Have you ever done it? A hole in one?"

Jordan smiled. "Holes in one are like playing solitaire. If you deal enough hands, sooner or later you'll win one. They've got more to do with persistence than skill, and I play a lot of golf."

"How many do you have?"

"I don't know. A dozen or so. Two of them on the third at Catawamteak."

"I keep hoping there. I've golfed for twenty years and I don't have one."

"You're way overdue."

They nibbled at the fruit and cheese and bread, and drank the wine, and talked golf; Jordan's family wound its way in and out of her stories, and Gillie remembered the first time they had come to Bethlehem, and how Jordan had told just enough to keep her wondering what she was keeping hidden. "Just a week ago," she murmured. "God, it feels like ten years."

"What?"

"We were just here a week ago today. It feels like someone else's memory."

Jordan looked up. "It is, in a way," she said quietly. "We've changed each other a lot . . . or allowed each other a lot of change."

"I brought the pictures," Gillie said. "Photographs. Excuse me, Park."

"The Sunday ones?"

"Yes."

◆

"My god — " It was a breath of something almost pain when Jordan realized what the photographs were. Park had captured them on the break-water, struggling with the beginnings of their feelings: pausing in pain, searching with looks, touching in trust for the first time; from the distance of the first one to the close-up of the last, the depths of the photos shifted like the nuances of her memory of that day.

"They're incredible," Jordan whispered. They were like a ballet, starkly, texturally intense as only black and white can be, the movements the ache of memories and hard questions asked too soon, apology and then the healing of touch that grew braver until acceptance lost its reluctant caution; they were two women ascending from acquaintances to friends, and she knew, looking at them now, that by the time she had said she might fall in love, she already had.

"No," she said softly. "That's not right."

"What's not right?"

"Not in love. Just . . . love. I just knew I'd love you."

Gillie's fingers slipped gently through her hair. "Come to bed," she said quietly. "That sofa bed would be like trying to sleep across a speed bump in a parking lot."

"Gillie, we don't have to — "

"I know we don't have to. Just come to bed."

◆

She came out of the bathroom in time to catch Jordan between dropping her robe and pulling on the long tee shirt she had brought for a nightshirt, in time to see the web of thin red welts that traced across her back. "Jordan, what — oh, god, Jordan, wait. Let me look — " She touched her fingers to the tracks her nails had left; a few of them were raw, the skin broken hard. "God, look what I did to you," she whispered. "My god, I didn't realize — Oh, lord. Jordan, I'm so sorry."

Jordan slipped into her shirt. "I'm not." She turned, picking her robe from the top of the dresser. "Which side do you want?"

"The left, if it doesn't matter to you." She found the TV remote and pretended to look at it, not wanting Jordan to see the blush that had risen on her.

"That's fine." Jordan draped the terrycloth wrap at the foot of the bed on the right. "You probably ought to keep the remote if we're going to watch Leno. I'll fall asleep."

Gillie pulled the sheet up under her chin. "No guarantees that I won't."

◆

They started out on opposite sides of the bed; sometime past two Gillie drowsed awake to the awareness of warmth against her. Searching that feeling, she knew that she had sought Jordan the way she had sometimes sought Phil when he'd been on a stretch of good behavior and would allow her to sleep snuggled under the weight of his arm, using his chest for a pillow, listening to the strange comfort of his heart and his breath.

She shivered a sigh. "I wish I could, Jordan," she whispered. "I wish I was, because I love you."

Jordan drew a deep breath and closed a tiny hug around her, and slipped back into the depth of her sleep.

Acutely aware of the undemanding presence beside her, too many thoughts chasing their tails through her mind to let her go back to sleep, Gillie tried to corral the thoughts, but they teased her, staying just out of reach. At last she gave up and let them run until they got tired and quieted, and finally, soothed by the subliminal lullaby of Jordan's heart and breath, she slept.

She was tired of the bar, of the hours, of the drinkers and the drunks; she hadn't known that she was until she had to face it and them again after a week away. "Michael," she said, when he came in for an after-dinner drink, "why don't you promote Cindy to night shift and give her a nice raise out of what you won't have to pay me anymore. I'll still do the management if you want me to, or train her to do it, I don't care, but I need out from behind here. I'm too damned old for double shifts."

He settled onto a bar stool by the cash register and loosened his tie and ran a hand through his hair, and suddenly he wasn't the owner and general manager protem of Catawamteak; he was just a handsome older gentleman in need of the momentary respite a quiet conversation with a trusted bartender might provide. "You know, when I hired you to manage the powerhouse, I never suspected you'd jump behind the bar. I thought keeping the bartenders honest was just something you could do in your spare time."

She got down a snifter. "What's your poison, Michael?"

"Mist." He felt his jacket pockets and drew out a slim green cigar, and hitched up on his seat to extract a tiny pocketknife from his trousers. He fussed with the end of his cigar and patted his pockets again; she slid a book of matches across to him. "Thanks." He traced his thumb over the blind-embossing on the glossy black cover of the book. "So I guess I can't see not paying you for not doing something I never intended for you to do in the first place." He lit his cigar. "Hire Cindy, if that's who you want to take your place, and hire who you want to take her place, and make me a memo with salary suggestions. I'll float it through Personnel."

"That would be Rafael. Thank you, Michael."

He tasted the drink she put in front of him. They had spent much of the day together, but in the presence of Stedman, or Bill Marston, or Carla, they hadn't had a chance to exchange more than pleasantries and their reactions to the news that a drinking buddy of Ray Phelps had been busted at a local car wash; the guy who ran the place was a twice-a-week member at Catawamteak, and knew bentgrass when he saw it. He got the plate number of the jacked-up, fat-tired 4WD pickup truck, and a description of the driver, before he salvaged a chunk of sod from the floor of the bay for evidence, and Ray's old pal sang like that proverbial canary when it was pointed out to him how very much trouble he was in. "How was Bethlehem?"

Rafael tossed an order to the bar on the fly. "Hey, Mr. G., how's it goin'? Back in two minutes, Jordan. I gotta hit the head."

She turned the slip to read it. "We did a lot of talking." She filled glasses with ice and tipped bottles over them with an automatic wrist. "Played a lot of golf. I put the house on the market."

"I think that's wise. I wanted to do it back when — " He coughed; 'back when you had your nervous breakdown' didn't seem very sensitive. "Years ago. But Aiga wouldn't let me. She said it was your decision to make."

"And I've made it, at long last. Have you seen Gillie?"

"She's in the dining room, with the most stunning woman I've ever seen."

"That would be Olathe. Isn't she gorgeous? Did you talk to her? Gillie, I mean."

"They were deep in conversation. We waved across the room."

"She'll probably come in for a drink. Ask her how she golfed. Have ten minutes to listen," she grinned. "She hasn't come back to earth yet."

"That sounds like an ace."

"On the eighth. I thought I was going to have to remember my CPR. It was funny; we'd just been talking about it the day before. But she played well all day. She was really nailing the ball, and she's finally figuring out her wedges."

He sipped his drink. "How much more improvement do you think can you offer her?"

Jordan slid Rafael's tray to the waiter's port. "I think Gillie and I have accomplished all we set out to do," she said quietly, "and more. She's an extraordinary woman, Michael."

"So are you, Jordan."

"Thank you. And yes. I do think she might care to have dinner with you. Of course" — she gave him a metallic smile — "that's if you still care to have dinner with her."

He cupped his snifter in his hand to swirl the liqueur in it, and tasted his cigar, and looked at her through a soft haze of fragrant blue smoke. "Why wouldn't I?"

"Does he know?" Gillie came out of the bathroom of her suite in a classic little black dress and presented her back to Jordan for assistance.

Jordan slipped the tab of the zipper up past underwear and pantyhose and bra strap, and folded it down at the top and smoothed the dress against Gillie's back, smiling to herself at the armor Gillie was wearing, dressing for Michael, that she hadn't worn when she had dressed for her. "Yes."

"And he still wants me to go to dinner with him."

"You're dressing, aren't you?"

Gillie turned.

"And you look wonderful," Jordan said softly. "Where are you going?"

"The Bayview Yacht Club. Jordan, I'm so nervous — "

"Why?"

Gillie jittered a laugh. "What do we have in common besides you? And he knows I've been sleeping with you? That's a great jumping-off point for a conversation."

"One could go on at some length about the semantic differences of sleeping in the same bed with someone or sleeping with someone, were anyone rude enough to inquire, which he won't be. Gillie, you both golf. You both love the course at Bethlehem. You both loved the back nine here. You know what we're proposing for the renovation. Talk about golf. That should take you into next month, but if it doesn't, Michael knows more about stocks and mutual funds than most investment consultants. Listening to him has made me a ton of money. Pump him for advice."

"What if he asks about us?" Gillie paced to the door of the bedroom of her suite.

"I don't think he will, but if he does, tell him the truth."

"What if he asks about Phil?"

"Tell him what you think he needs to know."

She turned, looking back at Jordan. "Will that make him understand?"

"I think he already does," Jordan said quietly. "Enough to accept, anyway."

"Does he, or is he using me to get back into your good graces?"

"He wouldn't take that risk. He knows how I feel about you. Gillie, if you don't want to go, why did you — "

"I do." She leaned unhappily against the door frame. "I do want to go. And that feels like — I don't know. A betrayal of you."

"Don't do that. I told you Monday morning — "

"I know what you told me. And it worked for me Monday morning, but I've had a lot of time to think about it — about everything! you and me and Phil and Michael and what I — " She picked a thread from the breast of her dress. "What I want. What I don't want. What I don't know whether I want or not. What did I do besides use you to get over my fear?"

"Did you use me to get over your slice, so I should feel used? Did you use me to get over your back pain, so I should feel used? I knew — "

"Apples and oranges, Jordan, and you know it. Teaching me how to hit a golf ball is a long damned ways from investing your heart and soul into teaching me how to be loved."

"I didn't teach you how to hit a golf ball without using my heart and soul. We were working on love long before we both got naked. Gillian, I'd have felt used if you'd checked out of here Monday and run away without leaving a forwarding address. I don't feel used by you checking out the possibility of a relationship with a man I know will treat you well."

"Always an answer for everything," Gillie grumbled. "You're a pain in my neck, Jordan Bryant." She found her wristwatch on the dresser and snapped it on. "So once again you manage to drag the truth out of me. What if this works? What if he asks me out again, and again, and finally we arrive at a point where something more than a handshake at the door might be anticipated? How am I supposed to go to bed with your uncle?"

"The usual way. Ask him in for a drink, or accept if he asks you in. Let him kiss you — "

"You are pissing me off," Gillie said evenly. "You know what I'm talking about."

Jordan smiled. "Yes, Auntie Gillie, I do. And I think that Uncle Michael's over in the East Wing tying his tie and asking himself some very similar questions. Take it a step at a time, and let it work itself out." She stood; she was in her bar uniform, that snug mess white with its pleated shirt and deep purple silk bow tie; Cindy couldn't swap shifts until Sunday, so she had one more night to endure. "I've got to go to work. Stop by if you get in before closing time. I'll buy you both a drink." She bent to kiss Gillie's cheek. "Have a good time. And stop worrying. My mother used to say that worry is nothing but interest paid on trouble before it comes due."

♦

They came in at ten-thirty; Jordan checked her watch and thought, *Oh-oh. They sure didn't linger over their brandy.*

But they lingered over it at a small table in a corner well away from the band, and Jordan knew, watching them out of a corner of her eye, that their evening had gone well, that they had enjoyed each others' company, that they had found common ground besides her. When Michael excused himself and headed for the men's room, she waved at Rafael to cover the bar.

"Hey," she grinned, squatting beside the table. "You two look great together. It's going well, I take it?"

"Do you have any idea of how much you and Michael are alike? How can I not like him?" Gillie shook her head with a wry smile. "And so I'm even more bumfuzzled. This feels more incestuous all the time."

"Wrong word, sweetheart. Not a drop of blood in common."

"You know what I mean."

"Gillie —" She stood, and reached to touch Gillie's hand on the table. "Michael's first wife wanted to take me away from my father," she said quietly. "I think it'd be wonderful if his second wife could be the woman who did."

ONE YEAR LATER

Dearly beloved, we are gathered together in the presence of God to witness and bless the joining together of these two people in holy matrimony. . . .

The chapel at Catawamteak was small, but big enough for the gathered dearly beloved: besides the bride and groom and their attendants, there were but a handful of guests. Of the bride's surviving family, only Meghann Benson had made the trip to see her mother married.

Meghann had inherited her father's height and black hair, and her mother's fine bones and soft brown eyes. She was attractive at nineteen, and would be a handsome woman at forty and sixty and eighty, Michael Goodnow had thought, meeting her for the first time at Christmas; he thought it again when she arrived at Catawamteak in June. He offered his hand and a smile he hoped didn't look too (as he had overheard her grumble to her brother six months ago) 'smarmy-charmy;' Meghann, he thought, was quite completely unimpressed with him. "Miss Benson. It's so good to see you again."

Meghann didn't understand his amusement, but sensed the deep affection for someone that was behind it when she said, "Meghann's cool with me, but if you've got to do the formal thing, it's Ms., Mr. Goodnow. *Ms.* Benson."

The union of two people in heart, body, and mind is intended by God for their mutual joy, and for the help and comfort given one another in prosperity and adversity. . . .

"I understand that 'this man and this woman' is how the Book of Common Prayer would have it" — Gillie offered their rewrite of the vows across the priest's desk — "but please read it as 'two people' in every instance. We've stricken all of that about the mystery of the union between Christ and His Church; we're not all that religious. And surely we can forego the part about the procreation of children. We're quite sure we won't be needing that."

Peter Jenkins turned a double-spaced page, not expecting to find the prayer concerning God creating us male and female in his image, and he didn't. "May I assume that you've discussed these changes at some length," he mused. He was a youngish priest, possibly forty, and his reactions were diplomatically impossible to read.

"We have," they said together. "We believe that we were created in God's image," Gillie added, "but we don't believe that God has gender, and we don't believe that any merciful god would discriminate against creatures made to such heights of love as we humans are capable of." She tilted a small smile at him. "Not that it's always practiced. Only that it's within our inherent capability."

215

"Secular humanism, if you will," Michael said in his gentle, rumbling voice. "As an Episcopalian priest, are you comfortable with that, Mr. Jenkins?"

The Reverend Mr. Jenkins leaned back in his desk chair. "As an Episcopalian priest, I'm comfortable with any spiritual belief that embraces tolerance and charity for all of the creations of God," he said quietly. "It will be my pleasure to perform your ceremony as you've revised it."

Therefore marriage is not to be entered into unadvisedly or lightly, but reverently, deliberately, and in accordance with the purposes for which it was instituted by God. . . .

Stedman attended the groom, affixing his studs, tying his tie, holding his coat, showing him the rings seven times when Michael asked that many times if he was sure he had them, telling him the time more often than that. "I feel like a schoolboy at the prom," Michael jittered. "You'd think I'd never done this before, Stedman — loved a woman, or married her. What is it the kids say? Been here, done this?"

"I've done it twice, and I'm here to tell you that once ain't enough to shake the nerves off it the second time." He drew his father's watch from the vest pocket of his rented tux and opened it: two hours to go. "If you ever have to do it again, do it earlier in the day." His gnarled fingers dusted off the shoulders of Michael's coat. "Celia was a good woman, Mick. She gave you a lot of good years." He found ice and two glasses and the bottle of single-malt scotch that Jordan had sent to Michael's suite. "Just let the goose walk over her grave, Mick. I remember her good enough to know she'd've liked this one. They'd've been out there golfing and telling truths about you that you'd've called lies, and they'd've been good friends." He offered Michael a grin and a glass full of rocks and scotch. "You've got to know it's love, Mick. The lady's got money of her own."

◆

"When were these taken?"

Jordan glanced up from the ironing board to see Meghann at the north wall of her bedroom, studying the five framed photographs Park had taken one July afternoon almost a year ago. "Last year," she said, and held up the iron so it could quit burping steam, not needing for it to puke brown residue all over Gillie's wedding dress.

"Well, yeah, but when? I mean — " She traced a finger over the glass covering the last one, the one of her mother touching Jordan's face in echoing, naked trust. "This is pretty intense. You must have known each other a while."

Jordan finished the last touches with the iron at the hem of Gillie's dress before she looked at Meghann; looking at her, she thought, was like looking in a younger mirror, and that was somewhat disconcerting. "Just about twenty-four hours."

"No." Meghann looked at Jordan, and at the photograph, and at Jordan again. "Twenty-four hours? You're shitting me."

Jordan smiled. "I wouldn't shit you."

"Yeah, I'm your favorite turd."

"Meghann . . ." Reproach from the bathroom, where Gillie was applying her face.

"Don't sweat, Mom. We're getting along." She spent a moment with the pictures before she turned to Jordan. "I guess," she said slowly. "Yeah. I've had a few people I got there with quick. Just — you knew, you know? There you were."

"That's about how it was. There we were."

"You look so totally cool, Jordan." Meghann flicked a disparaging finger at a speck of dust on her skirt; she was dressed in a kind of a Seven Sisters-L. L. Bean look. "I wish I'd've thought to wear a tux."

Jordan hung Gillie's dress and turned off the iron. She considered, and finally said, "I've got another one. It'd probably fit you."

"If anyone wears that lilac tux today," Gillie inserted from the bathroom, "it'll be you, Jordan."

Jordan went to the bathroom door; she leaned there for a moment, watching as Gillie smoothed a light foundation across her cheeks. "I have a black one," she said. "She'd look good in it."

"She'd look better in the charcoal." She capped the bottle, tossing it into her cosmetic case, and opened a flat of eye shadows before she met Jordan's eyes in the mirror. "And god knows I know how you look in the lilac."

Jordan looked away with a disbelieving half-laugh. "Are you sure you want me to wear that at your wedding?"

Seated at Jordan's vanity, wearing Jordan's purple silk robe, Gillie paused, brush in hand and her eyelids at half-mast, to wait for Jordan's eyes to come back to hers in the mirror. "If it hadn't been for you in that tux," she said quietly, "I wouldn't be having a wedding."

"Look, it was just a thought, okay?" Meghann's voice apologized behind Jordan. "It zinged in from outer space. I didn't mean to start a hassle."

Jordan unbuttoned her coat and slipped it off, handing it behind her without breaking contact with the brown eyes in the mirror. "Here, Meggie. Try this on. If this fits you, any of them will."

Into this holy union Gillian Benson and Michael Goodnow now come to be joined. If any of you can show just cause why they may not be lawfully married, speak now; or else forever hold your peace. . . .

"What did Mom mean, without you in that tux there wouldn't be a wedding?" Meghann waited while Jordan, trousered in deep lilac, finished the last touch-ups with the point of the iron against the cream-colored shirt front she would wear; the gray trousers Jordan had been wearing fit Meghann like a slightly snug glove. "I probably wasn't supposed

217

to hear that, but I did, so what the hell. No questions gets you no answers."

Jordan didn't look up. "You'll have to ask your mother that."

Meghann watched as Jordan turned her back to slip out of the white shirt front and into the cream one. There were three faint, interesting marks just under her left shoulder blade, the soft sort of scars that would remind for a while and disappear over time; they looked, she thought, as if someone had raked her pretty well. They seemed the sort of marks a woman would leave on a man, not vice-versa, and she grinned nervously as unbidden, a memory whispered at her: her mother sitting at the dining room table with that dazed, drawn look she always had a day after Phil had taken after her, working with an emery board to bring her nails to a smooth taper, the Valium shielding her from the pain as the morning paper shielded the teak table from cotton balls saturated with nail polish remover. She didn't remember ever seeing her mother without her nails done to perfection, or recall that she had to protect them; they were hard and strong, and rarely broke. Fingernails like that, she thought, could leave marks like that, marks that would linger against delicate skin rarely touched by the sun.

Jordan finished with her buttons and turned, catching Meghann staring blankly at her. "Hello?"

The question blurted out of her before she could catch it. "Are you a lesbian?"

Jordan found the cream cuffs in a dresser drawer, and undid her cuff links. "Yes." She put the white cuffs on the ironing board and the cream ones around her wrists. "I thought you knew."

"Mom never said — " Meghann glanced toward the bathroom; her mother was leaning in the door, arms and ankles crossed, an odd, small smile toying with her as she watched them.

Gillian met her daughter's eyes. Her voice was soft and gentle. "Any questions for me, darling?"

She looked at her mother, at that tiny, telling smile. "Mom — " and at the photographs on the wall, and at Jordan: "You — " and at her mother again. "Oh, man," she said faintly. "I'm not believing what I'm thinking, here. Mom . . . ?"

I require and charge you both, that if either of you know any reason why you may not be united in marriage lawfully, you do now confess it . . . .

"You have an idea of what I went through with your father," Gillie said quietly. Big-eyed, her glance flickering between her mother and Jordan, Meghann nodded. "It was worse than you thought. Worse than you need to know. After I — After he died, I . . . I just resigned myself to the fact that I'd never be able to get married again. I was — " Still in Jordan's robe, she went to the game table in the corner to open the gold cigarette case. Silently, Jordan went across the room to offer fire; Gillie steadied

218

her hand against Jordan's, glancing a look of pure gratitude into her eyes before she turned.

Jordan leaned against the table, her eyes, like Meghann's, following Gillie as she roamed the room, touching things on bookcases. "The thought of going to bed with a man terrified me." Gillie looked out the window that she knew afforded the barest glimpse of the tip of the lighthouse, with its muttering white memories and musing green future. "I didn't know what the words 'making love' meant. Jordan . . ." She hesitated, searching for words. "Jordan gave me that," she said softly, at last. "It was the most incredible thing that's ever happened to me, Meggie, besides you. She gave me the chance to know that I could love and trust, and that I didn't have to be alone because I couldn't do those things. Without her . . ."

She put her cigarette in the ashtray by Jordan's bed and traced her fingertips under her eyes. "Without her love — " She swallowed. "Without her gentleness. This never could have happened, Meghann. I never could have gotten here without her. Honey, please understand what it meant to me — " She looked up to find their attentions riveted on her, and she went to Jordan, first, to take her hand before she stretched her other one to her daughter. "What it meant to me," she whispered, Meghann's cool hand in one of hers, Jordan's warm one in the other, "was the rest of my life. Meghann, she gave me back the rest of my life."

Meghann looked at Jordan, and in those calm grey eyes she saw deep fog and hard seas and moonless nights; she saw the feathers of a dove and the fur of a sleeping cat and the touch of silk on private skin, and she saw that Jordan Bryant loved her mother without reservation or expectation, and she saw that because she was Gillian Benson's daughter, Jordan was prepared to love her, too. She blew a soft breath. "So my mother marries your uncle. What does that make us?"

Jordan looked at her, tall and lean and smooth in her own charcoal tux. "Family," she said softly.

Dark brown eyes held deep grey ones for a long moment. "So you're going to teach me to golf, right?"

A smile twitched to a corner of Jordan's mouth. "Just as soon as I've danced with the bride."

Meghann grinned. "You've got brass, girlfriend."

Jordan held out a cupping hand. "And this big. Let's get these tuxes sorted out. We've still got to dress your Mom."

Meghann turned to her mother. "Thank you for telling me, Mama," she said softly.

Gillie drew her head down for a gentle kiss. "Thank you for hearing us."

Gillian, will you have this man to be your husband, to live together in the covenant of marriage? Will you love him, comfort him, honor and

keep him, in sickness and in health, and, forsaking all others, be faithful
to him as long as you both shall live?

"Michael knows? That is so chill! I mean, it's weird, but it's chill. I thought he was a stuffy old fart, but man, he must be pretty great to be good with that. That would freak most old rich guys right the ff — f — frig out."

"If I didn't think he was great, I wouldn't be marrying him. Sweetheart, I can't believe how good you look in that tux. I'm going to send you to Jordan's tailor."

"Excellent! I always wanted to go to England. So like — god! How do you open that kind of a conversation, anyway? I mean, he's her uncle, right? And you guys were lovers and now you're going to be her aunt?" The look on Meghann's face suggested she had just taken a bite of something she wasn't sure whether she wanted to swallow or spit out, not because of the taste but the texture of the thing. "That's *so* weird! Did he know before he asked you to marry him?"

"It was one night, Meghann." Gillie scooped one silk stocking onto her hand so that she could draw it over her foot and up her leg. "And he knew before he asked me out the first time." She fastened the garters, not unaware of Jordan's eyes following her hands, also not unaware of the tiny stirring of her own reaction to that.

"How did he know? I mean — look, tell me to bag it if this is too personal, but god, Mom, I'm freaking out here. I mean, my whole perception of you as a sexual person is all warped because of what that subhuman sack of toxic waste I had for a father did to you, you know? And this is like, so one-eighty-out it's off the fucking — oops; sorry, Mom. But it is. It's off the planet for me."

"Did you ever blush at the wrong time and have that blush tell someone more than they needed to know?" Jordan asked, Gillie's dress ready in her hands.

"Well, duh. Hasn't everyone?"

"That's how Michael knew. I blushed at the wrong time."

"You blushed?"

Jordan shot her a smile. "I'm chill, sistergirl, but I'm not that chill."

"Anyways, Meggie" — Gillie looked for her other stocking; Meghann relinquished it — "we knew he knew, and he knew we knew he knew, and yes, that had its moments of awkwardness. But we — he and I — got along so well, and we felt . . . safe, I guess is the way to put it, with each other, because neither one of us was out for the other's money. One night in October — we'd gone sailing, and had dinner at the Yacht Club, and got back here late — we had a wonderful day. He walked me to my suite, and I asked him in for an after-dinner drink, and he . . . kissed me." She blushed, remembering the taste of Drambuie and why she had served it that night. "I knew he wanted to stay, and I wanted him to, but I couldn't just — "

Slowly, she gathered the silk stocking onto her hand. "I had to tell him about Phil. That led into what happened with Jordan. And he understood. He was so — god, he was so — " She drew a shaky breath. "God, I never thought I'd have this," she whispered. "He was so gentle. He — I — we didn't — we haven't — " She stopped, trying not to cry. "I'm sorry — "

"Breathe, Gillian," Jordan said softly.

"Thank you. I'm scared," she managed. "I know he'd die before he'd hurt me, but I'm still scared. Jordan, out in my suitcase in the pocket on the left-hand side is a blue jeweler's box. Would you get it for me? Please?"

Jordan trailed a touch from her shoulder to her fingertips, squeezing her hand before she relinquished the dress to Meghann and turned.

"Mom?"

Gillie looked up; gently, Meghann touched a tissue under her mother's eyes, catching tears before they could ruin her makeup. "Thank you," she whispered.

"Mama, are you sure you're going the right way? She really loves you."

"I know she does." She slipped her stocking over her foot and drew it up her leg; she fastened the garters and smoothed the silk against her skin, and stood to adjust the belt of Jordan's robe. "But so does Michael," she said softly. "This way I get them both the way I want them both. And they both get me the way they want me. Meggie, I know it's hard to understand — "

Meghann touched her fingertips to her mother's lips. "I hear you, Mom," she whispered. "If you're sure, I'm sure."

Michael, will you have this woman to be your wife, to live together in the covenant of marriage? Will you love her, comfort her, honor and keep her, in sickness and in health, and, forsaking all others, be faithful to her as long as you both shall live?

"How come Grampa and Uncle Richard and Aunt Jerri didn't come, Mom?" Meghann watched in the mirror as Jordan fastened Michael's wedding present, a triple strand of pearls, around Gillie's throat. "I mean, jeez. Four's been drunk and pissed off at you since Val left him, I didn't expect him, but god. You're getting married. Isn't Grampa supposed to give you away?"

"Grampa gave me away a long time ago," Gillie said quietly. "Would you go out and make me a cup of tea, honey? I need to talk to Jordan alone for a minute."

Will all of you witnessing these promises do all in your power to uphold these two persons in their marriage?

"I can swear on a thousand Bibles," Gillie whispered in Jordan's arms, feeling the warmth of her inside the coat of that lilac tuxedo. "But I'll always know how it felt to have you love me, Jordan Baker Bryant, and I'll love you until the day I die."

Jordan smoothed a hand up Gillie's back, traced her cheekbone, tucked a wisp of her all-colored hair back into place. "Auntie Gillie," she said softly. "Family. That's what you get when you fall into the love."

She drew Jordan's head down to her. "Oh, Jordan —" It was a warmth of breath against her lips. "Kiss Mrs. Benson goodbye."

Who gives this woman to be married to this man?

Jordan felt the gentle pressure of Gillian's hand on her arm. She came back to the chapel, to stained glass and sunlight, to the scents of new-mown grass and Shalimar and wild roses, back to the grave and gentle eyes of Michael Goodnow . . . she came back from the taste of Gillian Benson's love against her own.

Who gives this woman . . .

"I do," she said, and stepped aside to let Michael take her place.

"Hey, Carla." Jordan put her new coffee cup on the counter in the pro shop and turned the registration book to see what was happening out on the course; it was a brilliant day, as green and gold and blue as only early summer days can be, and the parking lot was thick with cars. "Any thing exciting doing?"

Carla aimed a thumb at the white board. "Happy days are here again. Lucky you."

"Oh, my achin' ass," Jordan muttered, seeing *P. Watkins* in bold red ink in her column for Wednesday morning. "Thank god Park and Olathe came for the wedding. At least I'll have someone to bounce off of."

"How long are the Goodnows going to be gone?"

"Six weeks. Three in Australia and three in Scotland. Meggie and I are supposed to meet them in Edinburgh August third."

"Tough life," Carla grumbled. "What's your cup say?"

" '*La seule différence entre moi et un fou c'est que . . . je ne suis pas fou.*' "

"Thanks a lot. I was kind of hoping you might give me a translation."

" 'The only difference between myself and a madman is that . . . I am not mad!' Salvador Dali. Gillie gave it to me." She took it to her office and came back wearing her spikes. "Speaking of Meg Benson, you spent a lot of time with her Saturday night at the reception."

A faint blush touched Carla's face. "Yeah."

Jordan saw the blush and smiled. "A lot in common?"

"A lot more than I expected. She's pretty down to earth for a rich kid." She straightened the stack of score cards by the cash register. "She sure thinks you hung the moon."

"We'll see if she still does after I've tried to teach her to golf."

"Yeah, she said she figured she'd better learn. I — um — " She cleared her throat. "Not trying to horn in or anything, but I said maybe I could help her, too."

"Sure you could. I'll work basics and you can work reinforcement. It'd be nice if she had someone to spend some time with while she's here." She glanced at the white board again; her entry for 8:00 was in purple, Carla's signal for someone who had alerted her gaydar. "So who's this Sam Hanson?"

"Your eight o'clock? What's to know? Callaway clubs, writes south-paw but plays right — "

"Thank you very much."

" — and dressed to the nines. Check the chipping green."

Jordan picked three Catawamteak Titleists from the barrel at the end of the counter and dropped them into her pocket. "Later."

"Break a leg."

She approached a meticulously-dressed, handsome blond man of about thirty at the chipping green, understanding Carla's purple pen. "Mr. Hanson?" She extended a hand. "I'm Jordan Bryant."

"Pleased to meet you, Jordan Bryant." He had a good handshake, and a pleasant, blue-eyed smile. "But I'm Bruce. I think you're looking for my much more talented twin." He looked over Jordan's shoulder. "Sam! Look who I've got."

Jordan turned. *Well, hel-lo,* she thought. *What's to know, indeed. Carla, you're just full of surprises today.*

Sam Hanson was definitely her brother's twin: thirtyish, with a lush golden ponytail tumbling out from under a Michelle McGann hat, she was as slender and well-toned as Bruce, with tiny black triangles in her ears and dark blue eyes that crinkled into a smile when Jordan offered her hand. "Yes you are, Jordan Bryant." It sounded like 'so am I;' her handshake was firm and warm. "Is it okay for me to tell you that you were my absolute hero when you were on the Tour?"

"Sam was so in love with you," Bruce grinned. "It was pathetic."

"I'm going to kill you, Bruce," Sam warned, still smiling; she looked back at Jordan. "I was — what, thirteen? Fifteen? Kid stuff." She left a last small squeeze against Jordan's fingers and let her hand go, but her eyes kept contact. "I was in love with golf. You were the best. Was I supposed to hang Bryan Adams in my bedroom when I had an autographed picture of you?"

"Sam . . . Sam . . . Sammie Hanson! All right; I remember." Jordan laughed. "'My name is Samantha Hanson but please make the autograph to Sammie.' You wrote me about a six-page letter." And her smile faded a little, not leaving her, just turning bittersweet. "You sent me a get-well card, too. Thank you. I'm sorry I didn't answer that one."

Sam's hand brushed Jordan's forearm. "I didn't expect you to," she said quietly. "I'm just glad you made it through." And she smiled. "So enough about my childhood crush on you. I think I'm beyond pathetic."

"Way past it," Bruce inserted. "You're so far beyond pathetic —"

"Bruce, go play with your balls while you still have some. So tell me, Jordan Bryant. Can you possibly please please please teach me how to control my driver? I don't want to play executive courses for the rest of my life."

"I don't blame you . . . is it still Sammie?"

"God, no! Sam, or Samantha if you're pissed off at me, but not Sammie!" She grinned. "If you hear Bruce and me get into our 'Sammie-Brucie' thing, just duck. We've been known to take our sibling rivalry to ridiculous depths." She slipped an arm around Bruce's waist and gave him an affectionate squeeze. "See you in a while, sweetie. Okay, Jordan Bryant! I've got a cart over there somewhere with my bag on it, and that crusty old foof of a starter you've got practically made me synchronize my watch with his. Let's go before he gives our tee time away."

"I'll get my clubs."

And on the deck of the pro shop Jordan paused to watch Samantha Hanson shoot her wedge into her bag and stretch as if she were just awakening to the glory of the day. The first fairway was long and lush before her, the bay brilliant beyond, and Jordan looked at the lighthouse at the end of the breakwater as it blinked white, and then green, and she smiled.

A SHORT COURSE*
IN GOLF
IN GLOSSARY FORM

* AKA "PITCH-AND-PUTT"

GOLF GLOSSARY

Ace: a hole in one.

Address: the stance of the player before the swing. Also known as the approach.

Apron: the area around the green that's mowed closer than the fairway but not quite as close as the green itself. Creates some interestingly difficult shots when the ball lies on the lip of the APRON, i.e., resting at the border of the two lengths of cut.

Banana ball: see SLICE. (See 70% of once-a-month golfers.)

Birdie: one under par on a hole.

Bump-and-run: using a lower lofted iron, such as a 7, 8, or 9 iron, and pitching the ball like a fast putt onto the green, usually with a short stroke as opposed to a full swing. The object is to pick a point on the green where the ball is to land, get just enough loft on the ball to miss all the rough or first cut around the green, and then run it to the cup.

Bogey: one over par on a hole. (Double-bogey is two over par, triple bogey is three over par . . . quad bogey achieved before the green is not only reason but demand to PICK UP.)

Chili dip: a shot where the swing cuts a swath of turf and barely moves the ball. Unusually embarrassing, and hard on your clubs. See FAT.

Chip: a low, short approach shot to the green.

Divot: a hunk of sod torn up by the club. Bad players take them behind the ball (see FAT). Good ones take them from the ball forward.

Dogleg: a hole in which the GREEN is either to the left or the right of the TEE BOX. A gay hole, if you will: either to the left or right of center, but not straight. A sharp dogleg right is a Log Cabin Republican. A sharp dogleg left is a member of ActUp.

Draw: a shot that veers slightly to the left. A draw is a controlled shot. A draw out of control is called a HOOK.

Drive: the first shot of each hole.

Eagle: two under par on a hole.

Fade: a shot that veers to the right, controlled as is a DRAW. A fade out of control is called a SLICE . . . also a BANANA BALL.

Fairway: the most closely mowed area between the TEE BOX and the APRON of the GREEN. The object is to keep the ball in the fairway. (See ROUGH.)

Fat: hitting the ground too far behind the ball with the swing, taking a "fat" divot and usually projecting the ball too high into the air — or not moving it at all. See CHILI DIP.

Gimme: a putt so short and makeable that the opposing player says, "That's a gimme," and lets you go without taking the stroke. (The stroke not taken, however, does count on your score.)

Good mis-hit: a ball hit poorly but with good results, i.e., a mild SLICE on a DOGLEG RIGHT, or a WORMBURNER on a level or downhill FAIRWAY.

Green: Golf's dance floor. Far and away the most expensive part of any golf course, the green is where players put the ball in the hole in the process of making (or, less often, avoiding) the most abominable errors of etiquette in the game. See YOUR GOLF PRO.

Grip: how the player holds the club. The three recognized golf grips are the interlocking (right pinkie finger intertwined with left forefinger, assuming a right-handed player), overlapping (right pinkie finger overlapping the left forefinger), and baseball (right pinkie finger abutting the left forefinger). See YOUR GOLF PRO.

Hazards: sand traps (a.k.a. bunkers), ponds, rivers, streams, oceans ("water hazards"), or lateral water hazards, which are bodies of water running parallel to the fairway. Many rules of golf apply to playing out of hazards, most notably: you can't move anything Nature made, and don't ground your club. ("Grounding your club" is touching the head of the club to the ground. In hazards, the touch of the club could cause the ball to move, which would incur a penalty.)

Hitting into: hitting your ball before the group in front of you is far enough away that you're not going to hit them. Serious injury may result. Requires immediate apology if done once; completely beyond the etiquette of the game if done a second time.

Honors: the player who scored lowest on the last hole gains the right to tee off first on the next one. Mandatory in tournament play, but in recreational play, many golf courses today encourage "ready golf," where whoever is ready to hit the ball does so, without offense to whoever has honors. Saves time on crowded courses.

Hook: a shot that veers sharply to the left, usually into an adjoining fairway or woods, water, or some other cussable hazard. Much less frequent than the SLICE.

Irons: golf clubs with smaller heads than WOODS.

Long irons: the 0, 1, 2, 3, and 4 irons. The lower the number of the iron, the more distance the player gets on the shot. (Theoretically.) Lee Trevino suggests that if you get caught on the golf course in an electrical storm, hold up your one-iron, because not even God can hit a one-iron. John Daly and Tiger Woods do quite well with it, though; in fact, John Daly was most instrumental in the development of the 0-iron.

Mid irons: the 5 and 6 irons. Pick one of them and learn to love it. Give the other one away.

Short irons: the 7, 8, and 9 irons, plus wedges. Wedges are sharply-angled irons used in specific instances: the pitching wedge for shots out of deep rough, the sand wedge for the obvious reason, etc.

Leader board: the scoreboard displayed on the course or on TV in tournament or professional play.

Lie: the position of the golf ball on the course. (But, of course, never the story you tell about it in the clubhouse bar.)

Mulligan: a freebie. If your first shot is a BANANA BALL into the woods, your playing partners may invite you to take a Mulligan, which, if you hit it better than your first ball, becomes your ball in play and doesn't cost a stroke. Used only (and, we hope, very sparingly) in recreational play.

Par: the number of strokes prescribed to play a hole. Commonly Par Three to 225 yds, Par Four from 300 to 425, Par 5 from 380 (Front TEEs) to however long they want to make it. I've heard of Par Sixes, but I've never seen one. (Willie Nelson, talking about his privately-owned golf course, says, "Par is whatever I say it is. I've got one hole that's a par twenty-three, and yesterday I almost birdied the sucker.")

Pick up: to quit a hole before completion. An automatic disqualification in tournament play, it is nonetheless often an act of mercy toward your playing partners in recreational play. Put an X for the hole on your scorecard and forget it. Birdie the next one.

Pitch: a high, short approach shot to the green.

Plus fours: a knickers-style of pants popularized by golfers in the 1920s, notably the sartorially-correct Walter Hagen, and, more recently, Payne Stewart. *Ne plus ultra* (no pun intended) when worn in a solid-color summer-weight flannel with matching argyle socks and wingtips with SOFT SPIKES.

Pre-shot routine: all the tics, twitches, shirt pullings, prayers and remembrances that precede a shot. Please keep it short unless there's no one waiting behind you, or you're playing for money on television.

Rough: the breakdown lanes of the fairway. The ROUGH can vary from grass an inch higher than the fairway, to Scotland's virtually unplayable gorse, to thickets of brush, to woods. Rough is just that: rough. Not to be confused with HAZARDs.

Short game: the approach to the green; i.e., the game played with the short irons from about 120 yards from the hole.

Slice: the nemesis of many golfers, the slice — a.k.a. BANANA BALL — is a shot that curves in varying degrees to the right. The longer the club, the more likely the slice is to get the golfer in trouble. Most noticeable on the drive, a slice may look like a beautiful shot upon leaving the TEE, only to soar 200 yards and suddenly take a hard veer to the right, landing in the woods, the water, or the next fairway. Individual clubs and entire bags have followed the slice into never-never land. (Throwing clubs is, of course, considered to be extremely bad form.)

Soft spikes: *de rigueur* at many golf courses these days, and soon to be the standard, as they significantly reduce wear and tear on the GREENs. One foot-dragging player in metal spikes can cause thousands of dollars' worth of damage to the delicate surface of a green.

Starter: usually a crusty old fart, the starter is the person who keeps track of TEE TIMES at the first tee. If it's your turn and you're not there and ready to play, he'll give your tee time away and you'll linger in hopeful obscurity until he decides to let you play. His decision may depend upon which dead president you have handy in your pocket.

Tee: a little wooden stick with a pointed end that goes into the dirt and a cupped end used to hold the golf ball off the ground. Also (and used exclusively in the) TEE BOX.

Tee box: the area from which the first shot (DRIVE) of each hole is taken. Traditionally marked with three sets of markers, the forward (red) markers denoting the shortest distance to the hole, the middle (white) tees being more or less centered between the reds and the back (blue) markers, which are most distant. Today, in an attempt to get people to play to their game level (handicap), many courses have at least four and as many as six sets of tee boxes, and state on the scorecard which tee box the golfer should use based on handicap. While the red tees were for years known as the "ladies" tees, that designation is less preferred these days, as it tends to keep senior, handicapped, inexperienced, or any other men from enjoying a shorter game more suited to their levels of ability.

Tee time: the time at which one is designated to start play on a golf course. You call ahead for your tee time. If your tee time is 8:12, be at the first tee no later than 8:05, ready to play but quietly respectful of those starting ahead of you . . . at the risk of teeing someone else off! No sneezing, no opening Velcro bag pockets, no running back to the Cherokee for that sleeve of balls that say "Special Aunt" that your sister's kid gave you for your birthday. Be on time, be ready, and be quiet.

Thin: a ball hit above the center of the club head. See WORMBURNER.

Two-putt, three-putt, etc.: the number of strokes needed to hole the ball once on the GREEN.

Up and down: "up" is making a usually short difficult pitch shot: out of a hazard, over a sand trap, on the fringe of water, etc., onto the green; "down" is then putting the ball in the hole on the first try, so that in 2 shots you have made a miraculous recovery.

Woods: woods, the heads of which used to be made of wood but are now made of metal, are the big-headed clubs used to DRIVE from the TEE BOX on long holes, and sometimes used in the fairway. (Tiger Woods, as we know him, came after the time frame of this book.)

Wormburner: a ball hit low and fast so that it skims hotly across the surface of the FAIRWAY. Often turns into a GOOD MIS-HIT.

Yips: a nervous condition resulting in a loss of putting ability. Lee Trevino said that nothing would give you the yips any faster than making a hundred-dollar bet with only a fifty-dollar bill in your pocket.

Your golf pro: the person who can teach you enough about this incredibly intense, complex, obsessive, compulsive, fantastic, (or is that spelled fanatic?), outrageously fun game to get you out there playing it. If you've never played before, see YOUR GOLF PRO. Get a few lessons on swing and etiquette. Buy *Golf Etiquette* by Barbara Puett and Jim Apfelbaum. Read *Harvey Penick's Little Red Book* (with Bud Schrake). At the very least, watch the Dinah Shore Classic on TV!

AUTHOR'S NOTE

It was pointed out to me by one of my trusted before-submission-for-publication readers that this is my third successive book in which rape/sexual abuse is a major issue for a major character. "Three rapes in three books threatens a formula," she wrote. "I believe that what you have written makes a great case on the domestic violence issue, particularly in that wealth and opportunity do not stave off the darker aspects of human behavior, but I wanted you to know how it could be interpreted."

I see her point, but does three rapes in three books threaten a formula, or does it explore three different perspectives of a threatening reality? Perhaps my perceptions have been skewed by the years I spent working in the battered women's movement; perhaps that experience makes it more comfortable for women who have been sexually abused to open their herstories to me. But it seems that a disproportionate number of women share that depressing similarity. The last statistics I heard were that one out of three women had suffered a sexual assault by the time they turned eighteen. (Statistics, of course, are based on reported cases; we all know that rape is horrendously under-reported.) From conversations with friends and acquaintances, I suspect that the numbers are appallingly higher for lesbians.

If my suspicion is true, then I hope that my readers will forgive the possibility of "formula" for the hope that through my books I might represent, in some way, the voices of women who have been victims of this brutal crime, but who have not yet dared to break silence, so that they might know that they are not alone, and by that knowledge, find some of the courage they will need to face and overcome the memories that are stored — but need not be locked — in their minds and hearts and bodies.

Tell someone. It's your story, not history.

ABOUT THE AUTHOR

Nanci Little received her degree from the University of Maine. A US Army veteran, she has worked as a truck driver, waitron, draftsperson, carpenter, cookbook editor, secretary, basketmaker, administrative coordinator for a battered women's project, home health care provider, massage therapist, and writer. She is an avid golfer and bicyclist.

She worked from her educational and military experiences in the writing of the well-received *Thin Fire*, which was nominated for the 1993 American Library Association's Gay and Lesbian Award for Literature. In *The Grass Widow*, she continued to pursue her affection for both the period piece and the thoughtful exploration of her characters' emotional development that won her critical acclaim for *Thin Fire*.

First Resort is her third novel. She has several more simmering in the hard drive.

E-mail Nanci at <yesiam1@bangornews.infi.net>

ODD GIRLS PRESS

P.O. Box 2157, Anaheim, CA 92814
800-821-0632 or 714-808-1608
http://www.OddGirlsPress.com
publisher@OddGirlsPress.com

Monologues and Scenes for Lesbian Actors by Carolyn Gage. Finally! A book for lesbians who are tired of "passing" at auditions and in acting classes and workshops! Here at last, from one of the most talented and inventive contemporary playwrights, is a book of more than twenty monologues and more than forty scenes by, for, and about lesbians. 1-887237-10-0, $11, August 1999

Pelt by Daphne Gottlieb. Using the language of the everyday to express the extraordinary, poet Daphne Gottlieb searches for the truths of human experience and finds those truths in relationships, childhood, and a woman on fire. From preying to praying, the loss of innocence and the innocence of loss, and the most cruel and unusual stuff of all — love — these poems represent a strong, fresh voice in contemporary poetry. 1-887237-09-7 $9.00

Bloodsong by Karen Marie Christa Minns. In lyric and erotic prose, Minns continues the story of the vampire Darsen, first introduced in her Lammy-nominated **Virago**. Against her will, Ginny has been given the bite that is transforming her into a vampire. As Darsen waits for her victim to weaken, Ginny's lover Manilla readies herself for the confrontation when Darsen returns to claim Ginny forever. 1-887237-08-9 $12.95

Checklist : a bisexual, gay, lesbian, transgender bibliography with synopses edited by Margaret Gillon. The last two bibliographies on gay and lesbian literature were published in the early 1980s, yet the late 1980s and the 1990s have seen a boom in the publishing of queer literature and studies. Books are grouped into seventy subject headings. Each title carries a brief annotation. An extensive index includes cross-references by Author, Title, Biographical subject, and Ethnicity. 1-887237-11-9, Fall/Winter 1999, cloth

Tory's Tuesday by Linda Kay Silva. Captured by Nazis while trying to flee Poland, Marissa and Elsa are shipped to the Auschwitz concentration camp, where they are separated. Through the atrocities and horrors both women face, their love for each other never wavers. They meet other courageous women who help them in their fight to survive and reunite. 1-887237-06-2 $8.95

Lesbians In Print : a bibliography of 1,500 books with synopses edited by M. Gillon. "If you are a librarian in any type of library — academic, public, or high school learning center — you do not need to read this review any further. Just go immediately and order this book.... It should go without saying that interested individual readers might want to purchase **Lesbians In Print** also." __*Feminist Collections*. 1-887237-13-5 $19.50

First Resort by Nanci Little. Jordan Bryant maintains an almost clinical distance between herself and the people she meets at Catawamteak, the grand resort on the coast of Maine where she is Director of Golf . . . until she meets Gillian Benson. **First Resort** is a meticulous exploration of the growth of the bonds of affection, love, and friendship between women. 1-887237-01-1 $11

ORDERING Our books are available at feminist bookstores, gay and lesbian bookstores, and some independent bookstores and mail-order services. If the book you are looking for is not in stock, the store will order it for you. We gladly fill direct orders for our books. Send a check or money order for the total price of the books, plus $3 to cover shipping and handling, and we'll get your books to you ASAP!